DEEP SAH

To Mandy,

DEEP
SAHARA

with warmest wishes,

Leslie.

LESLIE CROXFORD

THE MOMENTUM PUBLISHING COMPANY

Deep Sahara

First published in Great Britain in 2017 by The Momentum Publishing Company
www.momentumbooks.co.uk

1 2 3 4 5 6 7 8 9 10

ISBN 9781911475125
A CIP catalogue record for this book is available from the British Library.

Typeset by Davor Pukljak
Jacket design by Hamish Braid
Printed and bound in the UK by TJ International

Frank Sydney Frederick Croxford
Harry Abbott Williams
In gratitude and loving memory

PROLOGUE: MEMOIR

The front door has just closed. I'm finally alone in the apartment, using this morning's stillness to begin the account I've been wanting to write for days. It's a letter to myself after the battering I've received from the media – not to mention the anonymous death threats – for attacking our so-called "pillars of society".

I need to sift through all that happened out at the end of the world, coming back to me now like some dream. For the Sahara's a place of mirages you can actually photograph: palm trees, oases, expanses of cool water, silent cities – there, but unreal. Conjuring up the past, I want to reassure myself that all I claimed to have found among those shifting sands, on returning here to Rome, far from being the figment of my imagination critics allege, is actually the case: that the experience of unearthing – of understanding - what I have revealed has made me into a new person.

Silence holds heavy. The blankness of this page is as intimidating as the desert itself. Still, I've plunged in, covering the paper like a suspect instructed by the police to write everything down. And though I'm no criminal, I'm scribbling both as a release and for the reader I sense exists, but can't identify. This I do know: it's someone with whom the self I've achieved – as well as how I've done so – strikes a chord. He'll see me as the solitary figure I was, in a monk's habit like a Bedouin's burnoose, lost against the pitiless Saharan sky. And he'll find me faced with coming to myself in that emptiness to which life had finally brought me.

Yet, writing, so much I must recall is painful. I'm concerned that I've little more than my memory – that mirage – to rely upon, especially after all this time. Nevertheless, I know I must set out fully everything that took place, to see what was actually so, for my own peace of mind.

That's why I have set aside the book I keep telling myself I should be working on. I've no alternative now but to write and finally establish the *full* story of what happened in the deep Sahara.

1

I left Rome in the summer of 1980. The day before that, I went to see Father Carlo. He had asked me back for a final visit, although he'd already given me the travel information.

Late for my appointment, I hastened toward the German Catholic Church of Santa Maria dell'Anima, on Vicolo della Pace, not far from Piazza Navona. My mother used to take me there every Sunday during my boyhood. The rector had been German; now, its priests were not necessarily so. Yet even the Italian ones spoke the language, knew the country and were likely to have carried on their ministry in Germany at some point.

That was the case with Father Carlo. He was sitting in his office in the adjoining building. It gave onto the courtyard at the back of the church. The blinds were drawn against the summer afternoon glare when I finally entered.

Recalling the priest now, it's hard to bring him into focus with all that's happened since. Even then, I was still feeling the effect of the sedatives I'd been taking.

My wife Anja had died. But what I suffered was not only her loss, but the loss of myself, in a total breakdown.

I'd been in our apartment the week after she died. Staring vacantly at some mirror in the empty bedroom, I winced. Something had just moved in the glass. It was a stranger: me.

Father Carlo was waiting for me at his desk. He sat beneath a framed photograph of what I'd later come to know was the young Pius XII as Apostolic Nuncio to Germany in the 1920s. It was at one of the parties Pacelli – as he then was – threw for the political and diplomatic elite in the Tiergarten quarter of Berlin where he'd lived.

Father Carlo adjusted his monk's habit over an ample midriff as he shifted in his chair to look up from the desk. But he continued straightening its contents, then the rimless spectacles he was taking me in through.

I was sweating and out of breath. I apologised for being late, but explained that, having sold my car, I had walked all the way there from my apartment.

Mentioning it made me recall its shadowy silence, shuttered, too, against the city's brilliance and traffic. My possessions were half-packed there – the few I would be taking with me tomorrow. Standing alone, I had simply looked at the rest and left them to move only later if the owner absolutely demanded it. Anja and I had accumulated so much together.

"You're not very late," my spiritual advisor said. (For this was what the monk, now indicating the chair at the other side of the desk, had more or less become for me over the last few weeks, regardless of my lack of religious belief. With Anja's death I had soon found myself using Carlo as a secular Father Confessor, judging it better to rely on him than on the doctor, who'd been of little help.)

"Anyway, you're here now," Father Carlo said, "ready to move on. That's all that matters."

The priest told me how pleased he was that I had finally decided to undertake the publishing project I'd been offered; how personally helpful I was sure to find it; how conducive to work the monastery would prove. These were all things Father Carlo had said several times before, but which he nevertheless chose to repeat now, with this show of paternal concern.

"Look, I've written a letter of introduction to the Abbot for you."

Father Carlo passed me one of two envelopes lying on the desk. They were sealed and made of fine paper.

"He'll make sure you're well looked after. And then it occurred to me that while you're here for me to wish you Godspeed, I might as well also send a note with you for another monk, Father Erich. He's one of the Order's hermits, in permanent retreat even further south. I hope you'll meet him too. There's every reason why you should."

"How can I, if he's a hermit?"

"They come in when the monastery holds a chapter. And the Abbot will take care of giving him the letter. Or any of the monks should know how to get it to him."

"I'll do what I can," I said.

"It's most important that he should receive it," Father Carlo said, glasses glinting as he handed over the letter.

Taking it, I could not see beyond the opaque lenses.

That night, I had difficulty sleeping in the apartment. I finally gave up trying. I walked through moonlight to the window. The waiter in the bar across the street was closing up.

I'd given up taking the pills prescribed by the doctor in the weeks following Anja's death. They'd left me drowsy during the day without sending me to sleep at night. But my wakefulness continued even now, without the medication. It was especially hard given my thoughts on this long eve of my departure.

My mother had brought me to Rome as a child, after my father's disappearance in Egypt. I had lived here ever since. Yet, tomorrow, I would be leaving for North Africa. Staring into the deserted road, I wondered when I would be back. Now, writing this, long after returning, I can't help asking myself if I would have embarked on the voyage at all if I'd had an inkling of all that was to befall me.

I took a taxi to the airport long before necessary. Travelling across the dark city, then rising above it into dawn, I grew apprehensive.

Later, awakening in the plane, I was anxious again. It did not exactly register as nerves, but resembled a low-grade fever like that brought on by dysentery. My light-headedness and sensitivity to the sun even seemed a delirious clarity of vision as I trembled with the plane down over the Mediterranean towards a harsh white curve of buildings: the city.

Landed, I considered going up to the old Turkish quarter. I remembered it from one of those old films Anja and I used to watch. It had been shot on location, and showed crowds thronging the *kasbah* at all hours. In its tangle of dim alleys, I pictured myself seeking the Order's house. Thick stone walls must render it virtually indistinguishable from the rest of the fortress. I would fail to make out, in the pulsing human mass, a line of poor people queuing up to its door for the midday soup.

Jostled, unable to communicate, I might grow more and more lost among huge flies in the suffocating, covered passages. I'd surely long for a sudden brilliant point to look down from, gasping, across the *medina* with its sloping disorder of flat roofs.

Despairing of ever finding the Order's house in the *medina*, I made instead directly for the French city on the lower slopes near the harbour. Besides, I had to allow time to find the bus station, and could not risk missing the one coach I'd been told was scheduled for that day.

When I did buy a ticket, it was to depart at three o'clock. I went over yet again to another ragged official to ask which bay the bus would leave from, and at what time. I received the same answer, in the same guttural North African French, but also learned that in the meantime, I could store my heavy metal suitcase in the office. I chose not to.

There was the late morning and early afternoon to kill. I traipsed down an unshaded street. To either side, the walls were a mass of Arabic slogans and posters in what I'd later come to know was a struggle between Islamists and the state.

My hand repeatedly slipped round my suitcase handle. A patch of shirt stuck to my back, beneath my soaked linen jacket. A smell of charred meat drifted across from a kebab stand, with its bleat of Arab music. I felt empty but, faintly nauseous, I had no appetite.

On I walked, through wide colonial boulevards and squares deserted at this hour. Half their cobbles were missing. Tar oozed up in places. Palms drooped with splitting fronds.

I came upon a public garden, my head swimming. I sat on a cracked stone bench in the shade of acacia trees. An old man perched at the other end, a bucket by the hem of his tattered *djellaba* and cracked bare feet. It contained bottled drinks in liquid that had once been ice.

I bought a bottle of mineral water. The plastic top came off too easily. I gulped several strongly chlorinated mouthfuls. They were tepid. I poured the rest over my head.

The air was static – sickeningly so. Still, there was no question of moving. Awakening, I felt a stirring; a faint breeze, coming from the sea. Suddenly, I reached out: my case was there. The old man had gone. I looked at my watch. It was only two o'clock. Even so, I got up, drained, and returned to the bus station. I longed to be sitting, simply waiting an hour in my seat, my luggage stowed above me.

I entered the shed and walked over to the correct lane with its formless crowd. The coach had not yet arrived. I stood with men in burnooses, all smoking. Peasant women, hooded with towels the ends of which were held between their teeth as veils, carried large bundles.

Some set them on the oily ground. I kept looking down to make certain my suitcase was still there.

For an instant, my eyes strayed to another bay. A balding man with a gut, American to judge by his jeans and accent, was loading up a Jeep. He was helped by a woman, visible to me only as a shapely back bent to lift a box.

The bus appeared. There was a surge even before it was parked. I had to compete to get on, only to find, once I was at the door, that I was not allowed to take my suitcase aboard.

"But it won't fit," the ticket collector replied firmly when I insisted that it contained important items.

I pushed back through those pressing from behind and gave the case to the youth loading the hold, along with a worn note – though I was uncertain what it was worth, not having fully worked out the value of the currency into which I had changed my money at the airport.

Even when I was finally settled in my seat, I continued to wonder if the tip was enough to ensure that the suitcase was safely stowed. Was it free from pilfering, even though it was locked? I feared the Arab boy spoke too little French to understand that I did not want it to be added to that alarmingly precarious clutter on the roof. These questions were still on my mind as a matronly peasant woman with a raffia basket crowded in next to me. Inwardly, I was asking them of another woman. If Anja had been with me, *she* would have made certain that our luggage was beside us in the bus. She had always been the practical one.

I felt very tired. It was obviously the after-effect of the adrenaline needed finally to seat myself here. But I knew it was also the strain of travelling alone, for the first time since my marriage … and forevermore.

I was shivering again, light-headed, anxious without her – as I now finally recognised I had actually been since early morning.

The packed old vehicle set off in a dark cloud of diesel fumes. It swerved sharply out of the depot into a winding lane, barely avoiding the sacks of spices and cages of chickens fronting dim stores. With a prolonged honk it turned down a steep street, hurtling through the gloom, to come out abruptly into piercing light. I looked past avenues of palms on the corniche. The sea glittered painfully. Bathing rafts bobbed, empty.

I blinked, and in that instant recalled lazing with Anja on the beach near Ostia.

The coach jerked aside, past spacious colonial villas. White walls were peeling, thick with unkempt bougainvillea. The coach was speeding almost recklessly through a shantytown. Prayer mats were laid out in a ruined house: an improvised mosque. Another was installed on a building site with a running hose. A small girl and her even smaller sister were walking away from it, barefoot, henna in their hair, plastic water bottles in hand.

We were in open country. There were glaring expanses of red earth, yellowing fields and hills with cypress stands. Blinking, I smelled hot plastic from the seats, and diesel fumes. I yawned, hearing the opening crackle of the video player – the bus was equipped with one, although it lacked air conditioning.

I watched the blurred copy of an Egyptian film. Lovers were cavorting. The girl was shapely, swarthy, coquettish. She lived in Alexandria, to judge by the coastline, harbour and the kinds of looks I associated with it. But the video was inaudible, though it would, in any case, have been incomprehensible to me – in more ways than one.

The woman and her city were infinitely out of reach. They were in a place immeasurably far beyond whatever obstacle lay between me and that gleaming bay, where her lover displayed feelings it was impossible to imagine I could ever have again. The action was overcome by flickering on the video, a distant copy of the original. In my drowsiness, the scene became ash, falling steadily, relentlessly. It was after a cataclysm – the collision of a meteor in the time of the dinosaurs. The fallout, a cloud, blocked the effect of the earth's atmosphere. The barrier killed all life as surely as a nuclear explosion.

Eyes closed, I found myself on a planet that was now dark desert. It was as remote from the sun as if the solar system had never been. It was the only point ever to exist.

I woke as the video showed the closing credits. We were travelling through plains. I gazed out at monotonous fields and wide sky shimmering in this heavy afternoon heat. Even the flies seemed to buzz more lazily over the drowsy passengers.

Only my neighbour was awake. She offered me some of the food she was eating. I accepted from politeness, then realised how hungry I was. The taste of this white curd cheese reminded me of the latticed round my mother used to buy from an old Arab woman, coming to the door; it smelled slightly of ammonia and was wrapped in reeds. My mother, fanatical about germs, used to soak it in a solution of potassium of permanganate, as she did all the fruit and vegetables. One was always being bombarded with deadly microbes in Egypt, she would say, cutting me a piece of the now faintly purple cheese.

What I was eating with bread in the bus was pure white. I refused more of my neighbour's food – but not just from politeness – and turned to the window.

I cast my mind back to those distant days. Distant, too, I had felt from my mother, despite our closeness in so many ways, while my father was away for weeks, working. Then, when he was no longer with us at all, and my mother and I had moved to Rome, we continued living together – but somehow apart. Both of us silently studious by the same lamplight, we had actually been moving imperceptibly on different tracks. Once touching, now parallel, then diverging, they had been heading through seemingly similar terrain – to who knew what destinations?

She had simply come to a stop at no special moment, breaking down in the middle of nowhere. There had been no sense of conclusion, I thought, the road stretching on ahead of me. I yawned. My eyes watered and grew unfocused.

Night had fallen. The video was still playing. It might have been a second or even a third film. Scenes had appeared on the screen like senseless episodes from otherwise unremembered dreams, into which all that is evaded of life gets drawn: dreams expressing whatever loss or longing is eventually supposed to be left behind, but which one actually carries within oneself forever.

So I supposed, getting out of the bus with those arriving at their stop. I only wanted to stretch for a few minutes in pitch darkness. The air hurt my lungs. My chest ached.

Men sat in burnooses before a wattle café. They drank muddy glasses of coffee by the light of a hurricane lamp. There was the fragrance of hashish as I turned into the night to pee. I felt the steam condense against my hand. Distantly, a shred of veiled moon etched a further peak as I headed back to my seat.

On the coach went. So did the video. Figures moved incomprehensibly, ceaselessly, across a screen.

First light came. It was livid; sour yellow. But it was sand dashing against the window that fully awakened me. The wind was fierce. There were fewer passengers now. It was freezing, even inside. I had moved instinctively closer to the sole source of warmth. But no, this large bosom was only my well-padded neighbour's, rising and falling as she gasped rhythmically. The handkerchief that usually covered her nose and mouth had slipped down around her chin.

I envied her, together with the other snoring passengers. What I had been roused to, here on the high plateau, was a pane blank with gritty fog, barely revealing the occasional etiolated palm in that stony aridity. Or else there was the video continuing to run, although the film had long ended. All that was human had gone. It was just a blurred screen.

I awoke, sweating, to a seemingly new dimension. Bright, reddish plains with vast dunes stretched endlessly to a measurelessly wide, empty horizon. The sun climbed higher and higher over the sand. A hot wind made the bus roll and pitch. It blew on the hood with continuous thumps. Still the video crackled, blank.

Later, sick with hunger, wishing I had accepted more of my mother's curd cheese but fearing there was no likelihood of the woman offering additional food, I realised the dunes had declined. The sun was at its height. The track stretched on, blinding white.

Boulders appeared. I squinted at them. We were travelling over bare bedrock, gravel, sand. On and on it went.

It was giving me a headache to look out. I drew a thumb and forefinger over my eyelids. Sweat trickled over the back of my hand. I glanced up from my instant of sightlessness, met by what first seemed fiery dimness. Then I glimpsed stony desert. It spread to the very end of my field of vision and surely beyond, into blankness I could not even imagine.

I thought again of the video screen. It was still flickering. I yearned for an image and felt there must be one somewhere, but that it was being blocked. I seemed to be willing it into clarity, knuckles whitening with the effort.

Desert took hold of me again. My eyes were lost in it. One period passed, then others of which I was unaware except in retrospect. I awakened each time, whether from a moment of sleep or a full hour, to the same emptiness.

*

A faint shape gleamed in the window, barely distinguishable from the rocks and sand. Then I saw I was glimpsing myself.

I thought of the mirror in our flat – the ormolu one, given by Anja's parents and hanging in our living room. It reflected us both going unobservantly about our business, countless times a day. Too engrossed in one another's actual company, we had an unthinking sense of shared being, as if each supplied an element indispensable to the atmosphere we both breathed.

Only once Anja had gone did I consciously take in the mirror. It was a dead moment in which I faced its emptiness, only to be alarmed by what I saw there: a lost soul. The person I'd been had vanished together with the rest of our joint life, I now reflected in the bus, catching these spectral features of mine effaced by the desert glare.

I had thrown away our address book. Faces from twenty years together had been consigned to a dustbin to be incinerated. My memory of them reduced, too, in what my mind's eye saw as ash as I rattled on through the Sahara. It recalled images of Hiroshima, New Mexico, all from the photography book Anja had edited on nuclear testing. They also faded. It left me to unrelieved sand.

Dreary was the sameness as we drove unendingly, mile upon mile. But I was actually falling fast into an increasingly narrow place. From the vantage point of writing this, I see I was being drawn precipitately down into what I could never have imagined awaited me.

Moving deeper into this void, I severed whatever ligaments still held me to normal life. I'd begun drifting from my moorings once my father disappeared, then when my mother died. But with the loss of my wife, the bottom fell out of my life. A trapdoor had opened, landing me here in this limitless sameness without vitality or prospects. I could scarcely make out the blinding horizon.

The *I* I'd been, that paper-thin self I now knew had barely covered inner emptiness all those years, had simply flown off, like a flimsy kite losing itself in this burning desert sky. So, awakened in the bus, I felt deadened. The vital part of me had surely been removed during sleep's anaesthetic. It left only these dismal, drowsy remains.

How ever would I survive out here? I couldn't even be certain of having a roof over my head. I was not expected. Maybe I should have gone to the Order's house in the capital after all.

But I wondered how much use notice of my arrival would have been. There had been such a decline in communications since the days of the colonial occupation. The post was probably untrustworthy. Besides, I doubted that the telephone, even the radio telephone, had reached this far into the Sahara.

I would depend exclusively on giving my letters of introduction to the Abbot and another monk, a hermit – assuming they were safe in my metal suitcase. Again I worried that they might not be secure on the bus.

As for the monastery, I doubted my ability to withstand its rigours for months on end. Not for me, the novice's eager anticipation of hardship for his soul's sake.

Whereupon I could just hear Father Carlo say: "But the very simplicity of the place is the point. It'll allow you to pursue your project single-mindedly, without distractions or demands. What's more, it'll give you a chance to recover your balance. That will permit you to come into tune with yourself – and who knows what or whom else?"

The trouble was that, emptied of all I had been, I was afraid I would not have the resources left to survive in that silence and space. There'd be little more than a book in the making to sustain me. It could not match the strength the brethren derived from belief and a daily round, and carry me through to whatever was to become of me.

What was there to live off in this sterile calm? I asked myself among the snores of insensible passengers. For I was travelling with rising trepidation through these blindingly barren spaces to my personal zero point.

Later, gazing unseeingly out the window, a tree caught my eye. It was the sole living thing in that parched terrain. It spread the only shade hereabouts. I went on looking at it for as long as it remained in sight. Only now did I withdraw again from this desert, which, I learned some time afterwards, had water underground. It surfaced, doubtless, in a distant *wadi* into which the acacia's vast root system could tap.

*

It was late afternoon by the time we honked into the village. Children ran with the slowing coach through heavy glare. Others pressed round as the driver and his boy unloaded the luggage in the marketplace.

Repeatedly muscled out of the way by the other passengers, I was taken aback by the weight of my metal luggage finally swinging out of the hold towards me. I barely avoided dropping it.

I winced from the sand in my eye and stood there, rubbing the eyelid, holding the suitcase that, I hoped, still contained my fragile equipment – intact.

I heard Arab music. There were diesel fumes. By the time I looked up, the bus was on its way with its remaining passengers. The other arrivals had dispersed.

A radio crackled from a café. I paced over to it. There was a wave of mint at the entrance.

"Taxi. Monastery," I said, as I had been instructed, to the stern men inside over their glasses of tea. Was it already too late to have turned back? Would I, in any case, have done so if I'd known what awaited me beyond the monastery's door? Fruitless the questions may be, but I can't help wondering, knowing all that this raw self of mine was destined to undergo.

The owner of the café got up from a game of backgammon. Unsmilingly, he put out his hand to take the suitcase. I continued holding it, but followed him back out again. The market was closing for the day. An old woman was gathering up the few sprouting purple onions she displayed. A camel sat on its haunches in the sandy square, munching a bunch of limp clover while gazing into the trees of the oasis's orchard. We passed worn tires by a corner shop that was barely more than a cubbyhole; the owner cut them up to make sandals. Then we turned into a short road of single-storey red houses. Abruptly it gave way to rocky desert, reaching distantly to massive mountains, rimmed with scarlet.

One of the houses had a garage.

"Tax! Monaster!" the guide called to a man emerging from beneath a car. Its outlines, its colour even, were indistinct in the gloomy interior.

"Five minutes," the man said.

We turned back. A current of sand was drifting along the road. We re-entered the café. A youth got up from the game of backgammon he was watching and gestured to me to set down the metal suitcase and take his place. He went to prepare tea.

He took a flatbread from a pile by the kettle and set it, with a steaming glass, before me – the new occupant of the Coca-Cola crate. The others continued playing dourly, without acknowledging my presence. I did not look at the board. I was drinking, eating, fearing my queasiness had been caused by the little I had already touched in this country.

I went on staring at the glass, packed with bright mint leaves, here beneath a window. The sun was setting in the cracked pane. It faded away, hue by hue, from pink to black.

A naked bulb lit the game dimly as I finally looked up and out the door from where I was sitting.

"Taxi?" I said, sighing.

"Five minutes please," the youth answered.

I got up and walked into a foul-smelling cubbyhole, with its barely lit squat lavatory. A leprous shard of mirror faced me with tired, remote eyes. Blinking, I left to go into the street and stretch my legs.

Almost immediately, I stopped. Something was restraining me.

Unaccountably, confronting the owner, the youth, all those mutely seated around me beneath this flickering yellow glare, I felt a lack of will. I had stumbled into an opaque situation: one with absolutely no meaning for me, but which was strangely drawing me in. Passive, deprived of initiative, I sank onto my seat, only peering at the marketplace. It was dark, empty except for whirling sand.

I was drawn into a vortex. Instinctively, I raised an arm as if to acknowledge the youth, but actually to reach for another's hand. Yet Anja's was gone, and beyond it, my mother's.

I was in a daze when someone walked in. I did not have the slightest idea how long I had been distracted as I came to, recognising the man from the garage. So the taxi had arrived.

I reached into my pocket and heaped next to my untouched tea all the coins I came upon, having no idea what would be enough. I hoped it would protect me against any unpleasantness, which I felt unable to face. The youth instantly picked up the metal suitcase and headed off to load it into the boot of the car.

Following him, I was surprised the moment I stepped out of the café by the cold, windy night. Then, even in this light, I could see just what a beaten-up old car it was. Even so, the driver opened the back door for me to get in. Just as I was entering, the youth smiled, stretching out a hand and touching his heart with the other. I found myself reciprocating, half-surprised at my pleasantness to someone I did not know if

I would ever see again, and who could not possibly matter to me even if our paths were to cross.

The driver set off, asking: "Français? American? Italiano? Deutsch?"

I gave a tired nod, discouraging further conversation. But a cigarette was extended to me. I shook my head, barely taking in a sandy street, some loping mongrel.

We came out of the oasis, into vast openness – and amazing light, I realised, looking out through the dust-encrusted windscreen. The sky was huge, crowded with brilliant stars. I had never seen so many. They teemed without order, it seemed, as the driver sought to tune the radio.

The harsh crackle was quite acceptable, to judge by the man's smile. He must have thought he was obliging a passenger looking back from what, increasingly, became a bewilderingly random scatter of lights to formless desert. Blanched, the emptiness stretched on and on towards massive, moonlit peaks.

I wondered what we would do if the car broke down here. Then I was, again, rating my prospects of finally reaching my destination. Having no idea how much longer we had to go, or how much further across this lunar waste, I drew a breath and braced myself for the next burst of practical activity my arrival would require.

The car lurched to a halt unexpectedly. Stars were cut off by blankness. We had stopped just short of a wall. I judged that it continued for some distance, at a height of about two stories. Then I realised the driver had got out.

My feet touched sand. I shivered, closing the door behind me – quietly, given the hour. I found my suitcase beside me, coldly metallic. The driver had already shut the boot.

I gave him the fare with a whispered: "*Shukran.*"

We shook hands and the driver touched his heart, teeth glinting – and now eyes.

As suddenly as he had arrived, he sped off.

2

A cloud of invisible sand half-obscured the car's single rear light. The red was entirely lost. The whirring grind of tires had faded. There was a soughing as I went on standing there, shuddering, with my single piece of luggage, looking out over luminous desert.

Turning back to darkness, I proceeded alone, suitcase in hand, approaching a long wall. In its shadowy mass, softly shaped adobe as it seemed to me, I came upon a door.

Actually, it was more of a recessed gate. I ran my hand over what the texture revealed to be wood studded with metal. Varnish had bubbled, but was dry in this cold. I felt the jamb at shoulder level. Finding the bell, I paused, wondering whether it was electric or manual. I regretted having to awaken anyone. Even the Guest Master – doubtless used to such arrivals as they had from the bus at this hour – might be disturbed. He would surely be angry, albeit silently, appearing at the unlit entrance.

I rang. The bell sounded within, manually, hardly sonorous. It might have been ringing in some nondescript city apartment, such as that to which I felt, irrationally, I was going home.

There was no answer in what I instantly reminded myself was a monastery. It was deliberately simple: a place of work and service. I prepared myself for a wait, while the brother roused himself. My arrival was, after all, unannounced. I listened closely for footsteps, for the jangle of keys at the other side of the gate.

I heard the wind again. It was sweeping across what, from this hill, my night vision suggested were sandstone flats with distant dunes.

Silence returned. There was only the splutter of an electricity generator. The longer I waited, the more my ear edited it out.

The silence had become absolute. Not knowing how long I should allow for someone to come to the door, or how much time had already passed, I was uncertain as to whether or not I should ring again. Perhaps the Guest Master, expecting no one, not even having left on the entrance light, far from sleeping with an ear cocked for this late arrival, had fallen into the deepest sleep. The ringing bell might merely have been incorporated into his now-continuing dream.

Indeed, I half-wondered if I myself had actually heard that thin, reed-like peal, which could just as well have been the wind, whistling once more. Yet, no: I had definitely pressed the bell. It had sounded. I should be certain of that.

I must not allow an understandably slow response to make me doubt my welcome after such a journey. The Guest Master would be here soon enough to admit a late arrival on the basis of a letter of introduction.

I rang again – harder, longer. I stood closer to the gate, suitcase on the sand. Still, there was no noise. I breathed in deeply. It hurt, out in the cold air. My finger went back to that button, thrusting two, three times. I was right up against the door. There was no sound, not even of the wind.

I turned away from the studded-wood entrance and took up my suitcase, fist tight around the handle, and paced along the wall. It was some distance to the corner. Rounding it, I saw the short side of what was obviously the monastery's rectangular enclosure. It had window slits, though no door. I walked at an increasingly wide angle to it, near the edge of the shelf on which the complex stood. It gave me a better view, by bright starlight, of the shadowy tops of several trees. An inner building was surmounted by a cross.

I turned another corner, dismayed at the prospect of a further blank, unlit wall. So on this darker back of the enclosure, I trudged on over-packed sand, striving to reconcile myself to making a full, fruitless circuit of the building before giving in to alarm – or permitting myself, back at the unlit, unyielding front gate, to ask (let alone try to answer) the perfectly rational questions I was now preventing myself from forming in my mind.

This self-censorship must have turned my thoughts, for a moment, away from my pursuit of this long, back wall. But suddenly I shuddered, recoiling: I had just glimpsed a dark thing hanging from the wall.

It was a ladder.

Setting down my suitcase, I raised the ladder from sand to parapet. It all but touched the top of a tree.

I put a hand on a rung. It was made of bamboo, tethered to the side by what felt like raffia. Drawing on it, testing it for weight, I mentally balanced the idea of simply climbing up.

The brethren, roused as every morning at first light by their bell, would discover an intruder. So they would inevitably resent my stay, even if it was only to be for a limited period on the periphery of their lives. But without their calm acceptance, I couldn't take my surroundings sufficiently for granted to lose myself in my work, emerging with whatever final outcome.

Equally, however, I did not see myself slumped in the sand against the locked gate until dawn. Deaf dreamers all, the monks might well open up to find me out in that early sun, wondering why on Earth I had not done the obvious, sensible, thing and scaled this ladder.

Momentarily, I asked myself in whose footsteps I would be following. But by then I had already hoisted myself up to the bottom rung, and was concentrating hard on making further headway.

It was a precarious ascent, with that metal suitcase swinging from one hand. I kept trying to counteract the bias it gave me, especially the higher I climbed. I winced each time the flimsy structure creaked, fearing, with each step, to awaken those I had so recently longed to rouse and receive me. Yet then I had proposed myself as their guest; now I approached like a thief – one whose head, shoulders, upper arms reached the top of the wall at last.

I placed my free hand on the sandy parapet, still warm from the sun. Pausing, I glanced involuntarily past my suitcase, down the gleaming bamboo ladder off this sandstone shelf, and almost lost my balance. I looked up instantly, clinging to the top of the wall. Chest pounding, I pulled up the suitcase and carefully placed it on the adobe perch. Raising myself there too, I sat with feet dangling into what might have been a fig tree.

I continued atop the wall, taking in the sound of gushing water, the smell of jasmine, the indistinct masses of buildings set amid dark foliage and, again, the stars.

I became aware of the wind. It was cold up here.

I reached for the suitcase and set it length-wise between my legs. Lowering it, letting it slip from my hands, a face flashed into my mind: Anja, my wife, would have received it, I thought, grimacing at the risk to its contents, at the expected noise. But the sound was barely more than of a stray dog making its unruly entry through dense undergrowth.

There was no answering sound, no light. All was still, dead quiet. It carried on, it seemed, as I glanced back from the enclosure with the silence of moonlit desert planing endlessly away. Returning to the tree, I suddenly just slipped towards it, not conscious of any moment in which I had specifically decided to do so. I lowered myself to the ground.

I had landed by a bench, beside a large tank. Water gushed into it from a pipe. Nearby, the dark form of my suitcase lay cradled by branches. Maybe the contents were safe.

I went to collect it, feeling the remains of the day's heat, protected here against the wind. I found myself treading on soft earth, then between rows of tall plants that might be sunflowers or maize in this light. Pulling the suitcase off what was, in fact, a fig tree, I simply held it, not moving. Despite the effort of entering the dark enclosure, I found myself in the same predicament as I'd been outside it.

Certain, at least, that I must not awaken anyone, I was not clear what to do next. I just looked out over more shadowy vegetation to that adobe rectangle with its bell tower and cross. Then I began making for it, deciding to wait inside until morning.

I would hardly be the first outsider whom the monks, proceeding into their chapel at first light, had ever seen, quietly, respectfully waiting in a pew at the back for the divine office. I might be standing with other visitors, whose comings and goings the brethren would not question or even notice, simply leaving it to the Guest Master. Or so Father Carlo had told me to expect.

On my way to the building, across a path so thick with sand that it covered my shoes, my eye was drawn to the side. There was a space of framed stars: an open gate, smaller than the one in front. I would have come upon it had I continued along the back of the enclosure.

I trod on something, and flinched. Half uncoiled, it turned out to be a rosary. I continued for several steps, and came upon a sandal – then another, its pair. I left them there, moving on through dense shadow.

The chapel's moulded adobe wall still gave off heat. I climbed a step and entered through the half-open door. It was stifling, stale with old incense. There was the intense red point of the sanctuary light in the darkness.

I stretched my hand out to the side, to rough-grained wood. It was the end of a pew. I slid in. Lifting my suitcase in behind me, I put it down and sat with a loud creak.

I yawned loudly. The journey, the anxiety of coming here, of gaining access, had exhausted me. My chin lolled onto my chest.

My head jerked up from the dreamless pit into which I'd fallen. Stretching as I peered vaguely about me to see if it was getting light, I had no more idea of where I was than of how long I'd been asleep.

Now there was something to my left in this pew of what was again the chapel. It was at hardly any distance. Yes, it was a human figure.

I tried to look at him more closely. It was too dark to make out more than the person's mass, sitting there absolutely still. I had heard that a monk would sometimes pass an entire night in meditation, keeping prayerful vigil until morning. I would not disturb these deep devotions by peering too closely.

I turned away, satisfied that my unannounced presence had apparently been simply accepted by at least one of the brethren, although I soon grew uncomfortable at the idea of having to hold so still next to somebody for all the long, dark hours ahead.

I looked before me, again, at that red point of light. I was sweating in this used air. It was heavy with a smell like that of unwashed bodies.

In the utter silence, there was the muted sweep of a cold wind outside. I saw the sanctuary light flicker. It was a flame, lengthening, diminishing, settling to my accustoming eyes. It cast what I now found to be a trembling, fluctuating arc of shadowy visibility over the altar, a simple affair. On it went across several front pews – where I saw another motionless human form.

I gazed intently about me, coming into possession of full sight. There was another figure – and yet another. The chapel was full of monks.

The silence, the stillness, was suddenly oppressive. It was claustrophobically hot in here. There was no question of me sleeping, or of sitting out the night restfully, with all these presences.

There must be twenty or more of them, I realised – the majority of the brethren. I turned nervously back to the monk beside me. No longer seeing him as a formless mass, I made out my neighbour's head. It was settled at an angle on one shoulder. The mouth was open. Something was glinting, black, beneath the chin.

Gripping the pew in front, I leaned across, frowning. I gasped: the sound held in the silence. *The man's throat had been cut.*

Suddenly all the blood seemed to drain out of me. I was faint; I felt sick. Sitting with my head down, as far between my legs as the cramped space between this pew and the next allowed, I finally looked up.

I pulled out a handkerchief to wipe my face and put it back, drenched, into my pocket. I got to my feet. Numb, barely serving me, they carried me beyond my suitcase and out into the aisle. I lurched forward over the packed sand to the figure several rows in front.

The monk had not responded to my rasping cry. He sat hunched, motionless, in an attitude of deep meditation. I touched his shoulder, then tapped it. Finally I shook so hard as to draw the head back. The eyes stared. Again, I cried out. This throat, too, had been slashed.

Bent over the monk, I started, feeling something on the back of my hand, and recoiled. It was my own sweat falling from my forehead, off my nose, as I gasped, striving to bring my breathing under control.

I stood up straight, fighting panic lest my heartbeat, far from subsiding, were to grow more painfully frenzied with what I was now suspecting.

The realisation drove me further up the sandy aisle to another figure whom, this time, I did not bother to observe first from a respectful distance. I slid into the pew right next to him – and to what I hoped against hope I was not going to find.

I flinched from that blood-caked throat. There was buzzing as an invisible fly feasted off the gashed windpipe.

I paced on, moving without sensation. This might be a dream. The nearer I came to the altar, the more the monks could be found in groups. They had been hauled there, to judge by the way they were on top of each other. Some lay stretched out on the pews, with others piled over them. A few hung forwards across pews, limbs overlapping those of their fellows.

I stood up straight, rigid, taking in the whole chapel. Gazing at the frozen disorder of this, the brethren's final embrace, I heard a cry go up involuntarily:

"Is anyone alive?"

The question reverberated. The only reply was the droning generator, the wind outside. Then there was complete silence, in this crowded, suffocating darkness in which I somehow found myself, and into which my eyes had just begun to see.

*

I escaped the chapel. Again I called out my question, staring at the heavens with their massive disorder of stars.

This time the silence grew eerie. A voice – Anja's – welled up within me, warning that I, too, might be in danger. I took it in on the chapel step, before the shadowy path of sand, by the brethren's curved adobe quarters, the kitchen garden, the filling water tank. Such deceiving nocturnal serenity! The very calm was terrifying. The slaughterers might still be here.

Yet already, only seconds later, my panic had been swept into some distant, unreachable part of myself by a huge wave of fatigue. I knew I ought to be making decisions, resolving matters, but my will was paralysed. I could not think or act. This was a nightmare in which I was unable to cry out against coming danger. I yawned, mouth bone-dry, salty, with this further surge of exhaustion. It made everything remote in the moonlight, unreal.

I went to pick up my suitcase. It felt heavier than before. My hand was having trouble gripping, but I set off with it. The path led to the open gate and the desert beyond. I had only taken a couple of paces along it when I noticed something to the side of the sand: the sole of a foot. A monk was slumped over in oleander bushes.

Steps later, I came upon the sandals and rosary. The dead brother must have shed them in his haste to join the brethren in their supposed sanctuary.

Not sure where I was going, I found myself back in that area planted with sunflowers or maize. This time I noticed a group of the waist-high stalks dangling, broken. They had been caught in a fall. There, just before me, was another corpse, which I had walked right by. Earlier, though, I had only been looking for a way to survive the dark hours until morning, when all would be settled and clear. Now, with my unwanted night vision, I saw all – and knew such a morning could never come.

I noticed a light. A weak electric bulb was outside one of the buildings. I began carrying my suitcase over to it, presuming it had been on previously but that I had overlooked it too. Or had it been switched on since my arrival?

I trod gingerly, repeatedly seeking to judge how my footsteps sounded. I wanted badly to believe they were muffled by this sand, that I, less even than shadow, was vacant darkness from the lighted entrance.   On I continued, the non-being I imagined myself to have become. I shuddered in the cold desert night with fear of what lay in store in that fast-approaching, magnetic interior.

The door was ajar. I pushed it lightly, my free hand trembling. It swung back several more inches, hinges whining. I winced. There was no further sound, just a heavy inertness.

I was arrested before the lintel and jambs. My eyes had not penetrated the wash of lit space opened up by the diagonal door. Then, without awareness of having decided to, or needing to overcome fear, I simply entered the frame.

I came in at the side of a long, shadowy room with a low ceiling. A wooden table with benches ran down its length. Plates were set out for a meal – interrupted, to judge by the food remaining on them. A line of ants traced its way to a spill of olive oil, I noticed, walking down the refectory. It ended in a dim serving area.

Approaching it, I almost tripped. Someone was on the floor. The monk was slumped face-down in a dark red pool, a ladle in his hand, apron strings tied at his back. He had been slower than the brethren he was serving in fleeing sudden danger for sanctuary. I did not turn him over. I knew only too well how he had died. I merely sat heavily on a bench beside the stack of plates and the serving dishes.

Hinges creaked. Here, out of the cold, I knew I must think what to do next. I simply went on gazing at the figure before me. The limbs seemed, to my repeatedly closing eyes, stretched out luxuriantly in their stillness.

My eyes opened. There was a strong smell. But no, I knew it wasn't just food in the pale light entering the half-open refectory door. Getting up, stiff, I reluctantly remembered all I had gone to sleep over.

So it had not been a dream. Leaving my suitcase where it was, I walked out into the fresh, already warming air. Dawn was breaking above the gardens, the orchard, the pink buildings and walls. Through the open gate an early sun bled over the desert horizon, its distant mountains magnificent.

I stood alone among the running water and the flowering trees until I again glimpsed the sandals and rosary in the sand: the brother in the bushes, the one among the maize (not sunflowers). New to me was the monk frozen over the side of the overflowing metal cistern by an adobe bench. I viewed him distantly, as if in a painting.

There was rustling; I started. A cat made its way out of undergrowth and walked delicately past the barefooted corpse, oblivious to all but the scent it was pursuing. I had an inner glimpse of feminine hands gathering it up.

Once more, I grew aware of being the sole living person here.

This clarity of light, this early crispness, the utter stillness, made it inconceivable that any malign presence lingered from the night. There was tranquillity, a quiet solitude even in this cool hour before the day's heat.

Taking in the fallen brethren, I barely felt the savage strangeness of their murder. I had a fleeting impression – more sensation than image – of waking to a partner stretched luxuriously beside me as always, yet this morning lifeless. It suffused, half-erotically, the grisliness of a spectacle so massively alien to me that I could well have wondered at the situations echoing each other like this. Might I always have expected finally to confront multiple deaths?

Suddenly the present resurged with full force, and I felt tethered to its brute reality. I could no longer elude the problem I had arrived with yesterday evening, leaving the taxi. It had grown to enormous proportions during the night: *what must I do next?*

It was a pressing question, but only one of several. Who could have done this? Why? Where was he – were they – now? And were there any survivors, though I really knew the answer?

I looked round, taking in the plan of the monastery. I wanted to see how to notify others. I needed a telephone.

Back at the main building, I was about to open a door beyond the refectory when I stopped. A persistent noise had, until now, been just below the threshold of my awareness. A distant sound of electric grinding, not just the generator, was getting closer. It brought me nervously over to the gate. I went out and headed around the monastery to the point where the taxi had left me last night.

I searched from this point above stony flats, then dunes and cliffs, in the whitening light, and saw a plume of dust approaching from the direction I myself had come by bus, all that unimaginably long time ago. Beyond were the dwarfing mountains.

Nearer and nearer it came. I stood and squinted before the locked gate until I could see an old Berber in a burnoose, his head bound in a faded yellow scarf, on a motorcycle. It was fitted with a tray heaped with limes. The man was hailing even before his contraption ground to a halt. He held up a lime in each hand and came over, talking animatedly.

Understanding through the gestures, not the language that he sought to sell his merchandise as always to the monastery, I took him by the arm to lead him to the back gate. The old man, chattering all the time, ignored me, his chaperone. He preferred to make for the front door where he usually entered. He pressed the bell again and again, in rapid succession. It rang and rang.

He was now waiting, totally still. In an instant of utter silence, about to draw him away, I took in the old man's unexpected patience, his odour of tobacco and stale laundry, the vast noiselessness of the desert, increasingly brilliant, and all that had lain in wait for me since I myself, sublimely ignorant too, had been at this ungiving door last night. It was a deathly muteness.

Again, I took the old man's arm. It set off a further stream of sounds. I virtually pulled him until, face to face, I stabbed the air in the direction of the monastery. My index finger sliced my own throat. It did so repeatedly. I only stopped in order to hold up both hands. I did so again and again and again. It made twenty-four: the entire number of the slaughtered community.

The old man was staring intently. He looked up to the sky, the whites of his eyes widened, to invoke Allah. Several times he uttered the cry. He rushed, faster even than me, to the back gate.

Once in the monastery, he appealed to the heavens with each member of the brethren he was shown: by the cistern, in the maize, among the oleanders.

He would not enter the chapel. Trembling, he merely peered into its gloom, with a low moan growing into an especially disturbing cry once he made out the fallen forms. It set him running back through the garden before the refectory could even be mentioned. He was shouting incomprehensibly.

I followed him out of the gate, rushing behind him to the motorcycle. The old man had already started it up. In any case, there was no room on it for two. I was left to see him send up another column of sand. Smaller, fainter, it grew.

Once more, I was the only living soul in the monastery.

3

I walked round the deserted monastery to the back gate, pacing slowly, pausing on the way. I noticed tracks: the desert had not erased furrows in the sand made by the wheels of those latter-day dinosaurs, the great international oil-company lorries crossing the Sahara.

There were also the ruts of cars and a motorcycle; donkeys and camels; humans, certainly. Most would surely be of routine visits, villagers bringing produce to or buying it from the monks. They told no special story.

I wondered how, in this web of traces, one could disentangle those that began the account of last night's unannounced arrival. Was it, in any case, possible to reconstruct, in a way that made sense, a tale of such brutal slaughter? How might the story go on?

I could not imagine. All I was aware of was a sense of deepening unreality.

I walked back through the open gate, my mind a total blank, and sank onto a bench by the fig tree. Help would undoubtedly be on its way. I had no idea what I should do until the old man brought it back from the village.

Queasy, I realised how little I had eaten recently. I remembered the food still left out in the refectory. Instantly I recoiled from any idea of touching the least morsel claimed by the relentless columns of ants from the unseeing brother serving it.

Disgust turned my thoughts back to the old lime-seller. I envisaged him reporting what he had seen to whichever official was available, at the top of his voice, in confused order, encircled by a loud, gathering crowd. It would provoke a police or army visit to the monastery. There was no telling how long it would all take.

With my sense of time warped by shock, lack of proper sleep and now the strain of waiting, I could not decide whether or not last night's taxi had taken more or less than half an hour, let alone estimate what it would take a motorcycle. Besides, the local police could be delayed, needing clearance or reinforcements from the provincial capital. It simply amounted to the realisation that I might be here alone for an extended period, that I was therefore back to having to decide what I myself must do now.

Sitting on this rough bench, I knew, of course, that there could be no doubt about it: there was nothing for me now but to leave the dead monastery. Such a bitter thought! It meant abandoning everything for which I'd journeyed this far: a place to see me through, to come to myself, to animate me so that I'd finally emerge from the feebleness of will I'd always secretly despised in myself – as in not being able to summon the energy, the organisational power, to get up and arrange even for the departure sweeping the rug from under my feet.

Here on the bench, brooding on the contradictoriness of it just muddled me, further tightening a knot in my brain. A new tide of tiredness swept through me. My thoughts were a dark, irresoluble welter. Everything outside them, like that coiled rosary on the sandy path by my foot, was a dream. Only the sun, raining down with force for the first time today, felt real. I got up in search of shelter. It was purely instinctive.

A somnambulist virtually, I shambled back over to the buildings. I scowled against the sun and noticed the light was still on outside the refectory, weak enough in this glare. I opened the door. Without fully entering, holding my breath against what I knew must be increasingly heavy odours, I reached for the switch. The bulb faded.

It left me wondering at my reflex as I walked straight on. There was no conceivable reason for me to adjust such a small detail in the face of an enormity that would certainly close a monastery for whose condition I could not, therefore, feel remotely responsible.

I passed what I saw was the kitchen through its window. Scraps were left out on saucers by the door. Continuing on, beyond the generator, I came to another building, detached from the rest. Unlike them, it had two storeys. The lower level was not a proper room, just a storage space for gardening equipment beneath a curve of mouldy-smelling stairs. I panted up them, finding myself before bookshelves, wall maps, reading tables.

I glanced at a pile of newspapers. This was the one my mother used to buy. It brought back to me the atmosphere of the apartment in Rome where we had lived, just the two of us, during my adolescence. She read the paper nightly, almost studying it, so it had seemed, in the lamplit stillness as I did my homework.

Anja and I had also read that paper. We even bought it on trips abroad, usually for her work. That was what had taken us to Washington. She had been commissioned to do a photographic essay on the Holocaust Museum. She'd pressed for it, always the intrepid one. How often she'd told me I should be more forceful, decisive!

"Just act!" she'd say.

And it was true that I'd simply followed her to the exhibition. A group of high school students was there, apparently from New York. One girl had dark eyes like Anne Frank, but was prettier. She reminded me of someone, though I was maddeningly unable to place her, there in that crowd. There was such a crush that I suddenly found myself lost in it. Trapped with all those strangers among such photographic images, I escaped by the emergency stairs.

I stepped out of the library, feeling the sun on my head. I approached, at a right angle, the long back of the monastery's "L" of adobe buildings. It faced the chapel across sandy paths and bushes with the garden, orchard and cistern off to the far side. I felt a painful stirring in my bowels on entering the first of these doorways. My hands were cold. I paused, about to go into the monks' cells.

Deserted, they contained little enough: a dusty cross made from a palm frond; a garish saint's picture; a sickly potted plant; a Waterman pen; a dog-eared book. Any of these, even the button on that unvarnished table, might have been mementos invested with invaluable personal significance by the room's occupant.

Their meaning now shed, I also thought distractedly of our apartment with its remains. Just as deadened were all the lives lived here in this heavily inert place. Each awaited slow, soft, irresistible interment by desert sand.

I went on to an adjoining building, presuming it the guesthouse from the identical literature about the Order on the desk in each of the rooms. There were no personal items. The furnishings were better than in the brethren's cells, with locally woven rugs on the floors and pictures on the walls.

Seeing none of the rooms was occupied, I wondered which would have been mine. I sank into an easy chair. It faced a slit window, giving onto the blinding beyond. A fly droned. My head swam with the heat.

Closing my eyes, I felt, eerily, the pressure of the dead all around me. It was an almost physical sense of them in this graveyard of a monastery where, sitting back in this chair, my head was now filling with thoughts of Anja, my mother, my lost father. A tap had been turned on, with memories bursting out so forcefully that I wondered if my cranium, the cistern, could long continue to contain them in a location so disturbingly unconnected, polluted by the presences disintegrating within its fleshy pink walls.

Then, nauseous again, I was thinking once more of that only half-finished meal still laid out: warm, ant-infested, rotting. I saw, in my mind's eye, my suitcase on the refectory bench. I supposed I ought to collect it. I would get up and do so in a moment.

Sirens were sounding. They awakened me. I stood at the window. Two white police cars approached across the desert.

Even in the ferocious glare, glimpsing those revolving blue lights, I again noticed the tangle of tracks I had observed, walking back after the lime-seller's sudden departure. Now I also saw, to one side of the rough track serving as a road, something I had previously missed: several lines of writing.

I looked closer, shading my eyes with a hand. The message was in Arabic. I could not read it.

The police cars' wailing had grown deafening. Then the sirens fell silent in mid-phrase. They had finally pulled up to the monastery. All that could be heard was the old lime-seller's cracking voice, as he brought a group of uniformed men to the back gate.

Seeing them, I felt a stab of fear, irrationally supposing I might be the prime suspect.

The senior officer had a trim moustache and waist, unlike his paunchy subordinates. His features were clear against white, razor-cut hair as he strode through the garden to meet me. His French lacked the heavy Maghrebi accent of his colleagues, now all shaking hands with me too. Even the lime-seller did so, touching his heart.

"Precisely how many people have been killed?" the officer said.

His exactitude challenged my emotional slump.

"All of them, as far as I can see. Over twenty."

I pointed out the brethren in the cistern, the maize, the bushes. The police trooped wordlessly after me through the foliage.

"But most of them are in the chapel. And there's one in the refectory."

The officer preceded me into its gloom, suavely moving around the corpse. It was evidently a practised reaction. But his men remained outside, looking distantly at the buildings as they mopped their brows in the sun.

"Fundamentalists," one of them muttered offhandedly in French, slouched against the lintel.

"It's the obvious assumption," the officer said with a Gallic shrug, whether to concede or disdain the policeman's foregone conclusion.

"But what brings *you* here?" he said, eyes focusing directly on me. "What do you know of all this?"

I explained I'd come to the monastery to work on a book with a letter of introduction to the Abbot. It was locked away in my luggage here in the refectory.

As we moved over to it, I speculated that whoever climbed in on the bamboo ladder still leaning against the fig tree must have opened the back gate to the others. A single man could certainly not have killed so many people alone.

The officer did not answer. He waited for me to take out what were actually two letters from my suitcase.

I stood in silence while he slowly read the one to the Abbot. It was in French. The other, to Father Erich, was in German, clearly a language he did not know. The officer simply returned it, rereading even more carefully the letter to the Abbot before returning that, too.

I put both letters back in the suitcase without a word. I was too drained to resent scrutiny by the first person with whom I could actually communicate since stumbling upon such a situation. Moreover, I not only instinctively felt his trustworthiness from his painstaking yet hardly suspicious review of the correspondence he'd carefully folded and given back to me. I also told myself that, behind this reserve, there lay the humane understanding I badly wanted to depend on, not least in a soft muting of the tone in which he continued:

"When the Italian nuns were murdered nearby, the monks refused to move. They repeatedly turned down our protection. The Abbot told me they were against arms of any kind. And now ..." His eyelids were heavy. He'd fallen silent.

"Well, there's something written outside in the sand," I said.

The officer's brow knitted. We all went out of the open gate to see.

The officer read the message out loud in Arabic. The lime-seller said something in a rising voice. He remained unanswered by the frowning police.

"What does it say?"

"'Death to the intruder bringing death to our land.'"

4

The army took over from the police. By the time the military unit arrived, the sun was pitiless. Whereas the police officer and his men had been out on the sandy paths hours earlier, now the soldiers hugged close to buildings for their knife-edges of shade. They let the workers, Berbers in wide-brimmed straw hats, carry off the bodies on stretchers.

The corpses, in their brown habits, looked hardly different from the expressionless men in burnooses delivering them, faces glistening, to the front gate, which had been opened. There they were put into bags and loaded onto a lorry. The back was eventually covered with camouflage canvas.

Like the police, the army sent photographers. But whereas the police had focused on the assassins' message, army cameras sought out the darkness. Only occasionally did they risk approaching some blinding spot to record a brother as he had originally been found.

The first photographers had also consulted me, flashing away at footprints, while others in plain clothes took fingerprints from the bamboo ladder, the back gate, the chapel, the refectory. They had lifted items too indistinct to see – a hair, a fibre – into plastic bags.

The morning hours had drawn on. The police had long ago taken a full statement from me, which the officer had ordered after our interview. They had heard how, arriving here to overcome a breakdown occasioned by the loss of my wife, I had stepped unawares into the nightmare of so many more strangers' deaths in the desert's open grave. Then they left.

The army's questions were only occasional. They simply checked the precise position in which I had found this or that. They continued investigating, recording, so quietly absorbed in their procedures as to appear matter-of-fact, if not bored. What should now happen to me did not seem to concern anyone. I was surely irrelevant, forgotten, beside the point.

Nor was *I* sure what I was doing there. I should have gone already. Disoriented, lost as I had increasingly found myself since Anja had died, I felt acutely out of place. In spite of this I finally collected my suitcase from the refectory, and gravitated unthinkingly to the guest room where I had previously sat. Hovering by its slit window, I saw, without looking, the comings and goings of army vehicles. The entire ridge of sandy rock outside the monastery had become a car park.

There was a continuous crackle of walkie-talkies. They went on communicating meaninglessly, as I shrank from the sheer intensity of light in that scorching wilderness. Sitting heavily in the chair, I felt faint. I was floating in an endless present, which I no more felt inclined to explore than the initial waking from some reverie, a dream such as the unreality of everything I'd come upon here made me feel I was living. There was a creak. The door admitted a fiery wedge of light. Someone passed the threshold into shadow. It was an old woman, I saw, looking aside from where I was sitting. Swathed in the worn, multicoloured fabrics of a Berber, she might merely have chanced on a lost soul in his cell, though she – someone – must have known I was there, even when I had felt my existence here most in doubt.

She was carrying a tray of food for me, containing a plate of lamb couscous and a slice of watermelon. She placed it on the desk without the slightest sign of recognition. Even so, it made me realise quite how much I had missed a woman's attentiveness recently. I had a lump in my throat, finding "Thanks" emerging from it – incomprehensibly, to her. A wrinkled cheek nonetheless dimpled. Her tattooed brow creased. The door closed.

I supposed I should eat the food whose smell made me swallow. But, getting up, I became so dizzy that I had to steady myself against the desk for several moments. Only then did I take the spoon and fork from the tray in one hand, the plate of couscous in the other, and sink back into my seat.

I ate mouthful after mouthful, and felt almost human. Then I put the empty plate back on the tray and picked up the slice of watermelon. Holding it with both hands, I took a bite before hearing a knock on the door.

It was forceful. But with my mouth full, I could not answer. That did not matter, apparently. Here was someone just walking in, holding a plate of lamb couscous of his own.

"Ah! They told me I'd find you here. Are you alright?"

The man asked me this gently. Tall, wiry, dressed in khaki trousers, sandals and a creased, open-neck shirt, he stood there an uncertain instant at variance with his vigorous entry. Still receiving no answer, he volunteered:

"I'm Father Josef."

I blinked vaguely, hearing the innumerable comings and goings outside the window, where an army truck was drawing up with metal tureens for the guards' lunch.

My visitor, as if expecting to be asked quite who he might be behind that name, went on in answer to my surely implicit question:

"I'm from the community of Czech brothers twenty kilometres away. You don't mind if I have lunch with you, do you?"

A wooden crucifix swayed at his chest as he sat on the edge of the bed.

He settled into silence, eating several spoonfuls of couscous. It gave me a chance, perhaps calculated, to absorb his presence, here in this place of stillness where so much had to be assimilated. It also gave me time, as he was no longer in a blinding doorway or in the dense shadow immediately succeeding it, to see his large and handsome, if equine, face. In his early forties, with perfect teeth and a full head of chestnut hair, he gave what I found a tiring impression of health, energy, accessibility.

"It's rather good, isn't it?" he said gently.

He smiled, putting down the lamb bone he had been eating with his hands. The way in which he creased his face, batted his long eyelashes and carefully licked his fingertips made him appear momentarily effeminate.

"The same women have cooked for the brethren for years. They come from the village by donkey. They set out before dawn. Maybe they knew that one day they'd arrive and …"

Large, manicured fingers fanned out.

"You'd hardly need to be a genius to realise that, with the general situation in the last year or two, something would happen here sooner or later. Although their reaction's interesting: to make lunch as usual. Same meal, different mouths – that's all."

He said this in an un-ironic voice, watching me finish my watermelon.

I put the rind on the soup plate with its juice and seeds, supposing the priest might regret sounding so scandalously terse. Hence perhaps, his speedy following remark:

"But I believe you were the first to come upon it."

I made no response, so quietly, as considerately as he had been at first, he said: "It must have been –"

"It wasn't what I was expecting."

"Which was?"

"To get on with a book."

"About?"

"Desert insects."

"Unusual."

"Mm …"

I was thinking it might well have been, this project inherited from my wife.

Of course most of Anja's subjects were strange, though it had not been she who had decided, finally, where to pursue it. But she had been interested in deserts ever since visiting New Mexico, the Mojave and Australia for her book on nuclear testing.

"Who suggested you come to this monastery?" Josef asked, quite still.

"Father Barnato."

"*Carlo* Barnato?"

"Yes."

Father Josef set his plate aside on the desk. He was looking at me intently, saying: "Strange that he'd send you here. The Tuaregs' name for the nearest town is *The End of the World*. You can't even find a recent guidebook to the country, except for *The Ten Most Dangerous Places on Earth*. Father Barnato must know that. No one could be more politically aware – as I'm sure you realise."

The statement was actually a question. I had no response.

Father Josef continued: "Father Barnato's a major figure in Catholic Action: one of those powerful anti-Communist clerics who influence Christian Democratic politics in Italy. Most of them came to the fore under Pius XII, as did a number of other ambiguous churchmen during and just after the war – many of them German. And I wanted to get to the bottom of the work they did for the Pope. I even suggested it as the subject of my doctoral dissertation in Political Science. *Pacelli's People*, I thought of calling it. But it was soon after the Soviet invasion of Czechoslovakia, and I'd escaped to the States. My Provincial in the Jesuits there thought it'd be more logical for me to work on the Church under Communism. So I did. In fact, it's what brought me here. As I told you, I've just come from the Czech community. I spent the last year interviewing the brothers for my book. Not that I only came out here to do research."

He paused. It was quiet. Inert. The stillness indoors merged with the heavy motionlessness outside. It reverberated endlessly.

"I needed time to myself." Father Josef said this mutedly. It was as if he suddenly wanted to make amends for the talkativeness with which he'd reciprocated information about his own project. "I longed for time to reflect, after America. The mere sight of oil trucks out here … the very thought of company compounds like Midwestern towns jarringly transported from their world to planet Sahara … well, it all brings back the strident hurly-burly I had to escape. It was high time to treat myself to silence. And then I met Father Sebastian. He … he *was* Abbot here."

*

Father Josef went on to say that, shortly after joining the Czech brethren, he had been asked to say Mass at the Italian convent nearby. Father Sebastian was visiting the Mother Superior at the time.

Then Josef came to know him. Sebastian invited him to take a solitary retreat in the cave he himself used below the mountains, a donkey trot of several days away. He had fitted it with a stone bed and shutters against the freezing winds that blow down there.

Father Josef was looking at the tile floor as he talked. Nothing stirred.

He said that Father Sebastian negotiated with the leader of a group of fundamentalists who suddenly appeared here last year. They had just murdered the Italian nuns. The security forces said the leader had cut the throats of more than a hundred people.

Sebastian asked to speak to him alone, outside the monastery. He said this was a place of prayer, that he could not allow weapons inside. Still, the leader demanded to hide men and guns in the buildings, and to have Father Rolfe, the doctor, visit their wounded. Sebastian refused.

"You must," the leader said. "There's no alternative."

"Yes there is," Sebastian replied. "You've come here armed, just as we are about to celebrate the Annunciation of the birth of the Prince of Peace."

"I'm sorry," the guerrilla said. "We are religious, like you. But I'll be back. Or else I'll send my emissaries with a password."

Despite the miracle of their escape, the community had to take their situation seriously. They had difficult discussions. Should they go to the capital? Return to Europe? Or perhaps move to one of the neighbouring countries?

None of the brethren sought martyrdom. Sebastian said it would be evil to want the terrorists to break God's injunction against murder. The brethren must pray, instead, that their Muslim cousins would lay down their arms.

Neither the guerrilla nor his emissaries appeared again. Later, it emerged that the leader had been killed in a mountain ambush by security forces. But Sebastian was adamant that the brethren should not rejoice. They did not; they simply continued discussing their destiny, staying faithful to their contemplative Saharan vocation and to the local people with whom they had built friendships over so many years.

After all, they were in the same boat. Guerrillas raped and murdered women for failing to wear the veil. They repaid them for supposedly aiding the security forces by slitting everyone's throat in a village, including those of their babies, in the middle of the night.

Of course, there were persistent rumours that members of state were behind the violence. Soldiers secretly complained of being ordered to participate in death squads and torture. There was talk of rogue military hit squads masquerading as fundamentalists in order to draw international attention to Islamic terrorism. It was one way of fighting fire with fire.

Yet whoever was responsible for the violence, violence it was, and the brethren felt solidarity with all who suffered from it. They identified with the locals.

They stayed.

"I knew them to my profit," Father Josef said. "This morning I came to say goodbye, especially to Father Sebastian. My time is up here. Tomorrow afternoon I'm catching the bus from the village to the capital. Then I'm taking a plane to New York. But really, I hadn't expected to take my leave quite like ..."

The silence was oppressive.

"The police have offered us transport after lunch. But I'm staying here tonight, even so – *especially* so. I'd like to reflect on Sebastian and what he's meant to me. I want to pray for all their souls. Maybe it'll help bring back some peace, at least, to the place."

He drew himself up, seated on the bed as he said it. Taking me in, he added: "Why don't you join me? You're obviously …"

The words trailed off, though his eyes stayed on my face. It was enough for some trace of *amour propre* to resent the reference to my appearance, as I did the rest of the speech, typical of lectures on a place that some arrivals – sudden experts – foist on newer-comers.

"You need a proper night's sleep. Meditation and prayer will help."

"I've never meditated. I don't think I can pray."

"Stay tonight. Just being here will be a vigil."

I did not answer, or move. I watched Father Josef get up. The priest added his empty plate, with its lamb bone and watermelon rind, to the lunch tray. He picked it up and carried it to the door.

"Oh!" I called after him. "Father Barnato gave me a letter for the Abbot. And he asked me to be sure to hand one on to another of the monks, a Father – I can't remember his name. It was German."

"Don't bother about it now. Just rest."

Father Josef noiselessly closed the door behind him with his free hand.

*

I kicked off my shoes and slumped onto the rough blanket of what, in that instant, I thought of as my bed. Instantly, I closed my eyes. Overtired, I soon stirred, and went on tossing and turning: not quite awake, not exactly asleep.

I was raging with thirst; the couscous must have been very salty. The room was heavy with afternoon heat, especially in this dry desert air. I would go and fetch some water, from somewhere, soon. I stretched a leg onto the floor, too exhausted to check first for scorpions.

There was knocking. It roused me; I was still heavy with sleep, my foot on the floor. The light had lost its strength. I felt chilly. My stomach was acid.

"Come in."

Father Josef entered and said, "I'm going to say some prayers in the chapel in about ten minutes." Then he left.

I got up. Through the window slit, I saw a single jeep with two guards sitting in the back. They were all that remained of the day's security forces. Far away, across a darkling expanse, scarlet outlined jagged peaks.

I left the cell and, yawning, walked into the dim cloister. It was deserted. As I began crossing it, I noticed that the back gate was closed. The ladder had gone from the fig tree. But the sunset was too far advanced for me to see if there were footprints on the sandy path.

I approached the chapel. Climbing its stairs, I made out, through its open door, the red point of the sanctuary light – and a huddled form.

I gasped.

But it was Father Josef, kneeling.

Eventually the shadowy form got up and lit a candle at the altar. He returned to his pew. There was a long period of reflection.

I used it to probe a wooden bas-relief hanging on the nearby wall. Mary held the baby Jesus, overlooked by Joseph beside a palm tree heavy with dates. The head and neck of a camel showed across the trunk.

The Holy Family was resting at an oasis, during the Flight into Egypt. I supposed that the monks, having forfeited their homes to join this community, might, even so, have recovered contact with their parents through the medium of the carved figures. Indeed, the sculptures not only served as – but seemed to become – the mother, the father that the brethren had imagined them to be. It made of the monastery a place where the family, the inhabitant's world, was reassembled.

Father Josef began reading prayers for the departed out loud from a missal. As this was obviously for my benefit – I was the only other person there – I knew I should concentrate on the words, investing them with their full weight of meaning. But I could not stop myself watching the flame flicker. It elongated in gusts of the nocturnal wind, fitfully disclosing forms or shadowy parts of forms. Oppressive as it was standing there, hearing of the dead, shuddering, I was transfixed by repeated after-images, especially in this guttering light.

At last Father Josef got up. Without moving, he stood looking at the candle. He crossed himself and joined me on the steps of the chapel, now soundless, with its two inner lights.

We went to the refectory. Its weak bulb was on, as it had been the previous night – though yesterday evening's scene only existed now as a scarcely credible mental image. The woman had laid the table for two by the door with bread, white cheese, olives, yoghurt, honey and dates.

Seated beside the priest, facing the dim inner wall, I ate without looking at the denser shadow, which I mentally replaced at the other end. I barely noticed as Father Josef began talking.

The priest was informing me of the time at which we would be collected by the police the following day, to catch the bus from the village. He asked if I was intending to stay in the community's house in the capital for a while, or if I was going straight back to Europe.

"I don't know … I just don't know."

I could hardly wait to leave the long, low room, with this heavily static atmosphere still redolent of last night's mouldering. But Father Josef had been looking straight at the wall, at a framed lithograph of Père Charles-Eugène de Foucauld, the Trappist monk whose "case" he was elaborating.

A nineteenth-century French aristocrat, Foucauld had converted from being a soldier to a Saharan ascetic. He had lived among the Tuareg, like the Tuareg. He sought, working shoulder to shoulder with them, to dispel all the differences between his background and theirs, just as Sebastian and the monks had made this monastery into a place of Christian–Muslim understanding.

The Tuareg admired Foucauld's austerity. They helped him with his grammar and dictionary of their purely spoken language. Foucauld agreed to guard sixteen French rifles in a fort during a Tuareg insurrection against their colonial oppressors. Then he was murdered, but by Senussi Bedouin.

The theme of imperialist abuse of the country outlasted supper. Father Josef described France's nuclear testing in the Sahara while we cleared up. He carried the stacked plates to the dark end of the refectory.

The priest offered me a nightcap of plum liqueur: "I brought it as a goodbye present to Father Sebastian and the brethren."

"Thank you, but I'm exhausted," I replied. "I'm going to say goodnight."

I headed off, past the front gate, perfunctorily saluted by a guard. His evident boredom expressed the prevailing assumption that the worst was over.

I continued through the cold night air, the silence, the light of so many stars. On I walked, beyond the monastery's shelf of rock, over the rutted track, into sand. I raised my arms, stretching high, inhaling the evening. There was just the sound of distant wind, and a fast-fading reverberation of Father Josef's words.

Released at last from having to hear explanations of what had happened here, I retreated, too, from the shock of stumbling blindly upon it – a situation existing since long before me. Far from troubling me with its savagery, its sheer scale, it should not be allowed to draw me deeper into it, stranger that I was even to this remote European outpost in a wilderness with alien ways of being.

Besides, the terms in which the situation had been presented to me were empty, meaningless. No miracle had waved off terrorists, if those it saved were to be murdered last night. One could not claim to understand where there was slaughter. Here was a dead language, with words like *God*, *prayer* and *Christian goodwill* that had not figured in my vocabulary for a long time.

These gusts were hushing it all with their cold moaning. They hid signs of previous situations, comings and goings, as I walked alone in this clean-swept barrenness beneath the massive welter of stars.

I grew aware of feeling, not seeing, the thick sand slowing my passage. My shoes were full of it. I stopped at what might have been a concentration of the night: a large rock. I sat against it and my mind went blank.

Eventually cold was penetrating to the bone. I got up and turned, giving me a view of the monastery from here in the desert: shapely, compact, a *kasbah* almost, with a glimpse of fronds over the walls. Slowly, I wandered back.

I entered through the front gate for the first time. The guard, a soldier, straightened. I recognised him from that morning. He had a gash across his cheek, and gold teeth. The man slouched back sleepily beneath a blanket against the outer wall.

Within, there was the sound of water. I did not look over towards the fig tree and maize stand. I did not need to, that cistern ever-filling in my mind's eye. On and on it sounded.

I could even hear it, yawning, as I entered the cell and lay down on my bed.

*

Dawn was breaking outside my window. I got up to look out, at a dot in the luminous distance, far off from the road. Something almost appeared to be moving across the packed sand with those granite slabs like the one I had gazed out from last night. It seemed to approach as I watched, my stomach knotting, wary of the unpredictable human life of the desert.

I was distracted by a knock on the door. Father Josef was asking how I had slept, saying that we were up early enough to pray. The car was not due to collect us for over an hour.

I joined him inside what felt like a different chapel, with night gone. I entered the front pew, whether from politeness, passivity or the word-defying complication of explaining how a willing guest at the monastery might consider evading its central activity: worship.

Father Josef went up to the altar. Yesterday's candle had all but burned out. He lit another. The weak new flame joined day, straining through a high, unadorned window. Scarcely mixing, the lights imparted a grey visibility to the adobe walls and rough pews, where we were both now kneeling.

Father Josef was leaving so long for silent contemplation that it was a strain. I was too aware of the other's presence to sink into my own thoughts. I could smell the soap he used. He surely heard the rumble of my bowels. I longed for this Jesuit, trained for feats of endurance in meditation, to release us from silence.

Unexpectedly, Father Josef started reading psalms out loud. They begged for help against the enemy in a desert hiding place. Something of the wilderness made itself known here too, in that creak behind us: doubtless the last of the night's wind, before the breathless heat of the day.

Father Josef set down his book to recite from memory, in Latin, a prayer for the dead. He mentioned the Abbot, Sebastian, by name. Then he sought mercy on the eternal souls of the other brethren.

"Amen."

The word also sounded behind us. We turned around with a jolt. It was difficult to make out the figure standing in a pew at the back, by the half-open door. He was set against a rectangle of light that had been strengthening all the time we'd been in the dimmer chapel.

Only as we went on to say the Lord's Prayer – all three of us – did I, glancing round again, see that the bearded old man was wearing a tattered version of the brethren's habit. His cowl was up.

There were several concluding, shorter prayers; a final few moments for silent reflection. Father Josef and I made our way down the aisle. Mutely, the young priest embraced the arrival at the back. The old man's face was ruddy, stern. The eyes stared over the Jesuit's shoulder, measurelessly far-off, then heavy, brimful.

Not until we were sitting in the refectory, the three of us, having the coffee the old woman served, did a word pass between us. Father Josef introduced his "friend" Father Mark, one of the longest serving monks here.

"I met him on my retreat to Sebastian's cave. His own is in the vicinity … And this is a visitor to the monastery. He too came for a retreat last night, but was the first to find –"

Father Mark raised a gnarled hand, his cowl now down, revealing short, tousled hair.

"I know what he found," the old man growled in a clipped Oxford, even Edwardian, accent. "The guard told me as I arrived. He was *most* graphic. And he told me what's written in the sand – or, rather, what the wind's blown away."

Silence returned. Father Josef soon broke it.

"What brought you here, Father? It's two days' journey by donkey from your cell, isn't it?"

"Two nights'. The days are scorching. Tomorrow we'd have had a chapter to discuss the long-term prospects for our community."

There was another pause. Once more, it was Father Josef who spoke first:

"Well, we're leaving to return to the capital. You'll join us?"

"Definitely not!" Father Mark was adamant to the point of anger. "My place is here. It's my home. The monastery continues even with just one monk. Because it's a communion of souls. It includes all who've ever been part of it. And they will never be separated, even by death.

To leave now would be to spit on all my brothers lived by and died for: peace, prayer, charity, witness. Besides, we're an order of contemplatives. Some brethren live even deeper in the Sahara than I. In time, over years maybe, they too will appear, unsummoned. We're still a chapter of the living too – a community."

Father Josef did not answer. Only eventually did he say, in words that had difficulty leaving his throat: "Of course …" Then he got up. "I must see if our car's arrived." He left the refectory.

Father Mark was still shuddering with defiance. He plucked at his beard, with nails like talons. He looked at me.

"And what brings *you* to seek retreat here?"

"I lost my wife –"

"And your way, eh? So death's overtaken you too."

There was a ghostly sigh.

"I have an entomological project I intended to work on."

"Why don't you stay then, for whatever you've come for? What else would you do? D'you really suppose things could get any worse here? And the monastery's continuing …"

Father Josef returned. "Time to go. The car's arrived. Sure you won't join us, Father Mark?"

"Absolutely certain," he said, tugging on his beard.

"*We're* staying," I said, surprising myself.

I helped Father Josef bring his luggage from his cell to the main gate. Father Mark was waiting for us at the portal. The old monk insisted on loading the suitcase into the boot of the police car.

The white Peugeot set off. It faded into a blurred track of sand. I went on looking into the emptiness. Turning back from the guard, into the forecourt, I found myself alone. The generator sounded. Water poured. Foliage gleamed in the intensifying sun.

I walked slowly back to the refectory. The three places at the long table, with their coffee cups, were abandoned. I lingered for several moments, then turned back. Hovering at the door, gazing at the cloister, I squinted. My head was starting to ache. Uncertain of what to do next, my unformed plans to leave summarily abandoned, I trudged off to the cell.

5

Less than an hour later, I heard a noise: a car drawing up. I froze. I left my cell and advanced rapidly to the front gate, almost immediately supposing I would have done better to approach it gingerly.

The police officer was getting out of a jeep. The driver and an armed escort waved to me, slamming the doors behind them as I emerged from the monastery. They leaned against the vehicle on its shady side, smoking.

The officer came over to me and shook hands, touching his heart. Taking off his cap, he used it to fan his fine features.

"I always used to stop by when I was in the area," he said, walking into the monastery with me, virtually its sole inhabitant. "I did it for years. The monks were so hospitable."

The officer paused for an instant, taking in the emptiness, that sound of running water. Awkwardly, I led him to the cistern and offered him one of the earthenware beakers on its side. The officer accepted it and, greedily quenching his thirst, said:

"I'm surprised to see you still here. Why didn't you leave in the car we sent for the Jesuit?"

I frowned at the impulsiveness of my decision, the terrible obviousness of my reason for it.

"I've nothing – and no one – to go back to."

Feeling instantly strange to be confessing something so intimate to this official I barely knew, I instantly qualified it. "I'm exhausted. I can't think of heading back so soon on a journey like the one I've just come on."

It was true. I was so drained as I stood for a silent moment before the officer that I recalled how, in my moment of spontaneous decision, I'd treated the monastery as a welcome refuge – which was why, going to my cell, it had suddenly struck me as "mine" upon opening the door.

Although those few metres were so much less than what I – *we* – had called our home, to step inside was a huge relief. There before me, as if in confirmation of my decision to remain, I'd found invisible hands had delivered the case of personal effects I'd sent on separately from Rome.

"But the monastery's an anchor, not a springboard," I went on. "I still don't know if I'll have the energy to start the volume on desert insects that's supposed to help me get over my wife's death."

"Yes, you do look distracted, *Monsieur*. Accept my sympathy for your loss. But you must realise that you're about to put yourself through something even more tormenting by staying here alone."

Unexpectedly, seeing my vulnerable self through the officer's eyes brought me up short. I was ashamed to have exposed my feelings so brazenly. Abruptly, I changed tack.

"So do you know who killed the monks yet?" I said. "I've heard that some of the violence is actually sponsored by the state."

This apparent statement hovered between us in the heat as a question.

"It's a repeated claim, which doesn't prove it's either true or false. There's no firm evidence." The policeman said this, eyelids heavy, shrugging his shoulders at the implicit moral oppressiveness of the entire conflict. Then he half-smiled and half-sighed, shaking his head of neatly combed silver hair. "Well, I don't think it's the army in this case, if that's what you mean. There are over sixty Islamist extremist groups to choose from – that we know about. They range from small cells in the cities to militias. Up in the north, around the capital, they're so active it's called 'the triangle of death'. Further south, the terrorists base themselves in the mountains, as the freedom fighters used to during the French occupation. They ambush us on the roads, or in towns and villages, then retreat back to their hideouts. Have you taken a look at those mountains?"

They formed, vast and crenulated, in my mind.

"Tracking down the terrorists there is like looking for a needle in a haystack. They even make sallies deep into the desert – as we well know."

Our eyes met.

Once more, I was struck by the inspector's French, and his authoritativeness. He did not have bad teeth like the others around here, or the same thinning hair and heavy, staring eyes. Unlike them, he did not move lethargically in this heat. More than a local policeman, he had *monde*, however acquired.

"Of course," the officer went on, "we can never count on the local people's help in finding these groups. They're terrorised into concealing their whereabouts. It's the classic scare tactic: 'kill one to terrify a thousand'. The killings are ritual acts that the entire village is forced to watch. And they often involve settling tribal blood feuds and vendettas, as well as Islamic protests. Either way, honour can only be purified by blood, with witnesses present at the sacrifice. It's almost always the same story: throats slashed in the middle of the night."

The words held in silence, absolute but for the running water, here in this once-thriving community. The light was fading. I was staring at terrible images thrown by the magic lantern of memory.

The officer took up his thread again.

"No, with this kind of fear you can't expect the locals to provide the police with sufficient information to find, arrest and convict the killers. Besides, villagers around here are tribal. Why should they feel any loyalty to officials of a state that only recently came into being, once the French left? Under the best of conditions, it'd still be under construction.

"The desert has nothing to do with the political map. The only real boundaries are the natural ones the nomads follow, such as contours left by prehistoric watercourses and the vast salt flats left from dried up lakes. Here in the Sahara you can't expect a state to exist, any more than they do in those parts of the Amazon which South American governments have effectively ceded to guerrillas. Desert or jungle, it's the same: nature overwhelming anything positive humans seek to create, leaving ample scope for *in*human nature."

"But you do expect to catch whoever assassinated the monks, don't you? I mean, you *are* going to catch them, aren't you?"

"We're trying, of course. We work together with the army. That's the idea. But if we're successful, it'll only be a mixture of chance and luck. The Islamist movement is a Hydra with many heads. Catching this one group won't be very significant."

"Except for the people they murdered," I said.

"It can't make any difference to them."

"What!"

I was adamant. It surprised me. I didn't care about impersonal losses having nothing to do with the lesser (but to me, far more terrible) one bringing me all the way out here. How strange, for my feelings to swerve between personal bereavement and public atrocity, as if they were comparable, let alone interchangeable!

"They're dead," said the officer. "*A priori*. We learned logic, those of us who were sent for our training to France. In those days I was idealistic too, and believed I could contribute to perfect justice. It's been hard to find that justice is Allah's alone. Good luck in *your* discovery of it."

Listening, I strove to register what it meant for those deaths to go unavenged. All that would be left was their lives, or rather what they had meant, at least in the remembering of them. But it was painfully hard to reanimate a life in one's mind if its death created a feeling of equal deadness in one. Whoever it was must have gone to ground forever.

"Look," the officer said, "I advise you to move on, as I did the monks. That's really why I'm here. You'd best go home."

Yet I'd already despaired of where that might be, other than here, a place in which I would silently pursue my project all alone without involving myself in a situation having nothing to do with me.

"The monks were different," I said. "They were known in the whole area, scores of them: sitting ducks. But the killers are hardly likely to strike in the same place twice, are they? Especially not a passing hermit or foreigner."

"Maybe. Maybe not. But whichever, being a foreigner won't help. What happened here proves that."

"Why do *you* think the brethren were murdered?"

The officer frowned. Then he said: "Foreign consular officials and engineers have presumably been kidnapped and killed to deter investment from abroad. It's intended to destabilise the state economically. But long-term expatriates, like the monks, are a focus in the war too, probably for the reason you've given: they're so much a part of the place that they have no security and are thus easy targets. Although, as Christians, the brethren here doubtless also fell foul of Islamic xenophobia.

"Before the First World War, the Tuareg joined a Sufi-inspired crusade to free the country from Christian moral pollution. And remember the desert saying: 'The Great Sahara is the Garden of Allah.'

"Though exactly how the monks offended against the murderers' creed depends," the officer said, "on how one reads that clue, their signature, left in the sand. An intruder, a foreigner, has apparently been bringing death to their land. The colonialists did it literally, in the liberation struggle. The American oil companies are doing so figuratively, with their drills ripping up this God-given land. One might even say that the French atomic tests in the Sahara brought environmental death. But how," he wondered, "does this apply to the monastery? Is it the religion practised here that's diabolical – in other words, spiritual death? Or is something else about the place lethal?"

Again, we fell mute. Soon we did not hear the water gushing in this newly invading darkness.

"I should go," the officer said.

We walked together through the front gate. A brilliant vista of night surprised us. Both driver and armed escort were slumped against the wheels of the truck, one with his head back against the mudguard, the other with his chin on his chest. It was as if they had been overwhelmed by something in the atmosphere, in the very hugeness of the star-crowded sky.

"Promise me you'll leave." The officer said it gently. I felt his hand on my shoulder.

I watched as my visitor turned to rouse the others. They waved to me, driving off.

I stood there, registering the officer's solicitude in coming here to warn me himself with that final paternal touch.

I discovered myself looking into empty desert – and at the sun suddenly flaring out. It was cool; the temperature had fallen in the time I had been standing there, and continued to drop fast.

Shivering, I turned to go inside. Past the gate, hearing the water, I headed for the cell where I was deciding to stay, after all, in the most dangerous place in the world.

6

Father Josef had imposed such an early start on us that I simply slumped on my bed. Hardly hearing the lorries outside, my eyelids sank.

Much later, I blinked in a far hotter room. There was a grinding in my bowels that became urgent. I got up and opened my luggage to take out my sponge bag, a towel and clean clothes, then went to the lavatories, to one side of the guest quarters, in the washroom.

There were no mirrors, as in some hospital wards preventing patients from seeing what accident or emaciation has done to them. I was faceless, presumed but undiscoverable to myself among a row of identical laundered habits hanging from hooks.

I took a shower. For some time I watched tepid rivulets of soap run off my feet into the rough stone trough, refreshed by the precious desert water.

Back in the cell, I noticed literature about the Order beside my open luggage. I picked up a slim paperback with the silhouette of a monk, showing just his habit and hood. But I put *A Saharan Solitude* and the rest of the leaflets under the bed, having no idea that I would eventually keep the book open beside me – even now, as I write.

Turning to my metal suitcase, I lifted the microscope out of its box nervously and set it on the desk. It appeared to be intact, as did my camera and its two lenses. Beside them I arranged hardbound sketchbooks, carbon pencils and the X-Acto no. 11-blade knife with which I would sharpen them to a fine point.

I placed my watercolours, with brushes ranging in size to the tiniest, on one shelf of the cupboard. On the other, I put the cotton wool, vials and other collecting gear, including lighting equipment.

As for my clothes, well, they were best left in my luggage for the moment. Better just to sit at the space I had left for myself at the desk, writing the date in the first page of my notebook.

I could begin immediately, what I had come for.

Yet I gazed out the window. A strange vagueness had overcome me, forcing me to crystallise for myself again the reason I was here.

My project came to mind, although there would probably be a low diversity of insects in the desert. Soaring daytime temperatures and a severe lack of moisture made the existence of whole species unlikely. This was especially so of the potentially eye-catching *Lepidoptera*.

In such a depauperate environment there was surely no scope for a tome as extraordinary as those eighteenth-century books of Amazonian flora, with their amazing orchids and quinine-producing *chinchonas*; there would doubtless be scorpions, though, including the world's most venomous: the Deathstalker. Hardly more appealing were foot-long centipedes with lethal stingers at each end, to say nothing of the camel (or sun) spider whose anaesthetic saliva enables it to eat part of a sleeper's face without him knowing it.

It was not clear what else I'd encounter other than ubiquitous lice, mosquitoes and flies, not to mention the beetles and spiders likely to cover every thorny bush. My wife had doubtless conceived the project for a place with a more rewarding insect population. But I did not know exactly how far Anja had progressed with her plans. We each sat at a different desk to write, just as I once used to pore over butterflies and moths with my self-absorbed mother.

Separate, silent, Anja and I had nonetheless somehow communicated. So I felt, finding myself all at once quite alone here. I was aware that this was the first time I would be working exclusively in my own company. Here, finally, was that challenge to stand on my own feet.

I felt a stab of panic. I had nothing to sustain me except these paltry makings of a dull book of doubtful interest to the non-specialist intending to have it on his coffee table. Father Carlo must have known what this area would provide. Nevertheless, he had encouraged me to undertake the study. After all, sales were the publisher's problem. Presumably he simply believed in the curative effects of work – any work.

Then I recognised the echo of Father Mark's words about staying on: "What else d'you do? D'you really suppose things could get any worse here? And the monastery's continuing …"

Motionless, lingering for some reason, I gazed beyond the security force's vehicles, fewer than the previous day. I was now aware of the door opening behind me. It was the same Berber woman as before, with a tray of food.

It was surprising that it had not been served in the refectory. Feeling too queasy to taste more than a little of the chicken and rice, I left the fruit. Together with the tap (not mineral) water I had drunk in the capital, and the cheese offered me on the coach, it was presumably responsible for the state of my bowels. Napoleon's army had become sick from the watermelons in Alexandria, I remembered hearing at school there, my eyes far off.

Perhaps I should take the tray to the kitchen. Then again, I might leave it outside my door as I had the previous day. So I did, continuing in my room, wondering if, later, I would be summoned to chapel.

It was far too hot to go out. I stripped and lay down. Something buzzed around me, entering from its world that I was here to study. I could have tried to identify it. But waving it aside, I reached for the book I had found in my cell – very different from one I should ever produce.

It was *A Saharan Solitude*, which I had picked up from my custom of reading in bed whatever was to hand. I opened the cover. It was published by the Order's own press, only last year. The paper was rough, with pages of differing size and crooked print. The author was simply "A Saharan Monk". I started with the Introduction:

Years ago he left the monastery, like several other brethren, in search of even greater silence. And thus it is from the contemplative calm of his mountain cell that we receive these anonymous words. Simple but profound, they share an experience of God that is mysterious, powerful and haunting as the desert itself.

The reader, though a stranger from afar, will, if he opens his heart along with these pages, find here sentiments he might recognise. Thoughts that seem to arise from the very centre of his own being.

Turning the page, I began reading the author's Preface:

Here are a few themes that have occurred to me during my years of Saharan solitude. I've turned them over haphazardly in my mind from time to time, and so present them now in no particular order.

I simply offer them as I might in the course of meandering conversa-
tion, if you were to join me one night to feast your eyes on the desert's
harvest of stars.

Here, perched above the sand on a spot I know well on this rocky
promontory, where I have my cave, my home, we'd talk, you and I.
The words would simply flow until we'd notice dawn breaking. By then
we'd surely be each other's closest friend.

The sun would rise, and I'd have passed on the thoughts that have
come to me through prayer; through visitations, invisible but keenly
felt, in the mighty, undisturbed peace of this place. Thoughts they are
that I've noted down roughly in the following pages.

I offer, for what it's worth, these words arising from the desert sand.

I flicked on through the book. There was no continuous, chapter-length
writing. There were musings – here a paragraph, there several. Sections
were, at most, a page and a half. Drawn in by one string of passages, I
considered whether or not it was, in fact, a sequence.

The deep Sahara is sometimes silent and still for days and months
on end. But far from mere quietude, this calm can feel at times as
cold and harsh as the winter climate of the mountain heights where
I'm now writing these words. Sterile, uninhabited, the desert seems
forbidding, pitilessly other, like the rock itself; the endless, barren sand.

Yet there are moments, too, when the mind unexpectedly relaxes. It
might happen at the end of a day, during the mute drama of a sunset.
That is when prayer wells up in a flood of conversation with the Other.
Then the bounds of the self dissolve. The view feels continuous with
the beholder: I am myself and all that is beyond me. It gives one seem-
ingly endless extension, fused with the desert, the night, the heavens,
so infinite.

Wrapped in benign tranquillity, pure as this air, one feels fully
absorbed into what one finally recognises one had always somehow
known was one's destiny: this, the sole, all-encompassing reality.

A place of unforgiving isolation, the Sahara is also a human thorough-
fare. People entirely unrelated to one another travel it, as on any road.
Some cross it within sight of this hermit's cave, like phantoms in dreams.

There are those strange Blue Men; those long, jangling caravans with mores and beliefs utterly alien to Westerners; Americans, too, in their lorries, careering across vast tracts in hectic pursuit of oil, which the world never needed till seconds ago in geological time, and that must become extinct in moments according to the same clock.

What would happen if one group converged with another: hostility, curiosity, openness to change? What is certain is that a hermit must seem fantastic to any of them. He is a virtual madman, isn't he, choosing to exist on the minimum of food and contact, in the middle of nowhere?

So, you, too, reader, incipient hermit in that heart of yours which makes you turn these pages to seek, if unknowingly, the calm to discover what your own desert, your deep Sahara, has to reveal to your benefit.

Strange to ourselves even are these hermit's yearnings. Strangest, indeed, of all the alien forms appearing before our enclosed, protective cells, are we. When, in a rare, unpredictable moment in that dark cave housing us, we unwittingly find the key to our own being and fit it to the lock, the door will spring open, facing us with an infinite vista.

Desert, it is burning by day, brilliant by night. From its seemingly blank sand, we come to see, the longer we look, all that we are, just waiting to be recognised, for all the apparent unfamiliarity. We have been unwittingly seeking it across a lifetime: over years as seemingly measureless to our secretly attendant half-selves as the Sahara itself that the alien travels. But the Other must be recognised, piercing as the moment may be.

Do you remember the story of Abraham sitting at the door of his tent in the heat of the day, in the plains of Mamre? He lifts his eyes and looks, and, lo, three men stand by him.

In one he finds God.

Abraham runs to them, bows, and says: "My Lord, if now I have found favour in Thy sight, pass not away, I pray Thee, from Thy servant: Let a little water, I pray You, be fetched, and wash Your feet, and rest Yourselves under the tree."

He serves veal, curds, milk and cakes. It is a fine lunch. Would anything less befit so gracious a surprise visit by our Father?

And the Lord went his way, as soon as he had left communing with Abraham. And He was also the One who rained brimstone and fire upon the cities of the plain, and all their inhabitants, and that which grew upon the ground.

I closed the booklet, still holding it for a moment. It fell back to the floor as I thought of such ruin. Tossing and turning, I could not rid my mind of an image: someone turned, in that wasteland, into a pillar of salt. It gleamed eerily, melting and spreading across endless ashen tracts.

Eventually I realised what it made me think of: nuclear devastation in deserts, such as that photographed in Anja's book.

*

I woke, shivering, to waning light. Through the pinkish window, I saw that the vehicles had almost all left. I threw on my clothes, expecting to be summoned to chapel.

It had grown dark in the cell. Uncertain whether I should continue waiting, or of what ought to happen next, I eventually prepared to go out to the refectory. The woman must have gone by now, but a meal would surely be left out on the communal table.

I nearly tripped over the tray outside my door – not lunch, but supper. Turning on the light, I wondered how long it had been there. Here were yoghurt, figs, a piece of bread, milk.

Smelling the jug, I asked myself if I dared drink it, especially with my stomach so upset. It had a cheesy odour. Yet the earthenware was cool, as if it had been brought out of a refrigerator only recently. I raised it to my lips, sipping just a little. All the milk hereabouts had this strong taste, I supposed, imagining the goats from which it came clanking about in the woman's village.

I drank a few more mouthfuls. I peeled a fig, then another. I ate a third, slowly, seated on my bed, hearing a mosquito, though expecting a knock at the door or even the sound of a chapel bell.

The mosquito continued droning. It was joined by another. It threatened my night's sleep. I was, after all, not as drained as on my first night and day, when I'd simply tumbled into the stillness of the dead. I was now here to stay.

Yet while the noise was irritating, it did not remotely qualify as a disruption by the standards of all that had occurred here. Though was anything currently happening? Strangely, I found it disconcerting that nothing was going to disturb me.

There was an eerie lull in the monastery, with the deaths over – including such as I'd brought with me. A hyper-stillness was entering into me, momentarily paralysing my movements, restricting my respiration even, just as, following an earthquake, people hold their breaths to see if there will be more devastation: if life will return to normal.

I was unsure of my ground. Relieved to be delivered from Father Josef's forceful presence, I was at a loss, finding myself quite so abandoned as I felt without rituals, such as refectory and chapel, unbeliever though I was.

Left entirely to my own depleted devices, my experience of time here was formless, worryingly shapeless. I had now spent almost a whole day in this cell.

I got up, stiff, and opened the door, switching off the light.

In the instant in which I was surrounded by darkness, I had the impression of a shadowy form leaving the chapel. I did not move, straining to see in the forecourt. I seemed no longer able to fix on any such shape. I couldn't be certain that I'd made out anything, anyone. All felt deserted, as I again grew aware of gushing water in this utter stillness.

I followed the sandy path between the buildings. It led me to the main gate. I walked some way across the rocky ledge, taking in, once again, the painful purity of the air, the profusion of stars so brilliant that it struck me, although I had seen it before.

I stood there, looking far off, through the deserted vacancy, at the inky jaggedness of mountains where some lived in caves. Only on my return did I notice the shape huddled against the outer wall: a dozing guard.

The security force dwindled in the succeeding days. They did not enter any more. Even the guards at the gate disappeared. The scarred soldier was gone. The monastery was silent but for the generator and cistern, which I had long ceased hearing. It might have been deserted as I strove to settle to my work, to establish a pattern of existence.

Yet the food appeared regularly outside my door. My dirty laundry vanished, to return the following day, clean, in my cell.

Other items hung on the washing line. There were heavily patched, smock-like shirts and underwear. And walking out one sunset, past tended garden with brimming scarlet irrigation ditches, ranging further than usual with my nocturnal insect collecting gear in a belted pouch, I eventually did come upon their owner.

It had to be him. Spying him seated against a granite slab, just a habit and hood turned to the distance, I instantly took him for the author of *A Saharan Solitude*. He alone, with that silhouette, was available to fit the bill in one of those fragments of reality to which the mind, unknowingly, feels mysteriously prompted to assign its own player. For sometimes a person crossing one's threshold inexplicably has a resonance for one, a strange human density, suggesting, from the moment of his arrival on the scene that he will be of consequence in one's unfolding situation.

It must be what the novelist feels when a new character comes, unplanned, to the fore. Or so it occurs to me, writing these pages, recounting the tale to myself, to that other beholding part of me standing in for the God in whom I no longer believe, but to whom I apparently continue to have things to say.

Here they are, at any rate, these lines for the benefit of whoever else may unexpectedly surface as my best reader.

7

The old monk had a powerful sense of obligation to continue the community, I knew, but now he might be experiencing the equal pull of his hermitage. For out here, needing no torch beneath such stars, wasn't he hearing the call of still deeper desert as strongly as any grounded seafarer felt the tug of ocean tides?

Yet he had already responded by recreating in the monastery his place of isolation and solitude. Nothing, no one, dictated the organisation of his time there except the regular, imperturbable yielding of day to night.

My legs had carried me towards him, involuntarily, unseen, without my even being aware of their silent forward tread until I was all but upon the granite. Was the other conscious of my arrival, gazing into those depths of illumined darkness? He might be asleep, dreaming something tremendous though unknowable to the observer or, even, when dawn would break, to himself. So motionless was he that it suddenly seemed as if he had turned to stone; that this was no more than a craggy promontory into which I had been reading someone.

At the very instant when the human – the dreaming human – merged with desert rock, words sounded:

"Good evening."

They came distinctly to my ears, yet somehow as if not actually spoken here in this emptiness. Eerily calm, they might almost have emerged from part of myself.

"I come here at sunset, when the heat of the day has passed ... It's so much easier to find one's way by night."

There were stars all around us, lightening the lie of the land.

"I rarely leave until dawn breaks. Come and sit by me ... That's right."

We reverted to silence. There was no telling how long it was going to last, each of us looking out.

"Silence and prayer, prayer and silence: they weave in and out of each other here in the Sahara. They become indistinguishable, until all waking, even sleeping, becomes prayer. It simply wells up. You can't help it. And never more than at night."

We continued gazing, wordless, beneath this brilliance.

Yet, serene as I felt I ought to be, I found words forming within me that I feared, but felt forced to utter:

"Father Mark."

"Mm ...?"

"I have to tell you something. I myself don't pray. Actually, I don't have any religious beliefs. I'm not even looking for them. And I'm certainly not a would-be hermit. That's not why I've come to the monastery. I'm staying for, well, quite different, personal reasons."

The horizon seemed endless; the sky immense.

"I hope ..." My voice trailed off. I cleared my throat. "I mean, I hope that's all right." I said it lamely.

A wind was blowing; I felt it on my bare forearms. It caught a tuft of the old monk's hair. A momentary light, perhaps a meteor, flashed far off.

Father Mark said: "There are many ways of searching for God. Only a few, or none, of them are known to those questing for Him. But it's axiomatic that we're all looking for Him, whether we realise it, or like it, or not. Remember St Augustine: 'Thou hast made us for Thyself, and our hearts are restless until they rest in Thee.'

"Now, the onus isn't entirely on us. God knows we're here, and He's set the Hound of Heaven on us. It's chasing us toward Him through our personal circumstances, though we may not recognise it's what's happening. We may think our life's moving towards certain goals; that it's about certain themes; that it's succeeding or failing, as part of a certain story that's *our* story. Yet the narrative's part of a much larger scheme. So we'll see if we ever arise from that self-obsessed perspective that has our nose fixed firmly to the mirror.

"We actually live through quite a different plan from the little one we think our existences are about. The slavering mastiff has its teeth firmly in our darned underwear, deaf and blind as we might be to the fact. It keeps remorselessly on our scent, as if we were fugitives from justice. No sleeping dog, it drives us to the point where God's ready for us – though it might feel, from our perspective, as if it's we who are standing still and being approached. And by whom? Well, as I say, the One who's been reaching to us precisely through our unrecognised efforts towards Him – although we may yet have to recognise Him for who He truly is."

Silence had returned. I was looking at the old man. The monk knew next to nothing about me, despite which he had focused on me. His attention was at once intimate and impersonal. And suddenly I was aware of some unaccountable but indisputable tie between us.

It was strange, powerful, anonymous.

I was grateful. I felt his interest as a gift. Generous, it touched something within me: whatever had unknowingly been waiting inside, in the unrecognised absence of such closeness, to drink up affecting concern from an old Father.

Surprised, I quivered at the hands of my new, sterner spiritual adviser in these starker, desert conditions.

The monk held still. Impassive, he gave no impression of knowing the impact he was having. In spite of which I devoutly wished I could feel addressed by Father Mark, precisely because I did feel mysteriously tugged to him. I wanted to please him.

If only his spiritual statements were true, and had meaning for me! I felt such longing to believe. Yet I recoiled, as if from some long-yearned-for solicitude offered just too late. The priest's vocabulary, the ideas, the images, admittedly more vivid, urgent and feeling than Father Josef's, were ultimately of a piece with them. They came from a quite foreign sense of reality.

The monk's terms of reference, with their basic optimism, their assurance of eventual, all-explaining meaning, were utterly unequal to what I had come upon in the monastery. They were, in any case, no match for my indifference, irrelevant as the enormity was to me, no less than the general situation giving rise to it. No, they were of little consequence beside my sense of personal randomness, of drifting, amid this unrelated but intrusive burst of savagery.

Not that I could think what language would be appropriate to me. No words sprang to mind. I found talk, Father Josef's, even Father Mark's, just that: talk. For my own part, I felt capable only of muteness and withdrawal.

I had to force myself to respond to the monk, so generous in spirit, almost out of politeness: "Well, I can't help feeling as if I'm here under false pretences."

"You're hardly alone in that," the gruff voice said, unruffled. "Our community's like the Foreign Legion. We ask nobody his identity or background when he joins. Not even our guests. We're not what we were, but what we become here."

I took it in.

"We forfeit our names. The monastery offers us one not already assigned to the brethren, thereby enacting our Christian drama of new birth. So the traces of what we've been simply fall away like an afterbirth. They trail as shadows nobody notices.

"Apart from a new name, all that's required is loyalty to the Order. It doesn't even matter what transformations of self and belief do or don't take place. If we encounter God on one of His self-presentations here in the desert, walking out in the cool of the evening, rare, precious, but known, like our Saharan rain, all well and good. But otherwise there's just the unremembering of our old lives, under the guise of ritual, prayer, work and silence.

"Who knows what personal, what spiritual being our brother maintains beneath the community's freely given new habit? At most, there's the expectation of ecstatic self-transformation, amid waiting and absence, here where the wind bloweth as it listeth. Of course, now there's a new generation at the monastery … or there *was*."

He stared out, jaw fixed, then gulped.

"Our younger brethren were born in the liberal, democratic days since the War – people like you. They were more open about themselves than my generation, or Father Sebastian's, which lay between us. They saw self-revelation less as self-advertisement, as we did in my time with our Roman values of discretion and stoical reticence. They viewed it more as a virtue, guaranteeing personal authenticity. Theirs wasn't a dogma, but a psychological, exploratory faith. They were beloved of the locals for their good works and human availability. They were conspicuous for it. Yet none were more overtly political in this community, or nearby, than through standing shoulder to shoulder with the poor – although many in the Church, especially in South America, have 'advanced' social ideas. Doubtless you've heard Father Josef's."

He sniffed.

"Anyway, even with this new generation, the new brethren must've discovered an old truth: the more spiritually sensitive one becomes, the greater one's awareness of evil. It's one and the same Father who gives us these overlapping perceptions – although our juniors apparently haven't needed to go as far into the desert as we hermits to discover evil. They found out all about it here, in a most terrible way."

Father Mark was quivering. He went on doing so in tense silence. I finally broke it: "Talking about the other brethren, I wonder if you knew one of them. Father Barnato gave me a letter for him. I'll show it to you when we go back to the monastery."

That was much later, after more silence and sleep. It grew light. We walked back together, at Father Mark's pace. He was holding onto my arm.

An accident had paralysed one of his legs near his hermitage. When the doctor arrived, days later, after an eternity of agony stretched out on a mat in his cave, it was too late. He would be lame for the rest of his life, he told me.

I asked what had happened to the donkey on which he had arrived at the monastery we were now re-entering.

"The women took it. They'll return it when I want."

Father Mark told them to serve breakfast in the refectory. As they prepared to do so, I went to my cell to fetch the letter. In fact, I brought both.

"Oh! Father Erich's not one of the brethren here," the old monk said, squinting to read the elegant writing on the envelope already opened by the police officer. "He's a hermit too, but much further out." Father Mark said this with distant eyes, tapping the letter abstractedly.

"I haven't heard of anyone coming across him in years. He could have moved into even deeper desert – or died, for all I know. You might as well forget him."

"Well, Father Carlo insisted that he should receive the letter," I said simply.

"Insisted, eh?"

Father Mark gulped his coffee, then dipped his bread in the remains of it. The letter lay beside him, together with the one for the Abbot. The monk gobbled, crossing himself and standing up from the table.

But he paused there, staring intently at the envelopes. A moment later he sprang away, thrusting them with brusque decisiveness into the pocket of his habit.

We emerged from dimness into bright light. Blinking, I asked Father Mark if he was going to chapel.

"*You* don't need to. You're a guest, not a member of the community."

It stung me, despite my unbelief.

"Don't force yourself to pray," he added. "Leave it to the monastery – *all* of us!"

Father Mark was looking ferociously around himself, in the fore-court – that desolate place of departed souls. "Can't you hear?" the monk said, suddenly adamant. "The very stones are crying out!"

The old man turned sharply away. I saw him hobble off across the sand in his worn habit, putting up the cowl. But he, too, did not go into the chapel, that old hermit made for wild solitude.

8

I did not see the monk again that day, or the next, or on the days after that. Mentally, I pursued this Desert Father. Inwardly, I scanned that sandy terrain. But I felt his absence. The old man was lost beyond recall in the Sahara.

The guards, too, were all long gone. Even the Bedouin woman was nowhere to be found, for all her ministrations.

I was alone.

Back in my cell, I gazed out the narrow window. Barely aware that the army vehicles were no longer there, all I took in was the desert beyond. On and on it stretched, endless. I had no choice but to face it.

Not that I'd disliked being alone in the past. Even with Anja, I'd frequently preferred my own company. I'd withdraw to concentrate on some project as when, in earlier years, I had done my homework and pursued my hobbies. But out here, now, without those maternal presences nearby, I was encountering something sharply different from meditative solitude. Here was harsh, unremitting emptiness – before and within me. How would I ever come to terms with it?

I didn't exactly ask myself. Although looking back on it here in Rome, all this time later, I wonder if I wasn't somehow relieved to have come at last to the point of confronting this ultimate reality; to have stumbled, without quite realising it, on such as I was destined to find, at last, awaiting me in the Sahara. For I suspect that I felt disturbed, robbed of my necessary isolation, on seeing the police officer again driving up to the monastery late one afternoon.

"So you're not leaving," he said in the lengthening shadows. "If you insist on remaining, you must know that I can't take responsibility for you."

He pulled off his cap to shoo away a troublesome fly.

"I only hope you've a better reason for staying here than just the insects. Surely you're not relying on them to get you back on your feet."

I did not reply, though he was looking at me intently.

"Are you?" he said, continuing to wave the droning fly aside with his cap, in my tongue-tied silence. "Well, I trust you can come up with a really good reason for continuing in this, of all places. Because God help you in all you'll have to face here."

I suppose I might have been casting about for something more than the lack of an alternative destination: a home. What could be holding me in the desert, as in dreams when limbs are paralysed despite sudden danger? I could scarcely glimpse it, let alone express it. So, surprising myself, I turned the tables on the man, saying:

"If it's so dangerous, why are *you* staying?"

"I'm posted here. Orders are orders. I've no choice."

But sniffing at the wry tone in which he'd delivered his pat answer, the officer continued: "Besides, I'm *from* here. Not this place, exactly. I was born in the capital and became a cadet in the police academy, run by the French in those days. Yet the Sahara is also part of this huge North African country we paid such a high price to liberate. And the fresh struggle you're witnessing here is actually a national one. It's my struggle, too. I can't turn my back on it even if I want to. It's instinctive for me and all my brothers to try and find a way to live through it.

"You see, I'm thrown into this predicament by the mere fact of being born in this country. Even if I left the service and travelled abroad, living in a country untouched by these outrages, as I once did in Paris, I'd find myself haunted by it. I'd transport it as surely as the burden carried by camels in those caravans crossing our desert.

"Wherever one is, *Monsieur*," the officer said, looking directly at me, "one is actually in one's own situation. That's the case regardless of how alien one's surroundings are."

He replaced his cap over his clear features and prepared to leave. "So one would do well to understand what that situation is. It might save one a lot of trouble in one's new setting."

We shook hands and he got into his car. I watched it till it was swallowed up by the dying light of the sun.

How was I to survive here? Not, apparently, by asking myself. Nor by consciously visualising the image I find before me now, writing this: a man alone, without resources, standing in desert. I simply went to work.

I took to going out at sunset with a belted pouch and nets. Few insects were active during the day, when it was too hot to hold a bare hand to the sand. They mainly came out in the cooler evening.

I set up ultraviolet lights, using batteries. These lured the insects towards me. I made quick sketches of some, especially of physical features that were likely to fade if they were preserved.

Others I netted or picked up with forceps. Keeping the specimens on damp cotton in vials, I stored them in a dark cupboard, to draw them live in the cell. Several insects needed to be killed for final drawings or modifications. These I put into small jars with cyanide under a layer of plaster. The glass bottoms were fully taped so that the grey cyanide powder could not leak out. But occasionally I would notice a live insect in an empty jar. I'd watch it, observing its struggle to find a way out of the glass.

My collecting done, I continued on to the granite slab where I had first sat and slept a night out. Eventually, dawn would arrive. I tracked back alone to the tray that awaited me outside my cell. There it was, as on subsequent occasions throughout the day.

The monastery seemed very large and deserted upon returning. It was eerie, particularly as the consequences of my decision to stay percolated increasingly into my thoughts. Yet I refused to dwell on this feeling of worrying strangeness, insisting to myself that murderous intruders would hardly strike twice.

There was no danger – and perhaps no brethren to suffer it. I did not know whether or not Father Mark was even there. He might be in his cell, not to be disturbed. But he could have ordered the woman to bring his donkey back one night, to set off for his desert cave.

Did he, *had* he ever existed? Or was he a mirage, there but not there, like the invisible giver of this daily bread?

Inhabiting the place, with my sense of absent presence, everything took on a feeling of immense emptiness. I found myself floating in an atmosphere of unreality, here where the slaughtered monks could seem as much a delusion as any mirage or wild vision provoked by desert thirst: a mind I had undermined by this timelessness, until the hours, or mere minutes, suddenly pressed on me again.

So at this low ebb, I asked myself if I had the will power to sustain the tedium of painstaking study. For what would I be without work, that great calmer of anxiety, of emptiness? Pity those unable to fill their time with routine!

Here were questions to which the desert provided no answers. Equally mute were starry nights, spent against cooling granite; fiery middays admitting nothing but debilitating heat; blank, grey, shadowless late afternoons. No other sequence existed. Meaningful narrative, drama, depth, the very pattern and sensation of lived life, had apparently slipped away. Whirling sand, reeling clouds, soughing wind, were telling some story of their own: but a tale indecipherable and unrecognised, because measurelessly remote from anything of which I could be aware.

All that the rushing, sighing breezes meant to me, instinctively, was the resurgence of natural sound over speech – in other words, human silence. Yet upon first acknowledging my solitude here, my ears had heard nothing from any source. It was like the stunned stillness affecting all after a massive disaster. Imperceptibly, it had transformed into purely desert noises, so that in the wind, as the sand "smoked", there seemed to be distant drumming. I might have been passing under an ocean, at immense pressure, with only faint, filtered echoes of watery currents.

Without words, without those elaborate discourses, this silence meant that a thought, a mood, once begun, no matter how undermining of my tranquillity, encountered no external obstacle. Nothing would deflect it. It went on and on, till mysteriously dissipated like night by approaching dawn.

Mute, finding myself in this unpeopled place, untouched by its alien history, beliefs and present predicament, I – lacking the claims of an actively remembered past of my own – lost any real sense of my very being. I floated, faceless, like a babe-to-be helpless in its salty sac, or a departed soul drifting into the ether.

In suspended animation, out of body, out of mind, still here from little more than inertia, I had automatically taken up, as if without decision or choice, the humdrum collecting that had been my excuse for coming. Sending me out regularly into the desert, it reduced my weeks to much of a muchness. It made my efforts, concrete and precise, unreal to me. I went for long periods without being aware of what my hands, I myself, were doing here and now.

Abstracted, having surely outlived my existence, I simply drifted on, as if some more general life flow had caught me into its waves, too powerful and fundamental for me any more knowingly to recognise and so heed it than the basic movement of the Earth. It buoyed me, advanced me for purposes then barely suspected, leaving me to work in a virtual trance.

During and after my labours, my thoughts were blank. For long, indeterminately long, that vacant mental screen held good. In the mid-morning, of an afternoon, by night, it met a no less silent, dreamlike void, whether the sand or a star-speckled sky.

From my position against the granite slab, something was beginning to dawn on me, though too imperceptibly for me to be exactly aware of it. Yet it was certainly happening. But was it arising from the sandy vastness, with its barely audible sound of distant wind, or of the far-off shifting of massive dunes? Might it be some stirring within *me*, a being unexpectedly finding himself in the Sahara?

Whichever it turns out to be in this memoir, at the time it bore no apparent relation to my work. It gave me, instead, an unwitting sensation of something distant, impalpable, increasingly familiar but essentially strange. These sounds were possibly echoing from my inner ear – connected, perhaps, to breathing or pulsing blood. But, as I went on taking in the vibration, it seemed like an increasingly loud humming. I all but heard voices.

They were singing. And matching it in my mind's eye, I saw Tuaregs out in the desert.

Pitching tents in the moonlight, they must be throwing off their goatskin cloaks to dance against evil spirits. They gyrated round a fire too far off to be seen in this endless night, brilliantly lit by the heavens. Yes, they could be the far-off source of the dancing, these Blue Men if not Berbers, Foucauld's killers.

As I appeared to make out the murderers' descendants, within earshot, with their insistent rhythms, a pattern seemed to be repeating itself endlessly here in the desert. Yet I did not measure what was now barely registering against what had been or might come. Those tall, brawny people, with their yellowish eyes and strange ways, were suddenly incomprehensibly remote.

They must be as far off in that boundless space as a caravan passing. So it might have travelled at any time over the centuries, though now, far out of hailing distance, diverging ever more, the caravan had become what it'd always been: a world unto itself in the emptiness surrounding its passage. It returned me to a void of soundlessness and obscurity now my hallucinating instant of excited stirring was over. I was unreachably alone.

Late the next afternoon, I was again leaning against the granite slab. Last night's sounds were echoing in my ears, imperceptible, infinitely distant, though reviving this troubling sense of anticipation.

Then I found an irregular outer rhythm taking up my inner reverberation. The noise became undeniable as I noticed a fast-approaching black mass increasingly blotting out the sunset. Wind lashed the sand. Huge drops raised a stale, dusty odour.

Thunder crashed off the remote sandstone range in ear-splitting volleys. Whole root-systems of lightning made it painfully brilliant. Each time, the flares died into darkness.

I did not expect the rain to stop so soon, as I began heading back. But the respite was short-lived. Altogether drenched in a moment, I trudged through sheets of water turning sand into shallow marsh overlaying rock.

I was naked in my cell. I dried myself, trying to wipe the grains from between my toes with a damp towel. The window reverberated. The dark room lit up again and again. I heard rain pounding the roof, the foliage outside. Somewhere it was cascading furiously.

An hour later, all was still. The storm had moved on. The sky was more lucidly starry than ever. Silence had returned – within and without – except for loud dripping.

Dawn broke, glistening and soft-hued. Colour remained as the morning continued. There were swaths of tiny white flowers on the red sand. Low, vivid grasses with shin-high yellow patches flourished in the continuing humidity.

Insects appeared in this sudden lushness. They drew me out even in the day, though I was loath to sketch them there and then, given the mistakes in my previous attempts at rapid drawing.

But the next moment, wiping my forehead as I recorded one, the back of my hand dried instantly, salty now. The sun was as fierce as it had ever been in this once more parched desert. Withered remains of the verdant germination scattered in burning breezes. The very memory of them slipped away from me like a dream. It left me to lifeless silence.

Later, dark spots appeared before my eyes. I discounted them; but still that sense of expectancy returned with a strange tremulousness in the light. Then a large cloud sallied forth, sailing on in this eternal, unreal present.

I visualised what it passed in slow motion across the glaring blue. Such an interminable passage over sand, rocks, rough tracks and mountains! It never connected with the least, most isolated sign of life, leaving only its leisurely shadow on the ground.

Even that passed on, endlessly approaching horizons to traverse other continents, other immensities of sand, sea and perhaps an unimaginably remote, real world. Nothing was left behind, inert as the extinguished time between dreams in a single sleep; nothing, despite this unreasoning apprehension of mine, but aching emptiness.

Still there was that unsettling of the light. At once I realised it had been reminding me all along of the video screen flickering emptily on the bus coming here, an emotional age ago. Quivering blankness, effacing an unreachable Alexandrian girl and her city, had left me even more bereft, longing for an image, for the blur to coalesce into a mass, to form into some single being.

Out here the unstable light conceded nothing. Nor did the inner reverberations. No matter the sense of anticipation, of expectancy. Only blankness overcame me, a lone figure, bending to continue working with insects.

Absences of mind extinguished knowledge of whatever lay beyond me. Here were whole stretches of vacancy in which I lacked awareness even of myself here and now.

For I might be out at night, beneath the stars. But, equally, it was an illusion given the images again taking shape before me. I felt myself in an open-air cinema, the legs of folding chairs pressing into soft desert sand such as this into which I reached for a scuttling, solid black beetle. Moonlight deprived that hand of fleshliness, colour, apparent life. Ghostly grey against the dark night, it seemingly reappeared ahead, projected as part of an actor.

Milk-white, still, open, it filled me with heavy tenderness. The mood stayed with me. It wove in and out of stray thoughts; of concentrated inattention. By the time I was holding with tweezers the bluish glitter of a translucent wing flaking away from a somehow shrunken black body, the hand was no longer an actor's. I was remembering it lying on the outside of bedcovers.

Memory presented stills of the hand at different moments, unsought, unconnected. One showed it entire, immobile. A close-up revealed the gold ring catching the Mediterranean morning light, with a harbour glimpsed through jalousies. A further shot focused on the nails, well cared for, but here with a trace of clay against the cuticle.

One of Anja's recreations had been pottery. She had moulded vessels like these I was now taking to sketching after long hours collecting, then illustrating. I did so in the same notebook in which I made rapid drawings of live insects out in the desert. The grain of the paper allowed shaded areas to acquire texture.

I saw a still-life painting in the crockery on trays of food left out for me – the sole sign of the absent woman. For hours I drew the earthenware spheres, shading the surface of full-bellied jugs, so rounded and smooth. Most of the pieces had a pattern of black dots, made with fingertips. Fingerprints were even visible in cases where the paint had run thin. They were signatures that I sought to convey, here in my cell. It seemed to put me in direct touch with the maker.

I was being drawn back by pottery like Anja's, overcoming the amnesia claiming our incinerated address book, too. I had the feel of her again.

I saw her hand on the outside fold of the bed cover, ice-cold.

Then I understood that, far from whatever live being I'd improbably yearned to release from the shuddering light, it was now the departed that was resurfacing in my mind. Like it or not, everything I'd distanced with sedatives, then discarded with an entomological project supposedly launching me into the future, had suddenly invaded my thoughts.

So that was how I'd survived in the Sahara: by not being there, but rather mentally in the company of the absent I'd unknowingly spent my time summoning to life with the recurrent urgency of ecstatic dance, of changeable weather.

9

Memory took hold of me. It returned me to the Mediterranean in autumn. There was a blanket in our hotel room, though it still wasn't cold. Anja, always the energetic one, was to be active in photographing Alexandria's underwater remains for a German magazine owned by the international publisher providing most of her commissions.

She was especially excited to have received this offer. It was so much less grisly than her usual projects. But I had resisted accompanying her, provoking one of Anja's repeated criticisms of me for being too self-enclosed.

"Self-*sufficient*," I preferred to say.

"Maybe," she muttered tersely. "But perhaps you'd enjoy opening up a bit. Don't you want to know what they're dredging up from the sea?"

"Not really," I said, as I later remembered in the monastery's Saharan night. "Alexandria's a closed chapter for me. I've no desire to disturb the past."

The closest I needed to come to Egypt was an exhibition of watercolours by a young American artist Anja had met. She painted scenes of a monastery off the Cairo–Alexandria desert road.

I had been content enough in the full life we had made for ourselves in Rome: I, trained as an entomologist, now an illustrator of ecological books; Anja, a feature photographer. Our voluminous address book bore testimony to it.

Film buffs, we often went out with friends to late night movies. Seeing, for the third time, *Hiroshima Mon Amour*, we discussed together, over drinks prised out of the café shuttering below our apartment, the opening sequence.

The lovers' naked shoulders, arms, were covered in dew, sweat or even nuclear ash like that in the desert Anja's book showed. Were they in agony or bliss? Now in the Sahara's lunar waste, I recalled us considering it. It was one friend in particular that I seemed to hear again: Laura. Shapely, dark-eyed, intelligent, amazingly still unattached, this minor actress of a single (if remarkable) film had always struck me as particularly desirable.

She had been saying that the Japanese man was not uniquely himself. He *was* Hiroshima. The French woman was not just herself either. She *was* Nevers, scene of her German lover's death and her punishment for collaboration. Each existed, truly existed, merely insofar as he or she fulfilled a role, assigned only by the situation bringing them temporarily together in the film: namely to juxtapose, with glaring discrepancy, an unimaginable public and a quite personal hell. Yet the dramatic moment, the movie, their functions, would soon end. Who – what – might they then be? Must they simply relapse into non-being?

I had trouble seeing exactly what she meant. Perhaps my thoughts had been straying as I wondered under what circumstances she, apparently searching, might come upon a more complete role for herself.

I felt something: a hand on my arm – Anja's. She was indicating to me that we should now extricate ourselves from this social situation that could easily continue all night. It was time for us to go to bed.

Anja was always reaching out to me. She never liked to leave me alone. She had recently lured me to Washington, on that project of hers, despite my dislike for the United States. As for Egypt, where she was going regardless of her recent bouts of tiredness, doubtless from pushing herself too hard, she insisted that the trip would have the greatest personal interest for me too.

Taking her hand, I relented. We were surprisingly attached, considering we had met through my advertisement in the personal column of a local newspaper.

We travelled by coach from Cairo, along the dreary desert road. Eventually we passed the contaminated marshes of Lake Mariout. In late afternoon, we entered the sprawling outskirts of the city.

I was peering past her through the window. We turned at a right angle to drive between blocks of flats. Suddenly I saw it, down a side street: the sea. Blue-green, glaringly luminous as it had always been, it was there a block later as well – then again, roiled by this early autumn breeze. I thrilled with recognition as we continued parallel to the

Corniche, several streets up. I smelled manure as the coach lumbered onto the esplanade with its horse-drawn carriages. We booked into our hotel, which fronted the bay.

I lingered on the veranda while Anja got out her photographic equipment to go to Qaitbay Fort. She could hardly rouse me from my slothfulness. I would not join her. The door to our hotel room closed.

She passed below me on the pavement, several floors down, hurrying with her camera while there was still light. She would shoot the archaeologists' undoing of earthquakes, tidal waves, hidden tremors. Roads, foundations of buildings, an entire section of the ancient Greek city were being recovered. They were striving to draw up a woman of legendary beauty, a goddess surely, from the obscure deep.

On the hotel balcony, I seemed once more to watch a lowering and raising. A raffia basket, suspended from a rope, was hauled back up to a balcony, full of vegetables. The middle-aged woman, my mother, continued gazing silently, softly, over its edge for a long-awaited return in this balmy seaside air.

The apartment was nearby. I might as well walk there now, even if only to see it from the outside. We could return together tomorrow for a closer look.

I found myself having advanced some way along the Corniche. But, roused from the reverie that had brought me this far with such certainty, I had a moment of doubt. I stopped a couple of passers-by in *gallabiyahs* speaking Arabic.

"*Rue* Memphis?"

I was looking into a well of incomprehension. A group grew to answer the question. "*Sharia* Memphis!" someone finally said. He set me on my way, further down the Corniche, across the tram lines, into the road itself.

There all was familiar, yet not quite as I remembered. This was the building I wanted, surely. It felt right, didn't it? Then again, I did not remember it being in front of the Armenian social centre.

I walked on, recalling that there had been a garden in front as I noticed dusty ficus plants before a four-storey block of apartments. My legs carried me up what I suddenly, instinctively, knew was the correct staircase. They'd done so regardless of volition – just as now, later, they had brought me unawares, across sand, to a cell in a dark desert monastery, my head empty of all except the reel replaying this part of the past.

The door opened. I stood a moment on its shadowy threshold and took in the young woman in a flowered housecoat and slippers, summoned by my knock. She had a scarf around her head.

"*Bonjour, Mademoiselle,*" I said in what had once been the *lingua franca* around here. "*Comprenez-vous le français?*"

"*Mais bien sûr, Monsieur. J'ai été au Lycée Français.*"

I began by explaining that my family and I had lived here in the mid-Fifties, and the woman, whose name was Amina, bade me enter before I could finish. I had been drawn into the old place, which I had never intended to revisit. No more had I expected to recall this return months later in the Sahara: memory, pressing through mental blankness, of a time, an Alexandria, assumed to be over and done with.

The woman introduced her older cousin, Laila, here with her teenage son. Laila, too, often visited the house where she had once lived. She said it over a cup of Turkish coffee, which they invited me to share with them.

"*La nostalgie, vous savez …*"

Amina added: "A lot of people come back to their apartments in this area. They're mainly Israelis." She caught her cousin's eye.

"*Au contraire,*" I said. "My parents were German. My father was a scientist working on a project for the government here. My mother taught in the German school."

We were in the main hallway, cluttered and small. It was not at all the large space I remembered having been forbidden to race through. Now I was invited to look round, Laila's son serving as reluctant guide.

There was a room by the front door. I simply could not recall it. It disrupted my memory of the one beside it, and of those beyond. It did seem to me, though, that the next place I looked in on was where my mother had taught me to read. She had started me on homework before it was formally required at my – at *our* – school.

Valuing study, she was in any case in a position to give me a lot of attention, as we were alone for much of the time. We understood no Arabic; yet neither had we been here long enough to meet other European families in the city. And we made no attempt to contact neighbours in the area.

I never once spoke to the people living in the apartment below. I heard them talking in a strange language on their veranda, under ours.

When I asked what it was, my father said it was old-fashioned Spanish, but that I must keep myself to myself. It didn't occur to me to ask why.

I never made contact with the neighbour's daughter, a girl my own age – at least not verbally. Once, when my eyes met hers on the stairs, my father barked: "Don't!" But every further glimpse of her on the landing, in the street when I went out with my mother, made her even more an object of silent daydreaming, of solitary yearning. Her image reverberated in my thoughts as a focus for intense desire, only to remain unfulfilled. It finally went underground – except when half-emerging in some older form, say, the woman in the bus video, or that student, prettier than Anne Frank, in Washington's Holocaust Museum.

My father would often be away during the week, working in the desert. Only late on Friday afternoons did he appear, perhaps to take us, the following evening, to an open-air cinema outside the city. It would remind me of the relaxed, affectionate father he'd been when I was much younger. But now he did not seem altogether with us. He appeared abstracted, eyes far away, as we sat waiting for images to appear in the desert night.

Once my mother asked what was preoccupying him. He did not answer her. All he said, mutedly, was: "Let's see the film."

He had saved his anger for home.

"Never, *ever*, again ask what I'm doing! I've a lot on my mind. Scientists need mental breathing space. We have to think things out. Don't you know that?"

Now, years later, I felt the silence again in the apartment with its boy guide. I – the adult a once-terrified son had become – felt ill at ease appearing too curious. My mother had grown withdrawn, too, without a man permanently in the stillness of the apartment. Mohammed, the servant, no longer worked at this cracked, marble-topped table in the kitchen. At least it seemed the original one, but I couldn't be certain. It robbed me of the sense of having truly revisited the place from which Mohammed had been summarily called up, one evening, to serve in the army in the Canal Zone, during the Suez Crisis.

As a boy, I saw my mother spending ever more time alone now on the balcony, lighted and jasmine-scented, onto which my adult self now followed Laila's son. She had awaited a husband returning more unpredictably, less frequently.

Revisiting the veranda, I again seemed to feel the cool hall marble on bare feet on which I, that young boy, had left my bed to approach a woman sensing, from her wicker chair invisibly off to one side of the French windows, that her son could not sleep. All I had seen, halfway through the dining room, was a hand, outstretched. I had taken it, to be told by an unsteady voice one evening, on a balcony unlighted that night:

"Your father isn't coming home again. He's lost in the desert. They said they don't expect to find him."

I remained on the veranda, now as then, with my mother. Laila's son went inside.

There were pots out here, but the plants were all dead. There seemed to be no light bulbs or chairs. Once more, I supposed I should be feeling something. I strained to. Still I felt no more than when they had buried the empty coffin. I had held a handful of sand over it, as the priest suggested. But grains, slipping through my opening fingers, were gusted away by a sudden wind towards the desert – in which I irrationally supposed my father went on wandering.

Nothing was left on the balcony but absence, as I looked out. I had no reason to do so. No archaic Spanish was wafting up from the veranda below. The people walking in the street were all unknown to me. Most had been born since I had left the city. Never would I recognise anyone approaching this building. I made out a cacophony of warbling at the corner of the next road; it was a turkey market. Unsure whether or not I remembered it, my certainty about aspects of the past I had just been recalling wavered. The capacity for the mental reliving of infant scenes was apparently deserting me. Stepping back from the veranda, I was in a dowdy apartment redolent of little more than its current occupant's sour laundry and stale lunch.

I was anxious to go. Amina and Laila urged me to visit them again. They two would now be the sole incentive for coming back.

If I did return, Amina laughed, they would give me the water bill. It had been kept in my father's name, as their grandfather had always said the water would have been too difficult to reinstall once it was disconnected at the time of Suez. The receipts of the water bill, while a link to those days, were not themselves relevant to my memories – in spite of which, from politeness, I said I would of course be back.

My voice lacked strength. It had no body. It was ghostly.

I was not ready to return to the hotel. I needed to walk, and did so in a chill wind to the centre of the city.

Shops were open; some sold second-hand furniture, bric-a-brac. I stopped at one. The owner hovered, alert, several paces back from the entrance. I took a position just sufficiently far away on the pavement to prevent him from drawing a potential customer into an exhaustive, committing review of his wares, but which still afforded a view of the gloomy interior. I wondered if it contained anything from the apartment my mother had left upon her departure with me, soon after the Suez Crisis. In no time, she had found a new position at the German school in Rome.

I supposed one of those piles of crockery might include some of her Meissen plates. I seemed to glimpse the piano in a dark recess. Yet I could not be sure that I had recognised such things here.

I must have been standing there for some time. The owner finally emerged from the shop, ivory-handled fly swat in hand.

"Are you looking for something?" he said politely, in English.

I shuffled on mutely, like a homeless person. I walked blindly for a long time. My legs took me past *pâtisseries* with evocative names: *Délice, Trianon, Pastroudis.*

A tram was crossing. At its open window, boys gnawed watermelon seeds and spat the husks onto the tracks. I went down streets with broken gutters and balconies flaking from the salt sea air. It was darkling; starlings shrieked and *muezzins* called.

I came to a dead halt. I had no idea where I was. I lacked a sense of the city. My inner map was an illusion. I had no homing instinct: there was no home. Its memory belonged to others. Houseless, in a city not mine, I stood watching girls crowd a cake shop to eat *konafa*. They all wore the veil, dictated by the religious law providing each with the clear sense of self she took for granted. One glimpsed me, between unravelling bites; she saw a shadow, at most. She, they, dissolved into giggles as I turned away.

There was a smell of shellac. Someone in a furniture shop was weaving a rattan seat. Other chairs, strung but only half-finished, rocked unpeopled.

I walked on through the crowded, vacant night.

I reached the hotel. My wife had returned earlier. She had left Qaitbay Fort before the light waned. Her camera had recovered little enough of the original part of the city. She had abandoned those watery foundations, doubtless feeling utterly drained. Perhaps she was unused to the food, the microbes. Anyway, here she was in bed, so fast asleep that I did not try to tell her of my outing – about which words, in any case, would have failed me.

I lay on my back, next to her still form, just as I was now lying in a dark desert cell remembering it, alone. I looked up at the pattern of light the headlamps of traffic on the Corniche made on the shadowy ceiling, and fell into a dreamless sleep.

Sun was pouring through the shutters. Her hand lay on the downturned bedcover. I took it: it was rigid, icy.

10

It all came back to me as I continued drawing still-lifes in the monastery. I recorded the vessels I received on any given day from the unseen woman's hands. I caught slight variations in their positions on the tray, whether the earthenware was glazed or not, with heavier or lighter decoration added by blackened fingertips.

I started sketching the sand and brought out the forms, the graining, of whatever lay before me in the early morning and late afternoon. The wind made whorls, some solidifying overnight, others soft and soon scattered. Cursive script of a kind, I repeatedly copied it down. Perhaps a time would come when I would commit a single, definitive version to paper.

I went on to draw the granite rocks. Ten metres high or more, embedded in red sand, these brooding presences gave me a heavy feeling of being observed. In the vicinity of one, there seemed to be movement. Maybe it was the Tuaregs whose sounds I'd earlier almost seemed to hear. Or it might just be quivering in the air. My pencil rendered it briefly, indistinctly. It was no more than provisional, a sketch of heat haze from which I was called away by the return of my earlier sense of anxious expectancy to turn the page.

I returned to the insects. It was constant work, collecting, preserving, photographing, magnifying and drawing them. It proceeded night and day, whether in the desert or in my cell. Sometimes I was aware of what I was doing. Increasingly, I performed the tasks mechanically, my mind a blank. Unfailingly, I photographed each small specimen I came upon, regardless of whether or not it was perfect. But, hardly realising it, I was anticipating studying the sequence.

Nor did I recognise for some time that by returning to memories of Anja, I was simultaneously reliving an earlier review of images: our Alexandrian photographs. I had not sent them to be developed at first. Yet, one long day in our apartment, I had finally taken out the film left in her camera.

The shots had come back to reveal a glistening goddess. Actually a pile of stones once serving in humbler ways as antique road paving, it had been hauled from muddy obscurity onto the quay beside Qaitbay Fort. A picture showed it surrounded by soft afternoon light reflected off the cove. I looked at it for a long time.

I studied another photograph of the desert taken, I supposed, from the bus. There was another of the marshes, and several more of the quay, disordered with that paving recovered with the bulky raising equipment also visible. Children – urchins – had crowded into a further snapshot. Or perhaps she had agreed to photograph them properly, this once, in the hope of preventing them from disrupting the rest of her work.

Maybe. There were no more photographs.

I had been drawn back repeatedly to the series. Could I imaginatively widen each photo's frame to include what was beyond it as, say, in this one of featureless desert? If I went on looking at the photographs, perhaps I might now see what I had missed at the time: why these were to be her last.

No. There was no pressing through to the unreachable; no penetrating the unknowable. The snapshots promised no answer to mysteries. There were no mysteries. There *were* only attempted evasions of the brute fact of loss, by posing questions to a past the answers to which were fruitlessly expected to alter its outcome. The past was mute, inert. Speaking to it, with no hope of reply, could only worsen the original hurt.

I ripped up the photographs, every last one. I threw them all away.

They joined the address book, that other victim of my tug-of-war between wanting to remember and preferring to forget. Slowly, pensively, leafing through the record of all who had made up our life together, I had torn it up, page by page. I put it, and everything it contained, into the wastepaper basket. So it was with other reminders of our years together. Each – a book, a bowl – was pensively jettisoned.

These were stones tipped into a dark sea engulfing me, too.

Out there in the Sahara, remembering my rejection of the remnants of our marriage, collecting insects, I found myself also recalling my mother's failure to preserve mementos of her husband.

We had come to Rome soon enough after my father's death, bringing to the small apartment arranged for us by the school not a tie, not a pipe, not a book with his name. She had abandoned everything, making the packing easier, surely – lightening the load of her baggage. The man might never have been, nor the city where we had lost him. It remained equally unrecalled by souvenirs.

I had no snapshot of Alexandria, nor of my father there. Gone was the photograph album. I could form no image of the man. I even lost the sound of his voice. It did not mean that I stopped trying to see or hear him. At the burial of that empty coffin, my childish gaze followed sand blown far from my hand. On and on, my mind's eye had pursued it, that evening, on succeeding days and nights, at any and every moment. Far into the Sahara I stalked the faceless figure, a shadow, hardly a footprint, a mere notion – till, unexpectedly, it came out unimaginably far away, at some stony desert fringe, half-cultivated, in fabled Black Africa.

Or later, without me deliberately tracking the man, I'd be surprised by him in a Roman crowd. Direct as a Fayum portrait, he suddenly peered out of a glance, a head half-turned, on the bus, in a *piazza*, crossing the street – only to vanish. It was possible, too, talking to someone – a teacher perhaps – to read, for a distracted moment, the wanderer in the features before me. The next instant, a smile effaced them. He was gone.

Yet with the years, even fewer remnants of him stirred. They did so facelessly, in moods of being with him in earliest infancy. So swift were they, so fleeting, that only a moment afterward would I catch that I'd just been learning to swim in Alexandria's Stanley Bay, or to read with him in bed with my mother. Then, coming back to myself, I'd feel abandoned. I would wonder how accurately, as my father got older, I could imagine and recognise him as the person he had become. The question; the ever-growing, ever-empty interval since he had gone missing; the changing situation of my adolescent life: they muted my quest. I was scarcely aware of it in myself.

Certainly, my mother never mentioned anything that might reawaken it. Nor did she refer to much else. She threw herself into her new job and spent evenings preparing classes and marking at the dining-room table. Eventually, the dim lamplight would hurt her eyes. Only then would she tell me, looking across the green baize cloth, to leave the moth and butterfly collection I had brought out upon finishing my homework.

"It's time to go to bed."

We were silent, travelling to school together in the morning. We hardly came into contact with one another during the day: I was never in her class. I only saw her if there was a general assembly, as when a special speaker was invited.

One wore glasses. They glinted as he stood at ease in his crisp monk's habit. His face, smooth and middle-aged, wore a relaxed smile as he addressed his young audience. He warned, in German pleasantly inflected with Italian, of the encroachments of communism. The Holy Father was especially mindful of the problem. It had a special place in his prayers.

Mother and son, we never acknowledged one another on the few occasions when we chanced to coincide at school, except with a fugitive smile, or by fleetingly catching each other's eye. We tacitly agreed that it would embarrass me before my fellows, and make her appear partial to her students.

Yet when the monk had finished speaking, and people (mainly teachers) were queuing to receive his blessing, my mother crossed the assembly hall to take me by the hand. She led me over to meet the guest.

"So this is the young man," the monk said benignly. "You're taking good care of your mother now, aren't you?"

He made the sign of the cross on my head, and gave me a coloured card. It showed the Saviour on one side and had a text about the Christian soldier on the other.

I set off for my next class. My mother went on talking to the monk.

Evening after evening consisted of supper, followed by my mother's lamplit reading, my homework and hobbies. But increasingly, she would look up from the green baize and stare distantly into the shadows. What forms was she seeing there?

Recalled to the actual emptiness where she was gazing, she half-sighed, half-yawned, returning to her book. Later she was gazing up again – and soon again. Finally, she talked of bed.

That was the moment when, on one of those nights (of which my adolescent years seemed, in retrospect, recording these Saharan insects, to have been entirely composed), the doorbell rang. It was the monk.

The man was shown into the living room. There he talked to her, beside him on the sofa. It was inaudible to me, sent off to sleep. She was presumably receiving spiritual counsel such as he must often be called upon to offer in his monastery. I wondered how the monk had been able to leave the community at such a late hour. He should have been cloistered for the night, so far – so safely – withdrawn from the rest of the world that it might never occur to it that he still even existed. The thought continued in my mind barely longer than I was aware of hearing those confidential voices. I was soon asleep.

My mother received another late call from her priestly visitor, and another. Then she broke away from the table early, and she herself went out for the evening. I waited up a little longer over my butterflies and moths. I yawned for half an hour, then went to bed in the empty apartment.

When I woke up in the morning, I found her in the kitchen as usual, making coffee in her nightdress. She said she had something to tell me: she had joined a lay religious order. They were like nuns, except that instead of residing in a convent, they lived in the ordinary world. Sometimes they needed to join real nuns; that was what she would be doing for a week the following month. She had arranged for me to stay with another teacher who had a son of about my age.

Somehow, the days passed. I had no more of a distinct sense of them than I did of the passing hours in the Saharan monastery, a world away from my married life in Rome. Dragging for some periods, intense for others, they were now mainly lost in an abyss of the unremembered, because they had not originally been lived knowingly. Bovine, almost, I had once looked up unawares from whatever I was doing and saw my mother, back, walking into the room. She hugged me, setting down a souvenir she had brought home.

She said little about her time away; she had not needed to. The effects of her retreat were plain enough. She had entered a fuller, richer, silence. For long periods, she would just sit half-smiling, self-absorbed. Maybe she was praying with her eyes open. That was how I would always remember her, even once her eyes had finally shut and she'd arrived at that perpetual silence. I took her hand then, heavy in the coffin. It was bloodless: marble.

The funeral was attended by a few other teachers and my aunt, her older sister, a spinster, flying in from Stuttgart. The monk officiated. He came over to me at the reception of sandwiches and coffee offered by the headmaster.

"You can be proud of her. She was very courageous, battling on alone like that after leaving Egypt. She was one of several Germans who had to make new lives at the time of the Suez Crisis. It was cruel for people such as your mother, who'd already suffered the chaos after the war, to have to go through something so similar after Suez."

Then a teacher called Brigitte said: "It must have been hard for someone suddenly alone like that, with a young son. The poor woman was obviously lovelorn. Naturally, she took an interest in other men."

I did not answer, coldly remembering that my mother had always tried to avoid Brigitte, especially since the afternoon when my mother and I had been travelling home together on the bus. Brigitte had come to sit in the seat in front. She turned back to us, teasing her colleague about an advertisement she claimed she had seen her writing in the staff room for the "Friendships" column of the local newspaper, allegedly a letter to "that special man destined to form part of a family, no matter what".

Looking back on Brigitte's gaucheness years later, I told Anja I had not seen a shred of evidence for my mother's supposed interest in men during the evenings when she had left me to my hobbies to join her religious order.

"Well, the 'Friendships' column served *us* well enough." Anja said it smiling at me, her quiet husband who had who had found her through their mediation. She had replied to my advertisement for "a mature German-speaking woman with serious interests". At once attractively blonde, maternal and active, she certainly had had the required qualities. There was her pottery, her photography, her illustrating and writing. She received commissions from the international publishing company I was to join through her introduction.

It was there that I met the monk again.

The man was shown into my shared office one day to discuss the cover for his forthcoming spiritual autobiography. Naturally, we talked of my mother – what little there was to say. He made a point of coming up to me at the launch party for what proved to be his best-selling book, given its particular point of view on Italy's political as well as religious issues at that time: its student unrest, guerrilla movements and resurgent communism.

He spoke to me thereafter with great warmth at the authors' receptions to which he was now always invited, and became a great favourite with Anja as well. He was an especially valued part of our very full life. Inevitably, perhaps, it was to him that I turned upon her death. Or, more accurately, I found myself quite ready to submit to such support as my effective spiritual advisor offered.

It had been he who, hearing of my bereavement, had approached *me*, generously as he had apparently been preoccupied with the many attacks on the state and its foundations in Italy. Old wounds, dating from the war, were being needlessly opened, he said. The role of the Church was coming under scrutiny; he had been designated one of its apologists. He went on explaining all this, walking with me among potted plants in the courtyard of his monastery on Rome's Via Sicilia.

It was a hard task, given the vengeful spirit – often of a witch hunt – by people with little or no political wisdom. They did not appreciate that actions had to be considered in terms of their original context: rarely perfect, always complex.

The Holy Father's sacred duty had been to protect the Church above all else. If Pius had protested against what the SS were doing in Rome, he would have provoked a collision with Hitler. He did what was more difficult, and apparently beyond the capacity of his critics: he remained mute. It meant that the Germans could hold the Holy City until such time as the Allies were able to enter it, still fully intact. This prevented a Communist so-called "liberation" and occupation of Italy.

On we walked, round the marble fountain. With what the monk had doubtless intended as a preamble now over, he turned to the matter at hand: my immediate life. Outwardly, it was a success, given the offer recently made me by my wife's publishers to produce a book of my own. The firm was international, and had suggested that I take over Anja's project: a German edition of lavish entomological photographs. It would be a collectors' item.

I might have found this an exciting prospect until recently. But not now, not anymore, with Anja gone.

We turned to my breakdown. What could be done to bring me back to myself? He suggested doing the book after all. Never mind that, unlike Anja, I was not a photographer. I had the professional background to produce a splendid volume as a draughtsman. And why not illustrate desert insects?

Months afterward, researching by his order's Saharan monastery, I could again hear Father Carlo saying goodbye to me several days later, just as I summoned up from the sand my last day in Alexandria with Anja and my life with my mother. There in his shadowy office beside Santa Maria dell'Anima, Father Carlo asked me to make sure to pass on a letter to an old friend, a hermit, who might prove to be an intimate of mine too: Father Erich.

11

It was dawn again. The sky was an increasingly luminous grey as I sleep-ily gathered up my equipment from the granite ledge I'd been using as a base for my night's work out in the desert. About to head back, I once more sensed a disturbance of the light. But there was actual movement on the horizon this time, surely. It brought me up short, and I looked intently – though it was no use. Turning, unsure what to make of it, I blinked as if simply disposing of an inner image.

It reappeared just as I was approaching the adobe walls. I sought nervously to free myself of it, entering the wide open, empty monastery. It was still in my mind as I got up from several hours of morning dozing. Gingerly opening my cell door into fiery sunlight, I paced out, my feet noiseless on the sandy paths. Nothing disturbed the stillness of the shrubbery, the trees, as I made my way to the main gate.

I halted beyond the walls on the sandstone ledge, in this greater silence, squinting into the distance.

There it was. A quivering form elongated, reduced, then grew again. It continued dissolving and recomposing. Vaporous in this repeated blighting of my vision, it kept nearly though never quite solidifying. I shaded my eyes with a hand, advancing, drawn on, even in such heat.

I walked and walked. The form never seemed to grow any closer. It might have been a mirage, a figment of my imagination or, worse, evi-dence of what I barely dared admit I feared: that I was losing my grip on reality. Though a speck in my eye, it was as real as grit that had not worked itself free. Still, for periods while pacing mechanically ahead, I did lose sight of my reason for doing so, oblivious even to the danger I might be putting myself in.

Yet these were times that occasionally appeared to give me a kind of clarity. I would come to myself out of my stupor of heat and the effort of moving. Despite dazzling light, I'd appear to see the vastness ahead as if with enhanced vision. It was criss-crossed right up to the burning horizon with furrows that often ran between the granite blocks. How voluminous the traffic of those great reptiles, the oil trucks and geologists' jeeps! What cluttered emptiness their intrusively alien passage left, but for the form still moving, quivering, before me!

I had progressed far beyond the boulder that was my nightly base, though fatigue was dulling my anxiety. Now I could make out the figure more clearly – and a jeep parked nearby. Whoever it was kept moving. But the individual was pacing, bending, measuring, it seemed, all in a defined area.

I saw that the person wore a white shirt and blue trousers, and the blue of a scarf was tied protectively over the shoulder-length black hair of the woman I now recognised her to be from this other granite block against which I was resting. T-shirt and jeans repeatedly separated as she leaned down. I kept noticing her taut, tanned waist as I continued watching at this distance from my fraction of shade. She glanced up from the sand a moment and pushed her sunglasses onto her forehead to dab her eyes and cheeks with a handkerchief. It caught my breath. I'd seen her face. I had an unreasoning sense of already knowing her.

I made no attempt to close the sandy gulf between us as she loaded equipment onto the back of the jeep. She carried a box of tools. Suddenly she got into the front and roared off, leaving me by my granite block. Eventually, all I could see was the plain with its criss-crossing furrows of vehicles, of people long gone. Finally, I set off across that abandoned emptiness myself, trudging across its red sand.

*

Somehow I must have fallen asleep. Sun was pouring through the window. I got up, naked, and looked out: there was only desert. I sat on the bed, scanning the table covered with equipment and papers. I told myself I must bring myself back to them and what they seemed to show, after the ritual of eating breakfast, bathing and dressing.

I passed the window again, to put on something, at least, when my eye was caught by a quivering. It was the intervening hot air that made it – her – flicker, far off, in that aridity.

I would leave breakfast and washing till later. I went out in sandals, just attaching my pouch to a belt around what I was wearing. Leaving the monastery and walking on, I blinked repeatedly to draw the sweat away from my eyelids.

There she was at last, again in a T-shirt, jeans and headscarf. I stood nearby, watching her load a wooden tray of rocks onto the jeep.

"Oh! You scared the life out of me!" She said it in English, pushing her sunglasses onto her forehead. "How long have you been standing there?"

I wasn't wearing a watch. I had not told the time during the days (or perhaps it was weeks) I'd been here. I squinted in the rays of the only chronometer nearby, not answering, but now realising how long it had been since I had last spoken. I had lapsed imperceptibly into a self-enclosed silence where even what was without, in this Saharan solitude, seemed to float up from within – like an underwater goddess, perhaps. That is, until this woman's voice cut in bluntly from her own remote reality.

She was scrutinising me.

"You're a monk, aren't you?"

It was surprising that with her swarthy, seemingly Mediterranean features, she had this American accent.

"Not exactly," I said, noticing that hooded, faceless shadow on the sand. But no monk, I doubted if I was much else either. "I've just started wearing this for convenience."

"It looks like a burnoose – which is what I thought it was, at first. Hardly the best thing for someone to find herself facing in this, of all, areas. Where are you staying? It isn't over at that place where they, er –"

"Yes."

"What was it like? I suppose you knew the monks well."

"I arrived afterwards," I said, and blinked absently. "I'm the only one there now."

"I can't imagine how that must be," she replied, shuddering in the heat.

There was an instant of silence. Then I said: "I'm doing an entomological project." I announced this while sinking a thumb behind the pouch belted across my waist. It supposedly explained my presence before her, although I never came out to work in the day.

"Insects."

"I'm illustrating them."

"Who for?"

"A publisher. I've a commission for a book."

"Interesting."

"Not really. There's something the same about all the varieties. Not sure what."

"I'm a geologist, myself. I'm on contract to an oil company. There's a huge swathe of petroleum across the northern Sahara: the residue of prehistoric forest. Our team's here for six months. But the leader sometimes lets me steal away from our base to do what I'm really interested in. He's indulgent …"

I watched her grow vague, tracking the toe of her sneaker through the sand. She was from the world of those monstrous lorries.

"This sand's 350 million years old," she said. "But only 130 million years ago, during the forested period, the entire region was inhabited by crocodiles, fish, the great reptiles. Some dinosaurs would fall into rivers that eventually dried up. It covered them with dust. Then they'd turn into fossils. So it's a matter of tracking down buried riverbeds. You can still find dinosaur remains in the ditches around here."

"In the ditches. Really …? And aren't you nervous about being out in this area on your own?"

"I'm told I should be. Though I've been coming here for a while. I s'pose I'm too familiar with the place for the danger to feel real to me – except just now!" She grinned. "Anyhow, I'm from here. My family, that is."

"French?"

"Culturally. We're Jewish. There was a large community here before Independence, as in most Middle Eastern countries. We were from the capital. A whole section of it was Jewish, but we came from the European part. I've revisited our apartment several times, even though we left it before I was in my teens. Other people are living there now.

"Of course, in every town you can find a quarter where there are still a few, very old Oriental Jews. Not so long ago they were barely distinguishable from Arabs, like those Delacroix painted in Morocco. Even here, in the desert, there were Jewish villages, including one not too far from the monastery. Have you been there?"

I shook my head.

"The leader of our team heard about it last season. His family's originally from these parts, like mine. And he was brought up in New York, too. Brooklyn."

I flushed, suddenly short of breath.

"He thought of visiting it this year, whatever's left of it. Me too. And he was intending to see your community, but ..."

The desert seemed all at once very present. It was fiery, hostile.

"And where are you from?"

"I'm German."

"Oh!"

"But I've lived mainly in Ita –"

"Hey! Watch out! You look about ready to faint. You shouldn't be out in this heat without sunglasses, especially not in that heavy old thing. Be careful of sunstroke. I've got water. Let me get you some."

Regaining my balance, I followed her over to the jeep. She gave me a tin cup. My hand trembled as I held it out for her to fill. I gulped; she drank straight from the plastic bottle, gazing out.

"I'm amazed you can stay out in this heat," I said, noticing the scarf slipping from her head.

"I'll soon be packing it in for today. But I want to finish this bit of mapping," she said, screwing up her eyes to take in the rocky section where she had been working. Lowering her sunglasses, she went on: "I'll get back to it now."

I stood there, shaky from the sun.

"So you'll be back tomorrow?"

"Or later. Like I said, when I can steal away from base – and Boss. 'Cos I'm hard on the trail of them thar dinosaurs, ain't I?"

She might never have assumed a Western accent, nor turned to the area to which she wanted to get back to work. I was simply continuing to stand there, in that emptiness.

"What's your interest in them?"

She frowned quizzically, as if to say it was self-evident; so much so that the only thing it was necessary to ask was when she could get back to the job.

"They're dead, buried and were brutal," I said.

"When they weren't herbivores."

"Well, what's the attraction?"

"I rarely ask myself. I'm just carried along by my enthusiasm. It doesn't seem to require justification. I guess the quest creates its own momentum. The more you search, the more you want to find. Then again, I've always been interested in dinosaurs. I spent my summers excavating for them in Montana, as a graduate student, horrific as they all seem, in a way. They're in my blood – as they are in everyone's, aren't they? They're our relatives, regardless of whether or not we want to forget them or disown them. Besides, there's always an eerie fascination in penetrating an alien world, especially one that's so cold-blooded, at least according to some theories. Perhaps I just want to stare a pitiless monster in the face, see if I'm up to it.

"Actually, their whole era was destroyed in a terrible cataclysm. But we still can't ignore it even if we want to. Its remains are all here, if we just scratch the surface. In fact, they often stick up through the surface, in those ditches I told you about. It reminds us that nature, including human nature, is red in tooth and claw. Maybe that's why I study them."

She seemed to be turning it over in her mind.

"Who knows? … And what about you? Why do you study insects? What do they mean to you?"

"Not much. I just identify and draw them for a publisher. Although I'm trained as an entomologist and have experience as a scientific illustrator, I'm merely a populariser, like some nineteenth-century clerical naturalist."

"But aren't you curious about their world? Don't they seem like monsters in miniature? Instruments of war, with their armouring?"

"You mean the waterproof cuticle they have to retain moisture? Well, I've never thought about it like that. As far as I can see, they're mostly just trying to survive by reducing their activity during the heat of the day and living off the morning dew. It's a minimal existence under the least exacting conditions. All I'm trying to do is fulfil my commission and get myself from day to day.

"I'm definitely not pursuing an obsession," I said, looking at the young woman. "I've no vision, no exalted idea of what I'm studying. It's arbitrary. It might as well be the clouds."

"But everything has structure, deep structure, if one probes the least bit. That's where its interest lies."

"Well, as I say, I'm not motivated by interest. I'm just working to keep afloat personally."

"You make it sound like a problem." I did not speak. I went on looking. She was looking too. "Is it?"

The silence continued.

"My wife died."

"Oh!"

Suddenly I was aching for her again. I was all adrift here.

"Recently?"

The question sounded as though from a distance.

"Fairly."

"So I suppose you're thinking of becoming …" Her eyes combed me. "It's not just the habit. There's something silent, stealthy about … I mean, you seem to keep yourself to yourself."

"Well, no. The idea's simply that the monastery's an undisturbed base to work."

"Some idea! I wonder whose."

I half-considered answering. Then I said: "It's quiet now."

"I'll bet."

"If you'd like to …"

"Sometime, maybe. If ever I finish all my work out here. But you'd better be getting back there yourself. You look drained. Take a leaf from your insects' book and lie low during the day. S'long."

She replaced her sunglasses and turned back to her mapping. There was a twitching in my eye. I, too, turned, sent on my way.

*

I must return to work. My Saharan project provided the only reliable pattern for survival out here. The woman came from quite another human dimension, chancing upon me in my retreat. She had intruded upon this, my mutely musing, half-self, in its place of ultimate refuge. She – and the so-called "real world" she tracked in with her – would totally disrupt the protective quasi-life in which I sought both to exist and emerge as whoever I might ultimately prove to be, if I did not deny her access.

Work was my only hope. Yet I had first to rid my mind of whatever distracted me from the contemplative calm necessary to embrace the alternative: insects. I finally set out with my equipment late that afternoon. Resuming a routine, throwing myself into my project, I concentrated on what had hardly interested me from the outset, then seemed almost repellent. I looked to habit to provide me with momentum.

Walking into the sunset, I varied my route for some reason. As if purposely, though actually only following my nose, I found myself – in fading light – in an area of low, parched bushes leading into a gorge. Rocks blocked the entrance. I climbed over them. My footsteps were soon leading me through the increasingly soft, wet sand of a twisting ditch.

What did I hope to find there? Can it have been insects more varied, more reliably perfect, than the usual trove of ants and beetles? I might have asked myself had I not been filled with sudden dread by gleams in the darkness. There were voices, laughter.

Weren't these assassins, the ones who'd slashed the throats of monks in habits identical to what I myself was wearing?

The murderers had not been caught. They might never be, according to the police officer. The killings would most probably remain unexplained, poisoning the atmosphere further like corpses themselves. Reality, normality, existed more and more rarely in the unnaturally still lapses between terrible acts.

I continued holding back from the group of six or eight black men. They were seated round a fire of crackling twigs where the ground levelled out. Their eyes, their teeth continued glinting. One of them saw me. I retreated. Yet cigarettes, tea were pressed on me – an apparent monk from the monastery in that habit. Barely able to hold the scalding glass by its base and rim, I heard, in scarcely comprehensible French, that these were workmen all from the same village hereabouts – probably one of those small communities of ex-slaves of the Tuareg.

They said they'd been digging an underground canal in the gorge. The old one had been destroyed in a sandstorm. It would collect the water saturating this soft sand, then train it over to a nearby field of grain. They offered me part of their evening meal. A few grains of couscous were served with a species of big firefly. Supposedly the insect contained scores of medicinal properties.

It should have interested me, but I simply felt I was there under false pretences. Wasn't I receiving generosity actually earned by the brethren among the local people? And was it really for more insects that I was out clambering in this ditch, making me recall for a sharp instant the dried-up riverbed yielding fossils to the woman I insisted to myself I couldn't be going out of my way to meet?

They pressed more tea on me. I sipped it in silence. Soon I left them to go about my work.

I wandered on, finally bending to the ground beneath the stars. It could not have been for more than an hour: probably less. But it was enough for me to tell myself that I had returned to my routine.

I awoke to the dawn and went to the window. My eyes scanned the desert in a wide arc. Not a soul was out at this hour; of course not. I returned to bed.

Later, the sun roused me. I wrapped a towel round myself to collect the tray left outside my door, as every day. I would simply eat breakfast, then go straight to the washroom.

I'd barely taken a bite of bread when I found I'd moved, crust in hand, to look out the window – fruitlessly. Yet it was still earlier than when I'd sighted her yesterday. Of course, it wasn't certain she'd be returning. I wasn't sure any longer what she'd said about it, or what she had meant. The safest course was to carry on as if she were gone for good. Loss was something to which I'd become accustomed.

12

Work had always been the sole salvation for which I'd looked to the monastery. Could I complain, then, if that's how it remained? So I considered, returning to the insects.

Studying them took me through much of a long day. Then, getting up from my chair where I'd been increasingly frowning over the microscope, I glanced with studied casualness out the window. I went on looking into late-afternoon light. As I stared, eyes sore, I viewed a blank screen like that flickering after the video on my bus ride from the capital, and the open-air cinema before and after a film.

The day's heat was fading fast. It concentrated in a blood-red capillary dividing two endless, differently hued spaces – as the horizon itself was to do again, hours later, when night finally yielded to dawn. Then the burning fusion of land and sky could begin once more, recreating, by midday, that continuous screen. It was one on which my unfocused eyes, on succeeding days, began to read what was increasingly me myself.

The parched emptiness I was seeing became more and more my own. It stretched unremittingly. It offered nothing, silenced everything. It just held, detached. I glanced out at that wilderness whilst drawing more earthenware pots like the one on my breakfast tray. Instead of tracing outlines, I rendered form by shading and patterning. It brought Anja back to me.

It was like awakening to find a limb amputated. She couldn't be felt anymore, not physically. But the sensation of her kept returning from beneath the surface, through the guise of others, as in a dream. For losing Anja wasn't just a fact. It was a continuing event, an open-ended reality.

Nor could I hurry or sidestep the pain of lacking her, I'd discover. While the American woman or the Alexandrian actress in the video might each be attractive, how could either appeal to me instead? It was

Anja, my wife of so many years, who was still in my mind. No, in simply serving to represent my wife to me, the others obviously couldn't communicate anything specific of themselves, could they?

Absence deadened me to normal sensation. For a time it was as if I were under anaesthetic, blocking what could neither be nor be borne. My sole feeling was feeling nothing.

What was left but my project? I must rededicate myself to work. Yet straightforward as this seemed, the question arose: was it really just work – something I was starting to find strange about the insects – that held me? If not, what *did* see me through? The thought haunted me, especially when it was finally undeniable that Anja was gone; that our life together was over. I deliberately abandoned memories of her, all foiled attempts to recall her, thereby also losing the distraction enabling me to continue there.

So, not knowing what was afoot, I thought of my desert existence as merely that: survival through moods, endurances, lacks, all persisting, spreading, endless, and there was no taking stock of all that time I drifted through, like a sleepwalker. The desert itself kept no record. It could not have done so on terrain swept hither and thither by capricious weather systems driving around clouds as seemingly formless and unconnected as my thoughts.

I sketched both sand and sky. The drawings were brief, intermittent, undated. Many were unfinished. Should I keep a diary instead, just as I'm writing this now? It's to clear my mind, set my memories in order, establish the facts – though I'm aware of an urge to present what I'm somehow hoping will not only be read by the onlooking part of me, but also by an outsider.

Not that this is simply a case of seeking confirmation. For I know what it is to be marooned in a single mind – my own – which for another reader is the autobiographical writer's consciousness. I suspect I'm really hoping that someone else, in penetrating the sealed submarine of my self-enclosed recollections at these Saharan depths, will open them up to the fresher air circulating in the place from which he or she enters.

But mightn't the other also find something unexpected at work in what seems an oppressively static atmosphere? It's constantly advancing, like the sand dunes whose apparently motionless flanks are actually moving imperceptibly forward the whole time; or, indeed, the seemingly inert Sahara itself, which, having emerged from tropical forest and watery everglades, is unendingly engaged in transforming itself.

Be that as it may, I kept no diary. What I had to say about myself today was the same as I would have said yesterday or what I shall say tomorrow. Besides, it implied a reader – the cruel illusion of another presence. I gave the idea the cold shoulder, and begrudgingly conceded it was I alone who would be the reader.

I might scrutinise myself as I, an entomologist, did the objects of my study. In which case there could be no question of empathy – for which reason, apart from any other, the insects were wise to have self-protective shells. It made them hard, as resistant as the desert itself.

I would deny myself writing; let the ink dry in my pen, allow my feelings to parch. I would no more need to know I was being observed than those crawling, flying objects of my study, than the needle-sharp sand, the granite outcrops, the far-off peaks towering over the world's edge. I, too, could be an ant scuttling through centimetres of desert.

I *was* the deep Sahara.

*

One morning, I woke hugging the pillow. For several seconds I carried on the hyperreality of the dream, holding Anja from behind. Her hair was fragrant. I felt the warmth of her breasts, her belly; the softness of her buttocks and thighs. Then I was in bed all alone, emptiness in my arms. It fairly winded me. My coetaneous protection had been peeling off in the night unnoticed, under the emotional anaesthetic deadening my pain at her absence. It exposed raw tenderness.

Anja, my missing limb, was now a furious burning where the ligaments had been ripped through. She, and all the feelings I'd had for her, kept coming back to me throughout the morning. They ambushed me again and again in the blistering heat and painful white light.

This wasn't a case of simply remembering, of nostalgic longing. I was actually reliving our life together, complete with its atmosphere. It was mental bilocation such as desert visionaries – or madmen – undergo in their mystical experiences.

I was kissing her for the first time, in her room. I had an instantaneous impression that I was holding my mother. The phone rang. Anja ignored it. She continued embracing me, allowing "nothing to come between just the two of us".

She had made me a home every bit as much as had my mother, coming to mind out there in the desert sun. It was a regular life she, the middle-aged schoolteacher, had organised for herself and her teenage son. Almost no visitors were allowed to disrupt our daily schedule. Evenings were all but sacrosanct, spent in the dimness of our small Rome apartment, sitting round the green baize tablecloth and doing homework and marking.

A lump rose in my throat seeing my mother sitting there, her hair greyer, spectacles denser, eventually alone. At least Anja provided me with a settled existence so that, if she went abroad without me for her book on deserts, it still seemed as if we were the sole beings beneath an invisible dome, breathing an atmosphere all our own.

Not that the air didn't run thin. As the days approached for her return, I felt increasingly at a loss. Unable to cook, having eaten the food she'd left for me in the fridge, I was exiled to restaurants. I traipsed into churches, lighting candles for her as much as for my mother, to the God in whom I could not believe. I could hardly wait for her to return and resume our life, the feeling of which I once more keenly tasted this late morning in the monastery.

Now, blinded, staring at empty desert, I knew no one was ever coming back.

Much of the day passed. Then I realised something strange: I was holding my arm. And I understood I was reliving Anja hugging me at this evening hour, after our first kiss. She had drawn me onto her bed. I had never made love before. Recalling it made me think of all the lovemaking that had followed.

There were excursions to the beaches near Ostia. Anja had packed the food, brought the suntan oil and towels. We swam to a tethered raft bobbing far out to sea. She reached it first. Lying there, she helped me up onto the wooden slats. We lazed far from sight, kissing, naked, merging as the sky did with the sea.

On and on we floated, static, hidden on our backs. I glanced aside at the soft dome beside me. Its tight nipple obscured the view. Sand spread beyond our raft, out on the shore; sand she washed off me in the shower with hands that I, remembering our lovemaking from my moonlit bed in a Saharan cell, knew I'd never touch again.

I found I'd flexed my fingers – to grasp hers. It was no good. I must get up. I kicked aside the worn monastery towel I'd used to cover my legs against the infuriating flies, and went out. It was the only alternative to these tormenting relivings. Leaving through the front gate, I sought also to abandon the draining struggle to hold onto that vanished moment merged on a raft. Almost as an effort of will, I let it go – the instant, the raft. Untethered, they could float right out of my mind, headed into oblivion.

*

I was left with only the insects. Studying them was a real effort. Which of us recoiled more, the studier or the studied?

With Anja gone, Anja who'd always taken an interest in my work, I questioned whether or not I had the self-confidence to see my book through alone. Failing the following day to corral a scuttling spider – probably misshapen – I swept a hand over my glistening forehead, wondering what on Earth kept me pursuing a project with what I was increasingly finding were imperfect insects.

Might I, at least, find my way to the village? It was as much a mirage as Rome, after all this time here. They were all the equivalents of oases to the fevered mind of one trapped, parched, in the desert.

Sitting by one of the monastery's glassless windows, seeing a fly wing out into the desert it was fated never to outstrip, I felt instinctively restrained by a force as invisible but indisputable as that which had confined me to the closed, intense lives I had lived with my mother, then with my wife. So what, as the police officer asked, held me there, in a place where I was burying my feelings for my wife among all the emptiness I'd written off?

One evening, working just outside the adobe walls, my life with Anja came back to mind. It was as if ours had been a shared being at the time. I'd been unimaginable to myself apart from her. Then, raising myself from crouching for insects in the sand, I remembered another student at my university. How strange! I hadn't thought of him for years.

He'd been returning from a lecture when he discovered a letter addressed to him in his college post-box. Opening it, he found it was from a woman writing of their travels together, their love-child and her longing to see him again – not least for their baby's sake. He read the letter again and again, frowning more and more. He remembered nothing of this. He didn't know her. He'd never been part of the brief, passionate life she said they'd shared. But he couldn't detach himself from it, either. It all trembled on the brink of something he recognised, lay claim to in a dreamlike way, regardless of the mere coincidence of bearing what was also apparently someone else's name.

He couldn't resist replying. He said he wasn't her ex-lover, but that he'd opened the letter, an understandable mistake. She answered. They met. They made love.

So he, the one now bearing the name of the man she'd written to, assumed his role in her life. It became *their* life. They lived on happily, as far as I knew.

But, so I asked myself, stretching to my full height before the glittering heavens outside those walls, had it ever occurred to my fellow student that it was actually chance, *her* requirements, *her* past that created *his* seemingly inevitable existence? His only conceivable reality was a pure accident. Had he once, even fleetingly, realised that he might have it within him to lead quite another, fully authentic, life without her?

13

If something was preventing me from going into the outer world, that world came to Muhammad, as it were. It arrived in a form that may well have helped jog my memory of that letter a fellow student received: the mail sack left outside my door one morning with my breakfast tray.

Not that I did more than stare at it. It stayed unopened on the floor of my cell, a mute, shapeless presence neither welcomed nor sent packing. Then again, I didn't exactly ignore it either, given a sudden surge of interest welling up in me one afternoon when I simply couldn't work. Of course, I'd had access all along to the letters now tumbling out of the burlap. Yet with the formless, faceless thing standing before me, I'd had second thoughts about reading other people's mail – unnecessarily, with them all dead. And there'd been no need to use the knife left from my lunch tray to slice through the top of an envelope. It had already been opened for examination by the censor – or by the police, given the recipients' fate.

The post was of no further use to the authorities, or even to the poor locals who usually cannibalised what was discarded. If they could read, it would only be in Arabic, and they might be illiterate. So the bag had ended up at its destination – the monastery – for the Order to deal with. It sat at my door as if to say, "let the dead bury their dead".

My hand trembled, sifting through the mail, with a trepidation I realised I'd been feeling since the postbag arrived. I'd been battling the irrational expectation that I'd find a letter addressed to me from somebody, somewhere, too unimaginably unreachable to recall me, let alone write. How dare I even entertain such an unthinkable thought! Better to bury the very notion, leaving all that mail interred in the postbag.

My chest knotted. I found myself holding an envelope addressed to me.

*

What that dumb sack released was a typed envelope from Saint Xavier University, with several stamps showing the Statue of Liberty. I took out the letter, holding it at a distance, almost as if it could ignite something explosive. It turned out only to be from Father Josef, the Czech Jesuit:

My dear friend,

Ever since I left you in the monastery, I've been wondering how you are. You're clearly before me as I write: unshaven, exhausted from your long bus ride; weighed down by the cares that had brought you this far; so overwhelmed by the atrocities that you were all but tongue-tied.

Your face said it all. It left me to do so much of the talking that I couldn't mistake your impatient longing for silence and solitude. What a surprise it was to find you suddenly overcoming it and announcing you were staying there after all, thousands of miles away! I want you to know how much I admire your decision. God will grant you His grace in your harsh seclusion, advancing your entomological study. Perhaps you have even begun to feel it as the weeks have started turning to months – assuming you are still there, well, as I pray, and continuing to focus on your reason for going and remaining.

Maybe, too, you are finding changes taking place in you; strengthening you in unsuspected ways, real regardless of how hard they may be to describe or explain.

It's amazing how time has flown since I met you, only to return to the States. At least it goes at breakneck speed here, with my absurdly busy university life: teaching, advising students, sitting on committees, attending conferences, trying to finish my book – all to the hum of television and debate about public issues in prefabricated terms everyone ends up adopting, regardless of which side of the question they come out. It makes me long for a quieter place to pray; the one you occupy, with its packed sand floor and calm sense of an eternal standstill. You, in your cell, the chapel, the desert, the night, can have no sense of advancing time, but only of continuous recurrence, as with one of those Buddhist prayer wheels I saw on my trip to Bhutan.

You're unaware, I'm sure, of what's happening at such speed in this brash, banal continent I've returned to. The nearest you'll come to it, I suppose, is a glimpse of one of those American oil company trucks rushing away at a distance from you. I've repeatedly looked for references in the newspapers to your part of the world over the last few months. But the press, let alone the television, has never so much as mentioned the brethren.

I, for one, have had enough of not knowing – from the Germans who say they never knew anything of their horrors in the war, then from my own country, Czechoslovakia, which they invaded and where all questioning was ruthlessly suppressed by the Communists till we had our Velvet Revolution. But should one – can anyone – bury one's head in the sand? Regardless of what one takes as one's personal situation, one would be deluded to suppose matters can ever rest there. Sooner or later, doesn't the world always come back at us?

I ask myself here in an America entirely focused on its own violence: high school killings, serial murders, racial friction, terrorism nearer to home. You might as well not exist, in a desert that is not a reality for people here. The monastery, its inhabitants, are without meaning. Be that as it may, rest assured that you are known, whether it feels like it or not. Not a sparrow falls but that our Father in Heaven feels it. And you are remembered by your friend, who sends you his best wishes.

Josef.

P.S. Don't hesitate to write when you feel like it. I'll be sure to reply, although I obviously can't answer for how long it'll take each of us to receive the other's letters. The Sahara is almost outside time!

I put the letter down. I would never answer it. Josef was avowing his best wishes to one he'd merely left behind, not one he knew – really knew. I'd simply been commandeered to the priest's worldwide parish. I resented what was effectively a business letter, written from a sense of professional obligation, with its tired religious jargon. What it praised as eternal, like the turning prayer wheel, was not timeless but endlessly the same. As far as I was concerned, everything here had been rudderless, drifting on an infinite sea of sand.

Nor did I appreciate being reminded of trucks and the American oil company. It made me think of that other distraction from a routine set up with such difficulty, and re-established with all the extra effort of forgetting about her.

Again, I found the young woman bending in my mind. The T-shirt split from her jeans to reveal a lean, tanned waist. Now I heard an inner echo of her self-confident conversation: "… Everything has structure, deep structure, if one probes the least bit …"

I feared lingering over thoughts of her this second time. Nothing more could possibly be made of the feelings that had held in me as she'd spoken, or that had come back to mind, than of clouds hovering silently, unnoticed, over the face of the desert. Yet if I'd known then what I've come to find now, after all that's happened, I could have replied with confidence that nothing's formless: not even the massed sand, the rocky outcrops, mountain ranges and seemingly random dusting of stars.

Apparently amorphous, the clouds themselves were moving, growing, transforming. For regardless of how it felt, no matter how long the period of apparent inactivity, things were no more at a standstill than in that timeless dreamlessness of the larva, the pupa. Everything finally reveals its organisation, its direction, to eyes that can see. Change always breaks through.

Though even supposing I'd known it, I'd have wondered at the time if I would share the thought. For with whom could I do so? She hadn't said when, or if, she might return. It was just as well. I had work to do, which had been interrupted by Father Josef's letter provoking this inconvenient yearning in me.

*

I was determined to make headway with my project, concentrating on that alone. I peered fixedly down the microscope, categorising insects. Yet my eyes grew tired before I could see an explanation for the anomalies increasingly staring up at me.

I considered going out to collect insects that evening, but I had a blister on my big toe where the sharp sand had ground between the flesh and leather sandal strap. I sat in the dark cell, staring blankly out at the heavens with all thought of the project and whatever it might reveal clouded.

I became aware of the postal sack behind me. It was like the growing sense of somebody at one's back. I leaned round, pulled the bag towards me and took out several letters. What harm could it do to read them? I thought, putting on the light. The recipients were all dead.

Within minutes, the lamp attracted more insects than I'd have found if I'd gone out on my nightly search. They raced round the bulb as I took in fragments of others' lives. And lives they'd certainly had. Brother Paolo received a reply to his letter to Monica in Udine.

If only you'd come out more clearly about your feelings when we were having those painfully long conversations before you finally took your vows. It's all very well for you to write now that love can exist and grow in impossible conditions – "rigorous", you call them. And yes, I know there are life forms where no one suspected them, such as in the hellish heat and dark near the Earth's core. But I'm a woman with a woman's needs. Can you really expect to continue a relationship with a life that's no longer open to you, especially since it's uncertain if we'll ever even see each other again? What kind of loving could that be?

Father Aiden, whoever he'd been, was in correspondence with his niece in Galway. She wrote:

I know what you mean about letting go. It's just so hard when Jimmy's seeing that woman while I have all the responsibility for the children. If only I could let go of my anger – but it's my marriage that I keep telling myself I should drop, though I know it's not the Church's teaching.

It is dead, isn't it? In which case I should allow myself to smile back at the French master. I teach in the classroom next to his. He's very nice.

Out came more letters, more voices, more complicated situations. But then the thought that everyone addressed was lost oozed heavily into my consciousness. So did each correspondent's likely reaction to why there'd never be a reply.

The hemp sack was a bag of horrors. It might as well have been lethally radioactive, I thought, tipping all the envelopes back into the opening without touching it.

I turned off the light and sat staring into the night. The insects stopped racing around the lamp. But my thoughts went on wheeling.

Abbreviations of pained confidences, slogans almost, passed before me. There was *letting go; love growing in impossible conditions; life the ever-widening river connected to an infinite ocean* (as Padre Jesús's confessor wrote to the monk, lamenting that the monastery door had slammed behind him years ago with no prospect of another door creaking even ajar). What a welter of the irrepressible among the fated! I found myself summoned without apparent warning by the memory of that letter to my fellow student at university. Then I wondered if I had it in me to lead another, fully authentic life.

I fell asleep in my chair.

*

I must have gone to bed. But I couldn't remember, waking up there early next day. Nor could I recall ever having slept so deeply before. I felt profoundly rested. The morning air seemed crisper, more refreshing, than usual. The light gave a special clarity, even beauty, to the buildings, as I wandered among them after breakfast.

The strengthening sun brought out the pink of the adobe. It looked as soft as a membrane, with an aperture into the body of the chapel, as I walked out of the monastery to gaze at the greater redness of those distant peaks. They took on a fleshly appearance, alive almost, as I continued before them. Increasingly dominating my line of vision with their blunted pinnacles, they left me giddy. I went back to my cell to lie down.

I stretched out on my bed, naked – whereupon it occurred to me that the monks must have done the same at times. My glimpse into the postbag had revealed that they were not just spiritual beings. They were caught in webs of desire such as that in which I now found I was becoming entangled.

Was it surprising? All this time here since coming from Rome, I had known hunger but not appetite; heat, exhaustion, longing, loss, yet nothing more sensual than a repeated wrenching in my bowels. The least sensation of desire had been smothered, as if by this very cover on which I had stretched out – unexpectedly aroused.

I was returning to the solitary practices I had indulged before marrying. It became a habit for me to lie when the sun was at its height. I stretched out with a succession of images passing through my mind, trying but failing to match an exact thought to my desire. I would drift into a doze and awaken, only to give up again and resume in bed at night – with scarcely more success.

I simply couldn't shoo away the amazingly large flies buzzing virulently down as if in some private agony from the arcs they endlessly traced. Nothing could stop me from scratching away at my dark, desiccated arms, legs, groin. Half torment, half ecstasy, this was a paroxysm of picking into my exposed pink flesh.

Then, lying there, I unwittingly returned to a prior self, indulging like this. Once more, I felt the sharp passion aroused in me, decades earlier, by our Alexandrian neighbour's daughter, the one my father had scolded me for merely looking at on the stairs. It made me long all the more painfully for the girl, as later for the equally inaccessible student in Washington who resembled Anne Frank.

Then I thought of another desert woman – the one imaginatively able to reanimate fossils after eons of extinction. My thoughts returned to her, so much so that I, another denizen of the monastery, found myself inwardly composing a letter of my own. It hardly differed from the brethren's correspondence: it belonged also to the dead. Or, at least, it disavowed the moribund part of me in favour of what was increasingly coming to life through my yearning for her, the actual addressee.

Increasingly, she resembled the others physically, mapping the sand. I found myself wanting to hear more of her reasons for doing so. They arose, surely, from assumptions, a background, a world quite foreign to me. Their very strangeness gave me the thrill of danger as I heard her voice again – American, but with an unplaceable accent. She was telling me that her family lived in the Jewish part of the capital, and that she'd revisited the apartment she left in her teens.

It made me see her with my childhood self on my parents' Alexandrian veranda. In a city of my imagination we were suddenly neighbours, infant friends, boon companions. She was the Spanish-speaking girl on the balcony below. Only we spent all our time together, long summers on the beach, sharing – creating – secrets. She was as close to me as my own skin.

She it was, then, who had grown into the student in Washington and the attractive Egyptian actress in the video, a sequence formed of whatever, whomever it was that kept stirring me.

So I had known her in one form or another for a long, long time. We had conducted a subterranean love affair over many years. It filled every page so far of *My Book of Life*, the volume I had unknowingly been writing all along in invisible ink. Yet I had not fully known it until faced with this woman, whom I now saw in my mind's eye as no less beautiful than those lush, unexpected desert blooms.

I had not taken in the woman's resemblance to the others when we met, or permitted myself to acknowledge an attractiveness striking me so belatedly. It made me want to know more of her, of an inner self that would reveal itself in the tone of voice, the breathing, the silences, the most intimate being finally opened up in the lovemaking I was now mentally – physically – bringing into existence. I'd surged past a barrier such as that which had kept me from yielding to feelings for the Alexandrian woman in a faded video, long, long ago.

I wondered how I had ever crossed the line separating me from such longing. For cross it, I had. It was alarming. Nervous, I wondered again if I might have done better to linger in the memory of my secure domestic relationships than to cast recklessly adrift, taking me far out of myself, well beyond the scope of life as I had always known it.

*

I returned to my cell window at the break of each day, just staring into desert, that seeming mirage out of which all or nothing might materialise. I focused again on the encrusted insects emerging from glass-sharp sand. Observing them, scathed as they invariably appeared, was a routine more dependable than relying on phantoms to appear. Yet I still peered out at dawn. I couldn't have denied myself that, even if I'd wanted to. I glanced up from working at my desk several times, hardly knowing it. I looked off to a fiery vapour: the horizon.

Out at night, with its stellar flares, I realised I was trembling – but not only from the cold. It was anxiety: expecting a sudden arrival in the dark.

It never came. Repeated disappointment left me too shy, or ashamed, to expect it. So I had to face the fact that, having finally opened up to my feeling for her, regardless of how expectantly I waited, she was never returning.

Feverish with longing to hold her, I hardly knew how I could survive her eternal absence. I was filled with uncertainty. It reverberated through me – though was it with a dead echo, like a rock falling to the bottom of a waterless well? Or was this the precipitous scaling of depths so profound that no knowledge existed of what might be found there?

14

Drinking my coffee in the mornings, I still could not help looking out. Nor did I resist it after rising late in the afternoons – such as when I gasped, wondering by what miracle that spectre was now hovering in the distance. Wraithlike, she quivered in the blinding void.

I had to leave my cell, the monastery, at once and hurry over to her. Even here, by the window, I felt the adrenaline rush of departure, the breathlessness of speeding, my heart pumping wildly, sweat breaking out. I sank onto my bed, foreseeing myself arriving where the young American was getting up from her work. She would greet me – if only for a moment, as she'd want to continue in the limited time her team leader allowed her to devote to a personal project.

But I simply had to go, finally – well, not immediately. Mightn't it be better to consider for another hour the increasing strangeness of these insects? I'd arrive just as she was finishing, when she'd be most receptive to her desert visitor. And, delayed, the re-encounter would be more intense.

The worst of the heat had passed. The light had lost its fire. It was time, surely, to put on my habit. I attached my waist pouch to my belt like the accessory to some vestment.

I glanced a final time through the window. She was still there, but no longer a flickering spectre. The form had solidified into a woman, attracting me across desert.

Pink, the walls radiated the day's sun. I felt it on my back, heading past them. I continued on at a steady pace. The rhythm seemed to have speeded up of its own accord. Now I was going so fast that I was out of breath. I panicked, lest I lose my gamble. Instead of catching her just as she was about to finish, I might arrive to find she had already left for her camp.

I approached a granite slab. Deep shadow rimmed one edge, mica glinting where it veined the stone. I slid my hand over the worn grey, rushing ahead. There were several sandy hillocks. Beyond them, I came upon her, bending. I watched the late reaper she seemed, taking in the expected split between T-shirt and jeans, just a mark in this light.

Only now did she sense a presence, looking up in sunglasses, not having previously found the glare fading. She pushed them up above her forehead, lodging them on her hair band. Seeing her face once more caught my breath: she was startlingly lovely. Once more, too, I had an irrational sense of always having known her. It was as if this image of beauty were rising from inner depths where it had long awaited me. Indefinably thrilling, her qualities – my sharp desire – alarmed me. It must be why, observing still more intently the fineness of that face, the unstudied gracefulness of her movements, I felt nervous approaching.

"Hi again! I mean, it *is* you over there, isn't it? You look different. What's been going on inside you – behind that beard you've grown?"

I ran my hand through it. At least it served to hide me flushing.

"So you've come back to these parts," I said, breaking my nervous silence. "I often go to work at dusk. It's when the insects come out."

"Too bad. I'm just about done for the day. I could've offered you a lift back to your place. Well, see you."

"When?" I longed to say.

Fearing what she might answer, I dumbly witnessed her pack up in minutes. She got into her jeep.

"Bye."

Again, she was gone.

*

I would walk back, slowly, deliberately, in the waning heat. I might even rest at my rock, drifting into a long sleep. The light would be weakening as I approached the monastery walls; fading as I entered the gate. The sky would have coloured when I entered the enclosure with its smooth pink adobe.

Soon the foliage would have abandoned its outline to darkness. Standing outside my cell a moment, I would hear only the generator and running water. I would turn to collect the frugal supper left on a tray, going inside to eat and work by a weak lamp. I would continue my methodical classifying for hours.

Not so! I remained before that abandoned emptiness, not remotely ready to head back. Nor did I want to study insects out in the night. I kept trying to conjure up from the red sand the sight, the presence, I'd so often half-believed had only ever emerged from my imagination. For instants, now, my mind did supply her with such arresting vividness that it took hold of me as present reality, not mere memory. But they were fleeting moments. The best I could do for the rest was forcibly to remind myself of images remaining from what I had seen. I deliberately coaxed back the sight of her; of the face I had suddenly seen her unknowingly reveal to me, as she turned in whatever physical effort.

Again, I felt the alarming charge it had sent through me – and again. Now it was rooting me to the spot, worrying, once it faded, that she had gone for good, without my ever having really hailed her. Finally, I left. I crossed the sand in stops and starts, unable to give up thinking about that encounter, which kept bringing me up short but which I repeatedly resolved to move past.

Once in my cell, suddenly so small, there was no question of settling back to these puzzling insects. Rather, I was amazed at just how unthinkable such a brief episode had made the very idea.

I was dismayed at the disruption of my work. Though my excitement at what – at whom – I had seen made the research so humdrum that, from this perspective, I doubted if, even uninterrupted, I would have gone on with my dull routine much longer. And the thrill I'd felt was so intense that, as disturbing as it was, I did not want to be rid of it. I'd fallen prey to the sensation so easily that, yes, it must have been something I had really been awaiting all along.

I was trembling. But then, stomach sinking, I was afraid it was all in vain. I might never see her again, the woman whose small, shapely hands came back into my mind, perfectly manicured despite all her work among the Sahara's rocks and sand. I would never re-encounter her, to judge by past experience. It was just too dangerous to long for her return.

Waking and dream fused into a heightened, hallucinating consciousness in which I relived rousing to an ice-cold hand. I found myself back, quite alone, in our apartment with its defunct address book, no less than in the one with the green baize tablecloth.

My emptiness spread. It grew vast. It was this desert: sterile, glaring, ashen. It was achingly unpeopled, but for the girl miraculously bending again in red sand, her naked midriff inflaming as much as the pitiless Saharan sun.

My bedclothes knotting, I again tried to put the face out of my mind. It should not be hard. It was absurd to feel so much, so urgently, about one known so little, so unlikely to return. I had to try to reconnect with my impulse to work steadily, as a surgeon might skilfully join separated ligaments. I could not permit this kind of excitability to undermine the slow, patient reconstruction of myself.

It was no good. The face could not be set aside. Of a different order of attractiveness from others, of an infinitely rarer type, it had the special power to magnetise my thoughts, whether I liked it or not. As if that were not enough, its very potency for me, filling me with timidity, threatened my chance of ever knowing her.

My most perfectly desired one was surely lost to me.

*

She was there the following morning at the same time.

Once more, I spent the day forcing myself to work in my cell. Throughout the hours, I kept glancing out of the window where, after an eternity, the sun was finally reducing. The sky was streaked with pink.

She was still there when I had dressed and hurried out of the monastery across to her.

"Hunting for the insects?" she said, standing up straight to take me in with my collecting equipment. *Contre jour*, in sunglasses, a once-vaporous spectre now faced me as featureless shadow.

"Partly," I replied. "But I'm also out walking, to clear my head. It's a good time for that. And I saw you …"

"Not for long. I'm finishing now. But if you want that lift …"

I must have answered.

"Give me five minutes to clear up," she said, "and I'll be with you."

I sat on one of the dunes. I lounged against it, ready to wait for as long as she wanted. She had become tangible, moving to stow away her gear.

She was soon ready.

"Coming?" she called from the jeep.

I rushed over.

Off we jerked – surprising me with the assurance such a beautiful young woman had with a machine. She put a hand on my arm, smiling:

"All right?"

"Absolutely!"

The sky was reddening. As we raced over the sand, I looked out the open window and wished I could watch the sunset with her on the dunes. We might stay on and on, evening gradually overtaking us as we approached darkening buildings.

I had never seen desert night in this way before. It had only been a coldly glittering emptiness in which I worked and simply exchanged for these monastic walls – my cell's confinement.

She was delivering me. We came to a halt. I continued in my seat, drawing irregular breaths. Somehow, I invited her in.

From the jeep, she peered past the main gate. Her face compressed, perhaps with a sense of danger at the enormity committed within.

I was getting out as she said: "I've got something to do at base camp. Maybe I'll come over tomorrow."

She was gone.

"Maybe."

If anything made the uncertainty less tormenting, it was recognising that she'd kept all her previous vague promises to return. Even so, I couldn't allow myself to become attached to her. I had no right to suppose I could ever possess her.

She'd said she might be back. It had doubtless been in order to escape my disturbed reaction to parting, as I became painfully aware, considering it back at the dark monastery. I had been awkwardly, inexplicably unwilling to prise myself away from a woman too striking not to be skilled in dismissing men seeking to cling to her after even the shortest acquaintance.

If she were that resourceful, though, it was not only because she was attractive. She was hardly the mere apparition of beauty my imagination had colluded in conjuring up. So practical, energetic, probing; did she exist at all, I wondered, as the person to obsess me?

It was a question that would not let me go – not a single facet of it.

*

I was exhausted by the time I saw her again, late the following afternoon. From my slit window, I made out red dust trailing across the twilight desert.

I was at the main gate when the jeep drew up. I walked over as she got out into the evening.

"So this is where ..." Her bright words failed like a falling star. Her shoulders shuddered, just barely, as she turned to take in the sandy enclosure deserted in this gloom.

I feared nothing would appeal to her, or interest her sufficiently for her to stay longer than she had yesterday. I felt at a loss as to how to entertain her. My conversation – I myself – had so little to offer to this woman seeming already to have taken in the dim adobe exteriors, the closed chapel, the silhouetted garden, the dense, shadowy paths.

"And where do *you* live?"

I pointed. I knew that I should invite her to join me there, this being of whose warm physical presence I was so continuously aware, but from which I was so excruciatingly separate. For, absurdly tongue-tied as I was, she might, like the sand whence she came, simply slip through my fingers. Had I already lost this soft shadow?

"Can I see it?"

I was flooded with relief. I led her over to the cell.

A tray stood on the floor by the entrance. It had obviously been overlooked in the self-absorbed haste in which I had gone to receive her at the gate. She opened the door for me to carry it in and put on the feeble light as I placed it on the desk.

Not bothering – or daring – to observe her taking in my habitat, I said: "Would you like to share this with me?"

"Sure – but it looks like someone's beaten us to it."

Several pits had been left by the dish of olives.

"Must be the cook," I said, anxious to allay the doubt I could feel spreading about this now supposedly calm, deserted place. "Or maybe her daughter." Not that I knew if she had one, that unseen female presence. "We can take the food to the refectory, if you prefer."

"Is that where *you* normally eat?"

"I haven't since the last time one of the brethren was here. But he comes and goes without warning. I'd never know if he's around – unless of course *he* leaves olive stones. He might as well not exist. So I eat on my own."

"Well, this is fine. That way you can show me what you've been working on."

She tore off a piece of bread to take a pinch of white cheese. Settling on the bed, she said: "How far have you got?"

"I'm aiming to produce hyperrealistic illustrations of insects by blowing them up to over twenty times their natural size. I'll be doing it in watercolour, using tiny brushes to apply repeated washes of colour. It's a technique my wife helped develop. She was good at technical things ... I could do with her advice now."

I slumped onto the end of the bed. Taking it in, she partially changed the subject: "Is your project impressionistic? Or are you aiming for accuracy?"

"I wish I weren't. It would have made my suitcase lighter. And I'd be much further ahead by now. I measure every detail. So, apart from initial sketches in the field, and photographs, I do a precise rough drawing, transferring the content of each square of a grid on my microscope lens to an equivalent square on gridded paper. If the specimen's supposed to be presented symmetrically, I trace the rough drawing and fold the tracing paper so that I can adjust any mismatch between the sides. Then I use the symmetrical tracing, or even the rough sketch itself, to produce a detailed working drawing. Of course it also involves observing the specimen through the microscope. That way I can put in any additional details by eye. It forms the basis for the watercolour version."

"How far have you got?"

I gestured, beyond the microscope on the desk, to my cupboard.

"It's filled with insects, either alive or dead in vials. Some are pinned out on trays. And they're all awaiting me. But so far I've mainly been sketching, collecting and doing the initial drawings. I've barely experimented with colour illustration."

"Can I see your sketchbook?"

"It's very rough."

I handed her a book in which I had begun to draw insect parts. Genitalia and wings helped distinguish between species. She turned the pages to the first whole insect, a tenebrionid beetle. She craned her head.

"Strange. It's asymmetrical. Wonder why." She turned the page. "Same insect, I guess."

"No, but same vicinity." I was frowning. "Sometimes I ask myself if I keep making mistakes of measurement. Though these are only first sketches. I'm still trying to master the technique. Anyway, they aren't so interesting. They're imperfect."

"The typical isn't interesting in nature. It's the exceptions that are revealing – like these," she said, continuing to turn the pages to several that showed trials of my watercolouring.

"As I say, I haven't really got down to illustrating yet. The great mass of insects is in those vials and trays. And I've a lot more to collect."

She turned the pages of the sketchbook, leafing beyond the insects. "What are these? Abstracts?"

"I've been drawing the desert."

"And there are so many kinds of desert, aren't there?" she said with bright interest. "Seas of shifting dunes; steppes with slight vegetation; this kind of terrain, with granite outcrops … And what about the Saharan winds? The *khamsin*, called the sirocco here, supposedly raises the Drummer of Death. Apparently it held up battles in the North African campaign of World War Two. The *ghibli* feels as if it's going on forever. They say it makes camels pregnant without a male. Then there's the *simoon*, *haboot* and *irifi*. They all transport vast clouds of sand. Every grain becomes a diamond point, sculpting and smoothing the rock. And the sandstorms make the air so hot that camels' tails send out sparks … But how about this? It isn't desert, is it?"

"It's sand," I said. "I was thinking about what was written in the sand by whoever killed the monks."

"You saw it?"

"But I can't read Arabic. Or write it. I was just trying to recapture the cursive design of the script."

"Did you ever find out what it said?"

"The police told me: 'Death to the intruder bringing death to our land.'"

"What does it mean?"

I did not give an answer. Perhaps there was none, at least not that I knew. She herself did not even strive for one, turning on through the still-lifes, murmuring: "Are they getting anywhere with solving those murders?"

Again, I did no more than shrug my shoulders. The mystery of the deaths would simply remain like those tracks in the desert: disfigurements, till time, like the wind, covered them over, seemingly erasing what would have become an indistinct blur in someone's mind – next to nothing at all.

"Snap!" She had, at that very moment, both reached into the olive dish and come to my sketch of a similar vessel. "Interesting design," she said. "I've collected a couple of the bowls. They're typical of this area."

"But you also find them in Rome," I said. "African vendors sell them by the Spanish Steps, along with carpets, wood carvings and ivory."

"They might be common," she said, looking closely from dish to drawing and back again, "but I've not seen this before: only four dots. The local potter must have had a missing finger. It's another example of the variant being more fascinating than the normal."

"Or it could be a purely accidental difference," I said, "of no particular significance. Thinking it's random, or has meaning, is simply the result of a personal preference for believing one thing's the case rather than another. It's a matter of one's disposition at a particular moment."

"Sometimes," she said quietly, as if she had not heard me, "there's an irregularity in prehistoric or classical finds. It suddenly brings the clay to life. You seem to be touching the craftsman's hand, regardless of all that separates you."

The words reached me as I looked down at the rough-woven fabric between us on the bed where we were sitting. She was leafing through another sketchbook, of all vessels.

"It's good that you like still-lifes," she said. "They focus on what's usually overlooked. And there's often more to them than meets the eye. They sure can tell a tale at times. Kinda like rock: the way it shows us basic structures, and the cataclysms that created them – though it takes a geologist to open up the drama and find the narrative in the stone."

"I've simply been drawing," I said. "Just working, really, without looking at what I'm doing."

"That's because you're in the middle of it. An outsider can sometimes see a picture more clearly than the artist. It's possible to take in the organising principle at a glance – what it really has to say."

I was looking at her eyes, so searching, so striking

"But don't you ever touch human subjects?" she said.

"Not here. Not now."

"But not 'never'?" she said, abandoning the sketchbook, her hand, to the fabric.

The words hung. They reverberated in the deserted community, the dark desert beyond, with just us two in a cell on a bed.

She was holding still. So was I – too much. The moment had passed. I scowled, reproaching myself for lack of courage in not seizing it, regretting my solitary's lack of practice in taking hold of it and despairing of ever recalling it.

"Would you like to go out?" I said, knowing nothing more would come of remaining in this room with its tray of food barely touched by us. "Sometimes I just walk in the evenings."

"Sure."

She said it reaching for my sketchbook, as she got up from the bed. She added it to the others on my table. Carefully, pensively, she straightened the pile. She paused an instant before leaving, to take in the room.

"So you have your projects. And I see they absorb you," she said, stepping out into the evening. "But you must feel isolated. I know I couldn't stand being here all alone." She caressed her arms with her hands. The chapel loomed against the night sky. "The Sahara's a big place. You could lose yourself in it."

*

We went out the front gate, among that mass of stars. Night enveloped us, boundless, as we wandered past the jeep towards the desert. We walked and walked, wordless, until, tired, we sank onto a steep sand dune.

The day's wind had ceased its scorching and howling. The heat had faded. All was silent. The air felt utterly pure. We stretched out, side by side, in the softest breeze, gazing up.

"Look!" she said. "There's the constellation Aquila, the Eagle. Altair is its brightest star. It's bordered by the constellations of Sagittarius and the Dolphin. Sometimes, if you're lucky, you can make out the Andromeda Nebula. It's the furthest one can see with the naked eye – only 2.2 million light years away!"

"I think I preferred the stars as they were, before they were given Greek names. It turns the sky into classical drama."

"You mean you prefer chaos, seeing the heavens as luminous grains of sand?"

"But you've organised the sand, too. You've measured it, turned it into strata, shown what cataclysms caused it to settle as it has – what life it's thrown up. The sand isn't just sand anymore. It's whatever's made it, and it's becoming. The stars aren't the stars, either. They've been identified. They've lost their innocence. It isn't possible to unknow what one comes to know."

"Is that a reason for avoiding knowing anything? Remaining deliberately ignorant?"

I did not answer.

"I s'pose, when you get right down to it, it's just a matter of background," she said. "There are cultures that are driven to 'know', regardless. I guess I'm very American in that respect. Others leave well enough alone … Although sometimes you don't exactly have a choice. Someone can come along in life, when you least expect it, unlike anybody you've met before. You can't help getting to know him. 'Love at first sight.' It happens. The way the world looks to you, then, is completely changed. Nothing's ever the same again – regardless of who you go on to meet."

She was leaning with her back to the dune. It was cool, but she did not cover her bare midriff.

I felt a tightening in my chest and throat, and said, in a strained voice: "You speak from experience?"

"Sure do." She sighed deeply and pursed her lips, thoughtful. "We were students together. He went on to law school. I did my graduate work in Geology and Palaeontology."

"So what happened?"

"I went on field trips. One day I came back and he wasn't there."

"Do you still regret it?"

"I loved him … But 'we' were impossible."

"Why?"

"Someone else came along for him. That's the easy answer. The deeper one is: 'I don't know.' Things run their course. How can you account for it?"

"I thought you believed in explaining."

"When I can. Anyway …" she said, brushing it aside with a sigh.

Her breasts heaved gently, shoulders to the dune, eyes starward. Her hand extended involuntarily. I reached out, equally instinctively.

If I had thought about it, it would have required courage. But this was spontaneous – and must surely change everything. Hitherto we had just been skating on the surface with each other. We had referred only obliquely to our feelings. Now we might open right up to them.

She was shivering. Her hand was cold. I continued clasping it, the fingers still rigid. I swallowed, feeling the cold invade my palm.

"Love at first sight," she had said. It was a heady thing, like glimpsing those sudden desert blooms. But she'd also said there are some things you can't explain. In any case, it was far too early to talk about it. Besides, I doubted that it was even me, or still the lawyer, who was in her mind.

She must be given time, space and silence in which to reflect and catch up with her feelings – although, how long would she be here?

Wordless, I shrouded the woman in my habit. I enfolded her in my arms, with spasms of tenderness. It was the first time I had touched – *really* touched – anyone since kissing Anja's icy lips in a hot Alexandrian hotel room, then embracing her in a refrigerated coffin.

We held close, shadows, so remote among the stars. I felt myself drifting into ever greater obscurity.

*

I woke to find her lying beside me, eyes glistening, facing upwards. I felt both a stranger and intimate.

"Do you think we're safe?" I said, without quite knowing why. While there was always a possibility of terrorists reappearing, was it likely that they'd chance on this spot of the Sahara's vastness a second time? The question hadn't bothered me before.

"Tell me if anything's ever completely safe," she said after a while. "There's never a stable base, when you get right down to it. The Earth is a series of shifting tectonic plates. The crust could give way at any moment. And we're a sitting target for some meteor to come and shut us down as a species, as it did the dinosaurs."

"Lying targets, don't you mean?" I said, stretched back.

It was a grisly thought – making me see the two of us, a couple stretched out on a granite slab, as live sacrifices awaiting our joint fate on this natural altar. I had no idea which gods might choose us as victims, severing us, the one from the other, or why. But I did know, finally, that it was fear of just such an outrage against us as a pair that had prompted me to ask whether or not we were safe.

I snuggled back, holding her tightly.

*

I was roused by something grasping my arm beneath the habit. But no, it wasn't that wife's hand, slender, white as marble, haunting me from deep sleep. Nor was it the mother's flickering back into my mind from a lost dream: yellow by lamplight; stretched on green baize; cold, inert. It was the hand that had turned pages of a notebook – though not from this momentarily reconjured nightmare with illustrated insects all huge, hyperreal. One after another they reappeared in an increasingly rapid mental slideshow of the asymmetrical, the distorted. It was grey blur. There was no image.

Awakened, feeling the warmth of these elegant, manicured fingers beside me, I heard her say, yawning: "What's wrong?"

I found I had pulled on my habit to sit up. I went on doing so, my arms drawn around my raised knees. I was staring out into the dark.

"We'd better be getting back," she said, hauling herself up on an elbow. She raised herself away from the cover. Watching, I again felt a surge, noticing how shapely she appeared, this substantial shadow. She was alarmingly perfect.

We set off.

I yearned to take her hand, pacing across the sand. It dangled free in our continuing silence. I had been close enough to hold her beneath the habit. She had grasped my arm. But that had been in sleep. Awake, she might object. Something prevented me from risking it, going on with her, painfully desirable, totally beyond my scope, here among this harvest of stars. Yes, something was at work in that space between her free arm and my tense hand.

Looking back on it, from this distance in time, I seem to observe a strange field of psychic energy in that narrow channel. It was what converted a bright young American woman, never at a loss for a word of her colloquial speech, into the quivering spectre of beauty somehow making itself felt from within my consciousness. Intimidating, forbidding even in her very perfection, she at once charged me with longing and denied me the means to satisfy it. I could no more reach across that unbridgeable gulf, which might as well have been miles wide, to touch her, to feel a small, smooth hand with the lightest down, than on some remote planet, one of those unimaginably far-off stars whose physical laws rendered Earth's ounces as infinite tons.

I was hardly able to see her as we walked ahead together, side by side. She was a shadowy, all-but-featureless being between the young American woman whose words I remembered and the silently resonant apparition. Whoever, whatever she was in that intermediate space, that waking dream, she advanced there, invisible, substantial, illusive, where my longing for her increased, my desire raged.

Yes, the more I yearned, the more painfully I wanted the apparently impossible sweet receptivity of her mouth, the tender warmth of her breasts, the opening viscosity of her sex – and beyond that, as if to suck out the very marrow from the bone, access to such as she was to herself. Such inclusion with her in her solitude, her bath, before the mirror, in the paroxysm of her private moments of passion, or awakening to the disintegrating memory of her own dream at ten o'clock in the morning!

This was cannibalism of her self – frightening, it occurs to me, writing about it. And now I think I was also seeking to draw from her that essence she shared with each of the succession of girls and women to whom I had been similarly attracted over the years. It surely was, had I found it, what she radiated in the impossible space between us as the being I'd known long, long before ever having seen her, but who, by my emerging standard of impossible intimacy, I did not know at all.

*

It was dawn by the time we neared the monastery. The jeep was parked by the front gate. Closing our distance from it, pace by regular pace, I felt fear rising within me at the fast-approaching prospect of her simply driving off.

I searched frantically for words. As our steps eventually slowed down, I managed, mouth dry, tongue heavy: "Would you like to come in?"

It sounded like conventional politeness, so my relief at uttering the invitation mixed with anxiety, lest empty courtesy was all it seemed.

"For some coffee, perhaps," she said, yawning again.

Sandy paths described the cloister's rectangle. It resembled a stage. Perhaps I had unknowingly viewed it as such all along. But I wonder if I had ever seen this as a place of sacrificial drama chanced upon by the interloper I was, coming for his own experience of death and loss to be played out here.

They were all ghosts, brethren and bereaved. Though straggling now along the side with her, I doubtless also dared hope that, far from remaining in the shadowy wings of that morbid theatrical situation, we were inaugurating a fresh one with new protagonists. I surely yearned to throw off that dismal spectre of my self fully to be with her.

A tray awaited us outside my cell door. I bent to collect it. Straightening up with it in both hands, I used my elbow to lower the metal handle and let us in.

I placed the tray on the desk. She poured coffee and milk into the cup, handing it to me. I took several mouthfuls and gave it back to her. She sipped from it too, staring out from the edge of the bed.

As she bent to replace the cup on the tray, I picked up the yoghurt in its patterned earthenware bowl and offered it, sitting beside her.

"Do you want some bread to scoop it …?"

The words tapered away. I noticed crumbs on the surface. She put the yoghurt back on the tray, untouched, then keeled over on the bed with luxurious laziness, holding out a hand. It drew me back with her. Suddenly I came to myself, pulled past whatever within me had kept me apart from her, walking out here.

"I'll go in a minute," she half-whispered, nuzzling up to me. I drew my arm around her shoulder, kissing her cheeks, her mouth. But who was I touching this freely, looking at her face too closely to see it whole? It dissolved into parts of one face, then of another. Instant by instant it presented itself as this or that feature of one or other person, remembered, long forgotten, or unknown. Still, she was no composite. That which made her *her*, whatever it was, kept flickering back into focus.

I drank it in, overtaken by mighty surges of tenderness. Another wave swept over me. It turned to a wonderful fatigue, matching hers. I was holding her, eyes sinking, with her softness and warmth.

We drifted.

Real sleep it was, not that fitful dozing on the dune. I must have dreamed, but something wholesome. For I carried off from the now fast-submerging episode a sense of us slowly turning the pages of our address book – surviving after all.

The air felt clean, exhilaratingly pure, on awakening. And she, beside me here, had emerged with me from dreaming. She shared its continuing sweetness, and felt indescribably sweeter to me than all I'd ever held before.

There was no distance between us, let alone that unbridgeable channel of static energy. We drew closer with this unloosening of the bounds of myself – no! Of ourselves. For it had happened so naturally, my tongue slipping between her lips. I was kissing her neck, her throat. Her hands were in my hair, now smoothing my arms, as my mouth found her breasts. And then, how miraculous it suddenly seemed to be one, like this!

We just lay there, still, basking in relaxed naturalness. Maybe she could remain with me forever. I knew she would have to get up soon, that she must leave the country with her co-workers before long. But then again, she might delay the departure to be together a little – a lot? – longer.

Dream on, I told my infant self. *Out of the question!* Yet I contemplated this in the interest of something more ambitious and permanent. We could reunite once she had left the Sahara, to live our lives as one, far from Africa. Nothing need detain us in the monastery once I had finished my project. There was little enough to summon me back to Rome. Certainly not my past, the bare remains of which I had not the slightest desire to exhume.

My – *our* – horizons were limitless, I felt, feverish with exhilaration. So much more than the harsh line I saw now, as every day, from my cell window. It was, I knew, the first time I had actually looked up from these sands to realise that I had a life, not just an existence. And such a life! It was one to be shared, enjoyed, wherever we pleased.

I sought to picture the place. An image flickered, but faded before I could see it. My internal projector hummed blindly. Even so, whatever the scene, she would be with me. It must be what she, too, wanted, otherwise she would not be in my arms.

"I hope we can go on being together," I found myself saying.

Neither impulsive nor planned, the words abbreviated a train of thought that had actually taken scarcely a moment. For it had simply been implicit in that softening of desert horizon by my inner eye.

"But I'm leaving soon," she said predictably. "I told you."

"I mean in the future."

"We might …" Her words sounded on, tracing a whole scale of tones in my mind. They attenuated only gradually in the heavy stillness. As silence absorbed us, I, unmoving too, realised how little we had talked to one another. True, we had touched on many things. We had spoken of insects, dinosaurs, wind, sand, stars and even a lost boyfriend and wife. But we had never discussed the one thing that concerned us both: ourselves. What each meant to the other.

There had been something remote about her from the start. It was not only that, to my eyes, she was overlaid by so many others. The being with whom I was actually presented was noncommittal, elusive, be it over when she might enter the monastery, or in a distant, distracted air repeatedly coming upon her. Never fully of the present situation, she seemed to have a permanent foothold outside it.

Not that I could have expected her instantly to avow feelings for me that she needed time to discover. Possibly, she thought I was lucky to have persuaded her to come this far, that it was almost miraculous for me to have received this much from her. She might consider it out of the question to discuss future benefits with an ungrateful Oliver Twist asking for more.

Indeed, perhaps she was with me like this precisely because she was treating me casually. Maybe I was only the most recent in a series. I might merely be its latest representative, rather than just myself. In other words, I could actually be insignificant to her.

Then it occurred to me that it might be an accident of appearance, no more, that made her special for me: those dark eyes, the features I had from time to time glimpsed elsewhere. So she, having done nothing to deserve her looks, nor realising what they meant to me, could really be just "the American ex-graduate student" after all, conceivably just one in a sequence extending from an Alexandrian block of flats to a Washington museum, and then to a video on a North African coach. Facially similar to a neighbour, a schoolgirl, an actress, she was like each of them, desired and distant.

So I had not really talked to *her* any more than she had to *me*, with her casual, noncommittal responses. For here was another of those conversations that I had failed to have in my life. They were – or, rather, were not – with all the most important people: my father, long lost;

my mother, withdrawn to the point of virtual absence; my wife, now seeming to me really to have been a companion, soon slipping into the maternal role of just taking care of me. I had not spoken, opened up to any of them – nor they to me. All my talk in the past had been a way of not saying anything. Only now, in the silence of this desert monastery, was I acknowledging it, my beloved in my arms.

Suddenly I had another surge of feeling for the soft, warm being beside me, and all at once I knew inescapably, as though something dark were passing through this cell and casting its shadow between us, that she would leave this bed in a few minutes; the room in several more; the desert in a day or two at most.

I clung to her; she drew nearer to me. Again, our eyelids sank. Insensibility claimed us.

15

What was approaching? It was so faint in the stillness that it seemed the remnant of an extinguished dream. Maybe an animal was tracking through one of the sandy paths. It might be a cat living in the monastery garden; I had taken to leaving out scraps for them in this place, so deserted that they would have little else on which to survive. True, like me they were perhaps served from the kitchen – although there was no knowing how long one could remain certain of that.

The cat was probably nosing through the tray itself, set on the other side of the doorstep and containing one of those earthenware vessels. It was smudged black, but not only with inky fingertips. Ants would be there too, pouring over it. Domestic ants; I took no interest in them. My insects had to come from the untouched desert.

Cats had obviously explored this tray before. Yet did they eat olives and spit out the stones, or break off bread to scoop up yoghurt? I sprang up on an elbow to ask myself, looking over to my desk. The coffee, the crockery, was still there. I heard a throat being cleared outside, and the sound of our own sharp breathing in the next instant of silence.

My heart pulsed so painfully that I couldn't take in the air. I was winded. All my blood seemed to drain away. It left me light-headed, in a virtual trance. It felt, in that dreamlike moment, that something was finally happening that I'd all but expected. I might have been awaiting it all along without exactly realising it, having come so far into the Sahara.

Not that I understood what appeared to be taking place even then, as I do now writing this years later. I reacted impulsively as to an earthquake, a car crash, replaying in a passing second one's entire life up to this, its suddenly culminating, moment. I dived away from it and what it might mean, beside the warm body already buried far beneath the bedcover, at the sound of the door handle being turned. An abrupt knock reverberated in that desert void – by the hand of Fate, it almost seemed, down in our stifling darkness.

We froze, sensing deathly danger.

I sought my voice. "Come in," I heard myself say.

She was clinging close to me, ever closer.

A head appeared: a grizzled white beard, largely hidden by a cowl. Father Mark, surely. Eyes gleamed, taking in the cell, then me. It was a long, enquiring look, suddenly turning fierce on seeing that other head.

"*Raus!*" he bellowed.

He stood full before us, against the light, in his habit. It was an eerily improbable moment of *déjà vu*, with this angrily reproving being hovering on the fringe of an inaccessible recess of memory.

"Where do you think you are! You've no right to behave like this! It's our home you're desecrating!"

He stormed out, slamming the door.

The noise echoed on. Silence reabsorbed him. So, it felt, did the desert. There was no sound of his catlike tread through the thick, sandy path.

"Now we know who's been eating the olives," she said with a brave show of nonchalance, trembling, pulling the T-shirt down over her breasts.

"Mm …"

It had not been Father Mark: Father Mark, whom I instantly realised something within me had longed for in that first moment, and whom I've apparently now summoned up in the writing of these events years after. Equally fierce, a spry eighty-year-old too, and quite as passionate about the sanctity of the community, he comes back to me by contrast here in Rome as open, generous, on a human level. No, he would never have protested with such rough fury.

This was Father Erich, with his German accent and worn hermit's habit dusty from long desert travel.

"Well, thanks for the coffee."

"Eh?"

"I'm going," she said, lips white. "I think he was hinting at it."

"Really?" I said, struggling to overcome my vagueness.

"Oh, yes! I'd better leave you with your countryman. Good luck!"

Finding myself hovering awkwardly before her, it suddenly came crashing in upon me that, with her leaving this cell, the moment I had most feared facing was upon me.

Here, where nothing had ever seemed to happen, where all was forever the same, something – someone – had finally broken in on my long inactivity to change everything, to speed it all up. Now everything was in a rush, like that desert sand cascading in irrecoverable torrents through one's fingers.

Yes, all of a sudden I was losing this, my unattainable one, without arrangements for future meeting.

"So I'll see you again soon?" I muttered, head down.

"I always come back, eventually."

"Tomorrow?"

"Or tomorrow. Or tomorrow …"

We walked out together. We felt the full heat of the day.

She held a limp hand. I could never have extended it myself, not on the verge of having hers withdrawn. Such a wrench!

I dared not tell her how unimaginable the time before meeting her suddenly seemed, let alone the idea of having to return to it. Previously I had been in a dead, dreamless sleep: now I was tensely animated. I couldn't willingly forfeit the nervous consciousness that knowing her had brought me.

"It's not *that* bad," she said. "After all, he can't really do anything – can he?"

She received no answer.

We approached the walls, passed the gate, shielding our eyes. Her sunglasses on, she walked straight up to the jeep, briefly hugging me as she got in with that practised, graceful swing.

"Just keep at it with the bugs," she said from the window.

I barely raised a smile at the American graduate student that her forced jokiness made of her. Now, as the engine sounded, I was gazing out into the blinding infinity to which I was losing her in that ever more distant, diminishing, finally non-existent, vehicle.

*

I turned back. The monastery felt dead – *your* monastery, Father Mark. For resuming my account this morning, having just heard the front door of our apartment close, entitling me to a day's solitude before our balcony with its geraniums and distant view of St Peter's dome, I somehow seem to be back in my Saharan cell in your company.

Inexplicably, I sense your presence, receptive as you are to what I now realise I have, for some time, been writing to share with you. You hovered on the brink of my mind before. Yesterday you stepped right to the fore for a moment, with Father Erich on his arrival. But not till this point have you fully emerged: at the start of an increasingly breathless sequence badly needing to be honestly understood by at least somebody of your profession, a period marked by the arrival of one like, yet so different from you, Father Mark.

As I think over what I've just realised, I hope, Father Mark, you don't mind me contacting you out of the blue after all this time. That's assuming this reaches you, the mail being what it is in the desert. But I'll be sending you these pages on the strength of those long conversations of ours in the Sahara.

You see, Father Mark, you struck a chord with me out there among the sand and the stars – something I'm still sounding out. So you, if anyone, will know what to make of this account and whatever it amounts to. I'll be forwarding it to you as soon as I finish it, just as I've written it, unedited. And I look forward to the day when I'll wake up to find you, Father, responding at last, out of deepest desert, to confirm all that's real in the story.

*

I turned back then from that fiercely glaring desert to which I'd lost her. The monastery felt as dead as ever. Yet, passing through the cloister, I noticed that the chapel door was open. It created a rectangle of dark.

I stopped, looking over at it. Then my footsteps were leading me towards it. I entered the dimness. It smelled musty, enclosed. Incense had turned to dust. Despite the sun outside, there was the chill of a place unused, its rituals abandoned.

The old man was sitting near the altar, hidden by his beard and cowl. He was rigid.

My footsteps continued on, as if not my own. They led me towards the still figure in his pew as though by some preordained plan. I sat beside him, glimpsing that carving of the Holy Family on the nearby wall.

Aware of each other, but not reacting, we shared the silence. It was not clear how, or if, it would end.

"She's gone," I finally said, sheepishly, in German.

"Who was she?" the old Father responded in kind, unexpectedly subdued.

"An American geologist. She works for a US oil company – though she says her family's originally from here."

I added it quizzically, asking myself how such seemingly contrary aspects, Western and Oriental, could coalesce in the already bewilderingly various self she had shown me.

"Jewish," the monk said, tonelessly.

I did not reply.

"There are lots of them around even now," the monk said.

We continued sitting there. Then he said:

"My nerves are on edge. It's an emotional time for me. After so long buried away in my hermit's cave far off in the desert, it's hard to face a homecoming – and especially to find the place like this."

I coloured – only to discover he must also have been excusing his outburst. For he went on: "This killing's horrifying. I can't bear to think of all that innocent blood."

He half-whispered it, eyes staring unseeingly into the dimness. Neither of us spoke. Again, the silence grew heavy. Then the monk said: "In the desert, everything's pure, quiet – except for the wind. Though there are places of still greater quietness, like this chapel. I badly needed to come here after such a hard journey. But now there's no more peace, even here. How can I stop thinking of the last time I was under this roof, worshipping with Father Sebastian and all the brethren? The very walls seem to be crying out ..."

His words hung between us in the emptiness of the chapel. Eventually, they dispersed. I got up, leaving the monk to his pew and pondering. Exhausted, I walked, numb, back into the fiery emptiness of the morning.

*

I returned to my cell. Standing at the door, I took in the bed, unmade, still with depressions in its rough cover. I walked to the window, scanning all those dunes, granite slabs and blinding flats. Once more my eyes panned over the terrain, and again all the way to those distant peaks. Each time, I probed it more nervously. But I did not choose to scrutinise. Almost in a panic, I could not help trying to locate the one whose enthralling being I had this equally insatiable longing to explore.

But no. Regardless of how earnestly I looked at the desert, it held relentlessly void.

Actually, it was teeming. There were not just those buried stone-age artefacts, armies who'd lost their way, slaughtered caravans, misguided explorers. It was full of life. One only had to look hard enough, learning just where and when to peer. Any entomologist knew that insects were often timed to spend the most vulnerable stages of their metamorphoses in the least adverse seasons. Most only came out at night.

Desert earthworms and mites spent an entire part of their life cycles concealed beneath ground. Ants and termites divided their existence between the upper and lower worlds. Termites even built covered runways above the surface to avoid strong light, though there were next to none of them hereabouts.

What did exist, in plenty, were ants and tenebrionid beetles. They were solid black.

"It's asymmetrical," I heard her say, looking at one I had sketched.

Her voice sounded so clear to me that she might have been right beside me in mockery of the speed with which I'd focused on insects to make up for her absence.

"Wonder why," she seemed to say.

My draughtsmanship must have been poor, I told myself, as I had her.

I turned from the window, back to the room, to pick up the sketchbook from the desk. Passing from the first asymmetrical beetle we had seen to the next, I considered that, even in those many cases where I had gone beyond initial sketching to make an outline with a grid, I had yet to produce detailed working drawings.

Setting the coffee tray on the bed, I opened the cupboard to reach for the vials and trays of insects from my desk. Sitting there, I would observe each specimen through the microscope, putting in any additional details by eye.

*

Later, I walked over to the refectory, searching for the Father I had previously barely made an effort to divine in natural still-lifes of abandoned olive stones and crumbled bread. There, so long absent as to have been almost a false rumour, he was summoning up lunch – and her, our all-but-invisible source of food.

I took them in. The electric bulb was unable to compete with cracks of blinding sun invading the closed shutters. A strange blend of lights, it gave a visionary quality to the pair materialised now. He, known to the woman for years, was almost miraculously back in the flesh from deep desert.

The woman served us. The old Father perfunctorily crossed himself. Then he said, as she left: "I also once saw a woman I was attached to in the desert."

I thought of those letters revealing the unsuspected lives of monks, as I saw him hold the earthenware bowl. It was as if his were the fingers now making its four black dots.

"Even when she went, after such a short time, I seemed to communicate with her." He put down the bowl and picked up his spoon. Sighing, he loaded it with lentils. "What are you doing out here?"

"Studying insects."

"How's it progressing?"

"I'm not sure. I mean, the project's advancing, but I don't know what it all adds up to."

"For you personally?"

"Well, that's no longer clear to me."

"How did you come to start it?"

"I was offered a contract for a coffee-table book of hyperreal scientific illustrations of insects."

"You have the training for that?"

"I studied entomology at university. And I've done biological drawing for publishers in the past. Besides which, although my wife was primarily a photographer, she had a background in graphic as well as visual arts. She helped me develop some of the techniques I'm using. When she died, I was at such a loose end that Father Carlo persuaded me to take up the project she'd planned, refocusing it on Saharan insects at the monastery – and to discover what to do with the rest of my life."

"She died, eh? … And Carlo acted as your sort of, em, spiritual father? He's very responsible. Many of us owe him *everything*."

"Odd sense of responsibility, to send me somewhere so dangerous."

"Anywhere can be dangerous, depending."

"Perhaps."

"And how long were you married?"

"All but twenty years."

"A long time. How did she …"

"A heart attack."

"And are there children to make your parents happy in their old age?"

"No. And I'm afraid they didn't have much more than a middle age."

"Oh! So they died," he said, head – cowl – lowered.

"Before I met my wife. It's odd," I said, finding myself rambling before this attentive, strangely calming presence, "I was very timid. I met her through a newspaper advertisement. My mother was also supposed to have sent letters through the personal column in the local press."

Father Erich's eyes were lost in shadow: gleams closing an instant.

"So Carlo encouraged you to study the insects out here," he said, his tone rounding off the topic.

"Yes, but there's something strange about them."

"How?"

"They're lopsided – the majority of them."

"Not everything in Nature's symmetrical. A scientific training tells one that."

"Maybe. But I'm an artist now," I said. "Besides, these insects are deformed in one way or another, every single one. Some have misshapen bodies. Others have legs with limbs missing, or crumpled feet. Then there are damaged antennae, sometimes acting as legs, and stunted or missing wings. There's a cicada with blisters and huge eyes with abnormal red pigmentation. The right socket's weirdly disturbed. And they're all from a radius of just a few kilometres from the monastery.

"I'm supposed to be producing a lavishly beautiful book," I continued. "Instead, I seem to be compiling a catalogue of horrors for the German public. Can that be what it really deserves?" Drawn on by Father Erich's attentive silence, I said: "I've no idea whether to go on with the project, or what it means – let alone for me."

"Terrible," he said quietly, setting down his spoon and tapping the table.

"One fly has a cavity instead of a face," I said, "How could such a thing have come about?"

Father Erich had grown self-absorbed. "I remember them studying insects in the Egyptian desert," he said.

"You were there?" I asked, looking up at him.

How odd that those lined features, shadowy beneath his cowl, suddenly became a palimpsest of other faces, including some I knew but could not place.

"I was in a Coptic monastery off the Alexandria road," came the answer, distantly.

"Oh?" I said, wiping sweat from my brow. I recalled seeing the same place, surely, with Anja at a young American woman's exhibition of watercolours in Rome.

"That was in the days before it was reformed by a pharmacist-turned-monk from Cairo," Father Erich said. "It was used as an unofficial rendezvous for scientists working in the desert."

"I spent nearly two years of my childhood in Alexandria. My father was working on a scientific project for the government. I'm not sure what it was. Anyhow, he was lost in the Sahara. He died there. I wonder if you ever …"

Father Erich tilted his head abruptly, eyes gleaming beneath his cowl. A tired hand waved against what I would ask. "There were so many people. Lots of us Germans. We were only there for a short time – until Suez."

"So Father Carlo said. But what happened at Suez?"

"If the Israelis had taken Cairo, as seemed inevitable before the Americans intervened, just imagine what lies they'd have chosen to believe about honest Germans working in Egypt."

We went on eating. A fly droned between us, damaged too.

"Why were they studying insects in Egypt?"

"They were entomologists, I suppose," Father Erich said, stuffing bread into his mouth.

"Do you think they might have been studying the effects of radioactivity?"

"Who knows?"

"I've begun wondering if that's what I'm seeing. Do you think the government's holding nuclear tests out here?"

"The French conducted a series of atomic explosions in the atmosphere, then underground, but that was in the early 1960s."

"So I've heard," I said, suspecting that what Father Josef had told me about it in this very refectory had been at the back of my mind for some time now. "But surely the effects wouldn't still be felt to this degree. I'm talking about the present government. Is it still going on?"

"You say you're an artist. A fine drawing of an insect, or even of a few, isn't a scientific study. It proves nothing. Don't let your imagination run riot. Hydrogen bomb testing these days would be a frightful prospect. It'd mean the extermination of whole species, entire populations. Unthinkable!"

"Have you ever seen any sign of it?"

"Various types pass by me where I am," the old man said, adjusting his cowl. "Some are scientists, I presume. What other Westerners would be out there? I've always supposed they were working for the oil and natural gas companies. Naturally, I've never asked. I live alone. I'm busy with my prayers, my spiritual life. How *could* I have any information about destruction on such a scale?"

The words reverberated in the massacred community.

16

I returned to my cell. The breakfast tray had been removed in my absence. I was about to slump onto my bed, exhausted from so little rest the previous night, but couldn't resist first glancing into the desert glare. Empty, it left me painfully empty too. Then there was no question of sleeping.

I had to force myself to block her from my thoughts: she, for whom I had come to hunger so; I, who'd already entombed the mother, the wife I no longer brought to mind. My eye, unrewarded by the sandy haze, returned to the microscope.

I was surrounded by specimens and drawings I had been making before going to the refectory. Automatically I continued investigating, our lunchtime conversation filling my mind. I went on pursuing the train of thought begun over lentils.

By the time I stretched, the light was much muted. I got up from my concentrated study to scan the terrain. Yet nothing the sunset was doing through this window could redeem the view. The subtle metamorphosis of its tints; the delicacy of its pinks and scarlet; that rich violet; the dense indigo; the glittering sheen of early stars: all these suddenly seemed to me gaseous, toxic.

Everything here was deformed, diseased, doomed. What but inert vacancy could survive?

Sterile desert, this could be the surface of a dead planet, unimaginably far away, with nothing but time to pass. For I didn't see how my project with the insects, supposed to help me find myself, could still be viable. All that was here was remains of ruined life.

It was suddenly stifling. I turned back to the dark cell. Holding the door handle, I felt a welcome breeze, taking in the shadowy trees; the silhouette of the locked chapel. I looked over at the refectory. If I studied its exterior, I might make out light through a crack in its shutters.

There was a tray by my foot. It contained my supper. I stooped to collect it. Rising, I breathed in the jasmine-laden air. How it thrilled, this sense of inhaling someone's scent – till I coughed. It was lethal.

Opening the cell door, I carried in the tray, with its ever-decorated earthenware. It, too, resonated with memories, standing out in the cold moonlight, as I ate pensively without turning on the lamp for some reason.

Even after my supper, I remained lost in thought – rousing, still sitting up in my habit in this metallic glow. I undressed and got on the bed. I lay awake, preoccupied by what tomorrow would or would not bring. The next instant, drowsiness swept over me. I was submerged by sleep.

I opened my eyes. It was day. But I did not get up and walk straight to the window as usual. I lay writhing at the prospect of discovering she was not there. I anticipated having to return from scrutinising bright desert, a man condemned to a never-changing view, to all the time in the world, to a ceaselessly repeated cycle of light and darkness, dusk and dawn.

I would eat breakfast in my cell or, at best, pace over to the refectory, further brooding on my image of Father Erich and his conversation in the booming silence. Prepared for the worst, I finally got up. My eye lighted on something: the spectre moving around, at a distance, beyond her jeep.

I left.

"Hi!" she said, wearing her dark glasses.

"Good morning."

My voice sounded muffled to me as I wiped sweat from my face with the sleeve of a habit white from previous use. I was breathless, having hastened over to her, but I was also feeling the restraint that had overcome me. Not embracing, not continuing on from our intimacy, it was as if the angry interruption in my cell had permanently distanced us.

"I wasn't sure if I'd see you," I said.

"Well, you have. I've all these skeletons to find in Nature's cupboard. I'm kind of a paleontological sleuth."

We were walking over to the cover provided by her jeep.

"Anyway, I wouldn't have missed hearing about our *Intruder in the Dust* for the world ... What *did* happen?"

I was frowning into the sun, droplets trapped in my eyebrows.

"I'm not sure," I muttered.

"Huh?"

"He asked me about my project," I said thoughtfully.

"You mean he quietened down and turned civil? He sure had a ways to go."

"We talked about the insects here."

We were leaning against the shaded side of the vehicle. I was staring out, frowning.

"And?"

"You saw the drawing in my sketchbook. I told you the measurements have to be inaccurate, or else I'm a poor draughtsman. Well, I made a new, meticulous drawing, and it's simply that the insect's deformed. All of them are. I spent virtually the whole of yesterday checking. It's definitely true."

"You surprise me. I thought you prided yourself on keeping your nose so close to the grindstone, collecting and drawing, that you just kill time without having to see the bigger picture."

"Look," I said irritated, urgent, "I found all the insects only a few kilometres from the monastery at most. Don't you see what that means? Something very disturbing is happening here. It's a severely damaged environment. This is obviously an area with high radioactive fallout."

She was facing me, the dark glasses making her expressionless in the desert. Then she said: "I was going to say: 'I wonder if we're safe here'. But I guess recent events have taught us that you don't need to be an entomologist to answer that question."

I made no response. She broke the heaviness with deliberate triteness, as if it could offer consolation: "Anyway, everywhere's polluted since Chernobyl. Although what you say does seem to confirm rumours about nuclear testing out here in the Western Sahara."

"I asked Father Erich about that."

"Why would he know?" she said, lips puckering.

"He's a hermit. He lives in the far desert. That's exactly where the government could be expected to operate such a programme. He might've seen something."

"You think he'd be capable of recognising it?" she said with continued disdain.

"I got the impression that he has a scientific background."

"And *had* he come across anything?"

"He said that from time to time he ran into Westerners, probably scientists working for oil companies – like you."

"*I'm* not developing weapons of mass destruction!"

"But are *they*?"

Again, she was just looking at me in her dark glasses. More than ever, they made her appear impersonal, searching, pitiless even, there against the jeep, with painfully brilliant desert peaks across its roof.

She was a shadow, dimming her American, her Oriental, selves. It extinguished them, no less than the time when I had held her, kissed her – and all the beings I had kissed through her – so tender and comforting. Such inconceivably distant moments!

"I wonder if it's worth going on," I murmured, my head hanging. "The project's in question even at this early stage of sketching and drawing. I haven't so much as started colouring. And who'd want a record of deformity on their coffee table, raising the question of who's responsible for it? The idea's grotesque. I might as well stop everything now. But that'd mean leaving ... going back, I suppose ... though to what? I can't see any good coming of it. Matters simply seem to be worse than when I started. I wish I'd never begun investigating. If only I hadn't found out what I now know."

"You can't unknow things. Or let matters slide. You must feel some urge to report your findings – the scientist's impulse. Besides, it's important for moral reasons. Nuclear weapons are no joke. So much hangs in the balance. And people have to be brought to account."

"It's all abstract."

I said it flatly, scorning the invitation to self-importance.

"So you say. But isn't that the attitude we've encountered before, in those seeking to evade responsibility for murdering millions of people?"

"*I'm* certainly not responsible for anything of the sort. And others, far more qualified, will surely analyse the problem and take whatever steps they see fit. The whole business leaves me numb. I don't feel remotely involved anymore. I've no idea what comes next."

"But you felt sufficiently involved to re-examine your specimens, to draw your conclusion."

"Well, I've reached it. So that's that."

"How can that be? Doesn't it make a difference to you? To you, personally?"

"I don't understand. What *could* it mean to me? I told you: I don't feel anything."

"Not anything about anything?"

She took off her sunglasses. Her eyes were naked. Her face appeared softer, more fragile than ever, perfect.

My chest thumped.

"What difference could it make for me to feel things? It doesn't change matters. Things, people, go on, go off, fade, die, just as they would regardless of how one feels about them. Getting to know them, understanding them for what they are, seems a huge effort – and beside the point … don't you think?"

She was taking me in, loveliest yet. But her head tilted away, eyes half-closed in the sunlight.

"I don't know," she said vaguely, as though abstracting herself from all we had been discussing. "Seems kinda disappointing to me."

I went on staring at her: she was unreachable. We had come to an impasse in conversation – and with one another. Father Erich had apparently frightened us apart; we had failed to come back together. I longed to believe we would return, though our contact was born of a particular, unusual moment coinciding here in the desert. But I feared it had gone for all time, like those sudden, withered, scattered desert blooms.

This must be what she, too, was making of the present moment. Yet did she also regret it, weighed down with love for me? I asked myself where we, where I, must go from here.

I had silence in which to consider. We were standing mutely, each looking out into endless stillness, avoiding one another's eyes, as if past some uncomfortable matter to be evaded. Our wordlessness became heavy. Together with the space, the heat, the light, it grew as oppressive as the question of how to suspend this morning's situation.

I knew I should leave; our conversation had nowhere to go now. I also knew that the instant I turned to pace off, I would regret it and yearn to be back with her.

"Well, I should be getting on," she said, replacing her sunglasses. "I want to finish while there's still time."

"Of course." I found I'd said it with surprising force. But still I did not move. I was suddenly holding my ground, despite Father Erich, her remoteness and my own uncertainty as to what to say. "I'm sorry we didn't talk about *your* work here, and, em, your progress in tracking down dinosaurs."

"It's not as if we *haven't* touched on it – in a way. But another time, perhaps."

"Another time," I said, voice trailing off, to continue within, questioningly. "*Are* you coming back?" I said out loud.

"The team returns regular as clockwork. Just so long as there's a drop of oil left to find ... But our leader's strict about leaving punctually, too."

Not for the first time, I saw her grow vague, the toe of her sneaker tracking through the sand before her just as her company's lorries did.

"Look, how can I contact you?"

"I'll write."

"Do you have the address? I don't know how reliable the mail is out here. And I'm not sure of my own plans."

"I'll write soon ... Hey, you're not that far off the face of the Earth ..." She held out her hand and I took it. Her mouth smiled, teeth white, regular, beneath sunglasses. No, there was no chance of more. Not if she did not feel it.

She was striding off to complete her work when I looked back after only several paces.

*

I walked on, mechanically. I knew I must eventually feel something. Yet, afraid that I would, I fully submitted to this numbness. I was a somnambulist parting from a dream enactment of the worst. Arriving back at the monastery, I halted at my cell door to gulp water from the jug on the tray. I gnawed at a chicken leg and flung the bone into the nearby bushes.

Licking my fingers, I returned to myself with surprise. Neat and clean till then, as befitted a methodical quasi-scientific enquirer, I had previously treated this community, albeit ghostly, with more respect. Of course, the cats would soon get to the bone. But lines of ants must already be leading to and from it, black until indistinguishable from night.

I shuddered at the very thought of the myriad insects, every last one deformed. Inwardly, I turned my back on my image of them, as on my work. I did not want to keep getting up from the investigation

I would not now be performing at my desk, to scan from my window a view that would only reconfirm my aloneness.

I went into my cell, slumping onto the bed. My arm hung uselessly from the side. I'd failed in all I'd put my hand to.

I found my fingers touching the Order's brochures, stacked on the floor. I brought up *A Saharan Solitude* and opened it at random.

I joined the Order soon after serving in the Army Intelligence Corps during the War. My work had sometimes taken me behind enemy lines, in situations of extreme danger.

When friends knew that I was intending to become a monk, I caught the unmistakable disbelief in their eyes. How could I abandon the excitement, the thrill, of all I had done for ... well, nothing? After all, this is an existence without action; without anything ever happening.

Such, at any rate, is most people's view of monks. To them the life of a religious is a life lost. It is far from the hub of human activity; the centre of power. How much more so the existence of a hermit, buried and forgotten in the desert. Here in the Sahara there is not even the communal silence of our brethren enacting the Church's sacred fasts and festivals.

There are no momentous events – no events at all. Absolutely no drama. One is outside history, with no tale to tell, since every day is a replica of the one before; indistinguishable from the one after.

Time does not advance. In a real sense, it does not exist. There are only the returning cycles of the seasons. Oh! and the inner clock; those inward changes, with frequent regressions, imperceptible but to the sensitive soul.

For a Saharan solitude is governed by quite different standards: calm, contemplation, a reverent attentiveness. They give access to eternal truths, far from the cut and thrust of society.

The rising and setting sun teaches me its lesson, outside my cave. If its lighting of the desert, or the slow magnificence of its darkening, happened just once, we wouldn't believe them to be repetitions but extraordinary occurrences, miracles – as indeed they are. Yet pondering them, absorbing and feeling them every day for years and years, I see them, everything, miraculously. I can live as if everything were happening, truly happening, only once, outside time.

The desert is rocky, flat and soft by turns. Sometimes, without warning, the entire, enormously wide sky turns yellow. It is a disturbingly dark lemon. Then sand enters my cell.

It is everywhere. How did it get into the cooking pot, always kept with the lid closed against scorpions? I discover a grain in my belly button days after a storm.

Mere grit, these specks are too numerous for us to count. None is important enough for us to notice. Yet they are driven by a mighty wind. It scatters as it listeth.

Rightly seen, this annoying grit shows us the invisible Spirit blowing into our hearts. It enters their innermost recesses. It's at work there even when life feels most empty, most static. We could meet it there if only we bothered to peer within.

A grain of sand, the sun, mute things we overlook far from the hum of humanity: these chart our passage to the spiritual Ithaca.

*

I set the pyramid of the open book across my chest and continued lying on the bed. I might always have been motionless, without blood coursing, lungs pumping, thoughts streaming. Inert, I just stared out. Sometime later, I got up. What had raised me? Half-perplexed, standing there, I looked at my sketchbooks. Sighing, I turned away and opened the cell door.

On the threshold, I took in the afternoon light. It was painfully bright. But now I was restless, and set off unthinkingly. I found myself heading through bushes, then maize, for the shade of that fig tree. There was the sound of running water.

As I approached the cistern, I came upon Father Erich seated on an adobe bench. He did not look up from the tree's shadow. He was sunk deep in thought. What was he seeing inwardly? On and on the water poured. I felt the eyes upon me. Sitting on the bench too, I said:

"I came to the monastery for calm. I actually entered it right here: over the wall, and down this tree – although I haven't been back to this spot much since. It was quiet, all right. But not exactly the kind of silence I was expecting. Even when I seem most deaf to those mute cries, the Departed suddenly reappear in my thoughts."

"What did you expect?" Father Erich said, clearing his throat, as if overcoming a long habit of not talking. "Did you really suppose your mind could be a blank, like this desert sand?"

"Maybe. But obviously I was only ever numbed with amnesia. And they're back. I keep wanting to sketch some startling stare or gesture."

"Isn't it really *she* who's upset you?"

"What makes you say that?"

"I saw you from my window – both of you," Father Erich said, somehow vehemently.

"She's leaving now."

"Apparently," Father Erich said coldly. "And you're bereft."

"I've got my work, my drawing," I said flatly.

"Still-lifes."

"*Nature morte* – like the insects. That's the reality the monastery has to show for itself. Some mystery! Not quite miraculous, but certainly strange."

"Harping on it does no good," said Father Erich. "Anyway, insects are a pest. Vermin spread disease. And their species will take over the world if they're not checked. It's a war of survival. Extermination would be a benefit, if it were really to be successful. So don't worry about the roaches. That'd be pure sentimentality. Forget all about them, and the rest of what's happened in the monastery."

"That's not as easy as it sounds, as I'm sure you yourself have found. You returned to the monastery as soon as Father Mark gave you Carlo's letter and told you what had happened, didn't you? And now that you're here, have you been able simply to turn your attention to something else? After all, you knew the brethren well, didn't you?"

"Monks never get to know each other well. The monastic round leaves too little time for that. The most that's possible is to sense what one of the brethren is like from his general bearing, or some brief exchange."

"But you *did* talk to Father Mark, didn't you?"

"Somewhat."

He was staring ahead, half-frowning, as if at an unbridgeable gulf between them.

"And had you spoken before?"

"That was many years ago, soon after I joined the Order."

He said it quietly, almost to himself, eyes vague, as if the long-distant scene were recomposing before him. "We were trotting together on donkeys, before diverging to the separate cells where each of us had chosen to live, out in the mountains."

"What did you talk about?"

"Heavens! I don't remember. It was just after the war. And we never spoke again – till now."

"So did you feel you got to know him, then?"

"Not really. It was tacitly assumed that neither would pry into the other."

"Do you think he might have been in British Military Intelligence?"

Were you, Father Mark? Let me put the question to you directly in this account I'm finding myself writing to you – but with what likelihood of an answer, I'm simply not sure.

"I've already told you," Father Erich said sharply, in a response of his own. "We didn't dig into one another's past. That's the whole point of the monastery."

"I thought God was."

"Well, of course," Father Erich said, his mouth forming the smile with which he added: "We're all answering a spiritual call, aren't we?" Then his eyes grew quite still. "Who knows if Father Mark was in intelligence? Everybody was something in the war ... Anyway, we talked about the dangers of political heavy-handedness in Germany. Not just the Werewolf –"

"The Werewolf?"

"The Nazi resistance movement in '45 and '46," he said. "That apart, millions of Germans had been Nazi party members. They and their families could never accept denazification, or trials for war crimes. And they made up a huge bloc of voters that could – and would – cost parties elections. It's what Adenauer found. If you wanted the new, democratic Germany, with a broad-based majority government, you simply couldn't go on raking up what everyone had been. Memory's disastrous: silence counts."

The monastery was utterly still, answering with a silence of its own. Father Erich was looking at me. The atmosphere was uncomfortable.

"So," I said, eager to change the subject, "you may not have got to know Father Mark well, but you obviously had things to say to each other. And I daresay you became friends with the years, if nothing else."

"Yes and no. Monks don't go to a monastery seeking friendship, especially not hermits. The brethren aren't looking to one another for intimacy, or even to be understood."

"What do they want?"

"*La Vita Nuova.* A new start. That's the Christian promise, isn't it? They simply want a well-regulated atmosphere in which to be reborn, without having someone suddenly loom up to pull one back to the old, abandoned self." Father Erich stopped talking, slowing down his breathing. "No, a monastery's a place to let go of the past. To forget and be forgotten."

"That makes it sound deadening, like anaesthesia. But you must have felt something more for this place, or you wouldn't have returned to it now. You obviously miss certain brethren here."

"Mm ... It's true that you get drawn to some people," Father Erich said in the gentle shade of this fig tree. "They get under your skin – especially the young," he smiled, expansive now, touching me on the arm. We continued sitting there, hands, faces mottled by sun and leaf shadow. We were almost grafted together. Yet now the old man sighed. "But actually, they're all just phantoms from the past," he barely rasped. "Survival in the here and now keeps forcing one on." His voice was gathering strength. "It's a cruel truth. You can't allow yourself to get left behind. Only cripples and ghosts do that. You must have the determination to survive. Will power is vital. It's fatal to linger in the same place, no matter what life was there once. Its reality vanishes, like a star growing cold. There's nothing here except desert. Just listen to the wind when it scatters those lifeless expanses of sand. It's a death rattle."

17

I went back to my cell. Even if I had seen the point of working, the impulse could never have survived incessant playbacks of today's conversations. They overwhelmed all other thoughts, even later when I opened the door and stared at dark buildings.

Afternoon, evening, night: each faded in turn. They must have since I got up to peer into the dawn, with yesterday's haunting presences surviving my dreams to dominate my mind.

I stared at the desert, ever fiercer – apparently with one who had evaporated back into it. For now she was looming again just as painfully in my brain. She was absorbing my mental energy: she, and my feelings for her, no less than these strangely powerful images of the recent monk.

Finally, I set out a finished lunch tray. Leaving my cell, I approached the maize, the water, the fig tree. It was the same time as it had been yesterday. This afternoon, though, the adobe bench was deserted. I continued into monastery grounds remote from my daily round. I came to myself climbing mouldy-smelling stairs that led to the library.

I had been here before, on my first full day in the monastery, incomprehensibly long ago. Then I had become absorbed in my project by my sallies into the desert. Only now was I fully taking in what was scarcely more than a reading room. Looking past the four rows of shelves, with faded spines of volumes in the brethren's several European languages, I noticed the orderliness of the place.

Different newspapers were set in piles on one of the two long tables with chairs. I noticed the Italian daily my mother and I used to take. One of these was laid out – still, presumably, as when its last reader had been fatally disturbed.

There were maps on the walls. One showed vanished areas of national sovereignty; a multicoloured colonial world all gone. A globe on a bookcase was coming off its axis. I sank into a chair without so much as glancing at the press. Not going on with my project, not knowing what to do with the information I had amassed, not having the least idea of what I should do instead … I simply sat there.

It was as if I did not dare show interest in anything, fearing to pursue the least line of enquiry. My mind was at once heavy and blank. I stared out, eyes unfocused.

I was awakened by a crackling. I raised my head. I must have slept for hours. The sun was waning through the window.

The crackling stopped. There was a muted sound, a voice behind the shelves. I got up and, moving with quiet steps, found a door. I turned the handle and came upon Father Erich in the business office. The monk was standing against a roll-top desk, turning the knob on a radiotelephone. Startled, he switched it off, a small black address book open before him.

"I could barely get through," Father Erich said, looking over chipped horn-rim glasses. "Just tell me what *does* work in this country!"

"I thought you'd left. The refectory and chapel looked closed last night. My food was simply left out for me on a tray."

"I wasn't remotely hungry. I told Fatma to serve you as she usually does. All I wanted was to sleep – which I did, instantly. Coming here has exhausted me. Quite apart from the strain of having to leave the place where I've finally managed to live in peace, not to mention the travel by donkey, especially at my age, it's been nerve-wracking to come upon this situation."

"So you've pointed out," I said.

"Well, it's not easy to cope with it, you know, my boy," he said, putting a hand on my shoulder, drawing me back into the reading room.

"I see you've been using our library," he said, glancing around. "It's a bit antiquated, like some of us Fathers. We're fossils buried out in the desert, though not the kind worth studying. Anyway, the books are full of insects – all intact, as I'm sure you'd find. It means they died long ago, before your nuclear testing," he said laughing. "What an idea!"

I did not respond directly. Looking away, I muttered: "I'm going to have to give up my project. Everything I've found is monstrous."

Father Erich took me in, dejected. "And all the world is turned to ash." He might have been quoting poetry.

"*Nuclear* ash," I said.

"*Touché*," Father Erich said mockingly. "But it all started with the Manhattan Project – although German scientists were developing something very similar during the war. The Americans beat us to it. But then, the US went on to have a large number of German scientists who made their biggest advances for them."

He paused an instant, thoughtful. I blinked as he put a hand on my arm to continue: "The American public might be surprised to know quite what they owe us Germans. Although our scientists had few illusions about the gratitude they'd receive. They knew a witch hunt was shaping up. They left, many of them, for pastures some of their colleagues had considered greener even from the start. So many brilliant people Germany lost to so many countries after 1945! If these men had been given only a little longer, Germany might have *won* the war! Then things would look very different today. How awful!"

"The weapons they made are terrible."

"Mm ... Defeat's terrible, too. Who knows where good and evil begin and end? A nun from Bremen told me that one summer evening, during the war, she looked up from her needlework in the cloister. Staring up at the sunset, she saw a plane flaming down. It was the most beautiful sight she'd ever seen. Later that night, an SS patrol found the remains in a turnip field. The pilot had been cremated. They discovered his wedding ring glinting around a bone."

Silence deepened in the increasing gloom.

"What are your recollections of the war?" I asked. "Have you ever thought of writing about it?"

"The war is impossible to explain to those who didn't experience it. It had an indescribable atmosphere. People come to it with such preconceptions these days. Anyway, I only saw a small corner of it, as an unimportant pen pusher. I really can't tell you much about it. Certainly not as much as you can find out about it yourself in books. It's a dream we can't remember now we've woken up ... It's better not to dwell on those years. Don't let's think of who everyone was then, who was responsible for what. Some people are obsessed with it. It turns everything into the plot of a cheap thriller. No, understanding the war's impossible. It's no use trying to assign praise or blame.

"*If seven maids,*" Father Erich said, lapsing into singsong English, "*with seven mops –*"

" – *Swept the sand for half a year ...*"
"*Do you suppose," the Walrus said,*"
"*That they could get it clear?*"
"*I doubt it,' said the Carpenter,*"
"*And shed a bitter tear.*"

"You know the poem by Lewis Carroll, don't you, my boy?" Father Erich said it sweetly, returning to German. It transported me back to far-off infancy, in which I lay enthralled by a parent's bedtime story. "Like the Carpenter, all we can do is cry. Quite useless! My time alone in my cell, years of it, looking out with only endless desert before me, has allowed me to understand that." ("You will too, when you grow up one day," I all but heard him go on to say.) "And it's spurred me into regrouping – spiritually ... No, luckily I had such a minor role that I had no specific responsibility for anything. Only our general guilt."

The man's hands had been moving. I'd watched their arcs, the interlocking fingers securing them now the words were ended. I continued looking at them in these mute moments, with the old man's mixture of lingering contrition and detachment. How distant, finally unreachable, he appeared!

"I must be going," the monk said.

He led off down the library stairs. We walked side by side, across a path, sand filling our sandals. There was a great stillness, a strangely dreamlike sense of reality. The chapel stood ahead in the dusk. We halted before the adobe sheet of darkness, almost a screen. I had an unreasoning sense of something – an image, could it be? – about to lighten it. I was aware of Father Erich's hand, recently so other, suddenly this close to my own. A hair from the back of it touched one from mine – with a near shock. Holding there, I heard:

"Shall we say the Our Father together?"

It was he who did so, standing there outside the chapel.

Now we were looking out in silence, Erich's hand on my shoulder. His eyes gleamed fugitively, as if in a dream.

All at once, too gruff for more emotion, the old man turned off without warning. I was left facing blankness. I felt a sharp access of emotion as darkness total as sleep swallowed up the Desert Father.

*

I continued looking into the night. It was an obscurity continuing into the next day, despite the bright, then burning, sunlight. I lay, sat, stood, at a loss. My inner dimness sought its kind, taking me into the gloom of the chapel. I entered a pew almost in a swoon. I broke into a sweat, trying to focus – albeit with this feeling of emptiness, of inertness, beside the carving of the Holy Family. It left me heavy as a stone from the Saharan rock field towards which I had sometimes wandered.

I clambered out of the pew and left the chapel. The monastery was silent. The refectory was closed. Meals would obviously appear, disappear, reappear on trays.

I continued in search of Father Erich. He was no more: in my heart of hearts, I knew it. Here was unpeopled; inhabited only by shades. But I went on looking for the man in all the places where he'd been.

Once more I went to the library. I must have climbed the stairs too quickly: out of breath, dazed, I was facing a stack of newspapers. I could hardly focus on the pinkish pages by this dim, quivering light. Then I glanced again at a copy of the Italian paper we once read at home, opened out before me. It dated from about the time I arrived at the monastery, making me realise how long it had been since I used to read that particular newspaper. There was the personal column with advertisements for meeting partners. Messages, letters were also sent, as always, from God knew who to God knew whom or where, their identities and intentions concealed in initials and private references.

I blinked, again seeming to lose balance from wildly hunting down a phantom, here where my project, my reason for being, was aborted. I felt my headache surge, continuous after so many months in this heat. My eyes hurt from close, frequently microscopic study by glaring sunlight, mere torchlight or a dismal bulb such as this.

I squinted at the title on the opposite page: *UN Agency Reports Worldwide Increase in Secret Nuclear Testing.*

Of course I recognised the article's importance. It leapt out at me in answer to views already forming in my mind. Even so, I did not – could not – read the article continuously. Rather than following it slowly from start to finish, with its full meaning emerging gradually of its own accord, whole paragraphs confronted me in no strict order. The type itself vibrated, fiery, together with the significance one cluster of words, then another, abruptly took on in my mind.

I finally forced myself to reread the article carefully, from beginning to end. Even so, it radiated in my mind with a meaning for this place specifically, for me indeed, regardless of its simultaneous reference to other situations.

I'll give you the gist of the article now, Father Mark. Let me do so for the inherent importance of what it said, but also for all I shall go on to record of what was to happen as a result of it. And desiring you to know it, to see it as I have, now makes me realise, finally, quite how much my wish for your understanding explains why I have, from the outset, been writing this account for you.

The paper's Vienna correspondent wrote that, according to The International Atomic Energy Agency, a growing number of countries were seeking to develop nuclear capacities well in excess of their civilian needs. Despite their commitments under the Non-Proliferation Treaty, many were already operating heavy-water reactors and had the facility to produce military-grade plutonium. Developing-world states saw no reason why the possession of weapons of mass destruction should remain a Western prerogative. This was certainly the case with parties to long-standing conflicts such as those over Kashmir and Palestine. The Agency's director noted in his recent press conference that, given the apparently irresoluble nature of such disputes, participants were finding the nuclear option increasingly attractive.

This was at a time when the necessary expertise and materials had become more available. Such governments, indeed all groups with nuclear ambitions, now had access not only to Germany's wartime scientists but to a nuclear black market based in Pakistan. The result was an apparent surge in secret testing, whether atmospheric, terrestrial or subterranean. This clearly posed a challenge to international security, the Director said. But quite as troubling was the threat of nuclear terrorism. Increasing political fractionalisation had breakaway provinces, ethnic minorities and religious groups opposing the central state and the military programmes strengthening it. They repeatedly planned acts of nuclear sabotage.

For example, Islamists opposed the very idea of the secular state. They sought to destroy weapons programmes with spectacular assassinations of those developing them. Not least, they resented any pollution of their God-given Sahara. It smacked of the atom bomb tests by France, the colonial power, in the 1960s.

I rubbed my eyes and returned to the article, reading slowly, then pushed aside the paper – whose last reader had been a monk, though surely not a murdered one. I sat staring into the dim light, the window dark.

I had a feeling of oppression. It was apparently affecting my breathing, this polluting atmosphere – even here, where I had been talking with Father Erich. Deforming, making monstrous in no time, it was a contagion I had to escape. No project, no person, need detain me. Why! I felt unclean already, recoiling from my own skin.

I got up and walked into the business office. Without much expectation of the radiotelephone working for me any more than it had for its last user, I turned the knob.

I heard a woman's voice. She spoke in French. I began explaining where I was; she already knew. I asked for the police. The officer answered. Yes, they would arrange for a car to collect me, and take me to the bus for the capital, tomorrow. It was high time I was leaving. I should never have been staying on my own. Terrible things were happening out there.

I returned to my cell. I did not feel remotely like going to bed, though I knew I should. To sleep for eight hours, a whole third of a day, would stifle this anxiety that had mounted in me since speaking to the officer. It would help me through this otherwise endless final night.

I ought to pack, I thought. A heavy inertia fell upon me. Unthinkingly, I picked up a sketchbook. In the dim electric light I flicked past the early pages, stopping at the series of sand. They were too abstract to be read as anything in particular. Still, I went on looking at them – till the image was overcome by an inner sensation of sand flowing across my foot, firm against the sole.

I got up, switching off the light to look out at the desert. It was brilliant with stars as always. I wanted to walk towards it, as I had done night after night. But this evening it seemed almost to vibrate with danger – in spite of which I felt an irresistible impulse to enter it this final time.

Leaving the cell I felt light, invisible surges against my toes, bare in sandals, as I followed the path to the main gate. I made my way out onto the firm shelf surrounding the monastery, stopping just beyond it, before that glittering vastness. Less staring than taking it in, I felt it part of some inner, half-illuminated vacancy.

Holding still there, I moved the tip of my sandal through sand abstractedly. Backwards and forwards it travelled, making small arcs. Then I found myself thinking of the insects that came out in the night. I might be disturbing them now as I used to, collecting my quarry: ruined creatures all, though just a fraction of fated millions.

I realised that my foot was leaving curve after curve; I had another image of one of my still-lifes. A voice came into my mind asking what it was, with disturbing clarity.

"It's sand. I was thinking about what was written in the sand by whoever killed the monks."

"Did you ever find out what it said?"

"The police told me: 'Death to the intruder bringing death to our land.'"

"What does it mean?"

The sound of her voice lingered …

It was utterly silent in the dark, before the voided congregation of monks. Only after a time did my ears attune to this breeze. It blew through my borrowed habit, chilling me to the bone as, unaided, I sought a pattern in the stars. If I gazed at that infinite scattering long enough, maybe I'd glimpse the myths they supposedly embodied. I might even find my celestial bearings. And a dawn could arise that would take me, finally, into the world and a life lived fully as my own.

I headed back to the monastery. Entering it, I continued my wandering and came upon the brethren's quarters. I had been in them once before, some time ago. Now I sought the cell occupied by a man returning from the deep Sahara.

I came upon one that I supposed must be it. Deserted, its bedcover rumpled, it contained no personal items – except on the desk. I recognised the thick, cream envelope even before I saw Father Carlo's writing. I removed the paperweight, a desert stone, and withdrew the letter.

Dear Father Erich, I read.

It is too long since we last saw each other. This is, I know, because you are doing the Lord's work in the Sahara. But it is a state of affairs that should, even so, be rectified without delay, before death or any other dire circumstance abruptly intervenes.

The Devil is everywhere afoot, especially now. Snakes surround us, in the grass and in the desert; in the meadow and the valley. Take heed!

I commend to you the bearer of this letter. You will form your own impression of him. You will, I believe, Father, want to extend to him your most paternal sympathies.

Make haste, while I may still offer you all that fraternal love can provide.

Your brother in Christ,

Carlo.

*

I was up early next morning, packing. It would not take long. I took the letter together with my sketches and photographs, although I left all those specimens. Much else could be jettisoned. I'd carry only one suitcase, allowing me to emerge in Europe, my load lightened, as though from a dark dream.

Nevertheless, my packing done, I could not entirely leave well enough alone. Sipping coffee, a hand cupping the earthenware bowl, the four fingertips settling instinctively onto the black dots, I gazed unthinkingly through the window. No matter that I had forbidden myself to search the desert, with all its silent emptiness.

The trail of distant dust must have been approaching through hazy light for some minutes by the time I was aware of seeing it. I had not expected the police to arrive quite so early, although I wasn't sure why not: the officer had never said precisely when I would be collected. Perhaps, eager as I was to leave, I wanted just a little longer alone; a wistful hour, say, yearning to come to terms, finally, with all my monastic retreat had amounted to. I might even worry out a positive conclusion to my dismally inconclusive time there. For my intense scrutiny over the months had confronted me with terrible truths about the insects: nuclear testing. It had killed my project, my *raison d'être*, making it impossible to remain in this poisoned atmosphere. Maybe it could now leave me instead with something redeeming, in this brutally foreshortened period I'd apparently elected to endure in the Sahara.

In fact, I did no more than take off my habit and put on the clothes I'd set out. I had arrived in them, and would wear them for the journey back. I picked up my suitcase, turning away from the door to take in the room, its window, that achingly wide sweep of desert, this last instant. I had folded the blanket on the bed, left the breakfast tray on the desk and stacked the containers of specimens by the wastepaper basket.

The cell, its white walls, said nothing, revealed next to nothing of its departing occupant's passage there through the uncounted months.

I walked with my luggage over the sandy path, aware, without looking, of the trees, the bushes, the running water. I passed the chapel, turning to the main gate.

I dropped my case before walking through. Beyond the heavy shade of the portico I heard a vehicle approaching – with that same irrational hopefulness as ever. But I couldn't make out the mere police car it must be after all, dazzled for an instant by that large rectangle of light.

18

A jeep was parking. It had the garish orange logo of an oil company across its side. A middle-aged man got out: balding, with a gut. He walked over to the monastery gate, sweating profusely in his khaki company trousers and shirt. Dark hair showed at the open neck.

"Hi! You're the Bug Man, aren't you?"

He spoke with an American accent, chewing gum. It exuded the sweet odour of spearmint in short bursts of breath, giving him an air of barely controlled excitement. "You know Sarah, right?" It was a demand.

"If that's who she was, Mr, er ...?" Other queries were forming.

"Mizrahi. David Mizrahi. And you're ...?"

"The Bug Man, apparently."

"Look, why d'you say 'was' – 'who she *was*'? When did you last see her?"

"Oh, yesterday morning, it must have been," I said, casting my mind over that huge expanse of intervening time. "Yes, late morning."

"What were you doing, the two of you?"

I flushed, nervous, sensing his resentment. "Talking. Saying goodbye, in fact."

"And then?"

"She continued working. She'd been surveying a site about a kilometre and a half away. I just walked back here."

Saying it, I asked myself how Mizrahi had been able to take the conversational initiative. I shouldn't allow myself to be interrogated.

"And you're sure you didn't see her go off?"

"Yes ... But why do you ask?"

"She hasn't returned to camp."

"What!"

"Hey!" Mizrahi said as I leaned against the jeep. "Don't let's jump to conclusions here. She's stayed out nights before, without notice, including in previous seasons. Only, thing is," he said, and quietened, "she knew we were setting off today …"

His jaws had stopped working on the gum. His eyes were fixed distantly to the ground. "So, if she appears hereabouts –"

"I'm leaving, myself."

"Ah, yes! So I see," Mizrahi said, glimpsing the suitcase in the portico. He moved into its shade. "Been here long?"

"It feels so."

"That bad?"

"I thought you were going to visit the monastery before. And some village or other."

"I was. But Sarah was researching here. And I was investigating there. When you're together, real close, like we, er, are, you have to give each other space." Mizrahi was gazing out vacantly, mutely. "Then it got real dangerous out here," he said. He spoke very quietly, screwing up his eyes to take in the farthest horizon.

I squinted too, as what I was hearing registered – together with a sudden answer to that earlier query I was only now fully aware of having formed: *Where have I seen this man before?* It had been while waiting for my bus in the capital, endless months ago. And I had just realised who the woman had been, bending her shapely back to me to load luggage into their company jeep.

"Say," Mizrahi said with an alarming brightening of tone. "I'm surprised you stuck it out, after what happened in the monastery."

"I had a project."

"The bugs."

"Exactly. But it's over now. So I must go."

"All the projects round here seem to be coming to an end," Mizrahi said.

"Like the nuclear one?"

He glanced sharply at me. "What makes you say that?" His eyes narrowed. He was surveying me steadily.

"Among other things, I infer it from an article in the paper."

"Oh?"

"An interview with the director of The International Atomic Energy Agency. He all but states that the Islamists are making it impossible to continue the nuclear testing programme out here."

"Interesting," Mizrahi said, moving his head to one side as if to weigh the plausibility of the claim. "Of course, *if* it's the case, you don't have to be Einstein to realise there'll be a sudden secret flight of scientists. Not that I think Einstein would ever have been one of them. But then that's really the point, isn't it? Those likely to be involved around here would all be Germans of the war generation. But they didn't immigrate to the US like Uncle Albert – or, if they were naturalised, they eventually found themselves in danger of being *de*naturalised and came here. It doesn't take much imagination to know who they were working for till '45 – or with what beliefs."

"You can't paint *all* Germans with the same brush," I said tartly.

"I just excluded Einstein."

"Wasn't he Swiss?"

"Maybe. But there's so much information coming to light now, especially from the Wiesenthal Center, that there's little doubt about it."

"The What Center?"

"The Wiesenthal Center," Mizrahi said, bemused. "You must've heard of it – if you haven't been living, well, in some monastery in the deep Sahara."

He showed perfect American teeth. It was a prompt to laugh at his little joke. The cue was not taken.

In the face of a mere stare, he continued: "You know, the outfit in California founded by Simon Wiesenthal, the Nazi hunter. He caught Eichmann."

"I see."

"Well," Mizrahi said, almost embarrassed out of humour by such coldness, "these scientists are Nazis. What could please them more than to help an Arab government develop nuclear arms targeting Israel? And a mass murderer doesn't change his spots."

"Can things really be that simple?" I said, wondering whether this amounted to much more than the man's inventive assumptions.

"Perhaps," Mizrahi said, tonelessly. "Anyway, they'll be on the run now, if they know what's good for them – assuming what you 'infer' is true."

"*Is* it?"

"How would I know?"

We held there a moment, and he ended the stiffness between us by moving back to the jeep.

"So, would you like to come in and see the monastery before you – before *we* go?" I asked, perhaps at the prospect of finding myself quite abandoned now in the desert, or on behalf of an absent community that had extended its hospitality to me all this time.

Mizrahi looked over at it for a moment. "Don't see why not, since I'm here."

The sun was rising higher. We felt its presence, wandering into the cloister.

"That's the chapel. Would you like to go in?"

There was no answer. Mizrahi was looking up at it, his bare head wet, cheeks dripping. He sank onto the adobe bench, partially shaded by trees and flowering bushes. I joined him.

"Did you get to know Sarah well?" he finally said, gazing quietly off to the guest house.

"I realise now that I didn't know her at all," I said flatly, dejectedly even, half-looking at this unexpected partner of hers. "I don't think she even wanted to be known."

"Perceptive," Mizrahi said, possibly with an air of relief. "There were very few people she ever trusted sufficiently to level with."

Mizrahi, in warmer, increasingly friendly tones, to which I reacted by moving my sandal through the sand, went on to say that I had apparently become one of that select number trusted by the woman he had been about to marry – until, registering the tense into which he had slipped, he cut in upon himself: "I *know* we'll find her."

His rapid intakes of breath made him sound like a muffled horse. His temples bulged as he chewed harder, faster. Then he calmed himself, I observed, realising I myself was thereby growing calmer. Now Mizrahi said: "The police are out looking for her. Anyway, she's always turned up before."

Panic reined in, he looked deliberately around him. He took in the monastery and changed the subject.

"How do you feel about being involved with the Church?"

"I don't think about it. I'm not a practising Catholic. I probably don't even believe in God."

"But aren't you bothered by the Roman Catholic Church's behaviour? It's hardly been very Christian, has it?"

"You mean the Inquisition?"

"That, and all the help they gave the Nazis after the war."

"What help?"

Mizrahi went on to describe a vital escape route the Church provided: the so-called "monastery route" between Austria and Italy. Then transport was provided from Italy to South America, although some also came to the Middle East.

"Isn't that far-fetched?" I said.

"No. It's fact."

Now I was staring at Mizrahi. Neither spoke.

Still greater silence extended beyond our breathing, the water pouring into the cistern, droning flies. It was the silence of that expanse spreading endlessly beyond the monastery walls.

"I'd like to know about Sarah," I said. "When she comes back, I mean."

"Of course. But you say you're leaving here."

"Yes, I'm going back to Rome. But I haven't an address there yet."

"Here's my card." It was the oil company's address in California. "Drop me a line when you get yourself a place. Or else send me a letter through the personal columns of the newspaper."

He half-laughed at the silliness of his joke. "But it's not as crazy as it sounds. This friend of mine at the Wiesenthal Center says that's how some of the old comrades and their families stay in touch."

"I'll write to you," I said quietly.

We got up from the bench by some unspoken accord and walked to the gate together. Mizrahi shook hands with me, surprisingly warmly. He got in the jeep.

Now it was invisible in the engulfing brilliance.

19

I went back into the monastery. Barely a step away from the gate, I smarted with a sense of betrayal. But I simply had to stop thinking about her, halted there. I need not have feared she was in peril. It had been Mizrahi's soothing message: she'd always turned up in the past.

Besides, "going missing" had meant, from Mizrahi's unknowing point of view, time spent here. It was what had passed with her fiancé's undeclared rival – apparently only an adventure for her. It had held next to no significance as far as she was concerned. So if this was the definition of "missing", her disappearance was no more serious than I, standing by the monastery entrance, had been for her. And if it hurt me, it was only the pain of having her thereby confirm what Mizrahi had unwittingly revealed: that she was not remotely bonded to me. It certainly wasn't the torment of worrying that she was in dire danger.

There was no need to seek her in a Sahara extending infinitely beyond that gate, I thought, the air swimming before me. My thoughts were disintegrating, like remnants of dreams. I could get no part of them clear. I should simply turn my back on the desert, unremembered, unmourned, for all the good being brought face to face with it had done me.

I was very ready to go, my suitcase set just within the entrance. It would be safe there, though I did not know exactly when the police would arrive to collect me. Nobody was there except, perhaps, the old woman. Yet I doubted that I was more likely to see the maternal Bedouin cook than anyone else. She felt like another of those invisible souls. I wanted to say goodbye to her, to give her something in person, not simply to leave her, in exchange for all her trays, my own trays of dead insects – so many! For I'd also killed the specimens I had been keeping alive in vials. Nothing would survive my departure.

I looked back at the sand, barren but inwardly teeming with nocturnal creatures. The atmosphere they breathed was horribly contaminated.

Thinking of them, crisp and deformed out of recognition, I shuddered.

I could not identify a specific place from which the uncleanness radiated. But all, including the freshest, most beautiful and desirable, would be ruined. What seemed perfect must turn out to be monstrous. Such deception!

It was a power of corruption at work – just as when someone, seemingly well yet with a vile contagion, spoke: hearing him, fastened by his glinting eye, one could not know what droplets, like seemingly innocent words, would actually fall as venom from his mouth. They would issue beyond the discoloured teeth, microscopically spraying one. Lungs would inhale them. The heart would pump the infection all around the body. One's very being would be unknowingly impregnated.

I simply had to separate from this silent, covert source of horror! Anyone would have to leave this place, never to remember it, or revisit.

I was back to looking through the monastery gate at the expanse to be travelled. Its arid vastness was imposing. Those far mountains were magnificent. But they held in poisonous air.

The police had still to arrive.

I turned back, thinking of waiting in the chapel. My steps were arrested – as they'd been one recent dusk when I'd inexplicably expected something to lighten the building's dark adobe wall, perhaps an image. Still, I knew that within, I'd have sat quietly. Even so, calm would have evaded me in the pew. Again I would be straining to get my thoughts clear. Confused, I would take in sour-smelling shadows. The lethal effect seemed palpable, just imagining it. The feeling weighed upon me like an incubus: a being barely beyond my reach whom I here, outside the chapel, dreaded to imagine might unexpectedly face me.

The sun was a physical force. I retreated to an adobe corner by the gate, leaning there as if to hide from the alarming impressions of that apparition. It had, of course, already vanished, losing itself in new pastures, there to continue sowing its seeds of destruction.

Still, I remained a mere shadow, in this dim recess. I was suffocating here. Peering through the gate was just as bad; glare scorched the ashen expanse.

*

"Terrible things are happening out there."

The police inspector's words came unbidden to my mind as I awaited him, gazing out as I'd done so many times. How I'd searched those tracts from which, after each of my bouts of suspense, she had returned – supposedly just to excavate!

Wondering if she might suddenly reappear now too, longing for the miracle despite my angry resentment, I dared imagine that the young woman, tiring of her partner, also felt drawn again and again to a monastery's secular occupant. In which case she'd not have treated me as a mere diversion after all. She'd be taking me as seriously as I'd assumed at the time – truly caring for me, if passingly.

My feelings for the woman were surging back, and I panicked again at losing her. I trembled to think how I could continue without her – though even more pressingly by whatever danger might have come upon her.

Then there was no question of just saving my own skin, fleeing this, the most dangerous place in the world – not least with its lethal pollution. I must rescue her, too.

I had to find her. It was a wild compulsion, but, eyes arcing from shoulder to shoulder, taking in the fullest view from the monastery, I faced the obvious question: How? I had no idea where to look. I'd barely ventured into that wilderness the entire time I had been here. I'd held to the rim of just several largely nocturnal kilometres round the monastery.

I could simply let the army and police search, as they had for the monks' assassins; but they might never find them and this was a potential atrocity that really mattered to me, unlike the nuclear tests I was cold-shouldering, not to mention that slaughter of anonymous brethren with which, I barely dared admit, this might, after all, have some connection.

I could not turn my back on what was happening in the desert. I felt driven to hunt there – as I'd once done for my father. That had been in my infant mind, conjuring him up in a sandstone cave or emerging from a barely cultivated fringe of the sub-Sahara. Yet my youthful imagination was to fail. My mental screen had soon blacked out. Now, for the first time, I would search in fact. I could not resist it. I ached to find her.

How? The question arose again, leading me to suppose I should have asked Mizrahi to take me with him to look for her in his company truck. But it would have shown too much interest in the man's partner. Besides, the police officer was sending a car to pick me up. Not that he would hunt, except with his own men.

Of course the old woman, the cook, was safe, despite being nowhere to be seen – certainly not with her donkey surely ridden off long ago by Father Erich. And where was *he* in all that sand?

Holding back would, then, have been the rational thing to do. Not least because she would probably return to camp, unharmed, as Mizrahi had said. One should not assume the worst. I might do best to wait patiently for the police officer as arranged. And yet I was diverging from this suitcase, leaving it unguarded on the sand. My footsteps led me out through the gate. They brought me out into the open, where blind instinct forced me beyond the monastery in mounting morning heat.

On and on I paced, in a reverie so feverish that my mind kept going blank as to whom I was tracking down. I had illusive glimpses of several quarries. They repeatedly merged. All I knew was that something within me was finally propelling me out into desert, questing, driven to find.

*

The search hurried me away from the adobe walls, from my confining passivity. I coursed through the mental barrier I'd extended a kilometre beyond the monastery's perimeter. Behind it, I'd taken refuge in thought from the war being waged all around. Now, flexing my muscles, acting – inconceivable before – I rushed on breathlessly, in a near trance, uncertain if I'd achieve anything but driven to advance.

Here in limitless desert, unremittingly silent, static, dry, I raged ahead like the violent storm that had once caught me. I was a flash flood, arising inexplicably as a distant rumble beneath a hard blue sky, only to gush deafeningly through parched boulders. The torrent would deluge this geological record of time which, unbeknown to itself, had been eternally awaiting sudden inundation.

The ground was moist here – obviously prompting these thoughts. Unthinkingly, I had made past low mimosa bushes into a gorge where, one sunset, I had padded through wet sand in a twisting ditch. Unthinkingly – but not without reason. This scorched morning, I had an unexpected mental image of pursuing her seeking fossils exactly where she had once told me she found them: in a gully.

The last time I was here I was taken aback by voices that had panicked me, but which belonged to the men who had been repairing an underground canal. They had offered a seeming-monk tea, cigarettes, the food they were lounging round a fire to eat. Seeming to hear them again, I strode into the clearing.

I came upon three men, not workmen. They were standing, alert. They must have sprung up the instant before at the sound of my approach. Seeing me, they merely settled back on their haunches as I asked if they had seen a young woman.

They couldn't have understood my French. One pulled at my trouser leg for me to join them, sitting on the ground, as they continued talking in Maghrebi. The man rested a hand on an upright rifle, saying something that made the others laugh.

The joke was salacious to judge, from the way he sucked appreciatively with his tongue on his upper teeth. He lowered his eyelids heavily to further cackling. The hilarity took on a life of its own. So, preferring to suppose that they had not originally understood my question, I asked again about the girl. It was no good; but they would not let me go when, despairing of them, I started to get up. They insisted on me remaining with the group.

Anxious to move on, I found myself transfixed. They were forcing dried dates on me. How long I continued there!

A walkie-talkie sounded, its electronic noise discordant in the copse. The joker answered and started speaking into it, agitatedly. Suddenly, with a brisk movement of his hand, he shut off the machine, snarling something. I found a gun pointed at me. The others, standing too, seized me by the arms, weapons hanging from their fatigues and burnooses. They snatched my wallet and residency card from my pockets.

Protesting, I smelled the garlic and tobacco on their breath. My voice seemed to come from outside me, in a place where something was telling me I must resist. I was demanding that they release me, that they return what they had taken, that I had done nothing wrong.

A vice gripped my stomach. It paralysed, as I was led off into the one situation I had dreaded beneath the surface of my every Saharan second, aware of it or not. I had somehow always been certain that it must eventually come. Now it had opened up around me, closing me into it, for all the illusory normality of months in the monastery. I didn't know what felt more unreal: long suspended animation, or these night-marish moments.

Then, as if to counteract my passivity, I felt a powerful rumbling in my bowels. I nearly fainted with the grinding. I could not contain it. Loudly, I insisted in a language my captors did not understand, but for a purpose they did, that I absolutely must find a place to squat. I did not wait for permission by those bushes. They kept watch over them, on my head.

Off we set again, soon coming to a track. I was amazed that it was so near. It showed me how little sense I had of even this, my tiny fraction of the desert – revealing, furthermore, just how restricted my focus had been all the time I was at the monastery.

We came to a lorry. A guard tied my hands and pushed me into the back. Sitting there, under canvas, I had my feet bound together. Then the guard got in too, lounging with his gun over his knees.

Outside, the others were using the walkie-talkie again. A voice came through as a loud crackle. Was it giving orders regarding an unexpected prisoner to men who'd been awaiting instructions for who knew what, near their vehicle in a patch of shade?

Wondering how much longer I'd be kept in this stifling gloom, and whether it would only be to get out again here or be driven somewhere else, I kept glancing into the painful brilliance. I waited interminably, fading in and out of the awareness that I absolutely must escape; that I had to concentrate on how to do so.

A face came into my mind: hers. I was asking myself if this was what had happened to her – when the crackling stopped. There was utter silence. An instant later a second guard jumped into the back. The lorry vibrated. We were moving.

*

A twisted cloth was tied across my eyes. It was tight, acrid with sweat. I shied away from wondering how much worse things might get.

As the lorry moved, sand stung my skin. I felt a rush of air against the lower half of my cheek. It went on and on. It scorched each time a jolt roused me. Later, though I had no idea how much, fingers returned me to full consciousness. The bottom of the blindfold had fallen over my nose, and they were raising it. A cigarette was placed between my lips. It was thin, and must have been rolled by the man I could hear striking a match. I inhaled. The end took the light instantly.

I was not a smoker, so the cigarette made me cough. Still, I drew on it each time it was invisibly returned to my lips, gulping the air. My chest was bursting. After inhaling several times, I noticed the cigarette's odour, its taste. I was growing heady, numbed. It contained hashish.

Her face came to mind again. More than a likeness, it – the very atmosphere of it – filled the entire screen of my thoughts. I had an indescribably sweet sense of the feel of it. I was filled with tenderness for her now, in my arms, our hearts pounding, back in my cell. We ached with love. I was unbearably protective of her.

I was being fed water from a plastic bottle. It was warm. I guzzled breathlessly, thirsty from the hashish – a word my mind locked onto, recalling it had been corrupted into *assassin*. I wondered what refinement of sadism led the men I heard giggling beside me to offer these consolations.

Beneath the sound, the noise of the lorry now registered too. I grew increasingly aware that long-held, high-pitched notes had been approaching. My mind's eye gave them to a *muezzin* calling to noon prayer from atop a minaret. The hour was confirmed by the intensity of sun on my forearm and cheeks.

The lorry jerked to a stop. The back flap was released and my ankles were untied. Still blindfolded, I was guided down onto what I was surprised to find was a hard surface: concrete. It made me recognise how accustomed I had grown to sand underfoot, over the months.

My legs were leaden as I was stopped in a body of heat. Someone else had apparently joined the guards. I felt I would collapse if I had to wait here much longer, hearing the new arrival call out in French into a walkie-talkie the prisoner's name, residency permit number and other details. I entreated the man: I'd done nothing wrong; I should obviously be released. There was no answer, only fading footsteps. All was silent now, eerie.

I was led into shade. We were climbing steps. My blindfold was removed. Dim as it was, it still seemed dazzling and hot to me, especially with the overpowering, sweaty smell of my captors.

I blinked as I took in my surroundings. I was standing, hands bound, before a small shuttered store with a faded sign: a star. Looking round, I found myself in a small covered market, quite deserted. Here, I was standing on a balcony with other hole-in-the-wall shops like this, which overlooked the main floor below.

Several trees sprang from the earthen floor. They sent up twisting trunks to spread a canopy of leaves onto wire mesh serving as a roof. Other shops down there had stars on their shutters, too. Noticing them, I realised that the effects of the hashish had worn off, but for my thirst and heavy limbs. For, again, I was focusing strictly on her, wherever she was – and on my own escape.

The guards had undone my hands, but only to begin chaining my wrists too tightly to the balcony. Suddenly I felt an opening of the mental valve that had closed off, for whole periods, full awareness of the situation I – and presumably she – was in. In an instant I was drenched, with anxiety. Basic instinct, not courage or logic, set me flailing against my confinement. I was fighting to escape the pain in my wrists no less than my captors as I ran in my imagination along the balcony, out of the market, into ... where?

The men abandoned me. Minutes of shouting drained my strength. One of the guards came back and covered my mouth with electrical tape. Yet I'd already fallen silent. The valve had closed again. I was slumped over the balcony railing, numbed. The effect of the hashish had returned as heavy drowsiness, my loss of all sense of time, of troubled reverie.

It was just as in a dream that I came to realise I'd been joined, for a while, on either side of the gallery. Mutely they stood, lines of albino-pale, shrunken old people, backed by armed guards. They were dressed in out-of-date Western clothes. The women had headscarves on. The man next to me wore a trilby. I saw a black skullcap.

They gazed down from the balcony, waiting.

*

I was distracted by voices that came from below. Armed men, Islamists surely, were entering one of the market's side doors with several prisoners they pushed in. The captives' hands were tied behind their backs. They had on what I noticed were khaki company trousers – except for the one holding up blue jeans, her T-shirt ripped and hair dishevelled.

I gasped, a cry strangled into a screech by the tape covering my mouth, as I saw it also masked hers and Mizrahi's. A hand covered mine, gripping the railing. I felt the wedding ring. It belonged to the old man in the trilby hat. His face was impassive.

By a row of shops, the prisoners were halted. The guards were untying hands, while one, in his burnoose, barked orders incomprehensible up here. He reached to pull the T-shirt up from her jeans, above the dark hair falling onto her shoulders.

Mizrahi swung round, fist flailing, and hit him hard in the mouth. Those perfect teeth were visible, clenched, even from up here. So was the blood streaming over the guard's snarling face with what I seemed to make out as a scarred cheek and gold teeth. He was slamming back with his rifle.

Mizrahi crumpled, holding his gut. He had to be helped up and supported to take off his clothes. The jeans and T-shirt joined the company trousers on the floor. They lay beside the long stone trough, surmounted by a chiselled panel of squarish writing and taps, where I now supposed the prisoners were being brought.

So frail the bra, the scant panties, seemed, falling to the ground! Then I saw blood smearing her thighs. How unbearably pathetic was the embroidery, the sexual allure, as she stood by her stripped lover, head bent, hair over her breasts, perfect body quivering as if frozen in this heat!

189

Their hands were being bound again, this time with wire. Mizrahi was pushed, bellowing through his gag, to the trough. A guard took his head under his arm. He was made to kneel before the stone side, shoulders over the edge. It was as if he were feeding, feet frenzied. Scarface advanced – familiar, though I could not be sure. His hand glinted. Mizrahi writhed. There were stifled sobs on the balcony as his head dropped. Then he was still.

The guards made no effort to lug that naked bulk away from the spattered stone. It remained, contorted, at the place where the ritual sacrifice of animals was performed according to religious law.

I went on gazing down at that form, so pasty, shapeless, inert. To think that an instant ago it had been bursting with love, with powerless protectiveness for the one next to him! It had gone, a whole world of feeling, in the blink of an eye.

There she was, standing quite alone now, apart from the guards. I strained to see her more clearly, to contact her eyes with my own, across blocked mouths, to communicate impossibly all I felt for her.

Desperate, I drew on my chains. They rattled on the balcony. But she did not recognise me, a distant, distraught being. She was a self-absorbed image of dark tresses and clotted pubes on an unspoiled figure.

A guard put a hand on her arm. Almost solicitously, he guided her forward. Fingers splayed over the back he was forcing forward. He pushed her head down, and further down as her shrill whining grew terrifying. He was holding her, ready for another guard, across the buttocks and round her waist.

It was Scarface. He thrust out that gleaming fist. I winced as if *I* were being slashed.

My eyes denied me a clear vision of the shapely body gone slack. Hair drooped beside the formless neighbour at the trough.

I felt a grip, a ring. The old man in the trilby had been holding my hand all along.

*

My head, my eyes, drooped. God knows how long I stayed like that, distracted, as if something invisible were blanketing over all thought and feeling. Not even when I heard the Maghrebi voices, jovially calling to each other below, did I stare down at what I knew was there.

Someone was stomping up the stairs. He approached, past the people lining the balcony. My head fell even lower. I screwed up my eyes, aghast at what the footsteps now halted here meant for me, chained to the gallery.

Glancing up, finally, I saw the guard half-smile, throwing a handful of something at me. It was my wallet and residency card. There was also a metallic clink. The man clattered off, leaving the market with his comrades.

The neighbour in the trilby picked up a key. Hand trembling, he fitted it into a padlock. This loosened the chain binding my wrists to the railings. I myself removed the electrical tape from my mouth. I inhaled and sighed deeply.

"*Merci*," I said barely audibly, glimpsing, involuntarily, across the brim of that hat, the soft white forms strewn over otherwise deserted space below. Outside, there continued the harsh sound of voices. An engine started up. It ground away. The vehicle faded into the distance.

People were passing behind me along the gallery. Their silence gave way to pained whispering, as they hobbled down the stairs, past shuttered stalls – but well away from the trough. Yet the man in the skullcap was opening his shop. He and a boy dragged out a tarpaulin and started spreading it out. They covered the human debris.

"God protect us!" the man in the trilby said. "Come with me."

Putting a hand on my arm, he led me past someone telephoning agitatedly in the dimness of a half-opened grocer's shop.

Outside, it was blinding. Mizrahi's company jeep – and hers – were parked nearby. I could hardly make out the buildings except for a mosque rising ahead. I felt faint.

"Come," the elderly man insisted, holding my arm. We stopped at a two-storey stuccoed structure with a heavy wooden door. The man turned its worn metal handle. It was shadowy inside. Only after some moments, standing beneath a gallery like a pall, did my eyes adapt. I saw carpeted stairs at the end of an aisle dividing pews. These led up to a large cabinet set into a red velvet screen. Its half-open front revealed silver scrolls. The heavily ornamented metal glinted in the light of a hanging lamp.

The old man gave me a skullcap to wear. He took me to the far end of a front pew. Signalling to me to sit there with that ringed hand, he set a candle in one of the glasses on a side table, then another.

"You light these. I'll say *Kaddish*."

My hand was trembling so much that the man in the trilby had to strike the match, give it to me and guide my wrist, marked from chains to the wicks, all the while reciting in an incomprehensible half-chant.

It ended. The old man sat beside me, also looking at the flames They were hypnotic. At last he said: "I'm Maurice Sitbon, the president here. There aren't many of us left now." He was looking at the flickering glasses. "I spend half the year in Canada with my daughter. She's married there. Ever since they built the new mosque, the place has really changed. You should hear what they say about us – not to mention Israel – at Friday prayers ...

"It was bound to happen. That's what we told her last night. She said she had always intended to join us for Shabbat, and finally decided to visit just before going back to America. The Perez family put her up She must have come on the spur of the moment, because this morning that colleague of hers from the oil company came looking for her. They were telling me about their own temples in New York. That's where you're from, is it? ... You were with them, no? ... Never mind. It's best to stay quiet. Just thank God you hadn't arrived yet when the barbarians descended."

*

Monsieur Sitbon left me to sit alone until such time as the police should appear. Sleep fell upon me.

When I came to, I found myself in deserted shadow. A glass of water had appeared on the pew beside me. A cube of ice was all but melted beneath the crocheted cover weighted with beads to keep out flies. I sipped, yet barely touched the almond biscuits.

I looked back into dimness. Flaming prayer candles and gleaming silver hurt my eyes. I felt nauseous, and was afraid I would vomit. There was a ringing in my ears.

I held absolutely still. Maybe all would be well again if I did not move I must simply wait for this feeling of oppression to pass ...
I roused from another absence. Uneasily, I sensed that only a small part of me had returned to full consciousness. It was a narrow peninsula barely connected to whole dark areas: the greater part of me. They

kept threatening to reclaim it, rendering feelings, memories, almost as hallucinations, hyperreal re-enactments.

A scarred soldier lounged against the soft pink of an adobe wall. Sunset bled overhead in a massive sky. A hand was pressing a perfect figure down to cold marble, pressing ... The image was eclipsed.

There was a creak. The door was opening – from a seeming furnace. The police officer was walking down the aisle. He wore his cap. I wanted to tell him to take it off, but remembered the skullcap on my own head. In any case, I couldn't find my voice.

"I told you it was time to leave. And this isn't the end of it." The officer sat by me. I was not reacting. "So how did you come to be here?" he asked, more quietly. "Did you know the victims?"

"Give me time," I said.

"You have all the time in the world."

20

Outside, the officer's men had started their work. They were collecting evidence, measuring, photographing and interviewing, all before the army's arrival. I found it a wearying repetition of what had gone on around me in the monastery so many months ago. I well understood, straining to give my account to the officer in these dreamlike shadows, how mechanical it must be for the police. Here was just another of the crimes they probably never expected to solve.

I had taken equally little interest in the monks' murder. Now matters could not be more different. Inwardly, I was arrested again by the features – the eyes – that had captivated me from my first glimpse of them. The face had an unsettling beauty, stopping me in my desert tracks – but suddenly gone in this repeating image of perfectly shaped shoulders, buttocks, calves, shuddering frenziedly into stillness, rigidity, uselessness.

I ached. It could never mean the same to another living soul. Not now, with the single person sharing my feeling for her gone, with the same cold finality as jeered at my every mental manoeuvre to recall her to life.

My solitariness put me back in a cell – an inner one. A wall separated me from the rest of the world. I, only I, was on the wrong side of life.

I finished telling my story to the officer. It left me empty. It was as if I had used up everything of myself in recounting my feelings for the woman, the news Mizrahi had brought of her disappearance and my wildly absurd search for her. By the time I had described how I had been detained, loaded onto a lorry and brought here to witness the slaughter, I was parched. My voice cracked. The words would not even come out to say there was now an end to any idea of finding something of value, making me more myself, out here in the desert.

Under the officer's calmly attentive eye, I felt a withered lifelessness, as if detoxifying after taking narcotics. The invisible valve of emotion, of mental images, had once more been closed.

The officer said nothing, even now that I had stopped speaking. He was watching me retract into myself. The door opened, admitting another fiery wedge and an old woman in a headscarf. She carried a tray of food.

The situation upon my arrival at the monastery was apparently continuing to repeat itself. Everything was the same, except for my relationship to the killings.

I looked at the food distantly, not remotely hungry. But my stomach grumbled at how long ago I had eaten breakfast – though not only the hours. I had travelled a vast tract of experience since then, truly a desert, bringing me to this infinitely harsher emotional terrain.

"Eat," the officer said patiently, as if to a child. "You've still got that long journey ahead of you. We'll go when you've finished." He smiled at the old woman. It made me emerge from my self-absorption. Realising how complete it had been, I remembered my manners. I nodded too.

*

By the time we left the building, the army had arrived. The officer paused to speak to the colonel in charge. I thought I would faint, waiting for them to finish talking in the airless shadow of this narrow alley. The mosque loomed.

We set off for the police car. My metal suitcase was in the boot, beside the petrol can and plastic bottles of water. The officer explained that he had come upon it at the monastery entrance, going to collect me earlier that morning as arranged. Not finding me there or anywhere in the vicinity, they had loaded my luggage and driven back to police headquarters. There the officer had eventually received a telephone call reporting what the unattended suitcase had immediately made him suspect: another massacre.

"I assumed you were a victim. You don't know how lucky you were, arriving late for the proceedings like that and receiving a seat in the audience."

I did not react, sitting with the officer in the back of the car. We were finally being driven on the journey we should have taken earlier that morning. There were only the sounds of hot, sandy wind and the engine.

Off to one side, over red dunes jagged with great granite slabs, I thought I glimpsed something familiar. Squinting, without sunglasses, I saw it grow till I could make out a bell tower and treetops surmounting the *kasbah*-like compactness of adobe walls. Gazing at it from this unaccustomed angle, I also took in cloud. Huge, lofty, the airy mass had turrets, battlements. A world in itself, it appeared to bear witness to momentous events; a big story.

But what *had* happened? What did it all mean, I caught myself asking distractedly, instantly turning back from such idle thoughts to the pink walls below.

Now, finally, the eerily silent place to which I had been so tied stood absolutely empty, abandoned to whatever purpose. The knot had been cut this morning – together with all else, allowing these desert winds to sweep me off like that cloud itself. Even so, I couldn't help wondering what I might feel about it in the future, that sanctuary I would never see again.

I continued looking into the driver's mirror long after the monastery had faded. A mere mental trace, it was suddenly invested with something I unexpectedly recalled from the young American woman's art exhibition in Rome, years ago. The exterior of a Coptic monastery was surmounted by a geometrically stylised white star set in powdery blue sky. They appear in paintings in ancient Egyptian tombs, preparing their freight for the new life ahead. Here it lent lonely, immemorial calm.

Months afterward, I had heard more of the latter-day tomb artist: she had been killed in a car crash in Saqqarah.

The mirage, the star, disappeared from my continuing view of Saharan sand.

Later, I turned to the officer to say, as we continued driving: "Do you really think the fundamentalists were responsible for what happened this morning?"

"It bears all their trademarks: a ritual sacrifice, with throats cut before an entire village. But in this case it was a special audience, as befitted the occasion: non-Islamic, including you. It was the unforgettable killing of one, or two, to scare a thousand."

"Do you suppose the army's involved?"

"We've talked about this sort of thing before, haven't we?" the officer said tersely. "What makes you ask?"

"I think I recognised one of the assassins. I'm almost certain he was a sentry on duty outside the monastery after the monks were murdered. He had a scar and gold teeth."

The officer smiled in a show of weary patience, exposing, for all his dapper appearance, a gold tooth of his own. "Show me who hasn't a scar in this country. There's been continuous violence here since even before the French. It's all a bag of feathers. You'll never get to the bottom of it … Even if someone in the army was behind these latest killings – and I'm not suggesting that someone was – so what? Can you, a foreigner, do anything about it? What remedy do you propose? Are you expecting anyone to be brought back to life?"

The officer breathed deeply after the indignantly blunt repost, mopping both cheeks. Actually, it was brutal given all I, his hearer, had told him about my feelings for the woman. But I knew it to be defensiveness springing from embarrassment, national pride and a feeling, *au fond*, of brotherhood with one's countrymen in the teeth of outsiders.

I went on: "What possible motive could the army, agents of the state, have for murdering two employees of an American oil company bringing vast financial benefits to the nation?"

"They were Jewish, if we must speculate – unlike you, which is why they let you go." The officer said it coldly. He was quite composed now.

"How do you know?"

"Foreigners' religions appear on their visa application forms. These people could have been Israeli spies, returning year after year like that."

"Ridiculous!"

"That's what *you* say. Others may not think so."

"What's there to spy on?"

The officer did not answer. In his sunglasses, he looked quietly out at the passing blur of sand and light.

Then it dawned on me to say: "The nuclear programme, and those involved in it?"

The officer just shrugged.

"I mean, it'd be a threat to Israel, wouldn't it?"

"Who knows?" the officer said, as if to himself, without looking back.

"But you don't believe they *were* spies, do you?"

"I've no idea. It'd all depend on the evidence. Besides, there are spies and spies. It can be as little as passing on a snippet of information gleaned purely by chance to the right person. Anyway, what does it matter what I – or *you* – think? Somebody or other considered that they knew something helpful to the enemies of the state, whatever it might be. He tipped off the army – *if* that's what happened. Because all of this is just conjecture.

"What decides it is the light in which one wants to see it. So even if you have recognised the guard in your nervous state, he might as well not be what you say he is. He could as easily be a fundamentalist randomly slaughtering, in line with usual practice, Jews in jeans and American company trousers. All we can be certain of is the deaths."

21

We arrived in the village. The car stopped by the marketplace, deserted in this afternoon glare. Standing with the officer in the meagre shade of a palm tree, while the driver unloaded my suitcase, I realised that I had not bid Monsieur Sitbon farewell. I regretted it: I owed him something, that old gentleman in his trilby. But maybe it was just as well. I thought of how the others to whom I'd said two of my recent goodbyes had fared.

The metal suitcase was beside me. I faced the officer, summoning up the least that politeness required of me.

He forestalled me. "Goodbye then," he said briskly, bringing his hand to his heart. "God be with you." It was a ritual phrase in Arabic, though I weighed how much the man might also have meant it. For clipped, even dry, the officer need not have accompanied me personally to the bus. He had talked to me with some openness, more than once. Possibly he had been glad of educated company, especially now it was no longer available from the monks.

There was an instant's heaviness between us. Unexpressed, inexpressible feeling hovered in the scorching air. Was I unreasoningly expecting him to embrace me, calling me by my name? Although, in our continuing silence, might I somehow have sensed that he couldn't – not only from a distaste for brazen intimacy, but also because I was evidently still coming to myself? I had yet to answer fully to who I am.

"We shall never meet again," he said musingly.

"Oh?"

"You know it. This is all over for you now. It may not have been obvious why you stayed here, but there can't be much doubt why you're leaving – for good."

"You mean I've nothing to come back to?"

I can't be certain now, years later, that I actually voiced these words saying themselves through me, but I felt they were true enough.

What could survive my monastic retreat? Not my project with the insects; not my love affair.

"It's too dangerous, even for you now. You've no choice but to escape while you can. You're fortunate to have lasted this long. I just hope it's been worth it to you. I mean, have you finally found what you really came here for? Not the insects," he added, smiling reminiscently.

I didn't answer.

"Well, have you?"

I couldn't have said anything, so sunk was I in thought.

What I wanted to say was no, not only that in sticking it out, despite all the slaughter, I'd made terrible discoveries, but that something important had surely stolen upon me. Silent, immaterial, it was as real as the advance of dawn. Yet I simply couldn't explain what, strive within myself as I might to see it. So, seconds later, I was still standing, tongue-tied before the police officer.

All I could do was wave aside a mosquito and the man's unanswerable question, all in one gesture. And I thanked him for the concern he'd always shown me.

"I've appreciated our conversations over these months."

"Much good it's done," he said, shrugging his shoulders.

"Ah! But …"

Impossible as I found it to suggest the benefit, I took refuge in a ritual final farewell. We shook hands. The man walked off, leaving a painful lump in my throat.

Now his car was out of sight. He had vanished among his Saharan slaughters.

I went into the café, with its lethargic customers. Here I would wait for the bus. I hardly noticed mint tea being set before me. My eyes were magnetised by the television. I tried to avoid looking at the screen. Repeatedly, I was drawn back to that chaos of black and white, but I longed to give up trying to disentangle a plot from it.

I wondered how much longer I would have to remain here, reminding myself that I had just passed an untold period in the desert. It should not be so difficult to sit quietly, waiting.

I went to the squat lavatory, discovering I did not actually need to go. But I was held by its fragment of leprous mirror, my eyes meeting a tired yet unflinching stare above the tangled beard. I went on surprising myself with this new, stern defiance that had come upon it since I'd last been there, months before.

I was barely aware of the dark, buzzing stench.

A loud horn sounded.

A few people were waiting by the coach as I yielded up my suitcase. How long ago I'd worried about whether or not it was being put safely into the hold!

Entering the aisle, I smelled the heavy orange blossom oil with which one of the peasant women at the back had perfumed her veil. I installed myself near the front. The seat beside me was empty; I gazed out the window. The late afternoon light was weakening as we drove off. We were in open desert that spread endlessly, harsh, with the unremitting drone of the engine. The stony terrain returned nothing to the eye. No, there was nothing to feed the senses out there; I heard the video beginning.

It was the Egyptian film I had seen on the journey down, the one set in Alexandria. I found myself waiting for that actress to reappear with her striking eyes, now looking out at me. Like a memory, the movie played itself out again, image after arresting image. But the woman, especially beautiful both in herself and in her amazing resemblance to several others, was cold.

The actress, the *real* woman, was gone, long retired from films, a reclusive cocaine addict shrivelled and wearing dark glasses in a Nile-side Cairo suburb. She, now doubtless dead, only revived ghostlike in the cinema. After the flickering illusion of her animated self, the projection stopped. The screen abandoned her obsessed fans to darkness: nothing.

My eyes opened to night. Cold, I sought closeness, and strove to get her into focus. Yet she never came fully to mind: she whose image kept breaking up. She was a series of fleeting facets, partial views, competing profiles, all misleading – as was anyone in his view of who he might be for her. The thought stayed with me. I went on worrying it.

Suddenly my stomach sank. I felt queasy, not least with the petrol fumes. If I found something outside, something objective on which to fix my sights, maybe it would steady my innards. I peered through the window. There were no landmarks. Clouds obscured the stars. There was only darkness. I went on staring into it, mouth salty. I felt sick. Out there, a person was permanently lost in infinite obscurity.

I woke, as if from anaesthetic, only to return to sleep, wake again and sleep some more. Eventually I roused on the outskirts of the capital, with its half-finished, half-crumbling, breeze-block dwellings, skeletal animals and meagre plots of canebrake and corn. Beyond this shanty-town, the coach honked its way into a bedlam of streets clogged with traffic. We were caught behind a donkey refusing to carry its cartload of rubbish any further.

A wave of seaside humidity wafted through the windows. It smelled like drains. Then I made out a distant band of glittering blue. The beach was deserted. So were the bathing rafts. Looking at them, I just saw shadows.

Now the *muezzins* began making their taped calls. I was trembling with anxiety. We arrived in the bus depot, which was stifling, with a stench of diesel fuel. Collecting my suitcase, I paused to look at another bay. It was empty. I was overwhelmed by the crush of people. Crowds would be thronging the *kasbah*. Seeing them in my mind's eye packing narrow streets around the Order's house, I took a taxi straight to the Alitalia office.

*

I had a one-year, open-return ticket. There was a plane that day and several hours to wait for the flight. I did not feel at all like spending them in the capital. Nothing there caught my interest: not reminders of its colonial period or of past or present civil strife, or even of Alexandria, with that Corniche stretched out along the sea. I wanted to shrink from the city. Somewhere within, I was continuing to hold still in a desert monastery's silence, with only the sounds of evening winds.

I took another taxi to the airport. An official from the national carrier told me that I could not check in or check my luggage until someone came to open the Alitalia desk. That would not be for two hours. No, there were no left luggage lockers, for security reasons. I carried off my case, transported in an instant back months to the time I had done so upon arrival at the monastery. But once installed there, I had been free to walk out, unencumbered, beyond pink walls, into open desert.

I set my case down in front of a newspaper stall. The press was in Arabic, except for a week-old copy of *The Herald Tribune* and an Italian paper from the previous day. Reading the headlines, I expected the saleswoman, head covered in a scarf, to protest. My excuse was ready: she could not expect me to buy something out of date. She went on staring mutely into space as I skimmed the paper. There was mention of the generally disturbed situation in the south, but not of nuclear testing or specifically of further killing in the desert. The murders might never have occurred. An invisible membrane sealed them off from my continuing sense of Saharan solitude.

I put the paper back and went to the restaurant. I ordered a crois-sant and coffee served in a glass. Consuming them without appetite, indeed with slight nausea, looking through the full-length windows, I realised that, oily and bitter respectively, they were last night's dinner and today's breakfast and lunch.

The runway was deserted, surrounded by waste ground and dirty, whitewashed buildings. Despite knowing my plane would not appear for another two hours, I gazed watchfully at that emptiness. But how could I permit myself to expect her to appear there? The self-reproof occurred to me the instant I became fully aware of having this picture of her doing so. Then I was entertaining a series of memories of her, chronologically ordered. It was as if I might relive our time together, yet with each sequence now experienced differently, in light of what I had come to know from David Mizrahi had been true of her from the start.

Yet no. There was no point. She was gone, forever gone, drawn hor-rifyingly back into the mere spectre she had emerged as, on my first glimpse of her in the desert. She was just a memory, an empty image, like those precursors on a coach video, on the stairs of an Alexandrian block of flats, in a Washington museum. So I thought, still staring at the empty runway, the deserted fields.

Far, far away, the void stretched. Down it went, deep into the Sahara; and there a man, a Desert Father, had lost himself too. I had already begun involuntarily tracking over my acquaintance with him. How I wished, awaiting my plane, that there were something else to take my mind off it! Yet our encounters played themselves out compulsively, abbreviated into images. There was his anger; his calm enquiry into my life, my marriage and work. There had been his recollection of a desert romance, arms all but touching on a sandy path; the Our Father. Eyes had gleamed fugitively in dying daylight.

The moments nagged on unremittingly, seen, felt, at this distance. Then I grew aware of a snatch of conversation replaying itself. These were Mizrahi's words – displaced by a sudden roar while I was still striving to bring them fully to mind. I raised my head, vaguely. Out of painfully bright blue, the gleaming plane was finally arriving.

On board, I sat looking at the fast-disappearing capital, with the monastery, the desert, far behind me. They evaporated while I gazed down at a greenish-blue smudge, the sea, just as a Saharan mirage had dissolved months ago: the one beckoning me to pursue a project; to find myself; to be.

A vanished illusion, it had been replaced, I recognised up in the plane, by a brute reality. Unimaginable horror personal to me had finally come to match that to which I'd been a mere bystander. And horror it truly was, not simply a husband's bereavement arising in the natural, if painful, course of things. For it was as if mass murder had summoned up from me, during the months I lingered among its reverberations, what it eventually echoed, then merged with.

It was as if two drivers, total strangers in an otherwise deserted Sahara, found their cars, mere flecks in the distance, magnetised, careering towards each other. Regardless of my planned trajectory, I'd been made an inescapable part instead of all that had happened through this seemingly chance encounter. Now it was, of course, impossible for me to stay. I had no choice but to focus on the deflatingly practical question of what my life in Rome would be. I must find an apartment, though I worried how I would survive there alone, having glimpsed what living – living together – really meant, especially with blighting memories of how it had all been terminated.

It had been a severely damaged environment in more than the respect I must explain to my publisher. For yes, I would have to report how nuclear testing, surely, had made me give up the book. It meant paying back the advance, forcing me to consider what to do about employment. Insistent questions, they had no answers except my yawn, exhausted as I was from journeying through the night.

Up she was being hoisted. I knew who it was even before she began to surface, streaming with viscous rivulets. The expression was there: strange, beautiful, serene. But she was remote with that perfect, badly cracked lapidary smile. More than life-size, her broken limbs set before a darkling glitter, surrounded by bleeding sunset, she betrayed no impression of a particular life lived. She gave no clue of a specific personality. She might have been any one of a number of beings. She was all and none of them. The lips, the cheeks had been beaming for ages, unseen, in the murk. So did they now, smashed, recovered, always striking.

I awoke, recalling Mizrahi again. That snatch of his conversation – yes, about the desert – opened up to me when the flight attendant announced that we were about to land. I'd been looking out at valleys and cultivated fields.

All of a sudden I knew that, whatever the failure of my desert project, I had at least survived my ordeal. The Sahara had transformed me into someone glaring from a shard of mirror in a café's latrine. And such things I had become aware of behind the sand's seemingly sterile surface! So regardless of the practical matters needing my attention, there was something I simply must do first in Rome.

22

From now on, Father Mark, this account finds me in the Eternal City. With its historic skyline and Renaissance domes, as well as these thronged piazzas and crowded pavement restaurants, Rome should have made a greater impression on me than a remote patch of desert. But there are apparently intense moments in life, times of rapid awakening, that transfigure the place where they happen, regardless of how outwardly striking the context in which, self-absorbed, one restlessly sets about taking the measure of one's inner transformation.

That said, I badly need you here with me in Rome, Father Mark. It's where the controversy that's been dogging me for years will begin, a dispute for which I seek the very understanding that's made me unknowingly start addressing you in these pages. It's not just a matter of agreement over facts, hard as some of them turn out to be. So stark are they indeed that now, in retrospect, I suppose some self-protective impulse prevented me from seeing the whole story that will unfold by the end of this record, despite my having had all the necessary information whilst in the desert. No, it's not only the facts I want endorsed, Father Mark. It's what they imply. I'm sure you'll see it with that unsparing clarity I instinctively feel you possess about your Church – or at least about some of its members. And it's empathy I'd welcome, for the stance it will emerge I've adopted as a result.

Above all, I want you to meet the "me" surfacing in Rome, the one writing to you here and now. It's the self that started to appear, finally, in protest against all I'd undergone, everything to which I'd been subjected. I was outraged at what I eventually recognised Mizrahi's words really implied, in flight from Africa to Italy. My anger aside, though, I hope you'll be pleased to make my acquaintance.

So now you see me having just arrived, Father Mark, taking the narrow cobbled street to the back of the German church. I'm standing at the gate, ringing the bell. A novice admits me to the courtyard, with its potted plants in terracotta urns. He leads me to the adjoining building, past the rector's office, to this spacious room.

Perhaps you knew it once, before you retreated to the desert. And maybe you still recognise, after all this time, the elderly monk greeting me effusively as he rises from his wide, tapestried chair. He offers me its pair with an open palm.

The novice has brought us sherbets. I can still hear Father Carlo saying: "Yes, it's a real pleasure to see you, especially after your awful experience in the monastery. Such a glaring instance of man's inhumanity to man!"

"You've no idea how awful it really was," I said. "Or maybe you have."

I peered across a silver crucifix on the table between us. A box, an ashtray and the goblets of barely touched sherbets, all silver too, stood on the highly polished surface. Father Carlo looked down vaguely at his hand, fanning out the fingers.

"I saw my project through to the bitter end, all right," I continued. "My entomological investigations were very thorough. They showed that every last insect was deformed – the undoubted result of nuclear testing in the Sahara."

"Are you sure?" Father Carlo said, glancing through his gleaming rimless glasses.

"Oh, yes! My suspicions were confirmed by a recent newspaper report. But then, you'd know all about it."

"I may have come across something of the sort in the press. But there are always general allegations of that sort. Is there any real evidence?"

Father Carlo reached aside to the silver box. He opened it and, offering me a cigarette, which I refused, took one himself. He lit it, slowly exhaling into the dim distance.

"Of course, when I set out, with your encouragement, I believed I was only incidentally a messenger, if I gave it any thought. I assumed I was being sent to lose – and find – myself cataloguing insects in the calm of desert nights. I had no idea that I was being manoeuvred into the most dangerous place in the world under the pretext of a publishing commission turning into exactly what could have been predicted: a ghastly look into Nature's chamber of horrors. Some German bestseller!

"It never occurred to me that, with my inexperience and weakness after all I'd been through with the death of my wife, I was being deliberately manipulated." I paused to reflect protectively on that feeble being consigned to the past by this my strengthened self finally undeceived by Mizrahi's words.

How they have come to impress me since, Father Mark, with all I have gone on to learn about how that very monastery on the Via Sicilia served as a way station for Nazis. Organised by Alois Hudal, rector, Bishop of Graz, it arranged from 1945 on through Caritas and the Red Cross for asylum seekers to receive ID cards, complete with new identities and refugee passports.

I took a deep breath, girding myself for all I, newly aware and combative, must confront in Father Carlo.

"How could I have dreamed that all the time I was in the desert, thinking myself free to leave the monastery to work or wander as I chose, I was being controlled from across vast distances? But then what could have prepared me to expect that you, a man of God, were knowingly putting me at terrible risk – and for what? To deliver a letter to a Nazi nuclear scientist, a mass murderer, urging him to escape. Because you knew the press was publishing reports of nuclear testing in the Sahara, and that the Wiesenthal Center would therefore pursue the Germans working there.

"Your 'snakes surrounding us in the grass and in the desert', but especially 'in the meadow and the valley' – in *Wiese und Thal*. Very clever! Your letter to Father Erich was a tipoff – and he flew the coop." I swallowed, searching Father Carlo's face for a reaction. He was shaking his head, frowning. "Of course," I went on, "Father Erich didn't leave before telling the authorities that he was being stalked by a Jewish geologist. He must have said that if she exposed him and God knows who else, it would compromise the security of the government's weapons programme. So both she and another Jewish employee in their American oil company were butchered by an army hit squad. And all from his paranoia about saving his skin."

I was breathing deeply, having finally expressed in full the explanation I'd only now worried out and that makes undeniable sense – as you'll surely agree, won't you, Father Mark? "Where is he now?" I asked.

"How should I know, my dear man?" Father Carlo said, placing a soft hand on my bare arm, so rough and burned from the desert. "You're overwrought. I know novices are told: 'Go, sit in your cell and it will teach you everything'. But what your time alone in the Sahara has given you are wild imaginings in your bereavement. I simply thought you'd find much in common with Father Erich."

"As you said in your letter to him," I said tersely.

"And he is, when all is said and done, a monk."

"So? Are monks supposed to be any better than the rest of us?"

Father Carlo's eyes narrowed fractionally behind those finely ground lenses. He drew on his cigarette.

"The deeper people get involved with religion," I said, "the more demons it releases in them. They're taken over by them. Look at the monks helping Nazis escape. Or priests granting absolution to military torturers in Argentina."

"Aren't you generalising? Our brethren in the desert were pacifists. They died for it."

"They were obsessed with evil as much as the fundamentalists. They just went from one extreme to the other in presuming they could defeat it. It was a completely unrealistic attitude, as if an adult can revert to innocence and become invulnerable in confronting fanatical violence. Of course there's a reason why the monks were skewed like that: they were emotionally stunted. They were all deeply wounded in love. Otherwise they wouldn't have been monks, would they?"

I smiled acidly, offering the insight whose uncomfortable truth I'm confident you, Father Mark, are too knowing not to appreciate.

Father Carlo returned my look with hooded eyes. "These are hard things to hear about our martyred brethren. For my part, I believe they're an enduring example of personal sacrifice for peace. I can't accept that Our Lord would let them die for less."

"Peace? Oh no! I hardly think that's what they were sacrificed for. They were massacred because the fundamentalists rightly suspected one of the brethren was Erich, whose nuclear testing was making 'Allah's Garden', the desert, lethal. But Erich was far off in his hermitage – which, being interpreted, means 'nuclear testing site'. That is, until he was tipped off by your letter, given to him by Father Mark from yours truly." I bowed my head, sarcastically. "And so, returning to the monastery to order transport, he set off without a trace, this monk – if monk he really is. The cowl is the perfect place to hide, and lose, oneself. You can be anyone or anything under the skin, can't you?"

Father Carlo had been listening intently. Eyes still fixed on me, he skilfully liberated his wrists, with their starched cuffs and gold links, from his habit. Then setting down his cigarette butt in an ashtray, he clasped one hand in the other and leaned forward to speak so quietly that the ticking of the porcelain clock remained audible.

"I want to assure you of one thing, absolutely. My intentions in encouraging you to go to the monastery were entirely good."

"Crusader talk? To save the world against Islamic fundamentalism by arming the Arab state, just as you'd protected it against Communism by helping Nazis, both then and now?"

Father Carlo gave a sigh. He leaned his head to one side, adjusting his skullcap. It gave an impression of weary patience, with our eyes meeting over unfinished sherbets in this Roman heat. Such long experience of human nature!

"It was the best thing for you to go to the monastery. I pray that you'll come to see that. You were emotionally dead when you went. You can't deny it. But it gave you the chance to come back into contact with a large part of yourself; to re-encounter what's made you who you really are. Quite simply, it's returned you to life, whether you recognise it or not."

"How can you possibly know?"

"From the way you've been talking: the force of your conversation. You're wrong in what you say, but I'm glad to see you so assertive. It's a sign of health. And take it from me, I know …"

*

Father Carlo remained cool. He put a hand on my shoulder. He said that if I hadn't arranged my accommodation yet, he could offer me a guest room for a few weeks.

I did not answer, except to shrug. I had grown too heated. Still, I had been devastating, hadn't I? I'd surely annihilated Father Carlo. I must have, although he had evaded my every accusation. Strange, then, that I had made so little apparent impression on the monk. So suave, so seemingly caring, he'd actually never been more dangerous and evil. Well, I'd had my fill of religious institutions. I left the cleric standing in his well-appointed room, accepting neither his hand nor his offer. I already had somewhere to stay.

What I was prepared to accept was his comment that I'd become assertive. It was in this frame of mind that I strode through the court-yard, along the cobbled lane and into the main road. I was heading off to see my editor. It was a meeting that my discussion with Father Carlo suddenly made me decide would have a very different outcome from what I'd originally intended.

23

The publisher had moved to a new building. The foyer was surgically clean, with black marble and plate glass. The receptionist, new too, was like a model in her fashionable business suit. Looking askance at me in my crumpled shirt and trousers, she asked me to wait while she telephoned to summon my editor.

Actually, she made a number of calls, in a conspiratorial near-whisper. It gave me time to suppose, gazing at these gleaming surfaces, that in their white striations I might make out fossils, insects. But despite an instant's reversion to desert, my eyes simultaneously beheld the reflection of me viewing. The one kept invading the other. It made my head whirl. Almost in a swoon, suffering the after-effects even in this air conditioning, of having raced in Rome's humid summer heat, I slumped into one of the chrome and leather chairs. There I waited, eventually supposing my editor was nowhere to be found.

I was right. The person finally approaching over that sea of black marble was someone quite different from the pleasant man in late middle age who had dealt with my wife Anja, then me. He had retired – or, as I was told later, "been retired" for offering unsuitable contracts to authors whose books never sold.

A young man with a short haircut confronted me instead, dressed in crisp, well-ironed shirtsleeves and a brightly coloured silk tie. He said he was sorry I had been waiting so long, and guided me into his office. But it had taken him some time to find a reference to the project he'd inherited – together with its author, he added, glancing at me. Again I saw myself, this time in my mind's eye: dark-skinned, bearded, dishevelled in the clothes in which I was emerging from the desert. The truth was, I knew, that both my book and I had been long set aside, if not entombed in Saharan depths.

Otto Linge, as he was called, sat before me, consulting his predecessor's notes on my project with the cold scepticism of a bank manager reviewing a defaulting client's balance sheet. He read aloud what had appealed to my editor: the strange, almost surreal aesthetic qualities of a book of large insect paintings; extraordinarily precise and delicate lines; a subtle palette ranging from virtual shadow, through delicate tints, to bold black. Linge did not have to say he was less interested in what had engaged the colleague whose tastes had cost him his job. I told him I'd been unable to see the project through on the terms originally agreed since all the insects I had studied were seriously deformed as the result of nuclear testing.

"So that's that," Linge said, leaning back from his desk with obvious relief.

"It's what I thought, too," I said. "But no longer. I've decided this sort of secret testing must be exposed, together with everything and everyone making it possible. What better way than with images of insects deformed as a result? It would have a great visual impact as well as making a crucial moral and political point. This is the book I'll be giving you."

Linge was leaning forward now. A vein vibrated on his temple as he spoke in a deliberate, controlled voice. "I don't think that kind of book really fits into the company's list. People buy art books to use them decoratively. They leave them on coffee tables to create a tasteful atmosphere. Something deliberately anti-aesthetic, or plain disgusting, doesn't exactly do that."

"But it's making an important statement. And aren't the people who buy art books exactly the ones who'd worry about the environment – especially nuclear pollution?"

"No," Linge said, digging in his heels. "A few lefties might be interested. Yet they'd never have the money to afford the sort of book you're talking about. In any case, if this testing is so secret, how do we know it's actually happening?"

"The insects."

"Apart from them, I mean," he said with a flick of the wrist.

I gave the gist of the newspaper article I'd read in the monastery. I would have gone on to speak of Father Erich's role and Father Carlo's support for it, but Linge was already saying: "The Sahara's a very large place, you know. The director of the International Atomic Energy Agency could easily have been referring to secret testing anywhere across the whole breadth of Africa."

"I know how big the Sahara is," I snapped, stung by remembering when I'd last heard that line. "I doubt there's much you can add to my knowledge of it."

"But you were at a single point – a monastery, wasn't it?" he said, gesturing vaguely to the report on the project. "You didn't come into contact with other regions where the director might have considered they were as likely if not more so to be preparing for 'the ultimate catastrophe'."

"Wrong!" I said, infuriated by his mocking tone. "Quite wrong! I encountered the catastrophe of the entire place. Because I was in the eye of the desert: the deepest Sahara."

The new editor could not have been more grating. It wasn't just that he did not agree with me about the prospects for the book I'd proposed. Young and inexperienced, but without the intelligence to recognise it, his mind was closed about matters well beyond his knowledge and understanding. He was too condescending to see the repercussions of what had been going on in the desert: vast implications that I suddenly decided required much more than implicit mention in a coffee table book.

So you see me, Father Mark, a mere half-hour later, breathless and sweating at the offices of the Italian newspaper taken by the monastery library.

"Can I meet your Vienna correspondent, please?" I asked at the reception desk.

"If you go to Vienna."

Yet gruff as this middle-aged woman was, she put down the cigarette she was lighting from a glowing butt, picked up the telephone and told me: "Just wait while I find someone to help you."

A wall-eyed man walked into the foyer, and took me to his untidy desk in the large open office nearby. He simply stared as I sat there speaking of their Vienna correspondent's report on secret nuclear testing.

"I'm just back from the place it refers to. It's happening there exactly as the director of The International Atomic Energy Agency said.

The public must be made aware of it – and of the terrible danger it puts us all in."

"If the testing was secret, how did you know about it?"

I felt the wall-eye fix on me as I explained that, in the course of studying desert insects for a book of illustrations, I'd found they were all deformed. It proved the existence of nuclear radiation and thus testing. The milky pupil leaked, whether seeing what I meant or not.

"What's happening to the book?"

"For some reason, it's predicted that sales for an artistic exposé of the effects of illegal testing won't be commercially viable," I said tartly. "That's why there needs to be an article in your paper."

Still that eye was on me, opaque. The pimply tip of a tongue slipped through the man's closed lips like a lizard's and licked them for a moment. "Alright," he finally said. "Give me your telephone number. I'll ask our Vienna correspondent to get in touch with you. He'll be here for a few days next week."

*

I wrote out the telephone number of the apartment where we used to live. Our elderly landlady had not been organised enough to rent it out in the months of my absence. She was allowing me to stay there a while, possibly even for the foreseeable future. After all, it still contained some of our possessions.

Heading off to the flat, I rolled up the free copy I'd been offered of the day's newspaper. I was sweating. The city, humid, with traffic fumes concentrated by stone pavements, felt even more suffocating than the desert. Wiping my forehead on my shirtsleeve, I was about to cross the road when something held me to the kerb: a large Levantine girl's face. Her eyes, dark, searchingly intimate, were foreign, but disconcertingly familiar. They passed over an advertisement on the side of the bus for an exhibition of Fayum portraits from Egypt.

Egypt. The word remained, visible in mind even after the printed original departed, stirring thought or memory – I had no time to consider which. It was instantly stifled as I crossed the street, the sun plunging me into momentary darkness. Strange, that I could forget quite how hot Rome became, I thought, passing a pair of African street vendors ambling along with what must have been sweltering rugs slung over their shoulder. They carried plastic bags, presumably containing pottery and other wares.

I was exhausted by the time I reached my building. The walk, the heat, that succession of difficult interviews had all drained me. Entering the apartment, I sank into a chair beside my desk.

Yes, I still thought of it as *mine*, of the apartment as *ours*. I felt I'd never left it for an instant in which I continued our shared life, our shared being. These possessions that I hadn't packed or thrown away were all in their place. Even the same Faber-Castell pencils were there. They stood, green, all sharpened, in an earthenware holder that I recognised, oddly enough, to be similar to the monastery's pottery.

Then I simply rested for a few moments; but I couldn't go on basking for long in the calm of homecoming when "home" was from a time now extinct. My sense of being in my natural habitat yielded to reverberations from the desert, and my turbulent encounter there. Yet, tired as I was, I did not want to revive disturbing memories. I opened the newspaper, willing to read about anything – even Italian party politics or the personals column.

What distracted me, though, was a strange sensation. This was a light prickling, as of the hairs on my arm being touched by somebody else's. I brushed off the mosquito, but the imagined human contact remained in my mind. It set off an instant of intense recall.

I was walking along the monastery's sandy path, side by side with my old companion. But only now was the Father's image fully clear to me in the dusk: it appeared projected onto that open-air cinema screen, the chapel wall. It was the father the man had been when younger – yes! – when he had reproved me that first time for taking an interest in a girl, before he'd gone missing in the Egyptian desert.

Something was echoing in my mind. It was part of today's conversation:

"It was the best thing for you to go to the monastery … it gave you the chance to come back into contact with a large part of yourself, to re-encounter what's made you who you really are."

"How can you possibly know?"

"… I know."

I sat with the newspaper open on my lap and stared motionlessly into midair. Eventually, I tilted my head and took something in, on the circumference of my range of vision: the desk. The pencils were there in their holder.

I lifted up the unglazed earthenware pot. It bore finger marks: sets of just four dots I'd known about all along, of course, but not brought to mind till now. Cupping it with my hands, as I had those like it that I'd sketched in my cell, I was at last recalling that my mother had brought it back from her religious retreat – presumably arranged by Father Carlo. Then I discovered myself holding a thought: she had stayed in a Saharan convent, visiting her husband nearby in his desert monastery.

The realisation stayed with me, unfocusing, refocusing. Finding them back together in a cell, I, too, chanced upon their warm closeness. Mentally rematching them, I also felt embraced in an infant moment in which I'd crept between them in bed. It was an instant's recall of the absolute security of being loved, as I held the vessel conjuring it up. By the time I had put it down, more was occurring to me.

How protective I felt of the woman, sacrificing herself, alone with her young son, to conceal the man's whereabouts; protecting whom – what – he really was! Yet they had managed to stay in touch; husband and wife, wife and husband. So the old Father had told me he'd done with the one he'd cared for while in the desert, even during their long parting. For here, in my lap, was the personals column of the paper.

This it was, surely, that they had used to maintain coded contact, unbeknownst to their son; that mother and father, father and mother.

24

I got up and left the flat. It was dark as I waited on my landing for the lift. It ground down, storey after storey. Then, leaving the building, I entered the dimming light. In some distant part of my mind, I had the nagging feeling that I should be confronting the practical issues of finding myself a permanent roof over my head and a way of making a living. I awaited a call from the Vienna correspondent. But such anxieties were overwhelmed by a feeling of suffocating heaviness.

It was like the emotionally confused aftermath of a nightmare, not the weight of specific, worrying thought. It was driving me out for movement, for air. If I walked far enough, breathing sufficiently deeply, matters might simply dissolve like some fantasy.

I stopped in an unfashionable section of this city of magnificent churches. The one I was peering into was plain to the point of drabness. I was already sitting in a pew, in stale air, before it occurred to me that, having left the monastery, severing ties with all it represented for me, I was back in a church. It came naturally to me to think there – or, rather, to let thoughts course through my mind.

Perhaps it was habit. But surely not. Nothing could have survived of my Saharan ways. I had deliberately distanced myself from my time there, from the desert itself, with its contamination and slaughter. I might just escape my contact with it, free, un-deformed – only to find that I was the blood relative of its source all the time.

Suddenly the air here smelled badly used. I could not breathe. I gasped, supposing I had suspected the damning truth about the old hermit, the Nazi scientist, from the start. And hadn't I found, inchoately, in a Desert Father almost touching my arm before a blank chapel wall the parent who'd taken me as a boy to some open-air cinema beneath desert stars? Had the man, recalled to life from Saharan vastness, known his son? I strained to recall our conversations. That interested enquiry into my marriage, work and mother suggested it. There was his final near-embrace, as well.

If only I could replay the exchanges. But I was having to understand them, their true meanings, now that they were over, vanished. It left regrets; no second chance.

Hadn't the old man known, or at least suspected, that this was his son, with the mention of a scientist father in Egypt? Yet he had kept it to himself, for his own security. He needed to cover his tracks, to ensure his escape. Doubtless, that was why Father Carlo, too, had not admitted to me the full truth. He had not even stated it openly in his letter:

"... Father ... extend to him your most paternal sympathies ..."

This very ambiguity must have emboldened Erich to leave out the envelope. Unrevealing to others, it was safe testimony to a relationship he really wanted to communicate to the son he supposed must eventually seek his traces in his cell.

Nor had I known my father was alive, or where he was, from my mother. I thought of the relationship between my parents, secret from me all those years I was growing up. How I resented being reduced to a deceived fraction of that greater reality! Then I longed to have spoken further, fully, to the man who'd disappeared back into desert where he now existed unseen, unknown, after paths only briefly re-crossed and a tantalising farewell.

I had come so close to him. I had stood with him, sat with him, touched him in exactly the place where I visualised my mother once more returning as wife. We'd been a family again, the three of us, mentally reunited deep in the Sahara. I, the son, had conjured up my child's world, forfeited and forgotten, out of desert: barren desert presenting me only with a dire, apparently irrelevant situation on entering it.

Yet what had been brought back to life disappeared just as quickly this second time. All it left me with was grieving, absurdly belated but momentarily disabling. That, and the hurt of my undeceiving.

Why must it revive so tenuously, so remotely? It existed by implication at best. This was a Saharan mirage, seen but not physically palpable. It was an image on a movie screen: looming, realistic though never quite real, vanished.

Even so, I was left with a keen taste for speaking to the man, thanks to – well, it *could* be that thanks were due to Father Carlo. In which case, had the cool cleric been doing good or evil?

"It was the best thing for you to go to the monastery," I heard him say yet again. *"… it gave you the chance to come back into contact with a large part of yourself, to re-encounter what's made you who you really are. Quite simply, it's returned you to life …"*

"Me – and who else?" I asked myself.

Yet, this afternoon, Father Carlo had denied what I'd claimed about Father Erich. He said he'd only been helping me find myself by sending me to the desert. So how could he be expected to respond to this further assertion about the old monk's identity? Suave, dismissive, Carlo would remain sphinx-like. And with my mother dead, my father gone irrecoverably into the desert, who else was there to say for certain whom Erich was?

Father Mark.

Or so it occurs to me now – just as I'm suddenly aware, writing this, that here is the likeliest reason why I'm sending you my account. Regardless of what you once remarked about remaining deliberately ignorant of the previous identities of the brethren, maybe you can tell me who Father Erich is. Even if you're only aware of something about him, though not his relationship to me, you might, with your evident intuition, confirm to me what I feel is our blood-tie – what I'm sure I know it to be.

Memories would make it real, I had thought, sitting in that dismal church in Rome. There, in its stale dimness, I strained to summon up my father from infancy. There were those few pictures from the past, so faint that they were actually mere memories of memories: the man's anger; visits to the open-air cinema; his regular, then perpetual, absence. But little enough survived from childhood for me to recognise Father Erich specifically as a parent after all this time. He might not even be a scientist manufacturing weapons of mass destruction, let alone the effective murderer of two American oil company employees. He could be just a religious moved on by his concerned brother Carlo out of undeniably dangerous terrain.

There was, finally, no knowing. Short of irrefutable evidence, apparently unavailable, it was impossible to establish for certain who the being was that had materialised out of desert, dissolving back into it just as imperceptibly. He might as well be the one person as the other. In which case, was it possible to break through the ambiguity? What more was there, except suspicion about his identity and an inclination to view him in this way, not that, from a preference only recently coming to light for whatever reason?

You see your importance, Father Mark. You, if anyone, surely had the capacity to confirm so much about Father Erich's identity all along, even when I had yet to realise it. So you also have the insight I feel to know how likely it is that he's my parent. For yes, you hold the key to resolving for me the issue of my father.

Might you not accept what I again saw, in the church, in another burst of unreasoning certainty? My father, long absent, silent and lost, had not ceased to be. He was still abroad, stalking about, appearing in the desert, pulling a tent flap back on those least prepared for him. He was always a step ahead of whoever sought to lay eyes, hands on him.

Throughout the years, he had maintained contact with my mother. He possessed the power to contaminate, this one who had created me, planting seeds of destruction, of ruined nature. Every human coming under his sway carried within the same polluted strain.

Yet how I hoped that Erich was not he – or he, Erich! For all at once I dreaded knowing that the man for whom I'd had an instant of tender feeling in an affecting farewell was spoiling on an infinite scale. I shrank from a sudden surge of anger towards my father for being whom I feared he was. Such a legacy it left me, the son of a Nazi criminal! Could I ever outlive it? It threatened to overshadow my entire life. I dreaded finding myself condemned to sift obsessively through our remembered conversation for signs, the merest hint, of his repentance.

I yearned to clear myself from all connection with the man, just as I had sought to leave behind me the monastery, its poisoned environs, and all I'd discovered there. Was that going to be possible, I asked myself despairingly, seeing my hands in this dark pew, knowing they were my father's. We were the same flesh and blood.

*

The newspaper's Vienna correspondent was named Anton Stein. As I waited for him to telephone me, these nocturnal thoughts in the church possessed my mind like a hallucination. The details of ordinary life were the dream: my nightmarish consciousness dominated, ushering my father back to life.

I felt certain, beyond further need for proof, that even while buried alive in the desert, he had been out loose in the world. He was invisibly wreaking havoc from behind disguise after disguise, regardless of any final assurance that this or that was truly he. He might be anyone, anywhere now – or not. He and his child would never more make certain contact except through such as I have inherited of his nature. I bore it within myself, not sure what exactly it was, how potent, or if it might be altered or outgrown.

There were only images of the places into which he had disappeared. Desert: they were empty, endless, brightening, burning, dimming, starlit, only to lighten again, and so forth into infinity. Unpeopled, these phases went on circulating in my mind, regardless of my efforts to make a mental break with the Sahara. It was so deeply embedded in me now that I found myself virtually bilocated in my monastery cell and our apartment.

Then, suddenly, I was recalled to Rome. The telephone was ringing.

25

Anton Stein introduced himself on the phone and said he understood I had information I wished to pass on about nuclear testing in North Africa. He suggested we meet in his hotel. I accepted, finding his Viennese accent had made me switch from Italian to German.

Later that afternoon, I approached the Forum and walked over to his hotel. Passing the reception desk I entered the bar, deserted but for a man in his mid-forties. With sleek, thinning hair and marmalade horn-rim glasses on fresh, harmonious features, Anton Stein returned me for an instant to the company of that equally fine-boned Saharan police officer who'd heard me out. I half-expected him to touch his heart as we shook hands and sat down.

A hotel ballpoint pen and notepad were on the table before him. My name and the date, time and place of our meeting were written at the top of the otherwise blank page. Stein was drinking sparkling water. He suggested I might like something stronger, but I said I was thirsty – to which he remarked, in his pleasantly lilting German, that he, too, always felt parched in Rome. He had once considered getting an apartment here, he added, though coming as little as he did to the city with its summer heat and humidity, to say nothing of the tourists and Italian inefficiency, he found it more convenient to stay at the Forum Hotel.

His life was in Vienna, to which his family had returned in the 50s. He had a long-term project to write a study of its contribution to twentieth-century intellectual history and was making headway, preparing the lectures he gave as a part-time university instructor.

Since he had a living to make, he also worked for an American foundation with a centre in Vienna, as well, of course, as for the newspaper. Less of a journalist than a feature writer, he preferred to put his energies into longer pieces, writing on subjects that really interested him. They did arise from time to time, though it meant he was visiting Rome less and less.

"So …" Stein said, by way of a pause in remarks more general than my recent experience of interviews led me to expect. Expansive on private matters, which had little interest for me given my lack of personal experience of his part of Europe, Stein seemed more open, more human, than those tightly focused individuals I'd talked to earlier. He spoke comfortably, like the youngish professor he was.

Only now, of course, Father Mark, do I realise what Anton Stein's "So …" really meant. He was saying: *So let me hear whether you can tell me something interesting enough for me to devote my valuable time to writing an extended piece.*

Stein poured me more mineral water. "So … tell me about the nuclear testing in North Africa."

He watched the final drops fall from his own bottle into his glass. Then he looked at me as I repeated everything I'd said to Wall-Eye. I included the rejection of my book. His gaze was fixed by the time he heard me say: "It all has to be exposed in the press."

Only now did Anton Stein sip – so little that it was, surely, merely to provide a moment for thought. Without picking up his pen, he held me with eyes at once distant and direct. Then he leaned forward and said, in a quietly confidential voice: "How did you choose to do a book on insects?"

"I inherited the project. It was originally my wife's. She died."

"I see," he said, with those eyes so concentrated, enlarged. "But why study insects in the Sahara of all places?"

I explained how the location had been suggested to me, and for what supposed reason. As I revealed the actual motive, sidetracked for whatever irrelevant reason into explaining that I'd been in Egypt as a child and that my father had gone missing there, in the desert, I felt he was not listening *to* but *for*: for the detail that might prompt him to pick up his pen, start writing on the hotel notepad and turn the bald facts of the case into something sufficiently intriguing for him to take up the story.

No hack reporter, he needed to hear the unexpected in the account he was surely knowingly loosening from me. And how? By his mere encouraging presence as a watchful listener to one badly deprived – first by Saharan solitude, then by Roman brusqueness – of a sympathetic hearing for his tale.

It was the narrative of how a letter had been sent by Father Carlo, a monk, to Father Erich, a Nazi scientist who had been developing weapons of mass destruction in the Sahara. At least according to a certain Mizrahi and the Wiesenthal Center – whose mention sent a tremor across Stein's face.

Yet much as I had told the story, complete with my role, Anton Stein's pad remained blank. His features did not, however. His expression taut, he stared at me as he fingered the glass unseeingly. All the bubbles were bursting.

"And who *is* Father Erich?"

His words sounded especially clear to me. I felt a thud in my chest.

"No one's sure who anyone is in the monastery," I said. "They leave their pasts behind. That's what one of the old monks told me."

"But you know enough about Erich to say he's a Nazi."

Had I ever seriously imagined Stein, so pleasantly professorial, would not become pressing, I wondered, almost to distract myself from the oppression of being forced to pursue a line of conversation that I might also have wondered if I'd ever seriously expected to avoid.

"*Do* you know who he is?"

Once more the words were crystal clear – syllables anticipating what I asked you, Father Mark, only a few pages ago. But they seemed to come from somewhere far away. As in a dream, I knew that in this test I had no alternative but to speak. I heard a voice, my own, giving his name. Even before I had finished, Stein had reached for his pen and written on the pad.

He stared at the page. Eventually, he looked up, stealing a glance at me. "Coincidence?" he all but whispered.

I had a sudden intake of breath – apparently evident. Stein took it as an answer. Quietly practised, he said: "A close relation?"

Gently, he broke the silence. "Father?"

"Yes," I muttered gruffly.

He held absolutely still, taking me in. Then he said in a calm, neutral voice: "Are you sure about this – *everything* you've been telling me?"

"The evidence fits."

"Does that make it all true?"

"I definitely believe it's the case."

The barman came over to clear away our empty bottles. He asked whether we would like something more. Stiffly, Stein made the polite effort of breaking off from his interview to offer what I actually declined.

Yet even when the barman left, he did not give in to his evident impatience on being interrupted. Rather than returning immediately to our subject of conversation, he tapped the end of his ballpoint pen again and again on the pad, leaving only tiny flecks on the paper. Eventually, he said: "I'm thinking about what would be the best way of approaching your story. I don't want to write an impersonal news article attributing your allegations to an anonymous source. Apart from anything else, I think what you're alleging would have much greater impact if I do a profile of you."

He looked directly at me. For a second I saw myself through those eyes of his: bearded, tanned, dishevelled, with a fiercely gleaming stare.

"At least that's what I'd find most interesting," he said. "Would you agree to it?"

"Yes, I would."

"That's good. And it will certainly lead to further articles. Because there's bound to be dispute. You must prepare for some ugly controversy."

"Ah?"

"Of course. You're entering into highly sensitive territory – a minefield, actually: the Catholic Church, Nazis, illegal nuclear testing. We must be sure you're ready to stand your ground. Are you equal to the inevitable personal attacks?"

I breathed in deeply – a pure reflex – and sat up straight in my chair. "I'm up to it. I can stand on my own two feet."

"I'm glad you're so self-confident. Because I must ask you something else. Can I quote you on everything – *absolutely* everything you've told me?"

It was another question I knew I must answer. I'd never imagined it would be so difficult. "Yes," I said finally. "Quote me on everything."

26

The die was cast. Finally. Yet, writing these words, I ask myself why it had taken so long. Not in the sense of plucking up the courage to announce such shaming things to others or even broadcasting them through Anton Stein. Rather, I wonder why I had not seen the facts, the truths they embody, far earlier. They had all been available to me in my ghostly monastery.

I suppose it was a question of my responsiveness. Only when I started to come to myself, with my shockingly brutal, beautiful interactions there, was I ready for the discoveries that, I realise, I made at the same pace as I exposed the expectation of them in myself. And it took place, I now also presume, only when I'd overcome whatever in me wanted to hide these painful truths from myself, preferring to take refuge in that half-life of mine where they seemingly did not exist.

For all that, the truth was now out. I'd finally discharged all the desert's dark secrets. I'd purged my mind of their poisonous power by abandoning them to Stein, now seeing me off in the hotel foyer. I had no doubt that I'd done the right thing, making my revelations public, especially about my own father. For despite my natural reluctance to expose him, I'd also asserted the naked truth. But I had also finally found the strength of will to decide for myself how I would stand in relation to the facts of my life. I'd discovered the force of personality to act accordingly; I rated it a major achievement.

Feeling fully myself then, I walked out into the Rome evening, approaching the Forum, that presence of a fallen past. But I was drawing level to it mechanically. I paced dully on to what I foresaw as a dark, dismal apartment. Something was dampening the liberation I knew I should be feeling. I was still harbouring denunciations of my father at the back of my mind.

I had a flashback of walking out from breakfast in the refectory with Father Mark. We'd been talking about Father Erich, and halted in the deserted monastery forecourt. Mark told me – the guest – that I needn't go to chapel to pray. He was ferocious, demanding me to leave it to the brethren … *all* of them.

And why was Mark so furious? Because he was actually blaming Father Erich for the crime. Or so I concluded from my mental replay of the scene. Yes, Mark was clearly longing to pay Erich in kind: "Can't you hear?" he'd said. "The very stones are crying out."

The shout set off a wild thought in me. Hadn't Sarah also taken against Father Mark's enemy?" Sarah would have known as much as Mizrahi about Nazi nuclear scientists fleeing desert hideouts. So, telling her partner no more about what she intended to do than she had about her other Saharan adventure, she might have had an uncontrollable impulse to go after the German who'd broken in upon her, a young Jewish woman, with his brutal *"Raus!"* Hadn't she been aching ever since to destroy this raging father wanting to tear her from his son? She'd deliver the old man to, well, Mossad or the Wiesenthal Center.

I imagined how Sarah intended to implement her plan. She would pass her message about his identity to the Israelis, or to the Wiesenthal Center's agents. And what better way than to go on an innocuous Friday evening visit to the Jewish village? It would destroy the man. The very idea left me, the son, thrilling with a sensation of being absolutely free with her. Yes, suddenly tasting fully that liberation I'd somehow felt eluding me on leaving the Hotel Forum, I looked up at a sky blocked by an orange neon glow. Yet what I was seeing surely, far beyond Rome's pollution, was some other, crystal-clear night. It was amazingly brilliant, with so many stars, viewed lying beside her on a sand dune.

Ah! But this was reckless. I knew I could never feel complete just by mentally returning to the Sahara, least of all to recall someone else gone missing. She, no less than my father, was different from the person she'd seemed to be. It was pointless to suppose she could ever come back, the woman I'd last seen having a tarpaulin drawn over her slack body.

My saliva turned salty. I must let her go, as I had my wife. But it was so difficult in Anja's case … though Sarah's appearance had helped. Sarah, so seemingly free – Mizrahi's Sarah.

My old bitterness welled up again – also, beside the point. I must let it go too, I thought, finding myself back in the neighbourhood church where my footsteps had led me several evenings before meeting Anton Stein.

Sitting in a dark side chapel, I thought of writing to Sarah's parents. If the letter spoke of my love for her, fully expressing my feelings for their daughter, maybe it would at last release me from morbidly recalling her. I'd post it care of the oil company in California. The address was on Mizrahi's card. And I should send condolences to the man's family too.

The letter to Sarah's parents started itself in my mind. But as soon as I'd written the conventional opening, it began turning into a message to Sarah herself: *You have no idea how I'm aching to hold you close to me again! I glimpse your face, these features charging me on a sandy hillock; in a cell. Yet it's only one frame from the whole film of our past. And the rest of the reel's spoiled.*

She was gone. The letter lapsed. I was at a loss.

It was mad even to think of a union in the desert with that mirage of a woman who'd kept reappearing each time I doubted she would. But that had been before. Although no bond had ever actually existed there even then, exhilarating as some memories of us together in the Sahara may have been. So she'd never have returned to me even if she had been alive. I myself, as opposed to Mizrahi, could not have recalled her once she'd re-emerged. Found, she'd be annihilated forever.

Annihilation: the word lodged in my mind. As I sat in that deserted church, I saw it wasn't only a matter of her turning her back on me, or the way an ex-Nazi scientist snuffed her out to save his own skin. It was a case of a father murdering his son's beloved – and doing it before the son's eyes.

After all, I told myself, my father must have been behind the walkie-talkie's instructions for me to see the slaughter. That's surely why I hadn't been killed too: not simply because I was a late arrival, or because my papers showed I'm not Jewish. My father had intervened specifically to ensure that I, his son, would be a witness.

Suddenly there was a ringing in my ears. I was sweating. I leaned forward in my pew in the side chapel. My head between my knees, nauseous, I found images of that sacrifice surging in my mind. Though what conceivable reason could a father have for making his offspring witness his lover's murder?

All I can say, with apologies to you Father Mark, is that if God commands His prophet to slay his son, then crucifies His own child, it's a universe insane enough for a father simply to want to cut his son down to size and reassert his power.

My head reeled. A mental shutter dropped. I remained slumped in the pew, dizzy, vacant. Coming to from this absence, taking in the used, incense-laden air, I was thinking again of what had happened to that woman. I had no choice. It was clear that she would not be there to come home to. She could never be. Feeling it – not just knowing it – had coloured my mood, returning from the Hotel Forum to a dark, empty apartment. Only now, finally perceiving it, I could free myself from the heavy thought and take a different tack, heading for what I really wanted.

It allowed an idea to come to me from quite a different part of my mind. Couldn't I simply turn my attention to another person, someone who could attract me as unexpectedly and completely as Sarah, actually only the most recent in a sequence of those unknowingly – and unsuccessfully – appearing to be the love of my life?

Yet this time it would be more successful, I told myself. And there must be a next time; certainly if I were to achieve the depth of satisfaction enticing me on first leaving the Hotel Forum. Again, there'd be a first heady scent of freedom such as I'd drunk in with Sarah. But matters couldn't stop there. We would go on to live in its atmosphere, exploring all life had to offer in that bracing, unpolluted air.

For my father had gone, never to return. He might as well already have died, for all his absence meant. Whether perishing in the desert or at the hands of the law, he could never again deliver punishment such as he'd inflicted on me through my beloved. He'd done his worst to the son outlasting him.

The thought remained as I glanced from the side chapel across the nave. Those shadows on the other side must be confessionals. I continued taking them in as I weighed up my advance into the future.

I had a sense of victory over my father, tied up with a ruthless disregard for my faithless desert love.

Looking back on this line, just written here in Rome after all this time, I take it for what it is: a brutal settling of accounts. My callousness toward Sarah equalled what she'd shown me. It was calculating coldness well and truly making me my father's son, and more than a match for him. Taking a leaf from my father's book, passing a death sentence on him through Anton Stein, I was repaying him for wanting to annihilate me with my lover's murder. Newfound, this late self of mine overshadowed the man to extinction.

I've just turned back to the last paragraph. Thinking about it finally makes me understand why I've really been writing this account for you, Father Mark. I've not only hoped you'd agree when I identify a given person as Such-and-Such. Nor have I simply expected you to endorse the Saharan narrative I've pieced together, taking my revelations seriously, understanding my predicament. All along I have, above all, been leading up to this ethical audit, my secular confession, of what it costs me to move unencumbered into the future. So I need my moral accounts to be reviewed impartially. They have to be judged as balanced by a man of your spiritual sensitivity.

You, after all, are the sole person to whom I might apply. There's no question of turning to Carlo or Erich. Both are blighted, as these pages surely make clear. No, you, *you* alone, are the Father sufficiently virtuous to justify the actions I've had no choice but to take, recognising, as I finally have, the loss of innocence in all we eventually have to discover and do if we're to become fully adult.

I wanted to move straight ahead. But there was no avoiding the difficulties, as I see now.

I must have had a sense of it even in the side chapel, realising just how long I'd been gazing at a statue of the Virgin. There was an inscription on the plinth. It was too dark to read, though my thoughts improvised: *"To the sole mortal born free of original sin."*

Then I recognised a problem: my name. I couldn't write that letter to Sarah's parents, her Jewish parents. How could they accept condolences from the son of a Nazi criminal who murdered their daughter, as Anton Stein would show? Could they suppose I was, or might become, other than the name I'd inherited? Did I believe it myself? Was I just a replica of my parent, doing to the one who'd given me my face, my hands, the evil he'd done? What more was I, surfacing like my father from the most dangerous place in the world?

Entering deep desert at a personal zero point, my identity vanished, feeling like death, I'd burst into being with a vengeance. And to think I'd gone to a Saharan monastery specifically *not* to feel, still less to answer to someone else's name, but with a humdrum project allowing me time to become my old self! What, then, was this sudden other self? Just a strong impulse to self-assertion on the brink of a future where I was still a *tabula rasa*?

The question remained as I got up from the side chapel and walked out of the musty church. I carried it within me through the night, returning to the apartment.

I entered the living room. Standing there, I wondered whether to allow scenes from the past to go on conjuring themselves up or to simply hover, blank as this darkness, until whatever presented itself drew me on.

The answer did emerge, though first my eyes accustomed themselves to shadows and an item I'd brought back from the monastery: Carlo's message to Erich. Looking at it lying on the desk, beside the pencil holder, I asked myself if it was best to destroy the letter, return it to the sender or pass it to Stein. But suddenly it felt unexpectedly hard to lose the only token of my sally into the deep Sahara: the sole memento of my desert father.

Yet if I kept the souvenir, wouldn't it be hidden like a guilty secret, or endlessly polluting nuclear waste? Then again, it might be filed away as an historic document to reveal quite how different my forebears were. For I wouldn't consult it much. Why encourage a disturbing spasm of nostalgic tenderness such as I feel writing this, by exhuming the letter as if it were the photograph of some momentarily revived yet irrecoverable face? Even so, could I afford *not* to have that page in hand to bolster my case against my critics? Who knew? I postponed a decision.

I put on the light. It was harsh, revealing a room where, instead of squatting, I knew I should make permanent living arrangements. I needed to organise my life and forge ahead. Then an image came fleetingly into my mind. It was as if I'd flicked on the switch of some inner lamp. It gave an instantaneous glimpse of a luminous room, harmoniously decorated by a woman to whom I was longing to come home.

Heading there, I'd leave behind me the evening and night thoughts. For what was drawing me on far outweighed what I'd lost by releasing the past. I'd found the strength to overcome regret at unmasking a Desert Father; to leave an illusory liaison to the shifting sands.

In that instant of clarity, the self in the room held in my mind: name cleared, established, a self that needn't worry about the reactions of the parents he'd meet. Freed, advancing into the arms of the future, finding and embracing their warm embodiment, wouldn't he at last enjoy that sensation of liberty I'd failed to grasp on leaving the Forum Hotel after my revelations to Stein?

27

One morning, days later, taking the lift from the flat to the foyer on my way to the bank, I glanced at the row of occupants' post boxes. Merely doing so from habit, I didn't expect to find anything in what had once been ours. Yet envelopes were showing through a glass panel.

An advertisement announced an exhibition at an art gallery that must still have had Anja and me on its mailing list. It was the one where I had seen the young American's paintings of a Coptic monastery off the Cairo–Alexandria road. For the whole of this month it was showing the Fayum portraits I'd seen advertised on the side of a bus. Answering some powerful inner call, I decided to visit the Egyptian exhibition that afternoon. Then I opened a second envelope, which had no stamp.

You're the scum of the Earth, I read. *You and your kind, fathers and sons, are all the same regardless of how much you claim to have changed. Your very existence here pollutes the building. Haven't you damaged us enough already? Get out! Or someone will get you out for good.*

It knocked me off balance – not least because it made me realise Anton Stein's profile of me must have appeared the previous weekend. I had not been looking for it. I suppose I was still inwardly living like you, Father Mark, in the apparent newslessness of the desert. How deceptive, as revealed precisely by this trembling note in an envelope with regular, old-fashioned handwriting that was at such variance with the violent tone of the contents. The concierge claimed he did not recognise it.

Even if I had read Stein's article, I could not have been remotely prepared for the bitterness of the reaction. I'd naively assumed that, irritatingly controversial as I might seem to many, my evident honesty would win out, including to some only reluctantly coming to see the objective truth of my claims. Instead I found myself facing a firestorm of personal criticism.

I shan't linger over them here, even if, Father Mark, you're unaware of them out there in your hermitage. It's still too painful. Besides, I hope I can take it as read, after all I've laid out in this account, that you're sufficiently understanding of what I'm asserting not to want me to rehearse in detail each of the poisonous responses I received. A brief summary should suffice.

First one and then another American magazine picked up Stein's story. They had titles such as "Son of Ex-Nazi Scientist Unmasks Father's Current Work on Nuclear Weapons".

Then came the initial reaction to my revelations – apart from the anonymous neighbour's. It was on television; Stein rang me from Vienna to alert me. A Harvard professor of entomology, previously called as an expert to a US House of Representatives committee considering the public health hazards of nuclear accidents, was interviewed on the international news. Beetling eyebrows twitching, he revelled in the corrosive sarcasm with which he scorned findings that belonged, according to the professor, to the realm of fantasy, not science. In any random sample of a thousand insects, he said, there are all kinds of deformities, for reasons too varied and numerous for us to be certain which applies in a particular case. You would need a full statistical comparison between the frequency of mutations in the relevant area and others, he added, before being able to reach a reliable conclusion about a specific cause. Besides, the most affected specimens would die long before the adult stage. That would leave only subtle changes in the survivors, but the reasons for these would be extremely difficult to assess – not least because it's well known that insects generally have disabilities of all sorts.

The professor declared that deformities in insects, alleged by an uninformed dabbler, were far from conclusive proof of nuclear testing, and that experts had already assured the public that there had been no significant damage resulting from radioactive fallout from the disasters at Three Mile Island and the Sellafield reprocessing plant. And that was so for insects, as well.

Hard on the heels of this interview came a North African government's strenuous denial that it was conducting nuclear tests in the Sahara, or that it was developing a nuclear programme for less than peaceful purposes. The spokesman had previously defended his country to the International Atomic Energy Agency. Now, again on the television news, he referred to the American entomologist's remarks for support for his claim.

Weren't these attacks on me part of an orchestrated response, I wondered, as did Stein, hearing that my slander was nothing more than what one would expect from the kind of person helping to circulate a piece of sordid propaganda by Anton Stein, a known Israeli sympathiser. I, in my zeal publicly to disavow my affiliation with a Nazi father, had supposedly kowtowed to Israel, especially with regard to its strategy of preventing other countries in the Middle East from acquiring the kind of weapons it possessed itself.

If I'd felt I had finally come into full possession of my assured, assertive self in emerging from the Sahara, my confidence was now badly shaken – especially on this very public, indeed international, stage to which my personal life, albeit with its painful loves and losses, had hardly seemed to be leading me.

Bad as the ordeal was, it was made far worse by what Stein now prepared for me. It came after an article in the Catholic press denying my accusation of Church support for at least one Nazi.

It was an invitation to engage in television debate with Father Carlo, no less.

Never more suave, his spotless, rimless glasses glinted when, at the start of the programme, he offered me that soft, white-cuffed hand to exhibit a shepherd's concern for his wayward sheep. Why did I take it, just as he was saying with what a heavy heart he'd found me attack a member of the brethren, a hermit in fact, precisely when his saintly brothers had been so cruelly stricken? It was exactly now that the monastery, the entire Order, most needed support – not least by remembering the holiness of its monks, so many of whom had become martyrs.

But then, equally, he said he felt compassion for my personal distress on entering the Sahara. My wife had died, and I was suffering the long-standing, if little understood, pain of having lost my father. Father Carlo well appreciated what a pressing issue it was for me to find the man in the very desert where he'd gone missing. It had, perhaps, been inevitable from the outset for me to believe I had done so, rightly or wrongly – although it saddened him to know it must be in such accusatory terms. Certainly, it was a most terrible thing to condemn one's father, supposed or not, to the ultimate punishment.

Yet, once more, Father Carlo could understand my need to attack a Desert Father for what my infant self experienced as abandonment. In my overwrought state, bereaved, alone, at the site of an appalling massacre, he took on the shape of fantastic evil in my mind. No less unfortunate was the way this had led me to spin a whole narrative as fictitious as the entomologist had testified, wrongly hurting individuals, governments and Holy Mother Church.

I made efforts to interrupt; to say that the facts spoke for themselves; that it was a travesty to portray everything as personal. But what I was hearing was so coherent, though perniciously wrong-headed, that I barely knew where to begin or how to dismantle it. The studio lights were blinding and hot. Father Carlo was especially poised. He had the advantage of fluency and presence. He skilfully gave the impression of lamenting his opposition to one for whom he actually possessed only the most sympathetic understanding. Unfairly, it was not he who was under attack.

I could not bear to see more than the opening minutes of the tape the producer later played back. It showed a bearded, tousled-haired man seated, ill at ease, before a prince of the Church.

Many other interviews and articles took up one or other of the issues Stein's profile had raised. I see no point, as I've said before, in giving you an encyclopaedically complete account of them. But one intervention might interest you, Father Mark. That Czech priest, Father Josef, had written to me at the Order's headquarters in Rome. Some functionary there must have forwarded his letter to me at Stein's newspaper without Father Carlo's knowledge. Carlo would surely have opened it, or held it back.

Josef wanted me to know he had been closely watching the controversy I'd set off, on television at the American university where he still worked. Seeing the news or reading an article, he remembered our conversations in a cell, a chapel, a refectory, all a world away. For there, in the desert heat – and cold – we had discussed Carlo Barnato and *Pacelli's People*.

Josef wondered at all that had come upon me since he'd left. He prayed that I kept safe every time he beamed out his tidings. So do astronomers release messages into our infinite universe. Like them, Josef awaited responses in the continuing silence. Yet, listening to the silence, hearing its answer, so untroubled, so profound, the more he took it that, for me, all things were working together for good. That said, Josef could just imagine how hard it was to resist the pressure I was being put under. He knew from the experience of his country's Communist past how efforts were made to force individuals to deny reality; but I had every reason to hold my head high.

Father Josef might not have been aware of the details of all I had alleged, he said, and everything to be said for and against it. Something he did know, however, from his instinctive sense of the matter based on our brief but intense acquaintance: I genuinely believed what I said and did. He added that an honest man should never be vilified.

Such careful words! Not for the first time, I resented the soothing tone he adopted with someone he did not really know but treated in a professionally pastoral manner. Not even his claim that I was sincere carried conviction. How could it?

There was no way he could possibly feel what it had been to be in my shoes – or sandals – all that distance into Africa. Suddenly I ached with loneliness, recognising that nobody ever would, ever *could* finally understand not just the facts of my case but what it had been like to be *me* out there in that desert.

What I'd discovered had released such public clamour, so far from the vast silences, the solitudes I was all at once recalling. If only I could escape these disputes in which I was embroiled! I longed to lose myself among those enfolding sand dunes, as you, Father Mark, sought to do, far from life's afflicting busyness in your self-protective hermit's cave.

Yet that Sahara into which I craved to retreat was the very place that had yielded up all that drove me to confront the world, my critics and self. Deep in its recesses, in the most abandoned parts of that sterile wilderness, it had brought out, not least in me, all that propelled me into the place where I now found myself inescapably thrown. I knew it was fruitless, as Lot had found, to look over my shoulder, to crave the comforting innocence of being where I had been before I became what I was.

There was nothing for it but to steel myself in this testing fire. After all, who had cast me into it? I felt very vulnerable. I craved support. It came from an unexpected quarter.

Otto Linge, the young publisher, had been following the controversy, so he told me on the phone. Insects, especially deformed ones, were suddenly of great interest to him after the media furore – especially so in a volume with my illustrations. It should include a long introduction carefully arguing my entire case, he felt, though in a manner provocative enough to draw in the large number of buyers he felt certain awaited it.

And what a superbly conceived case it was! But I was more amazed than gratified by praise so transparently self-interested. Once in his office, Linge passed across a new, considerably more rewarding contract. I signed it – thereby finally bringing to a conclusion my reason for going to the monastery. Now I've started on the volume, though I'm interrupting it to write this memoir to make matters clear to myself, as I hope they'll be to you too, Father Mark.

There was one person from whom I did not hear: Erich. I could not allow myself even to imagine that I would, after what I'd done to him. Not that there was any point regretting it, feeling guilty or telling myself I'd had no choice, painful as it was. The bare fact was that the thread binding us over all these years and across so many barren miles, no matter how tenuously, had snapped. He'd gone for all time. Nothing of him remained except Carlo's letter, which, without my specifically deciding it, I was effectively retaining as ammunition against my critics. But even if I were to have glimpsed him out there among the granite and sand, whether in reality or in my mind's eye, it would only be to see his back, the hindquarters of a man – surely him – retreating, eluding me, disappearing into thin air, leaving just an unbridgeable emptiness.

We had lost one another. There was nothing he could do for me now. Not that he'd ever have supported my views any more than he'd already done in the monastery – though worse than not believing me was not believing *in* me. It was the feeling that no one was behind me, that I was on my own, without the least sense of him just being there.

What more did I have to rely on, I asked myself, than the emptily encouraging words of a Father Josef or the commercial self-interest of an Otto Linge? My Desert Father was more invisible than the North African winds among which he'd gone missing. They at least stirred, agitating that terrain. Yet neither I nor anyone else reported encountering him. There was absolutely no contact with the individual-turned-monk. He was buried in the dead silence of the Sahara, from which I hope these pages will nonetheless summon up a good hermit to acknowledge the value of what their author has done.

28

I saw Anton Stein the next time he came to Rome. Again we met at the Forum Hotel, but on this occasion we sat on its roof terrace. We ordered late-morning aperitifs overlooking the Coliseum and Piazza Venezia as I fell into giving him a detailed account of my time in the desert.

Stein listened pensively. He only interrupted when I said I sometimes thought it had been a mistake to let him reveal my father's identity, as it was causing me so much trouble.

"Don't regret it. *I* don't," Stein said firmly. "You clearly wanted to claim Father Erich as your father. You were so determined to that had you not done it with me, you wouldn't have rested until you'd announced it through someone else. The moment you found yourself going to the Sahara, the one thought that must have been in your head was to discover the father you'd lost there. That's regardless of whether or not you fully understood it at the time. In fact, your long-standing mission may only have become apparent to you, fitfully, later – assuming it's even altogether clear to you now."

I blinked. I had heard these words uttered by the man beside me, yet seeming strangely far-off in the balmy sunshine. But I knew I still had to take them in fully. I was registering what he said as a photographic plate does light, to form an image to be developed later.

Eventually I drew myself up and said: "So why didn't I realise it earlier – if what you say is true?"

"Isn't that a question you might ask of everyone?" Stein said. "We all have some such quest of our own. It's largely unrecognised, pursued undercover, without our consent. How could it be otherwise, with our Achilles Heel, the chink in our armour? The one thing we feel most vulnerable about revealing to our harshest judge: ourselves?

"Even if we don't advance it so dramatically, against such a large background, but only in a dark corner of our being, it's our abiding project as we sally through whichever private Sahara our life sets us in. We create the individual myth of who we are, our very self, around that personal search. So although in your case, it's caused you great trouble to make this and related disclosures, it's brought what's most important to you out into the open. It's given you the release you badly want."

I still hadn't come to terms with what Stein was saying. But, equally, I was disoriented by thoughts like these pouring out of this youngish man. He was no longer the person who had conducted our interview in the bar weeks ago, in that coolly calibrated way, although it did remind me somewhat of Stein's expansive personal remarks at the start of that fateful discussion, not to mention this morning's conversation. Here were large, self-confidently delivered conclusions not only about me – true or not – but about humankind. How had he reached them? From personal experience? Did he have a sudden flash of insight? Was it simply acquired second-hand from people and books?

Yet such questions were shelved by the need I felt to respond to him. I did so in a vague tone, coming naturally to me to avoid either defensiveness or my impossibly immediate acceptance of an unexpected interpretation.

"I recognise," I said, peering out at the Eternal City, "you come from that other former capital of empire, where our modern understanding of the self really begins. But aren't you mistaking your role? You're a journalist. Shouldn't you limit yourself to judging whether what I say is true or not, printing only what can be corroborated?"

"Not at all," Stein said, turning away from me to gaze unseeingly at the surrounding rooftops. "I was writing a profile, not establishing the facts. My aim was to present a given man's – your – self-image; what drives you, in other words. It wasn't concerned with the truth of what you claim."

"So a journalist doesn't need to be sure that what he's printing is true. It simply has to make an impact, preferably a disturbing one," I said tartly. "Hardly very ethical, is it? But," I went on, covering Stein's voice, "you surprise me. I've heard you've worked for the Simon Wiesenthal Center in Vienna. You even have the reputation of being pro-Israel. Aren't you committed to establishing that war crimes have been committed, proving it beyond a shadow of doubt in the face of those denying them? Don't you track down the perpetrators, successfully holding them to account in international courts of law? You're far from cavalier about facts. They matter intensely to you. You and your associates use them with lethal precision."

"True," Stein said. "But that's where facts exist, as in documents that have been checked against other documents; dates that have been matched against other dates; or testimony that's been confirmed against eyewitness reports. Yet there are no such facts in this story. All we have is your account, with nothing to check it against. There's no one to give another report of what happened. So many of the rest are dead: the monks, Sarah, Mizrahi. Father Josef is gone. The hermits don't communicate, as being a hermit means keeping to yourself – especially if you're on the run, as you claim Erich is. And the police, the army won't discuss matters publicly for reasons of national security.

"No. There's no independent verification for your version of what happened, with its usual clichés about Nazis, the Church and Islamists ... Sorry!" Stein added instantly. I'd been stung by his belittling description of what I claimed. "I'm not saying your account is unlikely as you tell it," he said. "But one good reason why it sounds so plausible is that you're the only source. I'm sure you're not deliberately intending to be untruthful, misleading or biased. It's just instinctive, as it would be for anyone, to frame the entire version to support your point of view, your argument about what happened. We have no way of settling on the greater likelihood of this or that element being the case. And yet, setting the question of other accounts apart, there *can* be no facts in this story in the nature of the case. Because the issue is not actually about something objective. It's about what you are to yourself: your inner reality. And that is the result of your internal drives, demons, self-myth.

"So it's constructed in the light of your emotional priorities, to support your personal sense of reality. What else should we expect? Doesn't everything come to us through a veil of illusion?" Stein finished his aperitif in a single draught. Then he murmured, peering at its remaining viscous strands: "We're all caught like insects behind glass."

Was Stein continuing some discussion to which he'd been privy elsewhere, I wondered. I could not have contributed to it now myself. I was nowhere near ready. Not that it seemed to matter. Despite having exposed his view through these words to me, he was actually carrying on a conversation within himself. So I sensed.

"We mistake this inner reality of ours for the world itself," Stein went on. "We don't realise we're battering our wings against an invisible barrier, striving unknowingly for freedom out in the open air. How many such insects did you encounter in that place of Saharan mirages from which you finally decided to try and liberate yourself?"

The words subsided before the late-morning vista. Stein was squinting at buildings, a city, blurred by midday sunlight. I watched him for a moment. But no, he wasn't awaiting a reaction from one outside his thoughts.

I, too, turned to the dreamlike view.

29

That weekend, I decided to visit the art gallery whose invitation I'd received just before opening that anonymous letter from a hostile neighbour. The idea of seeing faces from Egypt, such as I'd glimpsed on the advertisement for the exhibition, transported me to my Alexandrian infancy. I was back with my parents in our apartment. Again, I passed neighbours on the stairs up. There I glimpsed the daughter whose direct, dark features have stayed with me over the years as clearly as the young woman's stare from the bus.

That afternoon in Rome, I bought a catalogue to the exhibition. I lingered in the entrance to read about these funerary portraits recovered from the surfaces of wooden coffins, preserved by the dry sands of Fayum. Roman in their manner of coiffure, dress and ornament, the likenesses dated from the first to the fourth centuries AD. The artists used pigments mixed with melted wax. The result of encaustic painting, as it was called, was a beautiful, radiant, glow.

I walked into the darkened chamber, finding myself held by an impassive stare, as on an Alexandrian staircase. But it was the girl advertising the exhibition on the side of a bus who was facing me from a wooden tablet in a shaft of light. Her kohl-rimmed eyes gazed out from the same funereal gloom as the row of other selfless heads. Like them, she focused on nothing and no one. Nor was she intended to be seen. She was privately, insensibly, waiting.

I looked at her, mummified in some museum vault apart from her painted image. How calm, peaceful, perfect she appeared! There was no hint of how she – so young and desirable – had come to be shrouded in fine linen, fragrant with herbs. One could only guess at the manner in which death had laid its finger on her.

What did she await? As an ancient Egyptian, she expected her returning soul to recognise her from the portrait, and so rejoin her. If a modern, however, wouldn't she at best hope a soul mate would find and keep her – if Fate did not cut things off too soon? In that case, the haunting stare would be into nothingness. It was chillingly evident in some contemporary flesh-and-blood faces, in the living death passing for their lives.

But couldn't one attract a soul mate permanently? He or she might come upon another from all those with a family resemblance. So the soul mates' meeting resembled a rare conjunction of stars, seemingly miraculous. It happened only when each had achieved what I found myself thinking of as the personal wholeness fully to align with the other.

My thoughts subsided as I moved on through the gallery. I passed from one painted face to another. Then, following this lull, it occurred to me that, during an absence, over a great distance, one's full self must be forming. I considered it, caught short by those features – mine – glimpsed in a glass showcase, after burying myself away so long in deep desert. For one day, one afternoon, say, after God only knows what solitudes and sights, what eruptions and emotions, that gradually emerging being would step whole from shadow such as this.

I heard my name. The voice was familiar. It startled me. I turned to the woman approaching me out of the museum's near-darkness.

Laura was as attractive as always. She wore the same perfume as when Anja and I would lounge with her in a midnight café, discussing films. "'*Tu es Hiroshima. Je suis Nevers*,'" she'd quoted.

"I wasn't sure if it was you," she said, dark Sicilian eyes still narrowed. "You've been away, haven't you? Quite the Saharan!"

"That's right."

"And what were you doing there?"

"Becoming myself."

We walked out together.

*

Laura and I spent a great deal of time together over the following days and weeks. We found it amazingly easy to be with each other, Father Mark. We were inseparable.

I'd been far from myself. I was in pieces. But now everything came together in conversation, in her presence, in her arms. It happened so naturally that I was scarcely aware of it. This wasn't only falling in love – which we've done, of course. It was finally coming into a situation with someone where everything fits, without anxiety or struggle, in a complete life: our life together.

Laura and I married. It's a breakthrough. With her, I've discharged my memories of the others: those hidden presences, echoes. After all, I merely glimpsed them, lacked passion or embraced them only for as long as it takes to be betrayed. It took the Sahara for me to find that Laura is indeed herself, no mere reverberation of another; to make the one recognising it the "me" whom I've become. So now I see, hold, only Laura, with her dark eyes and clear features. I am not my self without her. We will never be separated.

Such bold claims! Or so you might think, Father Mark. For I hear you object in some inner court: "Is it credible that he's finding his true love with Laura at last? Isn't he simply having an affair to stifle guilt at abandoning a previous lover, just as he did to get over his wife?"

Though I'm inclined to answer, there is really no need. It's enough that I know our relationship is real. With Laura I have that marriage of true minds of which my other liaisons, all doubtless poignant, were lesser precursors.

No matter that there's no more evidence from others than for Saharan revelations, the credibility of which has been so aggressively challenged that I'm writing this memoir to set the record straight. In fact, maybe it's simply the impetus of penning such lines that makes me also assert the authenticity of our marriage. But even if there might have been corroboration for my desert discoveries, no such thing could be available with regard to my feelings for Laura. It's impossible in the nature of the case. All that's necessary is that *I* know they are lasting.

30

"I think it's high time you told your story," Laura said one weekend.

I'd been remembering some aspect of my Saharan experience, as I tended to do, when the words faded in warm afternoon sunlight. It left me staring unseeingly at the burnished domes of Rome's skyline through our sitting room window. Then, recalled by my wife's suggestion, I said, sipping an espresso: "But I've already told you what my time there adds up to: becoming myself."

"Exactly ... Though I wonder how you could show it? Isn't there more besides your sensational revelations in the press and whatever you've been able to hear yourself say in those loud media exchanges? No, I mean *really* tell your story, publicly."

Laura could not have been more sympathetic to my claims from the start. Intimate, she intuitively understood my entire situation. Yet it's precisely that closeness that made her suggest whatever might mute the hostile negative reaction disrupting the atmosphere in which she, too, has to live.

"Well, I'm making a start with the volume of entomological drawings for Otto Linge," I said. "My introduction is setting out the case fully, coherently, for the first time. It'll offer a complete review of the insects' defects and give the only logical explanation: nuclear testing. I'm sure it'll help us weather the media reaction."

"Perhaps," Laura said pensively. "But I was thinking of something less academic, more personal. Then people could feel empathy. And what's likeliest to make them identify?" she said, dark eyes widening as if, dramatically, to produce something from up her sleeve, actress that she is: "A film. Just think of the desert locale, the isolated monastery, the whole *mise-en-scène*. Nothing could be better designed to draw an audience right into your situation."

But in the instant I glimpsed myself returning there with a rowdy film crew, I knew I would never be going back – least of all in the company of Laura, with whom I specifically wished to avoid reliving my Saharan chapter. The whole point of her was for us to enter a new phase. Even so, no matter how much I may have wished to move forward with her, unencumbered by the past, I knew – as I do now writing this – that it's impossible to avoid revisiting the events, if not the place, mentally. The media keeps throwing my desert revelations back at me. And I've an ingrained habit of looking back at my life: at Alexandria; at my loves; at losing my father.

My discovery of the man and what he's been has revealed a nasty moral stain. It's spread into the present and threatens to ruin my future, at least in the eyes of others. But if I'm to discount them and avoid being haunted by the shadowy presence of that past of mine with all it contains, I've no choice but to come to terms it. And I've a vague, dissatisfied feeling that, even after all this time, there's still more to understand. Not that this can include making a film about what's happened, or even Laura. Which is why I said to her:

"Movies eh? That's a long shot. Most big directors aren't interested in making documentaries. And they're the only ones who really have their films seen. But a news documentary is what you're essentially suggesting, regardless of how it's dressed up as a personal story. Besides, anyone taking on the project would first have to be convinced by what I claim. That seems as much of a hurdle as it's been for me to persuade the media …"

"Look Laura," I said taking her hand as I sat closer to her on the sofa, "I appreciate your support. I really do. But while the idea comes naturally to you as an actress, it feels foreign to me. Besides, we'd need a major contact in the film world."

Her eyes flickered. "Well …"

But before she could continue, I said: "How long ago was your movie debut? It was remarkable. But hasn't most of your work since been in television and advertising rather than mainstream cinema?"

Laura looked at once crestfallen and unconvinced. Could she have hoped for a part for herself, expecting not only to advance her acting career but also to insert herself into the past of a man made thereby even more her own? Yet there's no way to bring back a lover's history, to make oneself part of it, to have more of the person than from the time of one's first real meeting.

Didn't Laura know there are only two choices available regarding a partner's past? You can harp on it, tormenting yourself with uncertainties and leave yourself feeling excluded. Or you can decide not to mention it, hoping this more civilised approach will prevent you from wondering about it, either.

"No, a film's out of the question," I said. "In any case, the place is far too dangerous."

Laura suggested alternative locations. She had us traipsing across North Africa. I remained opposed to the idea. Security apart, scenes played out in a different locale could never amount to *my* past. Unable to render it, how might they assist me in making peace with it? They would never prevent me from dwelling on it, from unknowingly repeating it. And that could not possibly be to the benefit of Laura, who had to listen to me.

"But you've an extraordinary story to tell," she insisted. "It makes its own case."

I'd reclaimed my hand. My fingertips were tentatively exploring my cheek, finally clean-shaven these days.

"Think of what you found in the Sahara: your father – not just the results of an entomological project, dry as the desert. Isn't he where all your other discoveries lead, be they the insects, nuclear testing, or murdered monks?"

As Laura spoke, I came upon myself back at the monastery. I was finally grasping something actually obvious. I explained it to her.

By the time I'd finished supper in the refectory with Josef and you, Father Mark, I'd felt, without exactly realising it, that finding myself in the very desert where my father had disappeared, I would encounter him here, deep in the Sahara. Hence my sudden decision to throw away an invitation to leave that treacherously dangerous place. So, too, my capricious impulse to remain with the Desert Father, himself soon absent. For using manic devotion to the hunt for insects as my reason for remaining, it had actually been the search for a missing parent I was finally, though unknowingly, fully committing to at this crucial moment in my life. Yes, that it was which had held me there, as I now understood the police officer had been right to suppose something or other had been doing.

"I wish I could let the man know he'd been right," I told Laura, picturing his silver hair and fine features, those dark, thoughtful eyes.

"And I'd like him to understand that on leaving the Sahara I need not have looked back on my time in the monastery as a total failure after all. Out there among the murdered brethren, with my mother and wife both dead, hadn't I unknowingly summoned up my father from the scorching desert sands?"

I paused, troubled, Father Mark, even if I should have been as gratified as I might expect to be now by that outcome of my retreat – dissatisfied as I somehow still feel.

"But too much of this," I said moodily, "is about levels of awareness; developing intuitions. It certainly couldn't work in the cinema. You can't have a film where so much of the drama goes on inside the main character."

"Are you sure?" Laura said. "The great directors are able to bring inner conflicts out onto the screen."

"Such as?"

It brought back sitting over late-night drinks to talk about *Hiroshima Mon Amour*. Soon I cut into our discussion of comparable movies with: "Isn't a film really just a short story?" I said it blinking in the Rome sun. Then I found the light had transposed me to the bright roof terrace of the Forum Hotel. My neighbour and I were drinking aperitifs, not these espressos after lunch. "But life can't be reduced to a single idea; not even a strong one such as the search for a missing father. And you mustn't only focus, as a screenplay might, on whether or not what I claim to have found is just the predictable fulfilment of a private emotional agenda. My quest might also have been about what actually proved to be the case – as it was, wasn't it?"

I looked to Laura, sitting so close beside me that our arms crossed behind our shoulders on the sofa, and said: "For doesn't a person always work out what's driving him in terms of the situation he finds he's been thrown into? That's just as influential as whatever one brings to it. Because it's not a matter of judging that what I'd unknowingly pursued in the desert was a phantom, nor if I'd chanced in an alien place, through an event having nothing to do with me, on what was objectively there. My life's been far more than just a struggle beneath the surface, as if I'm the spy who wrote *My Secret War*. Though neither has it all taken place in full view of the rest of the world. What's within endlessly combines with what's beyond. We're caught in the no-man's-land between. We're the Sahara desert: both mineral and mirage."

Laura was listening with watchful eyes. As if holding back her thoughts, they appeared to look beyond the words. "I see what you're saying," she then murmured with quiet knowingness. "Even so, don't you think recalling an episode can focus personal themes surfacing at a particular moment?"

"I'm not certain," I said, frowning as I shifted on the sofa. "There's too much to a life at *any* point to reduce it to a single episode. In any case, there are so many of them. "

I halted abruptly, not mentioning Sarah, who surged unbidden into my mind. Laura would not want to know of her, or what she revealed about my pursuit of the complete lover I've now finally found in my wife herself. Nobody wishes to hear in detail of a partner's past loves, or wants to suppose it's the subject of one's silent reflection. But Sarah, *that* episode, could not be discounted. She was too much a part of me becoming myself.

"And yet you can't even reduce a life to a series of episodes," I said. "That destroys its reality. One shouldn't expect to follow it through like the Stations of the Cross, telling one rosary bead for each stage of the story, while advancing to a predetermined destination."

"Of course," she said gently, her hand cupping my shoulder, "you're right. Yet ... is there really so much to feel ashamed of in needing a father? It's only natural. And no one can blame you for being disturbed by who – or what – you've found him to be. You can't, in any case, sweep it all under the carpet. The point is that describing how you discovered it, together with your feelings about it, might help others understand it all, too. That's all I'm saying."

I didn't answer. I was thinking. I gulped my coffee – or was it an aperitif?

"Well, episode or no episode," I said, "what I claim is true. And it means I'm not just self-enclosed, blindly pursuing inner themes like some trapped insect battering its wings against reality. There are, after all, those of us who finally come to terms with their inner selves and open up to the outside world."

Laura was looking at me without speaking. Did she sense that she herself was hardly the one I'd been addressing, even if she did not have access to that instant of sudden recall in which I'd been back among Fayum portraits, recognising the possibility of achieving personal wholeness?

Tactful, she chose not to pursue our discussion. Anton Stein apart, I take it she'd realised she would make no further progress with me on the vexed quest for my father. It was a closed issue, if in the way something denied nonetheless remains open. In any case, she has never again mentioned the idea of treating it, let alone the rest of my story, as a film.

I was the one to return to these things. But I did so obliquely, and on another afternoon. It emerged from what had become our continuous, free-flowing conversation, though it was the discussion of those who live together, which, even when it seems to dry up, continues through intimate silence in the subterranean way rivers flow below the very Sahara where I'd once lived.

Embracing Laura once my words about some aspect of that desert life had lapsed in the fading afternoon sunlight, I told her I regretted always being the subject of attention: "I don't want you to think I'm self-centred."

"Oh! But you're not," she said, kissing me, amused. "And it's only natural, with all you've been through."

Conversation resumed: Laura's, this time. Listening to her rehearse plans to find a new agent, to restart her acting career, I gazed vaguely at the reflecting window. But what I glimpsed was an unshaven man, his eyes stern. It was the stare confronting me from a shard of rusting mirror in the privy of a desert café.

I interrupted my wife's suggestion that we visit her parents in Sicily. We both badly needed a break from the fraught atmosphere here, she was saying.

"You know, Laura, there's something I really *did* achieve in the Sahara," I said. "I survived it. That was something far bigger than making those awful discoveries now seized on by friend and foe alike. Because I met the ultimate challenge the desert posed, but which I'd always evaded before. I finally faced up to relying on myself, not others.

"Far away, in that loneliness, I had no parents, no wife, and no lover it turned out, to depend on. I could no longer assume someone else is always in charge of life's situations, that life itself can ever be evaded by enlisting another's protection. And yet I endured every Saharan day, each desert night.

"How? Through work? Not really. It was by unexpectedly finding I simply had it within me to do so. I'd become myself, as I told you, on emerging from that exhibition. Buried alive in the desert, I'd nonetheless found personal wholeness of the kind the Fayum portraits suggested to me some people achieve. It was true, I'd supposed in the gallery, of those who attract soul mates – such as my parents."

Ah! So I'd caught myself reverting to my father, sitting here with Laura, as well, of course, as to my mother. I continued: "Then I thought that, like me, they'd held their own in the Sahara as much as the parents of that family, nestled beneath a date palm, on the monastery chapel's wooden bas-relief. Out there, unexpectedly, my own parents had invisibly awaited my homecoming – as something within me implicitly thought of it. But how could I have known it at the time, surrounded by heavily static desert? Only now do I recognise that I'd inwardly embarked on a long, arduous return. I spent day after seemingly dead day, moved motionlessly by the promise of that domestic abode. It – they – drew me on, seeing me through to all I'd already received from my parents, had I but acknowledged it.

"Surviving, then," I told Laura, "wasn't a matter of an episode, or several. It was a never-ending stationary advance to who I am: to self-realisation."

I said it, finding myself at a darkling Rome window: there, where another couple found themselves together, at home.

"That was the true reason why – how – I remained in the Sahara," I said. "I wish I could tell the police officer."

That night we made love. Exquisitely close, we fell into deep sleep.

Later, I awoke. I got up in the dark. It was utterly still. It was that time when even the garbage trucks, the street hosing, the cats have all fallen silent. Clear-headed, at peace, I looked out over the silvered domes, hearing the steady purr of Laura's breathing. But what I took in from the reflecting pane was not just our bed. It was the warm, sunlit image of my young parents in Alexandria.

They were as they'd been in my earliest childhood. It occurred to me that, later, after much time had passed during which they and that image had seemingly lapsed from my thoughts, I had, in addition to unknowingly anticipating meeting my father in the monastery, also sensed at the back of my mind that my mother was there too.

Recalled they were, these unseen presences, as once in their bright Mediterranean bedroom, only now out in the glaring heart of the desert where I found myself – though far from deserted after all. They lent me unacknowledged support, not only beckoning me home, as I'd already seen, but also in finally standing on my own feet to last out my months there.

Strange, that I'd felt so isolated in that case! Odd, too, that I'd continued on the brink of boredom scarcely fended off by seeking insects. For I'd been equally engaged in quite another, if seemingly similar, subterranean project.

I was bringing my parents back together after their many years apart, just as they'd been in that mental picture from far-off Levantine days. For yes, it was I who, focusing with such concentration on no mere memento of the past, no simply touching snapshot of a time gone by, conducted them thereby, in my very distraction, regardless of intervening decades, into one another's arms.

Then it occurred to me, in this first dawn light, how long I'd been standing before an eclipsed city; an Alexandrian imprint. Only now, with my previous thoughts, that image, still holding in my mind, I turned from the window to our double bed. I merged deliciously in her enfolding warmth.

31

I presume that Laura spoke to others about filming my story. In fact, I suppose she had done so before raising the idea with me. For once it was clear that I opposed such a project, it must have been obvious that there was no point in her going on discussing it with anybody else.

Not that I asked her whom she'd talked to, or when. I don't want her to feel defensive about speaking to those in her own profession. How would it seem, so early in our marriage, if I were to start overseeing relationships necessary for her career? It was, in any case, quite unnecessary for me to ask whether or not she had shared her plan, or if others were now talking about it. It became perfectly obvious one evening when we resumed our habit of movie-going.

A colleague of Laura's had given us tickets to the screening of a new film. He thought we would be interested in its subject matter. It began flashing distractingly between Western capitals and the Middle East; that was apparently more than enough to set off my neighbour in the audience on the side opposite to Laura, a man I'd never seen before. He started complaining about the kind of subjects being made into films these days, and specifically mentioned the Saharan project, my movie, saying people who are politically innocent can end up paying a high price for dabbling in that sort of thing when delusion is all mixed up with reality.

Did I know the man, I wondered, trying to get a proper look at him; but he was lost to view, there at my side in the dark, whispering: "God knows whom you might antagonise – and with what result." He said it confidentially, which only made his words nastier, more menacing.

I simply turned away and stared at the screen – only to find, once I looked back, that he'd climbed out of our row, shadow that he was, and disappeared.

I barely managed to sit through the rest of the film. It gave me time for a disturbing though highly significant ninety minutes of reflection. But I held my tongue as Laura and I filed out of the packed cinema into the foyer. Only when we emerged into the night air did she speak: "Who was that whispering to you? You seemed to be having quite a conversation."

"Entirely one-sided, I assure you."

Then, unable to say who he was, I told Laura what he'd threatened – abruptly bringing her to a standstill by our car. "But why did he say it?" she struck back, whether to him or me. "There's absolutely no talk now of any such film being made."

"I'm glad he said it."

Taking her hand, the car keys in my own, I saw Laura's adamant expression lessen as she absorbed what I'd concluded in that excruciating hour and a half in my cinema seat.

"Whoever threatened me did so for the best of reasons," I said. "He himself feels threatened. Because he must know that if the film's made, it will damage him – and whom or whatever he represents. And the explanation is simple: my Saharan revelations can't be ignored. They must be true. In other words, I'm not a man just bottled up in myself. I and all I've been talking about are far from self-contained. It must now be accepted that I and all I am are part of the world. We're open to each other. And there's no alternative to concluding that what I claim happened did in fact occur."

Driving home, my words, the menacing situation underlying them, reverberated. Not for some time did Laura break the silence: "Well, as I say, there's no chance of the film being made." But by then I'd decided to tell my story as a memoir.

I may have resisted Laura's suggestion that I should do so as a film, now obviously too dangerous an enterprise. Yet having spent the afternoon discussing with her the challenges of presenting my life, after reflecting that night on such an important aspect of it, I'd acquired a taste for recounting my tale – though in what format and to what end, exactly?

My memoir, as the private document you now see, Father Mark, will avoid making me more of a public target than I already am. It should not incite the kind of violence my fellow filmgoer threatened. And it isn't only setting out the evidence for horrors I've claimed to have found in the desert. My shadowy neighbour had surely already effectively vindicated my factual claims. As Laura and I agree, my volume for Otto Linge on Saharan insects will provide the necessary detailed corroboration. At least it will, once I go back to it after finishing this memoir.

Not that my specific desert discoveries can simply be left out. They're the basis for the story's emotional and ethical claims. But as for those claims, while I've come sufficiently into possession of myself to rely on my own judgement and cope successfully with what even my most odious critics say, I can't entirely ignore something Anton Stein told me. It is that my account will, of course, make perfect sense for an obvious reason: I'm its sole source. Even if that menacing filmgoer apparently provided support for the events it relies on, I, the inevitable commentator, construct it as anyone would, to fit what I wish to think is the case. As a result of which I need the corroboration that my growing awareness of dialogue with you, Father Mark, effectively invites.

Of course, requiring another's endorsement, regardless of the reason, might seem to undermine what I've just said about having discovered my self-confidence. But is there anyone who has not, finally, wanted to be believed in, no matter how secretly? I say this here in particular, because this is not only a matter of me asking for you to help me sift through my narrative of events, confirming my view of its participants, their motivations, their identities. The issue in my memoir – my life – isn't only what happened. It is, rather, what it all amounts to. And that, surely, is me becoming myself.

Well, if I'm to have this kind of moral support for my self, it must come from somebody evidently good like you, Father Mark. I could not have a more pronounced longing for it following my Saharan experience: a paternal reunion so brief, so ambiguous, with such a flawed figure.

So it is, then, that I've sat down to write to you, Father. I've done so over the last few weeks on mornings stolen from the volume on Saharan insects, while my wife has been out trying to relaunch her film career. Now, finally, I've come to the point where I've said it all. My account, my submission, is all but complete. I can just contemplate it in the mid-morning silence of our Rome flat, wondering how I might send you the manuscript out there in the desert.

*

Otto Linge telephoned, asking to meet me. Loath to leave my memoir, I answered my editor's summons to his new office apprehensively.

It was larger, more lavishly decorated than before, given his success in commissioning the best-sellers set out on the gleaming central table where we were sitting. I found the firm's latest catalogue facing me with the announcement of my own unwritten volume.

"We've just received an anonymous call advising against the publication of your book," Linge said. "Now, we're a big company specialising in works that tackle contentious issues, so it's not unknown for us to get threats like this. Many come to nothing. But, in any case, we'd never publish anything if we were automatically intimidated by them."

Linge, so businesslike, had a tic near his eye. "I've talked to our Managing Director and Legal Advisor," he continued. "They agree that there's no reason to halt your project. On the contrary, the call underlines its controversial interest."

"No less than the truth of what I'm saying."

"Maybe," Linge said, frowning quizzically and fingering his brightly coloured silk tie. "But your claims have been objected to before. It's never made the sceptics find them more credible."

"This is different," I said. "It's not a matter of journalists speculating, or specialists expressing a difference of technical opinion. Your caller was someone who clearly knows what I'm saying is true, like the man who threatened me weeks ago in the cinema. Otherwise it wouldn't seem so dangerous to him that he needs to suppress it."

"Unless the call is a hoax," Linge said. "Or coming from someone objecting not to what you say about the insects specifically but to the very idea of you, based on all he's gathered from media reaction to your entire case.

"Anyway, you're surely not suggesting we advertise the book by saying it's credible thanks to a threatening phone call," Linge snorted. "In fact publishing it, far from settling matters, will almost certainly intensify the controversy, engulfing the insects too. And if that has the effect of preventing the caller from being fatally damaged, as you say he fears, it will at least have drawn his sting."

"With dangerous consequences for you if you're wrong," I said.

"Not exactly," Linge said coolly. "It's not the company as such that the caller threatened."

I looked at him. He broke the strained silence.

"But don't worry about it. We've got a bestseller on our hands. I'm showcasing it at the Frankfurt Book Fair. So tell me, how soon will you finish the book?"

"Soon."

"That can't be soon enough – for either of us."

*

I am back at my desk this morning. But although the entomological volume urgently waits for me to return to it, I find myself strangely unwilling to cease these desultory remarks in the memoir. What could they possibly add to all I've already written? What else can I be looking for? Is there, after all, anything more for which I can be turning to you?

I ask myself as much as you, Father Mark, as I lounge in this sunlit solitude and see, from this distance, that I've finished all I'd gone there to do – awakening from what's felt like a dream. Yet maybe it's not so odd after all. I'm aware of a light humming, glimpsing some winged insect such as I'd studied in one of those desert cells to which I feel recalled and where my parents had reunited, though I'd scarcely realised it till later. So perhaps I also unwittingly savoured even at that time what I'm only now fully aware of having shared with them as an infant. I'd stumbled on the love I feel brimming up in me here too, in my mentally recalled cell, as this moment I now recognise holds me in its engulfing calm.

But did I really only chance upon it? Isn't it, rather, love that's remained part of me long after the abrupt end of my life with my parents? Not that I was separated from my mother until much later. And my absent father, the one I missed, continued for me in my thoughts. A fond figure, he was, whom I could still recall from snatches of memory: luminous moods transporting me back to our beach cabin at Stanley Bay; long Alexandrian summer mornings when, buoying me up on bronzed shoulders, he taught me to swim in that immemorially glittering sea. He was there well before that brusque man, his other self, so preoccupied, inaccessible, soon to leave my mother and me alone. And he remained alive in my mind even when we left Egypt. He travelled within me, although I hardly knew it, throughout the shadowy half-life in which I'd never come to myself in Rome.

He still existed when, later, I went to the desert. For I had only seemingly lost him, the man supposedly disappeared decades before in Egypt. He'd gone on, I now see as I write, regardless of my encounter with my harsh parent, Erich, reappearing in the monastery.

He is the one I still await here and now, in spite of everything: the one to embrace what I am – as surely emerges from the memoir with which I long to evoke your Saharan response, my Desert Father.

And wasn't it to taste some such thing that the brethren submitted themselves to the Sahara's welcoming stillness, after all the conflicts and disappointments of their previous lives? They'd describe it, I imagine, as a spiritual homecoming. Was it in search of this, Father Mark, that you yourself drifted dangerously beyond the monastery, even, casting off its anchor to enter yet remoter solitude? Were you drawn beyond your past – all its situations, romances, ambitions and remorse – to a cell not of rock or adobe, but of the mind?

Finding form in your hermit's cave, out in that greater beyond, with its infinity of sand and sky, are you waiting, solitary – knowingly or not – to be visited one noon? Are you Abraham sitting at the door of his tent in the heat of the day, on the plains of Mamre? Maybe in such a place, the ultimate cell, the being all along awaited, so desired, whom it has never been possible to cease anticipating, eventually appears ... Oh! tell me so, Desert Father, responding in some boundlessly deep Sahara.

POSTSCRIPT

The memoir is complete, ready to be sent to the person its author now considers its true audience. But with the typescript before him, beside a book on the Sahara's prehistory that he'll return to when he resumes writing about desert insects, he continues lounging in his Rome apartment. He's taking in the late morning sun. It's a contented lassitude at having finally told his story. And he seeks to bring it to mind, though not by focusing on any particular thing he's said, but as a general impression.

Yet the account, with all its situations, its many transitions, none remembered exactly, simply hovers vaguely, like the afterimage of a dream. His eyelids grow ever heavier, squinting away the bright light; his thoughts grow more tenuous. Then, in an alarming burst of clarity, he sees something utterly unexpected.

The Sahara is spreading out before his inner eye. It curves with the Earth's circumference. But that sandy immensity, its many rocky eminences, have all been stripped away. Exposed in this moment of sudden vision is what lies beneath the sterile, abandoned surface.

It's a place into which ancient seas have overflowed. A vaster Mediterranean reaches far down into Africa. Powerful ocean has swept right in from the east. Huge bodies of water glitter before him, here at his lofty vantage point. Vast lakes, they abound with fish, turtles, snakes. Amphibians, whales, swirl in their depths.

Down there, mangrove swamp stretches endlessly instead of a shoreline. Its canopy of wide, interlocking trees is deafening: flocks of birds shriek among dinosaurs feeding off the high foliage. Below, crocodiles and the great reptiles lurch out of glassy stillness in the rich plenty of barely moving streams. A fecund world, it sustains eons of interdependent life. But his glimpse of it is starting to fade. The sky has darkened. The sun is black. Massive storms are gathering. They rage on and on.

Now calm has settled: utter calm prevailing across an unending sandy surface. Parched, desolate, it might always have been so, he supposes, shrugging away the light dazzling his eyes. Yet he knows something, doesn't he, sunk in this chair? A diviner, he feels in his very being that the Sahara's profoundest water sources are continuing in abundance.

And he knows instinctively just where to tap them.

*

Each morning, Father Carlo has breakfast after mass in the noisy silence of brethren passing plates in the refectory. Then he has a further reflective coffee, alone for an hour or so in his study, reading the newspaper.

Today, however, he is not glancing idly at the window, turning a page, to take in the courtyard with potted plants behind the church of Santa Maria dell'Anima. He puts the paper down, still holding the telephone receiver on which he's just answered a call from Klaus Werner, that disturbed man who stayed at the Order's monastery in the Sahara. Slowly returning it to its cradle, he prepares himself for the visit to which he has just agreed. They will meet here in the study, informally, rather than in the guest salon where Werner, returning to Rome, had been so hostile.

Father Carlo has almost an hour to wonder what Werner wants, to consider what he will say to him, to recall the man's state of mind the last time they met, on television. Though, answering this knock on his door, he finds the visitor, now clean-shaven, much less fierce and angular than he expects.

They shake hands and the monk indicates a chair, saying how pleased he is that they're meeting again. Settling for a silent moment into his position beneath the photograph of the young Pius XII as Apostolic Nuncio to Germany, he looks up from his empty cup and a manila envelope being placed opposite him on the table. Then, adjusting his rimless glasses with their spotless lenses, he says:

"I want to offer you my sincere thanks for giving me this opportunity to explain what I said before the cameras. I meant absolutely no lack of personal respect or affection. It's important to me to stress that I was speaking strictly *im*personally, on behalf of the Church. I particularly regret that in a role hardly of my choosing, I was obliged to make some unfortunate, if not actually wounding, remarks. I only hope you haven't been unduly bruised by my pointing out that whatever you alleged about your father in your now-infamous interview was actually to repay him for leaving you in the lurch, years before, with your mother. I well realise it's all too human."

Father Carlo notices the calm way his visitor crosses one hand over the other on the envelope, listening to him.

"I'm not hurt," Werner says quietly. "I'm not even offended anymore by the way you sent me to meet my father." He says it remembering his swingeing attack on the monk in the Order's grand reception room on returning from the Sahara – but apparently so as to think, in marked contrast, of how he'd come to find himself in a drab church in an unfashionable part of Rome. There he'd supposed that, far from seeing the cool cleric as performing the Devil's work in sending him – a broken man – to the desert, he might actually thank him for having done him the greatest possible service. "All's well and good," Werner says.

"Amen to that!" Father Carlo says, surprised and relieved. "Though don't you regret all you've put yourself through, by going public with such terrible accusations?"

"Sometimes. My wife Laura still finds it disturbing. By the way, you *do* know I've married again?"

"I've heard."

"Yet I'm discharging the entire Saharan business in a book about desert insects. I have you to thank for helping me with it, sending me off to your monastery. And I've told the whole story in a memoir," Werner says, tapping the envelope.

"Have you, now?" Father Carlo says, adjusting his glasses.

"The fact is, there was no other way but to bring everything to light. Not if Laura and I were to come to the point, at last, of living on our own terms. That, we're pleased to say, is now finally the case. We've found our reality: our personal space beyond the reach of the rest of the world and its worst. What brought us to it now lies outside it, as far as we're concerned. It's a mirage, evaporating in the Sahara."

Father Carlo continues in the silent attitude in which he's been taking in Werner. The man's expression, his whole manner, is so much calmer, more genial and self-assured than ever before.

The monk finds the envelope being passed to him across the table.

"Here's my memoir. Reliving everything so long after has given me the distance I need not only to find what was real about my time there, but above all what it means. I want to send it to Father Mark. But I'd rather not entrust it to what serves as the mail service out there. Would you have any problem about arranging for the Order to deliver it?"

It takes a moment for Father Carlo to answer. He knows Werner fully expects him to read the package and confront himself with what it says. But *amour propre* prevents him from seeming defensive.

"Of course I'll send it."

Then Werner, explaining how he's come to see that what he's written is for Father Mark, also acknowledges to himself that his implicit reconciliation over the last half-hour must always have been as much the reason for coming here as to pass to this monk an unsealed envelope containing his account of being sent to the most dangerous place on Earth.

*

Klaus Werner has asked his editor, Otto Linge, to send Father Carlo the work he's just published on Saharan insects. The monk undoes the package. The book lies beside his newspaper and morning coffee. Father Carlo stretches to pick it up; it's heavy, and he stares at the exquisitely delicate watercolour of an insect on the cover. Its legs and wings are meticulously drawn – and subtly deformed.

Adjusting his glasses, Father Carlo frowns his way through several plates, beautiful and grotesque. Then, holding up an inside flap of the dust jacket, he reads:

> *A major introduction, with matching texts in English, German and Italian, sets out Klaus Werner's controversial case fully for the first time in what is no mere book. With its extraordinary and generous illustrations, it is a Pandora's Box.*

Father Carlo releases the cover. It sinks. He lights a cigarette, barely moving as it turns into a precarious column of ash. He waits until the last of the smoke disappears, then finishes his coffee.

That Sunday, Father Carlo opens up the newspaper's bulky weekend supplement. He reads a review:

> *Many will see and admire this extraordinary publication as an artwork. There can be no dispute about the quality of the illustrations. There may*

*even be some, like this reviewer, who, having seen these plates, are now
inclined to believe Klaus Werner's allegations about nuclear testing in
the Sahara. There are, however, several distinguished entomologists
who will surely continue to part company with him. Moreover, it is clear
that even people tending to be convinced by Werner's conclusions drawn
from the insects must remain unsure about the rest of his claims.*

*

Some time later, Father Carlo receives another visit from Klaus Werner.
Greeting him in his study, he puts his newspaper aside, next to the book
on Saharan insects.

"Has there been any response to my memoir from Father Mark?"

"Your memoir. Ah, yes! Of course." Father Carlo feels the visitor's
eyes on him. They stare, at once inward and watchful, with lashes lowered in a habit surely acquired in the blinding Sahara. "Well, no," Father
Carlo says, with a stare of his own: direct but impenetrable. "The Order's
received no response. Though trying to make contact with one of our
hermits is always risky. It's a bit like throwing a message in a bottle
into a sea of sand … Even so, maybe you yourself might hear from him
directly. Have you, by any chance?"

Again the monk's glasses glint.

"No. Not by post at any rate. But you know, it sometimes seems as if
he has replied. There are moments when I feel the response radiating
through me. And I know he's confirming all that's real about what
I've come through in the desert. Not just the details, or only for an
instant, but powerfully enough for me to be certain that the day will
actually come when I'll finally feel him embracing all I've been – and
have become – in the Sahara. I even feel in contact with him now, if
I hold very still in this room, as though you yourself were my Desert
Father, and I'm basking in you just being here with me."

Werner continues looking at Father Carlo.

Perhaps unthinkingly, the monk stretches out his hand. With its
starched cuff and gold link, it covers the seemingly silent reproach of
a damaged insect on the cover of his visitor's book.

*

Anton Stein's visits to Rome are becoming less frequent. He is here this week, less as his newspaper's Vienna correspondent than to focus on the serious journalism he prefers to write nowadays. He hopes to interview knowledgeable people for his monograph on the Vatican's response to the creation of the state of Israel.

Opening the paper over breakfast at the Forum Hotel, he reads:

Klaus Werner, author of a recent high-profile book on Saharan insects, was the victim late yesterday morning of a motorcyclist firing at short range near the Piazza Navona. He was driving as usual to the television studio where his wife, the actress Laura Casati, has been filming a new series. He died on his way to hospital.

Police have issued a statement saying they are conducting an investigation to determine whether or not this is just the latest in the recent spate of drive-by shootings in Rome or a reaction to the controversy Signor Werner's book and previous notorious allegations have provoked.

Stein rereads the article several times. By the time he puts down the paper, his welter of thoughts has settled on a single issue: what must he do now for Klaus Werner's wife?

He has never met the poor woman. He knows little of her personality. Even so, he suspects she'll hold him at least partly responsible for her husband's death. For the man's revelations about his father in Stein's interview have done more to stir up criticism of him than anything else – except, of course, his book on desert insects and nuclear testing.

Yet had Klaus Werner ever told Laura about a later conversation with Anton Stein? Stein had questioned the objective reality of his claims, in which case it would remain highly unlikely that they'd excite a murderous reaction from the outside world. Shrill dismissiveness by experts was one thing; assassination, quite another.

Nevertheless, while Stein feels exonerated, he also considers it best not to meet Laura in person, emotional and accusing as she might well be. Least of all should Stein do so at the funeral where, besides, he himself does not want to run whatever risk there might be of becoming a target also.

He must write to her – though what? Can he restrict himself to a statement of conventional condolences? Well, merely penning a note of sincere sympathy for her great bereavement would be just too brief, if not downright cold, given the significance of Stein's role in the man's life – and, could it be, death?

Yet that very question, the problem of what has in fact killed him, finally, on this depends whether or not there is something more to say to the man's wife. More exactly, Stein considers, it would be the most meaningful thing he could tell Laura. So what is it?

The waiter has appeared. He's asking Stein if he wants more coffee. It rouses him from his thoughts, but, sipping as he returns to them, he finds something still awaiting him: the image of a disturbingly blank sheet of Forum Hotel writing paper.

*

A distant shape, barely a spectre, grows clearer now in the dawning light. It continues its slow, undulating descent down a dune, wind scattering its trail of sand. The old monk's grizzled beard is all that shows from his black cowl. Head bent, rocking dozily with the rhythm of the donkey's hooves, he's been carried from his hermitage through the long night. The animal knows the way to the monastery without direction. Unthinkingly, too, the monk – so many years after his novitiate – sets out for the annual chapter in that state which has finally become habitual in him: between prayerful distraction and daily focus, dream and reality, dimming awareness and increasingly blind instinct.

As involuntarily as the need to satisfy hunger or quench thirst, his reflex at sunset had been to set out for the ritual gathering of the brethren, taking him far into the knifing cold of massive starlight. Then, dark hours later, well on his way, an instant of consciousness had flickered in him passing the cell of a hermit who had joined the Order with him almost a lifetime ago. Not that he succeeded in remembering exactly who his nearest neighbour was or had become these days, any more than he'd been able to see if he was there now in the cave blocked like his own, with roughly woven thorn tree branches to keep out animals when he's sleeping or gone.

It's in another of his intermittent moments of lucidity that Father Mark awakens to the day with its sight of the monastery. But the next instant he's blinking, though not from the bright early light. It is from the sight of the pinkish adobe walls, the overtopping trees, the chapel tower – and his difficulty in placing them as the donkey nevertheless continues trotting down the dune and over to them like a proxy for his lost memory.

He arrives. Wincing, he hoists himself off the animal. Managing to stand despite his leg injury, he takes a tottering step to lean against the jamb of the front gate. It's been ripped from its hinges. They hang from the wall plaster. The heavy lock, with which the police or someone from the Order in the capital had secured the door to the abandoned site, lies in the sand.

Peering through the framed emptiness, he takes in the cloister. It's still as a snapshot, except for a moment's eddy of sand. Despite the wind, it seems strangely silent to the old monk, who has not quite realised he isn't hearing the generator, the gushing of water, that something within him unreasoningly expects.

He sees right into the chapel, strangely large and empty. The stone altar is bare. The pews, like its front door, too, have been stolen in this desert with its shortage of wood. The nomadic former slaves of the Tuareg must have been here. Not that he speculates, failing to come to himself while walking blankly into the orchard. Large, curling leaves sail in the air from un-pruned fig and avocado trees. Magnolia flowers, their white petals curled and rusting, litter the sand.

Wandering on through an unruly expanse of shuddering sunflowers and maize, he enters the kitchen garden with its patches of un-harvested melon and squash. Their stalks have been used for the campfire he comes upon in a circle of charred stones. A glass lies shattered beside it, with just enough of the base intact to hold sediment of dried tea leaves. The squatters had cooked there, using that sheet of paper as a fire lighter. There's typing on an unburned part of it. It's still legible.

So is it on another sheet not used for the fire at all. Still more pages – many more – unnecessary for preparing the nomads' meal and night's warmth, have landed in other parts of the vegetable garden. And the large brown envelope, once holding all the sheets, has simply been hurled away into collapsed bamboo tomato frames.

The old monk picks up a page. He screws up his eyes to read it as it flaps in his hands. It addresses Father Mark with regard to "the memoir about which I long for your Saharan response, my Desert Father".

He picks up another sheet, trying to keep that straight too. It asks if he's "Abraham sitting at the door of his tent in the heat of the day, on the plains of Mamre".

The old monk frowns, searching his mind to match the page to anything of which he can make sense. Then he just stands staring hard at the print, real pain on his face as he struggles to find himself in the latest destruction he's stumbled on here where, even now, it's undergoing a further slow, mute and final cataclysm of total eclipse beneath desert sand.

The wind catches the paper. He tightens his hold. But, in the instant that his concentration fails, the page is snatched from his hand. There's a flurry of other sheets raised from the ground. Off they fly, scattering far and wide.

He's left seeking answers to questions he can now no longer bring back to mind, staring deep into the Sahara.

Acknowledgements

To Carlo Carretto's *Letters From The Desert* (Darton, Longman & Todd, London, reprinted 1978), for suggesting elements of the setting and story;

To Father Christian, Superior of the Community of Notre-Dame de l'Atlas in Tibhirine, Algeria, who, together with his Trappist brethren, was abducted in 1996, for words attributed to him and spoken by Father Sebastian in this novel;

To Cornelia Hesse-Honeggar for her provocative paintings of damaged insects.

I wish to make it clear that I have used and altered the above elements entirely for fictional ends. My purposes in no way include intended portrayals of real situations or people.

My greatest debts are acknowledged in the dedication.

ABOUT THE AUTHOR

Leslie Croxford is a British writer born in Alexandria. He resides with his wife in Cairo, where he is Senior Vice-President of the British University in Egypt. He obtained a doctorate in History from Cambridge University and has written one novel, *Solomon's Folly* (Chatto & Windus). He is completing his third novel.